JACK'S BACK
Murder returns to Whitechapel

Mark Romain

Copyright © 2018 Mark Romain.
All rights reserved.
ISBN-13:978-1-7310-9771-2

The right of Mark Romain to be identified as author of this work has been asserted by him in accordance with sections 77 and 78 of the copyright, designs and patents act 1988.

This book is a work of fiction and any resemblance to actual persons, living or dead, is purely coincidental.

For my wonderful wife, Clare, and our two amazing children, Mitch and Lauren – you guys are my raison d'être.

And also, for our first grandchild, little Archie, who arrived in January 2018, bringing so much joy and love with him.

ACKNOWLEDGMENTS

Edited by Yvonne Goldsworthy
Cover design by Woot Han

I'd like to say a special thank you to my little team of test readers: Clare, David and Martin, for all the feedback you provided while I was writing this story.

ALSO BY MARK ROMAIN

Unlawfully at Large

The Hunt for Chen

BE AFRAID.
THIS IS ONLY THE START.
JACK'S BACK...

PROLOGUE

20ᵀᴴ December 1995

Connie Williams – or Willow as she was known in the trade – led the punter she'd just picked up along a narrow, cobbled alleyway just off Shacklewell Lane in Hackney. The place smelled rank, but at least it was out of the biting wind and away from prying eyes. Despite the bitter cold, the twenty-four-year-old, leggy brunette wore a lightweight coat over a low-cut black silk blouse, which was so thin it was almost see through. A red leather mini-skirt, a laddered pair of black fishnet stockings, and a pair of ridiculously high heels that she could barely walk in, completed the tacky outfit.

The night air was so cold that her breath came out as a thick cloud of vapour every time she exhaled. The bookies were giving great odds on it being a white Christmas, but only a mug would take that bet – she had never known it snow in London over the festive period.

Glancing over her shoulder, she smiled seductively at the gormless pervert who was blatantly ogling the curves of her arse. Seeing the lust that burned brightly in his beady eyes and the bulge that stretched the fabric of his stained trousers, Connie laughed. "Be patient, sweetheart," she told him, exaggerating the sway of her hips for his benefit.

The punter, an unshaven Turk with a thick moustache, leered in anticipation of what was to come. Even from a distance, she could smell the alcohol on his breath.

It was the wrong side of midnight, and business had been painfully slow for most of the evening. It was probably a knock-on effect from the sting operation that Stoke Newington police had recently carried out to target the area's kerb crawlers and working girls. She had read all about it in the latest edition of the Hackney Gazette. In the article, the neighbourhood policing Sergeant had boasted about the fifty-three arrests his team had made in response to local residents and businessmen complaining about the prostitution problem that was blighting the lives of decent law-abiding citizens. Yeah, right. Would that be the same citizens who regularly used her services because their fat, whingeing wives were either mind-numbingly boring in bed, or had gone off sex altogether and were no longer willing to lay there, legs apart, pretending to enjoy themselves while their inconsiderate husbands selfishly satisfied their own carnal urges?

Luckily, business had picked up during the last hour and she now had enough money to buy the crack she needed to get her through the coming day. Her teeth started chattering, and she decided to call it a night once she relieved this creep of his money.

Willow wondered what he would ask for once they were alone: a hand job, a blow job or a quick knee trembler. Her money was on the latter. She stopped by a line of garages at the far end of the alley; it was as good a place as any to rock his world.

Less than five-minutes later it was all over, and she was following Mr Pump-Pump-Squirt back out of the alley. She had been right about the knee trembler.

The Turk hesitated at the mouth of the alley, glancing around furtively before stepping onto Shacklewell Lane. It was funny how they didn't care about being seen on the way in – when all they could think about was getting their end away. Now that his wallet and his ball-sack were both a little lighter, and he was thinking with his brain again, and not his dick, the punter was keen to leave the red-light district without being seen by someone who might recognise him or – worse – being stopped by the Old Bill. Perhaps he had read the article in the Gazette as well?

"Hello," a voice behind her said, startling her. Willow spun around to see a white male in his early forties standing a few feet away, half concealed by the shadows. "Don't be alarmed," he reassured her, seeing the uncertainty that crossed her face. "I'm not with the police." He sounded educated, unlike most of her usual clients, who either had local or foreign accents.

"What do you want?" she demanded as he emerged into the light. The man was clean shaven, and of medium height and build. She could see wisps of dark hair poking out from beneath the old-fashioned Fedora he wore upon his head. The collar of his long grey coat was turned up, successfully masking the lower part of his face, and a pair of expensive looking black leather gloves protected his hands from the cold. "I want you to do for me what you just did for him," he said, indicating the receding figure of her last client with a jut of his chin.

Willow relaxed. A copper would never have propositioned her like that; it would have amounted to entrapment. She had planned to call it a night, but in her game, you never looked a gift horse in the mouth. Besides, he didn't look like the type of man who would know what the going rate was, and she sensed there might be some scope to squeeze a few extra quid out of him. Smiling, Willow waved him towards the alley. "Why don't we step into my office, where we can discuss your needs in more privacy," she suggested, rubbing her arms briskly to keep warm.

She led him back down to the garages. The full moon had broken through the clouds and was now bathing them in a silvery glow. It was almost romantic, she reflected. Well, apart from the freezing cold, the cluster of bins overflowing with trash and used condoms, the smell of urine and the sound of two Tomcats hissing and spitting at each other as they had a bit of a ding-dong on the garage roof.

The punter wanted to do her standing up, but not from behind. "Okay, but I don't do kissing," she told him. It was better to get that straight, right from the off.

He pulled a face. "I have absolutely no interest in kissing you," he assured her in a derisory tone that implied he found the thought repugnant. "I just want to be able to see your face."

"Fair enough," she said, holding out her hand for payment. "We can do that."

He handed over the money and they got straight down to it – she had charged him fifteen pounds over the odds and, to her delight, the fool had actually coughed up the cash without batting an eyelid.

Willow tried to make him hard by using her hand, but after several unsuccessful minutes of tugging, she grew impatient. "Is there a problem?" she demanded, irritably. Her hand was growing tired and she was getting bored, but at least all the yanking had warmed her up.

"I'm just a little cold," he told her, but she could tell he was lying.

"Are you having trouble getting it up?" she asked, raising an accusing eyebrow. If he was, she had no intention of giving him a refund.

"No," he said, a little too quickly. "It's just that...well...perhaps we could play a little game to help get me in the mood."

An alarm bell went off inside Willow's head. Some of the other girls were willing to indulge the perverts with so-called 'special needs', but she had never been into that. "I don't do kinky," she told him, releasing his flaccid tool and taking a step backward. "I'll fuck, suck or wank you off, but that's where I draw the line. There are plenty of other girls who are willing to play rough or whatever, but I'm not one of them."

His demeanour changed abruptly, and he lunged forward, grabbing her arms aggressively. "Don't you dare start acting all virtuous with me," he warned, slamming her back against the garage door with such force that it made her bones rattle. Willow gasped as the air was knocked from her lungs. She opened her mouth to scream, but he had anticipated that. The punter clamped a leather gloved hand across her mouth and squeezed so hard that she thought her lower jaw was going to break. He smiled at her pain, and there was a spiteful glint in his eyes that told her that the sadistic bastard was getting far more pleasure out of her fear than he had from her hand. "Make a noise and I'll kill you, do you understand?"

Willow nodded, terrified. Her heart was beating so fast that she thought it might explode inside her chest; this was every sex worker's worst nightmare, and she knew that her survival might depend on keeping calm and doing whatever he said, even if it meant remaining passive while he roughed her up.

He was studying her dispassionately, the way that a cat toying with a mouse does just before killing it. "I like to say and do certain things when I fuck," he explained, as though that made the way he'd just manhandled her okay. "You know: things that I can't say or do when I'm with my wife." Their eyes locked for a moment and she thought she detected a glimmer of sadness in them, but then his face contorted into a mask of hatred. "And I'm going to do all those things to you, right now." The words were spat out with such malevolence that Willow nearly wet herself with fright.

The punter's wife had been raised as a strict Catholic. For her, sex was an unpleasantness that married couples indulged in purely for the purposes of procreation; it was always done in the missionary position and never – ever – with the lights on. He respected her views because he loved her, but love or not, he still had needs, and when it became apparent that she wasn't going to satisfy them, he quickly found an alternative outlet. He'd happily used the services of prostitutes in his younger years, and it seemed a better solution to his predicament than taking a lover. After all, when you thought about it, having sex with a prostitute was no different to relieving yourself with your hand; it was basically just another way of masturbating.

The trouble was, he wanted to do more than just fuck them; he wanted to hurt and abuse them. He wasn't sure why, but the desire to beat up one of the working girls had finally become too powerful to resist, which was why he had travelled here tonight, to an area where he was unknown. He was finally going to act out his secret fantasy.

"Here's how it's going to work," he told her, grinning with a maniacal intensity that she found terrifying. "You're going to stand there and take whatever I do to you without complaint, and when it's over you're going to go down on your knees and thank me. Do you understand me?" Before she could respond he removed the hand from her mouth and slapped her violently across the face. Willow cried out in pain. Suddenly his hands were fastened around her throat, cutting off all sound, and she could feel him thrusting his shaft against her stomach. He was hard now, aroused by her pain and fear.

"You filthy harlot, I'm going to fuck you till you bleed, and if you ever tell anyone about what I've done I'm going to come back and slice your nose off, and then your eyelids and then your lips." His voice was quivering with excitement, and she suddenly felt him enter her. *No! Wait!* She wanted to cry out. *You're not even wearing a condom!* But he was too far gone to care. "And then I'm going to slit your worthless throat from ear to ear," he panted, his eyes bulging with excitement as he approached climax, "and watch you bleed out as I fuck the hole in your neck."

Unable to breath, Willow lashed out in terror, at first clawing at his face and then trying to gouge his eyes out, but he was far too strong and he simply swatted her feeble efforts aside.

She could feel the life being squeezed out of her. As she vainly fought to pull his hands away from her throat, tiny yellow spots flickered before her eyes and the world began to swim. Within moments, her hands fell to her sides and her legs buckled underneath her.

And then he had finished, and she was lying on the floor gasping for breath as he stood over her, trousers around his ankles, wiping his manhood with a handkerchief.

"Now thank me," he told her, breathing heavily from his exertions.

Willow struggled into a sitting position on the cold floor, rubbing her bruised and bloody neck. As she gulped down air, the world slowly came back into focus.

She was still alive!

When she didn't immediately comply with his instruction, the punter reached down and grabbed her hair savagely. Using both hands, he dragged her to her feet, ignoring her cries of pain. "I told you to thank me," he snarled.

"Thank you?" Willow sobbed uncontrollably. "What for, raping and half-killing me? You sick fuck, just get out of my sight before I call the police." As she spoke, Willow tried to back away from him, but the punter had no intention of allowing that. He yanked her hair upwards, forcing her onto the tips of her toes. Despite the searing pain in her scalp, Willow shoved him hard in the chest with both hands, sending him tottering backward in a series of penguin-like steps.

She kicked off her shoes and tried to run past him, but the punter rugby tackled her to the ground, landing on top of her chest with a heavy thud.

His brain was on fire as he pinned her writhing form to the floor. As she struggled to break free, something inside his mind snapped and he lunged for her throat, hands outstretched like grotesque claws.

The punter continued to wring Willow's scrawny neck long after she was dead. At some point during the attack, he couldn't remember when exactly, he battered the back of her skull against the dirty cobbled floor, cracking her head open like an eggshell.

Afterwards, as he sat astride her body, perspiring and gulping air down hungrily, the seriousness of the situation began to sink in. Staggering to his feet, Willow's killer wiped his bloodstained, shaking hands down the sides of his coat and hurriedly pulled his trousers up.

"My God, what have I done?" he asked himself, hardly recognising the sound of his own voice. In a moment of pure madness, he had done something utterly reprehensible.

Taking a last look at the unmoving form on the cobbled floor, the man who had ended Willow's life so prematurely turned and ran down the alley.

CHAPTER ONE

Saturday 30th October 1999

Although the pale-yellow glow from the brass table lamp illuminated his lap and most of his torso, it was nowhere near strong enough to reach his face, which remained firmly ensconced in shadow.

Beyond the small pool of light, the darkness that filled the rest of the room was cold and foreboding. From deep within it came the steady tick-tock of a large clock, providing the heartbeat of an otherwise silent house.

The man sitting motionless in the red Chesterfield opened the thick, leather-bound tome in his hands and began reading.

...As it is written in the heavens above, so it is reflected on the mortal plain below. This is a fundamental truth that lies at the heart of all occult teachings...

"As above, so below..." He voiced the magician's motto with reverence. The maxim comes from the Emerald Tablet of Hermes Trismegistus (*meaning Hermes the Thrice Greatest*). Also known as the Smaragdine Table, the Tablet's cryptic message is considered one of the bedrocks of Hermeticism.

The Tablet was purportedly discovered by Alexander the Great in a cave at Hebron, which contained the tomb of Hermes. The short work contained thirteen sentences in Phoenician characters, and these are considered to be the basic principles of alchemy.

In essence, 'As above, so below,' is an esoteric proclamation that the Microcosm – oneself – and the Macrocosm – the universe – are fundamentally one and the same, and an understanding of one leads to a greater understanding of the other. According to Hermetic doctrine, there are no autonomous strands in our existence; all things on heaven and earth originate from a single source and they remain forever dynamically interconnected. From the individual quarks, protons, neutrons, and electrons that populate an atom to the largest galaxies that make up the limitless universe, all things are joined.

The reader, a self-taught disciple of the Left-Hand-Path, was obsessed with all things occult and esoteric. Having studied books on arcane practices for many years, he knew that it is precisely because all things physical and spiritual are so intimately bound that the sorcerer is able to cause a transformation in or of a thing without any physical contact simply by possessing the will and the imagination to make it happen.

Sinking into the soft leather contours of the armchair, he turned a page and read some more.

...Powerful incantations provide the means to harness the unseen energies that pervade every breath of air and every grain of sand. Properly channelled, these forces can be used to advance the goals of the skilled Mage...

He was acutely aware that dark magic increased the practitioner's psychic energy and allowed them to manipulate the world around them for their own gains. The specific words and symbols used during powerful incantations create frequencies that influence outcomes by aligning the energy of the participant with the person, object, or situation they are trying to influence.

The Disciple surveyed the exquisite book with great fondness. It was one of many in a collection that had taken over three decades to accumulate. There were two other books on the coffee table beside his chair; a rare edition of the 1854 'Dogme et Rituel de la Haute Magie' (*Dogma and Rituals of High Magic*) by the occultist, Eliphaz Levi, and

'The Clavis Inferni' (*The Key of Hell*), a late 18th century book on black magic.

A cruel smile flickered across his face as he turned to the first of several chapters that dealt specifically with sacrificial rituals; if he ever appeared on *Mastermind* this would definitely be his specialist subject.

The Disciple had undergone a period of fasting in preparation for the impending ritual, allowing himself only enough liquid to survive on. The lack of sustenance was starting to take its toll, but he was confident the adrenalin rush would keep him going until it was safe to resume eating normally.

He glanced down at the engraved Rolex that adorned his left wrist; a gift from his – soon to be expired – wife, given back in the days when she still professed to love him.

It was ten-thirty p.m.

In ninety short minutes All Hallows' Eve, or Samhaim as the Celts called it, would begin. For the majority of people Halloween was a time for making jack-o'-lanterns out of pumpkins, dressing up in silly costumes, and taking the kids out 'trick-or-treating'. For those in the know, however, it was one of the four High Holidays, or Greater Sabbats. In fact, it was the most important of the four and was sometimes referred to as The Great Sabbat. He could not imagine a more fitting date to commence his work. The thought triggered a sudden surge of adrenalin, making him feel excited and anxious at the same time. He took a deep breath and released it slowly, counting to ten as he exhaled. This was a night in which calmness needed to prevail; he could not allow his emotions to get the better of him, even for a moment.

Twisting the book sideways, he attempted to study an intricate occult diagram, but after a few seconds of staring at the page blankly, he realised that further reading was pointless. Carefully placing the heavy book on top of the others, he continued to focus on his breathing as he ran through the plan for the millionth time. During the coming hours he intended to perform the first in a series of ancient dark rituals that were as powerful as they were obscure. The successful completion of each one would make him significantly stronger until he finally reached a point where he would be able to bend the powerful forces that shape destiny to his will.

The Sheep would be horrified, of course. To them, his actions would seem unforgivably brutal, but to him, the sacrifices were simply a means to an end.

Well, that wasn't quite true. Every slice of his knife would bring him exquisite pleasure, but that was merely a fringe benefit, and he wouldn't allow it to distract him from seeing the bigger picture.

He had carried out experiments with minor hexes and charms before, of course, but he had never attempted anything as dark and as powerful as what he had planned for tonight. Of course, he had been preparing for the coming events for a very long time and he knew exactly what was required of him. The documents he had read had been very specific:

...The chosen organs must be consumed within a single cycle of the sun or their power will be spent. The organs taken must directly relate to the corresponding zodiacal region of the body. Thus, the heart of a Leo will be eaten; the intestines of a Virgo will be eaten and the genitals of a Scorpio...

At least identifying and removing the organs shouldn't be too problematic. His anatomical knowledge might be a little rusty after all these years, but he was confident it was more than sufficient for what he had planned. What worried him was that if he consumed the wrong organ – for instance, if he killed a Scorpio and then ate her liver instead of her genitals – the ritual would not work, which was why it was so vitally important that he establish their star signs before killing them.

...Only by spilling the blood of the damned, which must be released through ritual mutilation and offered as a sign of worship, can the necromancer obtain true power...

Those who practice diabolism understand that a ritual sacrifice releases an instant burst of power that can be harnessed and channelled to assist particularly complex spells. Animals of varying description are most commonly used, but the most effective and powerful sacrifices require the offering of human life. In these rites, the victim's blood is drunk and their flesh is consumed.

The rituals he intended to carry out represented his last chance at salvation. Success would lift the curse that blighted his life, and prevent the controlling bitch that ran it from depriving him of the rewards that were rightfully his. It was a last throw of the dice in which he risked everything, from his freedom to his immortal soul.

The stakes were high, but to do nothing was to lose everything anyway, so what choice did he have? Besides, taking petty revenge on the heartless bitches who had done their utmost to destroy his life was just background noise; the bigger picture was that he was embarking on a mystical journey in which he would discover his true self and gain the power he needed to live his life to its true potential. It was his coming out party, only instead of doing something conventional, like confronting the truth about his sexuality, he was finally acknowledging the darkness in his soul; if he didn't forge ahead with this voyage of self-discovery, there was a very real risk that he would lose what little remained of his sanity.

The Disciple stood up, swaying slightly as the blood drained from his head. His blood sugar was low, he realised, and he told himself to be strong; he could eat as much as he wanted in a few short hours. He checked his watch again, and his stomach immediately constricted. It was getting on for eleven.

The planning and preparation phases were finally over.

It was time for the killing to begin.

The tube ride to the East End proved singularly uneventful. Emerging from the bowels of Bethnal Green station, he turned his collar up and tucked his chin into his chest to counter the chill. He left the main road as soon as he could and was quickly engulfed in a blanket of darkness. Rubber-soled shoes carried him soundlessly through the cobbled streets that led to his sanctuary, and he scuttled from building line to building line like a sinister shadow, avoiding the sporadic puddles of light generated by the area's few working streetlights.

A security light above the adjoining lockup, activated by an overly sensitive motion sensor, came on as he crept beneath it, and he quickly shielded his eyes to prevent his night vision from being completely destroyed. He cursed his security conscious neighbour as he fumbled with the key to his lockup, eager to escape into the darkness within.

Once inside, he lit the candles and the incense. He had prepared them himself, just like everything else in the ritual he was about to begin.

The Disciple knew that a magician had to craft his own instruments if he wanted his magic to be successful, and over the past couple of months he had fashioned a number of crude but functional magical accessories. These included pens, ink, a water sprinkler, an inkwell, a sand shaker, and, of course, the candles and incense burners.

Earlier in the year, he had purchased a thirteen-inch serrated Bowie knife and a razor-sharp Finnish skinning knife. In accordance with ritualistic custom, he'd replaced their respective wood-effect and rubber handles with elegant wooden ones he himself had made especially for the task ahead. Both were lovingly engraved with arcane symbols.

He had cut the wood he used from the living tree with his own hand, felling each of the branches he'd selected with a single stroke – an almost impossible task requiring a keen eye, a sharp axe, and split-second timing. It seemed as though half the trees in Epping Forest had been decimated before he'd finally got the knack of it but, once he did, the sound of the wood splitting as he severed the bole of each limb from its host had resonated through the forest like a series of gunshots. Ignoring the excruciating blisters his endeavours had spawned, he begun fashioning his wand and staff that very same day.

Practitioners of the dark arts place little value in the printed word. They believe the most important ingredient for performing any magic ceremony is the will of the magician; the words used are nothing more than a conduit through which the sorcerer's will is directed.

Over the years, The Disciple had learned that to be truly effective the hand of the person who wishes to use it must copy out the text of the ritual. And so, a few days ago, he had meticulously handwritten the words of the ritual on parchment made from the tanned skin of a lamb he had slaughtered and skinned himself.

The animal's death had not been a pleasant experience for either of them.

He looked around, studying the cavernous space of the archway in the flickering glow of the candles. The van was as he had left it last night, fully prepared for the task that lay ahead. But that was for later. Right now, he had to concentrate on getting through the opening ritual, in which he would summon the demon and pledge his immortal soul in return for the gifts and privileges the coming sacrifices would bring.

Black magic is most effective when carried out during the waning of the moon, which is the point in the lunar cycle that comes after a full moon but before a new moon – and tonight there was a waning gibbous moon. In addition, he knew that performing a ceremony on All Hallows' Eve, in a year that has a three-fold repetition of a single number in it, would create very powerful magic – which was why he planned to commence the opening ritual on the stroke of midnight, kill his first victim before sunrise, and consume her organs after sunset.

And there was a very important precedent for what he was about to do; the rituals had been successfully performed in Whitechapel once before, exactly one hundred and eleven years ago – another thrice repeated theological number.

The Disciple believed that the man the word had come to know as Jack the Ripper – whose five canonical murders were committed between 31st August and 9th November 1888 – had been one of the highest echelons in late 19th Century Freemasonry, and that he had used dark magic and sacrificial rituals to bring about the destruction of his closest rivals in order to influence the decision-making policies of the Government. His ultimate ambition had been nothing less than to alter the very fabric of the British Empire.

Dark rituals are generally performed to enable the necromancer to communicate with the dead, force malevolent entities to do their bidding, or to achieve power and influence over others. They can also be used with a view to achieving an extended life span, considered the first step in the search for immortality. The Disciple was very clear about what he wanted: money – lots of it, influence and, most importantly, freedom from the controlling bitch who ruled his life, and the other whore-bitches who had made his existence so miserable.

It is paramount that the appropriate measures are in place before the ritual commences, to protect against unwanted evil spirits. The pentagram, or circle of power, was already marked out in chalk. He sprinkled salt around the perimeter to keep out the dark forces he was about to summon. He knew he would need its protection during the incantation. Then he traced the circle with one of the engraved knives. He inscribed it with the pentacle and other symbols from the Kabala.

He was careful to start the ritual invocations on the stroke of midnight.

By the end of the ceremony, The Disciple felt mentally and physically drained. He crossed to his workbench on wobbly legs and slumped down in the padded chair that stood beside it.

As he sat there gathering his thoughts, The Disciple realised he was shivering from the cold, and that the temperature inside the old railway arch had dropped considerably during the ritual. Had the unseen forces that he had conjured caused that, or was it merely an untimely coincidence?

Despite the cold, he felt strangely exhilarated as he sipped mineral water from a plastic container. It was as though the atmosphere around him had somehow become charged.

The invocation had been made. Now he was obligated to kill five women. Failure to do so would bring about his demise in an unspeakable fashion and was therefore not an option.

An uncomfortable sensation rippled through his bowels. Hoping it was just wind, he switched on the lights around the stage mirror mounted on the long workbench in front of him.

"Here goes," he said. Taking a deep breath, he picked up the powder puff and went to work on his face. Next, he donned the wavy-haired black wig and attached the matching coloured moustache with theatrical glue. When the makeup was fully applied, he studied his face in the mirror, searching for any imperfections that might give him away. Satisfied there were none, he stood up and moved into the darkness of the inner chamber.

As he approached the cab of his van, he glanced up at the inverted cross that was mounted on the wall directly above the double doors, sticking out so dramatically from the semi-darkness that surrounded it. He stopped in his tracks, and for a long, troubled moment he wondered if the Catholic God of his misbegotten youth was angry with him for turning to Lucifer. Looking away guiltily, he concluded that God was probably much better off without him.

He opened the wooden doors as quietly as he could, and then slipped back inside the lockup to collect his things. A few moments later, cursing next door's security light – which had come on again – he nudged the van out into the chill night air.

Breathing deeply, he looked up at the scattering of stars that glistened in the clear sky above. Not a single cloud threatened rain. All in all, it was a fine night for bloodshed.

CHAPTER TWO

Sunday 31st October 1999 – All Hallows' Eve

Tracey Phillips sat on the edge of her bed and stared listlessly at her reflection in the dressing table mirror. A sallow-faced young woman, with puffy eyes surrounded by dark shadows, met her gaze with all the enthusiasm of a dead fish.

Up close, her heavily made-up face looked farcical, clown-like even; the mascara was too heavy, the lipstick was way too thick, and her blusher looked like it had been put on with a workman's trowel.

Tracey despised what she had become, and after several seconds of intense soul-searching she tore her eyes away from the painful image, biting her bottom lip in shame and trying to fend off the stomach cramp that was threatening to strike. Tracey had been released from the local nick an hour ago. The Rozzers had kept her there for eighteen hours while they tried to prove that she had been kiting stolen cheques. And even though she had started clucking almost immediately, that heartless bastard of a Police Surgeon had flatly refused to give her anything but paracetamols to ease the pain. When they finally realised they were flogging a dead horse and released Tracey without charge, she had rushed straight home, changed out of the sweat and vomit stained clothes she'd been wearing, and phoned her pimp to come and collect her as quickly as he could.

Staring down at the frayed and faded carpet beneath her feet, Tracey reminded herself that the skanky, hard-faced bitch in the mirror had been a real looker once, turning heads wherever she went. Of course, that was before she had traded her soul for the chemicals that had ruined her. She snorted, dismissing the self-recrimination. After all, what was the point? The fucking addiction owned her.

In an effort to take her mind off the craving, she tried to recall what life had been like before, but her memories of those drug-free days were elusive, like half-forgotten childhood dreams in which reality and fantasy blurred into one.

Just then, the mother of all stomach cramps hit hard, doubling her over. *Please help me*, she prayed to a God she no longer believed in. Sinking to her knees, Tracey clung to the rickety dresser as she struggled against the rush of hot bile that rose to the back of her throat, determined to keep the meagre contents of her stomach down.

She tried to pull herself up onto the bed, but another wave of pain washed over her, and she stumbled into the side of the dresser, scattering makeup onto the threadbare carpet.

Tracey squinted at the blurred hands of her cheap wristwatch through a pain-induced haze. By a sheer act of willpower, she forced herself to focus on the tiny numbers:

00: 55.

Her pimp would be here any minute now. If she was lucky, and she put herself about a bit, she should just be able to scrape together the money she needed to buy enough crack to see her through until tomorrow night. Claude would have a few rocks on him, and Tracey definitely needed a hit before she would be fit for work, if that was the right word for it, selling herself in some dim and dingy alley for thirty pounds a time.

The fly in the ointment was that Tracey didn't have any money to pay for that all important first rock, and Claude Winston wasn't the type of man to let her have anything in advance. Claude looked after number one. Everyone else was there for him to screw, one way or another. That was his philosophy.

The bedroom door opened a fraction, and a sleepy-faced child cautiously poked her head around it. An infectious smile immediately lit up her young face as she caught sight of the woman kneeling by the dresser.

"Hello mummy," she said, rubbing the sleep from her eyes with her knuckles.

"Go back to bed, April," Tracey managed, using her sleeve to wipe a string of dribble from her chin.

"But I heard a scary noise," April protested. As she stepped into the room something scrunched under her foot, and she bent down to retrieve a tube of lipstick, which she examined inquisitively under the weak glow of the room's forty-watt bulb.

"Put it down," Tracey said, irritably.

"Can I play with it, mummy?" the girl asked, brushing the long blond hair from her face. Clad in a pair of tomato red pyjamas that had little yellow teddy bears imprinted all over, the child possessed a purity of heart that her mother could no longer recognise or appreciate.

"No, you bloody can't." Tracey snatched the lipstick from her hand and viciously threw it onto the dresser.

Tracey's eyes clouded. "What did you say you wanted?" she demanded impatiently.

"Mummy, a scary noise woke me up. Pooh was scared too, and he wants to stay with you tonight?" She indicated the worn bear tucked into the crook of her right arm. It had been a constant companion since she received it on her first birthday, four years previously.

"No," Tracey said, averting her eyes from the child's piercing stare.

"Pleeeeeaase!" April's tiny, tired voice was both hopeful and demanding.

"NO!" Tracey all but screamed. She didn't need this. Not now! Why did the kid have to pick this night to have her nightmare? Couldn't she see that Tracey had more important things to worry about? "Look, I've got to go out to work, so stop pestering me and go back to bed." Her voice rose dangerously as she tottered on the verge of hysteria. Suddenly, the room reminded her of the stifling cell she had recently vacated; the very walls seemed to be closing in to suffocate her. Tracey staggered to her feet; dismissing her daughter's outstretched arms, ignoring her tear-filled eyes.

Where the hell was Claude? She needed some stuff. Right now! Tracey pushed past her child. Oblivious to the pain her rejection had inflicted, she stormed out of the bedroom without a backward glance.

Tracey's mother, Rita, had been fast asleep, but the shouting woke her up and she rushed across to her daughter's room as fast as she could, arriving just as Tracey charged out. Powerless to do anything, Rita could only watch in anguish as Tracey stomped off along the narrow hall. After grabbing her coat from the back of the door, she stormed out without saying a single word.

The street door slammed violently.

Little April was sitting on her mother's bed, hugging her teddy and trying very hard not to cry when Rita walked in. "What did I do wrong, Nanny?" April asked in that angelic little voice of hers. She looked so sad, and it broke Rita's heart. "It's alright baby. Come to Nanny." Rita's voice was thick with emotion as she fought back tears of grief. *Dear God*, she prayed, *help me to be strong for the child's sake.*

April fell into her Grandmother's outstretched arms and began to cry, her little body racked by giant sobs. *It just isn't fair*, Rita thought, as she carried the girl back to her own room and tucked her into bed. It was hard enough for an adult to cope with having a drug addict in the family, let alone a child. She found herself shaking with anger. How could Tracey do this to them, her own flesh and blood? Wishing she knew how to make things better, Rita sat on the edge of the bed, stroking her granddaughter's hair and whispering soft words of reassurance. Gradually, the sobbing faded and blessed sleep came, wrapping the child in its protective embrace.

Little April hadn't been planned. The father had vanished, never to be seen again on the day that he found out Tracey was pregnant. Tracey, consumed by her inadequacies, had been an absent parent from day one, leaving Rita to raise the child alone. As she tiptoed out of the child's bedroom, all Rita could think about was what would become of her beautiful granddaughter if anything ever happened to her.

Tracey slammed the street door shut and repeatedly jabbed at the button for the lift. She knew she ought to feel bad about the way she had treated April, but all that mattered now was finding a way to persuade Claude to give her some crack. Perhaps if she offered to blow him in the car park, he would let her have a little something on account. She doubted it though. He had long since ceased to find her even remotely interesting in that way.

The lift door opened and she went in. The light in the small metal box was dim and flickered constantly. She half expected it to go out before she reached the ground, five floors below. The inside was covered with graffiti, and the smell of urine was overpowering. This place really was a shit hole. It always had been, but at least when she had been a kid the lifts had been cleaner.

As she emerged from of the lift and entered the main lobby area, Tracey noticed two skinny white youths sitting by the stairwell. The older of the two couldn't have been more than fifteen. They both had dirty, matted hair and looked like they hadn't washed or changed their clothes in days, the dirty bastards. They gave her a nervous glance, weighing her up. "What you staring at, you fucking pussies?" She shouted aggressively, making sure they saw her as a threat, and not a potential victim. They turned away quickly, and she sucked her teeth at them in disgust.

Tracey couldn't help wondering what the fuck their parents were playing at, letting them out at this time of night, and then she spotted the bright red sores around their mouths and noses and caught a whiff of the glue fumes. Suddenly everything made sense. Solvent abuse had become commonplace around here. Well, let them get on with it, she thought as she left the block. Life was tough, and she had her own problems to worry about.

Tracey stopped at the edge of the kerb, shifting her weight impatiently from foot to foot as she watched the traffic going by. She nodded at the elderly woman from number twenty-three, who was walking her little Jack Russell on the small green in the middle of the estate. As she watched, the mutt squatted and began to defecate. Its owner patiently leaned against the sign prohibiting dogs and ball games and waited for her pet to finish its business.

Where the hell was Claude? she wondered. There was hardly any traffic on the road at this time of night so there was no excuse for his being late. Why did he always keep her waiting when she needed the gear? It was as if he sensed her need and deliberately kept her on tenterhooks. That would be just like Claude. He was a cruel man who took pleasure from other people's suffering. She wrapped her flimsy jacket tightly around her shoulders, hugging herself to keep warm against the autumnal chill. It had been a very wet month, and although the sky was currently crystal clear, she suspected that before too long it would cloud over again and piss down.

She had just started to pace up and down when the black BMW 3 series with tinted windows pulled up beside her and the passenger door was pushed open.

"Get in, bitch," a deep, gravelly voice ordered.

Claude Winston was a physically imposing man. The Jamaican stood well over six-foot-tall and weighed in at a smidgen under nineteen stone. True, he was carrying some flab, but only a fool would underestimate him because of that. The beaded dreadlocks he sported were his pride and joy; no one touched the dreads. Tonight, he wore a black three-quarter-length leather coat, a black silk tee shirt, and black trousers. He liked black. It was his trademark.

Winston liked to think of himself as an entrepreneur who dealt in marketable commodities. The commodities in question were drugs and women, and he was pleased to announce that business was booming.

As the car moved off Tracey turned to Winston. "Claude, I'm really hurting. Can you let me have a little something in advance? I'll pay you back as soon as I turn a trick, I promise."

She did her best to sound provocative, and as she spoke, she gently placed her hand on his left leg and began to slide it upwards towards his groin.

Winston didn't reply. He didn't even look at her. *Fucking cheek*, he thought, gritting his teeth. It was bad enough that she'd had the front to phone him up and beg for a lift, without expecting him to throw in a freebie on top. And what the fuck was the stupid little slut doing over in south London anyway? She should have been out grafting hours ago; her laziness was costing him money.

Tracey was almost at the end of her tether, and instead of putting her out of her misery, as he could have done so easily, it looked like Winston was just going to ignore her.

It was too fucking much!

She had to shout to be heard above the car's sound system which was blaring out the live version of Bob Marley's '*No woman no cry*'.

"Claude, sweetie, don't do this to me. I'm good for it. You know I am."

She tried to undo his fly. When she had first started working for Claude, two years ago, he had liked for her to suck him while he drove her to work. It had given him a buzz. Maybe that would loosen him up a little, make him more amiable towards her.

He slapped her hands away.

"Stop squirming, you worthless bitch, and save your breath. If you want the merchandise you pay for it up front like everyone else. What do you think *I* am? A fucking charity?"

Tracey sat back up and turned to look out of the nearside window so that he wouldn't be able to see the desperation in her face.

As they turned onto Tower Bridge Tracey glanced down to her left at *HMS Belfast*. As a child, London had seemed such a wondrous place, full of excitement and adventure. Her father, who was a bit of a history buff, and the local pub quiz champion, had regularly treated her to days out in London. They had spent many a happy Sunday afternoon exploring the Capital's famous sights together. Her father was a font of knowledge and seemed to know everything worth knowing about every landmark they ever visited. Tracey hadn't thought about her dad in years, yet suddenly, she could hear him, clear as a bell, recanting with great pride how the retired WWII Cruiser's revolutionary new radar system had played a major role in sinking the *Scharnhorst* during the famous Boxing Day battle of 1943.

London Bridge provided the backdrop for the Belfast, and to its right stood the pencil-thin Monument. Beyond that, she spotted the cupola roof of St. Paul's Cathedral. And there, right in the distance, stood the bizarre, aerial infested Post Office Tower. She welled up as she recalled her dad telling her that Anthony Wedgwood Benn, whoever the fuck he was, had once proclaimed it symbolised 20th Century Britain.

The London she knew now was a very different place from the magical one her father had shown her, a dark and violent place that brought her nothing but pain and despair, a place controlled by pimps and gangsters. Now, not even the cherished memories of those distant, happy days could ignite a spark of happiness inside her chest.

They caught a red light at the Tower, and Tracey forced herself to endure the long wait by counting the small cross-shaped slits in the massive stone structure on her left.

The lights changed to green and the BMW moved off with a lurch.

Tears of desperation streamed down Tracey's face.

She needed a fix, *NOW!*

Winston reached across to the Blaupunkt, pressing a button to rewind the Marley tape. Apart from a dull whirring noise as the tape rewound, the car was filled with an awkward silence that was so loud it was almost deafening.

A few year-long seconds later, there was a loud click from the cassette player and Bob began to sing again. Winston adjusted the volume until the bass vibrated through her entire body.

'*No woman no cry*'.

Her mind raced as she fended off another bout of stomach cramp. Surely, he wouldn't send her off without a fix? There had to be a way to persuade him.

But how?

She was running out of time.

When Rita finally returned to her own bed she couldn't sleep. Instead, she found herself wondering where her daughter was and what would eventually become of her. Would she even bother to come back home in the morning, or would she gravitate back to the East End squat where she had spent most of the last year dossing?

Rita knew that things couldn't carry on like this for much longer, and a familiar coldness engulfed her fragile body in its icy grip as she contemplated Tracey's probable fate. She tried to rationalise the growing fear, to dismiss it as the mindless dithering of an old woman, but deep in her heart, she knew exactly what would become of Tracey unless something drastic was done. The dreadful realisation made her ageing flesh crawl.

―――

Somehow, Tracey survived the drive around the outskirts of the City and into Aldgate High Street without breaking down. Music continued to blast out from the German car's powerful speakers, making her head hurt. It seemed to be throbbing in time to the beat.

Boom, boom, boom.

Tracey wanted to scream, but she forced herself to take a deep breath instead and looked at her face in the vanity mirror. *Shit!* Her mascara had run. Why hadn't she bought the waterproof stuff the prissy sales assistant had recommended?

As they turned into Commercial Street Tracey made one last effort. "Claude, I just need one rock, to take the pain away. Please! Just one measly rock! C'mon Claude, just this one time," Predictably, he ignored her, and in growing desperation, Tracey's trembling hand reached out towards his arm, gripping it tightly, a drowning swimmer clinging to a lifeline in a storm.

"Please, Claude," she begged him for compassion, knowing in her heart that the concept would be repugnant to him. He brushed it off and gave her a warning glance. She knew it was dangerous to push Winston. He wouldn't hesitate to hit her if he thought she deserved it. She had seen what he was capable of more than once.

Winston glanced at her out of the corner of his eye. All he felt was contempt. She was a pathetic little junkie whose life was a wreck. He might sell the stuff to others, but that was business. Only a fool would mess with that shit, and he had no time for fools.

Winston wondered how long it would be before he had to get rid of her. She was starting to become a real pain. Imagine asking him for credit!

Silly fucked up cow.

Even if Winston felt any sympathy, which he didn't, he would never let it show. He had a reputation as a hard, ruthless operator to think about. Going soft would be bad for business. Not that there was any chance of that.

He slowed down along Commercial Street to observe the competition and quickly spotted several girls from rival stables plying their trade.

As he entered his own territory his practised eye picked out a steady stream of punters with ease. It wasn't hard to spot them as they as they cruised past the girls, looking to score.

He pulled the BMW up by Quaker Street, and nodded at two of his girls across the road, lingering outside the used car sales lot. He turned to Tracey, looking at her properly for the first time that evening.

"Right, off you go, bitch," he said harshly. "I'll be back in an hour or so, plenty of time to earn the money to buy what you need from me."

She started to protest, to beg, but his hand reached out with surprising speed for such a big man. Fingers the size of sausages dug into her upper right arm. He twisted it hard, pulling her towards him, his patience at an end. His face was inches from hers now, and his foul warm breath bombarded her as he whispered: "It's not good for your health to argue with me, bitch. Now go and earn me some fucking money or I'll tear your skinny white arm off."

Tracey gasped with pain as her shoulder nearly popped out of its socket.

Winston had expected a submissive response and, under normal circumstances, that's exactly what he would have got, but Tracey's dysfunctional mind had pushed her over the edge, making her as unpredictable and as emotionally volatile as nitroglycerine.

In an explosion of unfettered panic, she lunged out with her left hand, clawing the side of his face as hard as she could. The world was closing in on her, making it difficult to breathe, and all she knew was that she had to make him release her; she had to break free and get out of the car. Her long nails were sharp enough to draw blood easily and, with all of her remaining strength, she raked them downwards, gouging the side of his face. She could actually feel the shards of soft flesh getting trapped under her nails as she shredded his skin.

With a surprised howl of pain, Winston released her arm. To her absolute horror, she could see, even in the dark, four fresh tramlines running down the side of his face. A trickle of blood was already seeping out of one.

Winston raised his hand to his face in disbelief. He winced at the contact with his lacerated skin. When he examined his fingers, they had fresh blood on them. His blood!

The side of his face was burning like he'd just been branded.

"I'll kill you for this." The words, spoken in quiet fury, chilled her to the bone. She jumped out of the car and ran blindly across the road. A passing motorist sounded his horn angrily as he swerved to avoid both her and the open door of the car.

Winston was already half out of the car, intent on following her across the road and thrashing her, there and then, as a lesson for all to see. No one fucks with The Man and walks away to tell the tale. But he was as cunning as he was brutal. There were people about, and he could do without the complication of witnesses. Besides, it might ruin trade for the night, and that would never do.

No, it would be smarter to make the bitch suffer later when no one else was around. Before the night was through, he would teach her a lesson she would never forget. He would make an example out of her for all the other bitches to bear in mind: don't fuck with The Man.

Fighting to keep his emotions from spilling over, Winston slammed the passenger door with enough force to make the BMW rock. He eased his great bulk back into the car and performed a lazy U-turn, pulling into Quaker Street, where the two hookers had converged on Tracey.

The BMW stopped by the kerb and the electric window slowly

wound down. The sound system blasted its loud music into the quiet night air, reverberating off the building walls opposite.

Boom, boom, boom.

Seeing the look on Claude's face, the two working girls immediately distanced themselves from Tracey.

Winston leaned across the passenger seat, his eyes locking with hers. The intensity of his gaze was unbearable. His black orbs seemed to burn deep into her head as if he were peering into her very soul. She recoiled from the aura of malice, instinctively edging backwards until she could go no further, coming to a halt with her back pressed into the wire mesh fence of the used car sales lot.

"I'm sorry, Claude, please don't hurt me," she begged, almost wetting herself with fear.

Still staring malevolently into her eyes, Claude reached up and placed his right forefinger just below the left side of his chin. Slowly, and with great feeling, he drew it from side to side across his neck. With the same finger, he then pointed directly at Tracey. The message was clear, even in her state of withdrawal, and she reacted as if she had been slapped.

As the BMW drove off her knees buckled with relief and a small whimper escaped her quivering lips.

What had she done?

How could she have been so stupid?

What would he do to her now?

Shit, shit, shit!

As she stood there, contemplating the pain that Claude would undoubtedly inflict on her, desperately needing a fix and knowing that things could only get worse, Tracey Phillips reached the lowest ebb of her entire life.

She found herself wishing that she was dead and that her life of pain and suffering would finally be over. Sadly, before the night was through, her wish was going to come true.

CHAPTER THREE

The Disciple sat motionless in the cab of his battered Sherpa van, which was parked between two cars midway along Quaker Street, and wondered how the situation outside the car lot would develop.

The girl had taken a big chance, playing chicken with the traffic like that, but the gamble seemed to have paid off because she now had a thirty-second head start on her pursuer. Incredibly, having just risked her life to get away from him, she immediately surrendered the advantage by stopping on the other side of the road.

What the hell was she doing? It was a no-brainer that he would come after her.

And he did. But instead of unfolding into the high-octane drama the build-up had promised, the situation simply fizzled out; for instead of leaping out of his car and laying into her, as any self-respecting thug in his position would surely do, the big lump merely sat in his BMW, made an 'I'm gonna slit your throat' gesture towards her, and then drove off.

The whole thing was a total anti-climax.

As the BMW tore past his van, The Disciple caught a glimpse of the marks on the driver's angry face. *That must have hurt,* he thought, taking perverse pleasure from the fact. *Good.* He didn't like pimps, for what else could the man be, any more than the odious product they marketed.

As the dust settled, he began taking stock of the three whores loitering outside the used car lot. The black girl had a long scar down her left cheek; an eyesore that marred an otherwise pretty face. The white middle-aged whore had a stern pig-like face, a bloated figure, and peroxide hair. He shuddered; she was more Marilyn Manson than Marilyn Monroe.

Neither took his fancy.

On the other hand, the scrawny white girl who had just joined them showed real promise. Even tear-streaked with mascara, her face was pleasant and inviting. Her hair looked natural, too, which was more than he could say about her plump companion. The third girl's body looked reasonably firm from a distance; although he knew that close up, she was bound to be a little frayed around the edges. At least she was endowed with good size tits, a quality he liked in his women. She had nice legs too, and he suspected that she had been a real stunner once.

In his previous, weaker, life he would have wanted her badly. But, like all the rest, she would have mocked his feeble efforts, making him feel even more useless and inadequate then he already did.

Thankfully, The Craft had taught him how to control and re-channel such urges, enabling him to focus all his energies on completing the ritual without succumbing to the distractions of the flesh.

As he watched, a blue Cavalier pulled off the main drag, slung a lazy U in the mouth of Quaker Street, and stopped by the car lot. Scar Face and Miss Piggy were at the driver's door in an instant, each trying to out writhe and out gyrate the other. The Disciple found their brazenness positively obscene. It was interesting to see that Nice Tits, the girl he had taken a fancy to, was hanging back.

At the conclusion of a short, businesslike, conversation Scar Face waved to the others and slipped into the passenger seat. Miss Piggy, having lost out, could only stand there looking dejected as she waved goodbye to the receding car.

Excellent, The Disciple thought, *one down and two to go!*

It struck him that Nice Tits was becoming increasingly jittery, and he wondered what was bothering her. Did she sense what was coming her way? He smiled. Now there was a thought.

Miss Piggy and Nice tits were so engrossed in their conversation that they failed to notice the police car that glided into view, headlights dimmed to make it less conspicuous.

He watched anxiously as the patrol car crawled to an inevitable halt beside the two blissfully ignorant whores. He held his breath, feeling powerless to prevent the inevitable vice bust. *Go away!* He willed them, knowing it was never going to happen. *Just drive off and leave them to me.*

The driver unwound his window, and from the way he started giving it some with his finger it was obvious that he was reading the riot act to them. The Disciple rolled his eyes. *How Pathetic!* The cop was wasting his breath. Well intentioned words were wasted on feral creatures like these.

The female operator got out of the patrol car and started taking down their details in a little notebook. In stark contrast to her earlier behaviour, Miss Piggy was now trying to look like butter wouldn't melt in her loathsome mouth.

When she was done, the operator handed over the notebook to her driver, who began speaking into his radio. The Disciple reasoned he must be doing name checks, to see if either girl was circulated as wanted. Just as the reply started coming through, the transmission was cut across by someone who sounded like they were running flat out. The Disciple quickly gathered that an officer on foot was chasing someone in Roman Road.

The driver, who up until now had looked rather bored, suddenly became very animated; he tossed the notebook aside and started signalling for his operator to forget the whores and get in quickly. As soon as the bemused looking passenger closed her door the car tore off, blue lights and siren erupting into action simultaneously.

Realising he was still holding his breath, The Disciple released it in a long whoosh and uttered a silent thank you to the gods above. He wondered if, perhaps, it would be better directed to the demons below.

As the patrol car pulled out of the side road, doing a wheel spin that would have left most boy racers green with envy, Nice Tits gave it the two-fingered salute. Miss Piggy walked over and gave her a big hug, then whispered something in her ear. Whatever she said seemed to cheer Nice Tits up considerably. There was another brief conversation, in which Miss Piggy nodded several times, and then she blew Nice Tits a kiss and waddled off towards the main road.

"Please be as quick as you can," Nice Tits shouted after her friend, and there was real desperation in her voice.

"I will," Miss Piggy promised, and waddled even faster. Within seconds she had vanished from sight.

Two down and one to go.

Things were moving fast, perhaps too fast. His heart pounded as he scanned the street, but other than little miss Nice Tits it was completely deserted.

He doubted that there would ever be a better opportunity, and it struck him that if he were going to act, he ought to do so now before the moment passed. He took a deep breath, thinking: *by Lucifer, I'm really going to do this!*

The Disciple's hands were shaking as he started the ignition and turned on the lights.

It was show time.

As the van jolted away from the kerb, adrenaline surged through his veins like liquid electricity. God this was the most exciting thing he had ever done. *What a ride, what a thrill,* he felt like singing. *All I wanna do is kill, kill, kill!*

The words echoed in his head. He had a score to settle and now it was payback time.

He felt no guilt about what he intended to do.

Why should he?

Harlots just like the one he intended to gut had laughed at him, cheated him out of money and finally infected him. The memory of being treated for venereal disease at that dreadful clinic still made him cringe. He had waited; hoping it would go away, suffering in silence. In the end, the pain had been too much. The shame had been worse.

Much worse.

He shuddered at the recollection of what whores like her and her filthy parasitic friends had put him through. How he hated them, all of them. *Fucking bitches!*

They had affected his health, ruined his marriage and made his life a total misery.

After years of suffering, he was finally going to put things right and move on.

What a ride, what a thrill. All I'm gonna do is kill, kill, killllllll!

The words had such a nice ring to them.

Tracey Phillips was swaying like a punch-drunk boxer as she stood on the corner staring at passing cars and waiting for a punter to show some interest.

The arrival of Old Bill had sent the kerb crawlers scuttling back under their rocks, but they were nothing if not predictable, and she knew that if she gave it ten-minutes, they would all come flocking back.

A part of her was grateful for the enforced reprieve; she desperately needed to score some gear before letting anyone score with her.

Fat Sandra had nipped off for a quick piss; she had a bit of a bladder problem, and would be backward and forward all bloody night like a urine fueled yo-yo. The good news was that Tracey had got the gullible old cow feeling so sorry for her that she had agreed to pick up a couple of rocks on the way back. The old piss pot had even swallowed the line about Tracey paying her back as soon as she turned a trick, like that was going to happen.

The sound of an engine coughing into life startled her, and she turned around to see a battered van lurch away from the kerb further along the road.

It crawled along the road towards her.

Fuck, she thought. *A punter.* She wasn't up to this, not by a long stretch, but she desperately needed the money, so she smoothed her mini skirt down and tried to look as interested and seductive as she could.

The driver suddenly flicked the headlights onto main beam, and she raised a hand to shield her eyes. "You cock," she cursed under her breath, "like I don't feel bad enough without you trying to blind me."

Tracey took up a half-hearted pose by the driver's door as soon as it slid back. Through eyes that wouldn't focus properly, she tried to give him the once over, taking in the fact that her prospective client was a middle-aged white man with waxen skin, dark, wavy hair and a moustache. He was a little overweight, and his small hands were encased in leather driving gloves.

It struck her that he had nervous, shifty eyes, but most of her punters had those. "Hello, handsome. Looking for some action?" she asked, trying not to slur her words.

The Disciple smiled. At least his mouth did. The eyes remained cold and remote. He had recognised her clucking for what it was and knew it would make her easier to handle.

The important thing was speed. If he could spirit her away before anyone appeared, he was home and dry. "Maybe," he said, guardedly. "What's on offer?"

"I can do most anything you want. Cost you though."

Was it his imagination or was she starting to sway a little as she stood there?

A dog barked in the distance, and he glanced nervously in that direction.

Still all clear.

"How much you want to go all the way?" he asked, licking his lips nervously.

"That'll cost you thirty. It's not negotiable, and you've gotta wear a rubber."

It always amazed him just how matter of fact these people could be about such an embarrassing subject. They quickly agreed on the price and he beckoned to her to get into the passenger door of the van. Her bum had barely touched the seat before The Disciple drove off.

"I know a quiet place just a couple of streets from here," she said, pulling her seatbelt on. "The Old Bill never checks round there, so we won't be bothered."

"Sounds perfect," he said. "Show me the way."

Three minutes later, she directed the van into a loading bay at the rear of a nearby warehouse. There were no streetlights, no CCTV, and it was completely off the beaten track, just as she had claimed.

She leaned tantalisingly close to him and whispered, "Do you want me in the van, or are we going outside for a knee trembler?"

Her cheap perfume filled the front of the van, intoxicating him. His hands trembled and he was aware that he was hard. He wanted this, needed it. He felt a shiver of excitement run through his body. "Tell me," he croaked, "what star sign are you?"

"Who cares," Tracey replied; she just wanted to get this over with as quickly as possible so that she could get back and buy some more drugs.

"I do," he said. "It's important to me." That was an understatement! He couldn't kill her until he knew for certain.

Tracey shrugged. *What a weirdo.* "I'm a Virgo," she told him. "So, are we doing this or what?"

"Oh yes," he told her. "We're going to do it right now." The Disciple climbed through the dividing curtains into the rear of the van and motioned for Tracey to follow. She shook her head and stayed put.

"Money first," she demanded, holding out her hand. She could see he was annoyed, but Tracey wasn't going to do anything until she was paid. She had been on the game too long to make that mistake. Cash up front; those were the terms. She told him so.

For a moment the impulse to grab her skinny little throat and throttle her where she sat was overwhelming, but, somehow, he managed to resist the voice in his head spurring him on to squeeze the life out of her. He decided to permit her the illusion of control. His breathing grew laboured as he removed the money from his wallet and passed it over with a quivering hand.

After carefully checking the money she slipped it into her purse with a shaking hand. She found it hard work, climbing into the back of the van. Dizzy and out of breath from her efforts, she noticed that the whole of the inside was covered in sheet plastic. "Kinky," she said, thinking: *You slimy fucking sicko. I bet your wife would be seriously freaked out if she knew about this little set up of yours.*

"What's your name?" he asked.

"Tracey. What's yours?" Searching her bag for a condom, she thought he looked like a 'Keith' or a 'Kenneth'.

He smiled as he reached for something just behind him. This time it did reach the eyes for he was about to begin his work, and that made him truly happy. His song was being played at maximum volume in his mind. It was so loud that he was sure she would be able to hear it.

What a ride, what a thrill. All I'm gonna do is KILL, KILL, KILL...

He remembered that she'd asked him a question. What was it again? Oh yes, now he remembered. "My real name's not important, but I suspect after tonight most people will be calling me... Jack. I'm sure you can guess why."

She stopped fishing around in her bag and looked up, concerned by the nasty tone that had crept into his voice.

"Ta-da!" The man announced theatrically. At first, she thought he was doing Jazz Hands at her until she realised he was brandishing a huge knife in his left hand.

"Oh my God!" she murmured, dropping the bag.

Sandra Dawson was a bit of a mother hen to the younger girls in Winston's stable. She was always looking out for them, forever nagging them to eat properly, constantly encouraging them to get fresh needles from the needle exchange in Cambridge Heath Road rather than reusing or – worse – sharing; and she never tired of preaching about personal hygiene and the dangers of not using protection.

When Tracey had come flying across the road, as though the devil himself were breathing down her neck, she'd instinctively known that something terrible had just happened. As soon as Winston drove off Sandra tried to get her to talk about it, but Tracey was clucking so badly she could hardly string a sentence together.

Sandra detested drugs. She had seen too many lives ruined by them, but seeing the state Tracey was in she had agreed to get her a couple of rocks to prevent her body from shutting down. How ironic, Sandra had thought, taking drugs would kill Tracey, and sooner rather than later, but her dependency was so great that she could not function without them.

As she hurried back towards Quaker Street, she tried to avoid handling the foul cellophane covered substance in her pocket, as though contact with it alone could infect or contaminate her. She almost soiled herself when a police van drove by.

There was no sign of Tracey when she finally arrived back at Quaker Street, out of breath and sweating despite the chill. Angela, the black girl with the scar, had returned, and from the glazed look in her eyes had already spent the money she had earned on crack.

"Angie, 'ave you seen Tracey anywhere?"

Angela gave a lazy shrug. "She's probably off with a punter." She didn't give a fuck about Tracey and couldn't, for the life of her, understand why Sandra did.

"Poor fucker's gonna want a refund, state of her," Sandra told herself, conscious that she would have to keep the awful stuff in her pocket for a little while longer. Still, it shouldn't be a problem as long as the fuzz didn't come back.

In her peripheral vision, she registered movement and realised a car was pulling up beside her. Sandra had been so lost in thought that she hadn't heard it approach. For a moment she assumed the worst: that the police had come back, and that she had tempted fate by thinking about them. *Shit!* Sandra thought as her heartbeat returned to normal, *I'm definitely too old for this game.* Pushing her tits out, she took a deep breath, sucked in her stomach and went into the old familiar act.

"'Ello dear. Fancy some fun, do ya?" Sandra flashed her best smile at the driver, hoping he would only want a quick wank.

CHAPTER FOUR

As he entered the ground floor briefing room at Whitechapel Police station, Inspector Ray Speed surveyed the ensemble of bleary-eyed officers sitting in three neat rows facing the lectern, and then glanced down at his watch. It was a minute before six, and he was half hoping that someone had overslept; it was customary for latecomers to buy doughnuts for the rest of the team, and a Krispy Kreme glazed original really would go down a treat this morning.

They all stood up as he entered the room, but he waved them back to their seats. It was far too early for formalities.

The briefing room was a mess, he noticed, which was hardly surprising seeing as the cleaners hadn't been in since Friday morning. Under the chairs, he spotted crumpled newspapers, old copies of *The Job*, sweet wrappers, soft drinks cans and even a sodding pizza box.

His Section Sergeant did a quick head count, and then checked the numbers tallied with those in his duties binder. "All present, sir," he said with satisfaction.

"Thank you," Speed said, nodding curtly. He made his way down the centre aisle to the briefing lectern at the far end of the room, only to find it cluttered with polystyrene cups containing foul-smelling coffee dregs. He wrinkled his nose in disgust. "This place is a bloody pigsty," Speed said, passing the offending items to his Section Sergeant for disposal. "Right, let's begin," he said, wiping his hands on a tissue.

The team had already been stripped to the bone in order to meet a heavy aid commitment up town, so, when Speed announced that the flu epidemic sweeping through the station had claimed another three of their colleagues overnight, there were a few disgruntled groans.

Speed ignored them. In his experience coppers were only happy when they had something to moan about, and by that rationale his remaining troops ought to be bloody ecstatic this morning. He started by posting his officers to the various patrol cars and beats. Once that was done, he asked the Section Sergeant to play the latest briefing slides that the Borough Intelligence Unit – or BIU – had prepared. This included a list of suspects who were currently wanted, and Speed told his four walkers that the team needed to show a few extra arrests to its name this month, so he wanted them to go through the warrants register and spend the first part of the morning making arrest inquiries.

The alarm list was next. The Section Sergeant drew their attention to several premises that had faulty alarms: ones which either didn't work at all or, as was more often the case, went off every time anyone so much as looked at them.

Some officers took notes in their pocketbooks; recording details they felt relevant, while others sat quietly as if it were an effort just to keep their eyes open at such an ungodly hour.

One old sweat, thinking he wouldn't be spotted in the back row, had the temerity to start flipping through the sports section in a copy of yesterday's *The Sun*, which he'd found on his chair. That earned him a right earful from the Section Sergeant and a 'fine' of doughnuts from Speed. "And I don't mean those cheap five-for-a pound stodgy things you get in the supermarket," he warned the offending officer.

Speed finished the parade with a note on officer safety. Night duty had been called to a spate of robberies in and around Hackney Road, in which the same pair of addicts had cornered their victims and brandished blood-filled syringes, before threatening to inject them unless they handed over their money. Luckily no one had been harmed, but it was only a matter of time before some brave have-a-go-Henry ended up as a pin cushion.

With so many HIV, AIDS, and hepatitis sufferers drifting through the ground, there was a very real risk of infection if anyone was stabbed by a junkie's needle. Speed emphasised the need for extreme caution if there were any calls like that this morning. "If in doubt, restrain the fuckers first, and ask questions later," he advised. "But, if you do have to use force, make sure you write it up properly," he added as an afterthought.

After parade, the drivers went out into the back yard to check over their vehicles while everyone else made their way up to the canteen on the top floor to grab a quick, much needed, cup of coffee. While the kettle was boiling the CAD – an acronym that stood for Computer Aided Dispatch – room started to call up various crews and assign them to outstanding calls. They were all non-urgent and could be delayed for a few minutes while the coffee began to work its magic.

When PC Nick Bartholomew entered the canteen a few minutes later, having checked over the RT car – or Pursuit Car as it was now known in modern parlance – he was met by his partner, who handed him a chipped mug that was filled to the brim with steaming hot black coffee. They sat down together at an otherwise empty table.

"Thanks, mate," Nick said gratefully. "Let me get this brew down my neck and we can go out and start playing hunt the bad guy." Bartholomew hated early turns; he would have preferred to park up somewhere out of the way, snooze for an hour and then find a nice quiet cafe to have a fry up in. Unfortunately, the kid was desperate to impress their boss, and Nick didn't want to let him down.

Terry Grier, the younger of the two by eight years, had his gangly legs splayed as far under the table as they would go. He beamed at the suggestion.

Inwardly grimacing at the thought of driving around looking for prisoners, when all he really wanted was to be curled up in bed with his nice warm duvet snuggled around him, Nick took a tentative sip of the boiling liquid, and let out a long appreciative sigh. "Thanks, Tel. I really needed that," he said, and from the look of him, he really did.

"Late night?" Grier asked, tentatively.

Bartholomew shook his head. "I was in bed by eleven," he half said, half yawned. "Trouble is I don't sleep well on earlies. I'm always so worried I'll sleep through the alarm and be late for work that I spend half the night clock watching." As he spoke, he undid the top button of his shirt and began rubbing at an angry looking shaving rash on his neck.

"I've got some moisturiser in my locker if you want something for that," Grier offered.

Bartholomew shook his head, wearily. "It'll be fine," he said, taking another sip of coffee.

"So, where are we gonna get ourselves a decent collar at this time of day?" Grier asked, getting back to the business at hand. He didn't want another drink drive; they were ten-a-penny.

"Don't you worry, mate," Nick assured him, sounding far more optimistic than he felt. "I've got a feeling in my water that today is going to be exciting."

Speed entered the canteen and, after pouring himself a drink, sat down between Bartholomew and Grier. "Late night was it, Nick?" he asked, studying the dishevelled man slumped in the chair before him.

"No, guv, I just didn't sleep well."

"I can see that. I reckon my wife could fit her weekly shopping in the bags under your eyes. Not coming down with this flu bug, are you?"

Bartholomew shook his head. "Only thing wrong with me is a dose of early-turn-itus."

It was at this moment that the first 'all units' call of the day came out. The dispatcher informed them that a watchman doing his rounds at the building site next to the railway tracks in Quaker Street had just called in to say he'd found what he thought was a dead body beside the site office.

"Bollocks!" Nick cursed, casting a wistful glance at the coffee he would now be forced to abandon.

In contrast, Grier looked expectantly at his partner, like a puppy waiting for its master to throw it a ball.

"Come on, Terry," Bartholomew said, buttoning his shirt back up. "Let`s go."

Grier propelled himself out of his chair like a sprinter leaving the blocks, his lanky legs jarring the underside of the table so hard that the three cups resting on its top were violently upended. There was no time to do anything about the puddle of dark liquid that quickly spread across the table's Formica surface and began to drip down onto the canteen floor.

Nick glanced down at his wristwatch as they headed towards the lift.

06:23hrs.

And another day in the city begins, he thought, ruefully.

Speed followed close behind, his face taut. "I'd better come with you. Sounds like I'm going to be needed in my capacity as Duty Officer."

The lift's descent was painfully slow, and Grier used the time to bombard them with useless speculation about what they would find when they arrived on scene. Speed did his best to tune out the kid's voice as he mentally recited the critical incident checklist to himself. Hopefully, if there was a body waiting for them out there, it had died from natural causes, but if something more sinister had gone down, he wanted everything to be done by the book so that it wouldn't come back and bite him later on.

As they sped out of the rear yard, siren wailing and lights flashing, they were already receiving updates from the control room. The informant was waiting at the site entrance and had been told not to let anyone in until they got there. Their ETA was six-minutes, but traffic was light and Nick, tired or not, was a superb driver. They made it in just over three.

As the area car screeched to a halt by the site entrance an elderly man began waving frantically from just inside the gate.

Here we go again! Nick thought, removing the ignition key from the Golf VR6.

Grier and Speed were already out and running. As he brought up the rear, Nick Bartholomew noticed that the old timer was shaking violently. His skin was the colour of faded parchment and he was clutching at his chest with a gnarled hand. Selfishly, Nick found himself hoping their informant would be able to tell them what had happened before he keeled over from a heart attack.

...I've got a feeling in my water that today is going to be exciting.

Young Terry took hold of the old man's arm to steady him. "It's alright pops, I've got you," he said gently.

Albert Grayson, Bert to everyone who knew him, was in charge of site security for the construction company. At sixty-nine years of age, he was still a remarkably active man who often bragged about being fitter than most men fifteen years his junior. Right then, he was feeling his age, and then some. He tried to describe the sight that had greeted him when he strolled through the gates a few minutes earlier, but the words just wouldn't come out. Instead, he pointed towards the yard with a trembling hand.

Speed took control. They had to find out what was going on here, and quickly. "Terry, stay here and look after this man. He's either in shock or suffering a heart attack, so you'd better call an ambulance for him. Nick, you come with me." In the distance, he could hear the sound of sirens as other units made their way to the scene.

Together they moved into the yard, treading cautiously.

As Speed pushed the corrugated metal gates backwards, Bartholomew drew and racked open his gravity friction lock baton, or ASP as it was more commonly known. The baton's metal shaft made a satisfyingly loud thwack as it extended to its full length, and Bartholomew griped the rubber coated handle tightly as he crept forward cautiously.

Inside the construction site, it seemed eerily quiet, as though the high perimeter fencing had magically cut off all noise from the outside world. Ray Speed branched left; Nick Bartholomew, baton held at the ready, moved off to the right.

As Bartholomew scanned the shadows for signs of a body, he couldn't shake the sinister feeling that someone was there, watching his every move. He wondered if it might be better to wait for backup, but dismissed the idea almost immediately. If a seriously injured victim was in here, finding them quickly could mean the difference between life and death.

"Nick, over here, quickly!" Ray Speed's voice shattered the silence and made Bartholomew jump. He spun around to see Speed standing beside a Portakabin to his far left. The Inspector was staring down at a shape on the floor.

Fearing the worst, Bartholomew sprinted over to join Speed as fast as he could. As he skidded to a halt, he saw that the dark shape was, in fact, the body of a young woman. She lay so deep in shadow he could barely make out her features, even up close like this. Nick fumbled for the torch at the rear of his utility belt with unsteady hands, and as he shone the light over the prone figure, he felt the colour drain from his face.

"Jesus Christ, gov'nor! Look at the state of her," he said, breathing hard. Nick had dealt with plenty of dead bodies in his time, some still fresh, others badly decomposed, but he had never seen anything like this. No wonder the poor old watchman was so traumatised.

The open-eyed stare of the dead woman sent a shiver down his spine. The poor thing was lying flat on her back, with her shoulders tightly wedged between the side of the Portakabin and the perimeter wall. The one arm he could see was branched out to the side at an unnatural angle. There was a frightful gash across the woman's throat, from which a river of arterial blood had shot up the wall during exsanguination. Her face was frozen in an expression of unmitigated fear, the likes of which Bartholomew had never seen before.

He guided the beam from his flashlight downwards until he reached the dead woman's abdomen, at which point he almost dropped the torch. The torso had been torn open, revealing her innards. It was as if she had been ripped apart by a wild beast. A pool of blood, already congealing into a foul looking jelly, had spread out to form the dark pool in which she now lay. The victim's miniskirt had been pulled up over her hips and there was no sign of any underwear. Another pool of thick clotting blood had formed between her open legs, although a small dune of sand had absorbed most of it.

"Who could have done something like this?" Nick asked in disbelief. He was grateful that he hadn't eaten yet; even with an empty stomach, he felt like throwing up.

"Whoever it was, they ought to get the death penalty," Speed said, donning a pair of latex gloves. Moving carefully, so that the crime scene wouldn't be disturbed any more than was absolutely necessary, Speed knelt down and felt the waxen face and hands of the victim. They were cold. She had obviously been there a while. Speed stood up and carefully moved away from the body.

There was a lot to do.

"Nick, go back outside. Absolutely no one, not even the Commissioner himself, gets inside this yard without my direct authority. Get the watchman's details and a brief statement if he's fit enough. Then get him straight to hospital. Make sure someone goes with him, and have them seize his shoes. No, wait. We'd better seize all his clothing, just in case. Then get on the radio. I want the HAT car called and I need more units for a search. Oh, and I want the On-Call Superintendent informed at home. We might as well spoil his day too." He gave Bartholomew a wry smile.

Speed borrowed the torch from Bartholomew. As the junior officer left to carry out his instructions, he began to examine the area in which the body had been found. There was nothing of obvious note on the floor so he let the flashlight roam up and down the sides of the Portakabin and adjacent wall to see if there were blood patterns that indicated a struggle.

There was plenty of blood all right, but not all of it was in the form he would have expected.

On the side of the cabin, in big bold letters, was a message from the killer. Unless Speed was very much mistaken it was written in the victim's blood:

THIS IS ONLY THE START.
BE AFRIAD...
JACK'S BACK!

Speed stared at the message in disbelief. He carefully read the words several times, feeling his stomach tighten a little more each time.

Before long the crime scene was awash with people. The East Homicide Assessment Team (HAT) car arrived first, and they called out a Crime Scene Manager, Sam Calvin, who in turn summoned the on-call photographer.

A Blood Pattern Analysis scientist from the Forensic Science Service was en route, and when she arrived, she would be tasked to measure blood spray patterns and angles and carry out tests on depth and velocity.

The early turn divisional Scenes of Crime Officer, or SOCO, had volunteered to help out, and CSM Calvin promptly put her to work dusting for prints.

The Coroner's Officer had been informed, and he had dispatched the two sombre looking men in dark suits who waited patiently beside a dark van with blacked out windows, and the legend 'Private Ambulance' along its side. at the edge of the cordon, ready to transport the corpse to the morgue.

A number of samples had already been placed in brown paper bags. In the absence of a dedicated exhibits officer from AMIP – the Area Major Investigation Pool – these were being indexed in a green A4 exhibits book by Calvin.

Outside, the area surrounding the building site had been sealed off with police tape, and over half of Ray Speed's early shift was tied up dealing with cordon control.

Territorial Support Group officers from the Commissioner's Reserve had been called to conduct a flash search in the surrounding area for the murder weapon.

The local crime reporter, who routinely monitored police channels, had just turned up and was snooping around outside the cordon, firing questions at Speed in the hope of uncovering some gritty details. Ignoring the man, Speed closed the gate and made sure it was secure.

A detective from the HAT car was making frantic phone calls, switching between the Serious Crime Group Reserve at the Yard and her DCI, providing updates and trying to organise further resources. The second had joined Inspector Speed and the Forensic Medical Examiner, a tetchy old Scotsman called Andrew Mackintosh, who had just arrived and was about to examine the body.

"So, what can you tell us doc?" DC Kevin Murray asked. In his early thirties, Murray seemed unhealthily thin. He had a pale complexion, cropped brown hair and a goatee beard, which took some of the sharpness out of his features. His suit was rumpled, as though he had been sleeping in it.

"I can tell you that she's dead," the FME said.

Murray glanced at Ray Speed and rolled his eyes theatrically. These doctors were all such prima donnas. "We worked that much out for ourselves, doc. What I mean is can you..."

Mackintosh cut him off with a raised hand. "Young man," he said irritably, "firstly, it's not doc, it's doctor. That's the title written on all the fancy diplomas hanging on my surgery wall, and that's what I like to be called. Secondly, I am a GP, not a Home Office pathologist. My job is to pronounce life extinct, nothing more."

"I understand that," Murray persisted, "but if you have any idea how long she's been brown bread it would really help."

"This isn't an episode of Quincy, laddie. You'll have to wait till the pathologist gets his hands on the poor wee thing. He won't appreciate an old fool like me making wild guesses, that's for sure."

"Please, doctor," Speed intervened, "you've been doing this a very long time, and you're highly respected. Any observations you make would be gratefully received."

"Are you playing to my vanity, Inspector?" Mackintosh asked with a raised eyebrow.

Speed shrugged, "I'm just asking for some help."

Mackintosh sighed. "I'm not sure how valid any opinion I express here is, but if you really think it could help then the least I can do is indulge you." Squatting down beside the dead girl, he carried out a visual examination in silence. When he was satisfied he had seen all that he needed to, he gestured towards the lifeless figure with an open hand. "I'd say that she was in her early to mid-twenties. I can tell from the needle marks in her arms that she had a substantial drug problem." Mackintosh turned the girls left arm a fraction for them to see. Track marks ran the length of it. "If you look very closely you will see the walls of the veins in this section of her arm have collapsed, undoubtedly caused by over injecting. I'd expect to find similar track marks along the upper legs and in the groin."

Speed winced. As a man with a needle phobia, he could never understand how people did that to themselves.

Gently lowering the arm, as if wishing to spare the dead girl any more pain, Andrew Mackintosh continued with his clinical observations. His voice was calm, professional, and both officers found themselves hanging onto his every word. "The injuries are truly horrific. I've seldom seen worse. Look at her neck. The wound appears to have been caused by a single, powerful, cut. The incision goes clean through to the vertebrae and has severed the carotid. There are bruise marks around the jaw area. One assumes these were caused by finger pressure, where the killer held his victim during the act of slitting her throat." He pantomimed the action for them. "Whoever did this is either very strong or very mad." His eyes locked with Speed's.

"Maybe both," Speed suggested.

Mackintosh nodded slowly. "Aye, maybe," he agreed.

"I take it that's the cause of death, doctor?" Murray asked, making rapid notes in his blue day book. There were other injuries on the body, but he figured they were all inflicted post-mortem.

"Not for me to speculate," Mackintosh said firmly.

"What about the other injuries, Mack?" Speed asked, thinking this was all so surreal, the gruesome tableau before him could easily have been a waxwork scene depicting Whitechapel circa 1888 lifted straight from The London Dungeons.

"They are interesting," the doctor allowed. "The main abdominal wound appears to be a single incision that runs from just below the sternum at the top to the pubis at the bottom, although there are at least two additional transverse cuts. The cutting appears anything but random, and I can't help wondering why the killer did this unless he wanted to access the organs inside."

"My God," Murray exclaimed, "Do you think this girl was killed so they could steal her organs to sell on the black market?" He'd read about cases where this had actually happened but didn't know anyone who had ever dealt with one.

"Highly unlikely," Mackintosh said. "I think anyone harvesting organs to sell would be much better organised. For starters, they would want to operate in a secure, sterile, location, not in the open like this."

"I take it those are her intestines?" Speed asked, pointing at the loops of bowel protruding from her lower abdomen.

Mackintosh nodded sombrely. "They are, yes."

"What's the story with all the blood and gore coming out of her fanny?" Murray asked, oblivious to the look of disgust that appeared on the two older men's faces. "I mean, it's obviously not just a case of having the decorators in, is it?"

"Having the decorators in?" Mackintosh asked, and his voice was acid.

"You know, on blob. Having her period," Murray explained.

"I would suggest that the haemorrhaging was caused by a large bladed instrument being rammed into her vagina with tremendous force," Mackintosh said, slamming his fist into his open hand several times to demonstrate.

"Jesus," Murray said, now regretting his earlier flippancy.

Mackintosh, who was still kneeling down beside the dead girl, stood up. After dusting his clothes down, he turned to face Speed. "I hope you catch the bloody swine that did this." The outrage in his voice was evident.

"I know it's asking a lot, but can you estimate a time of death for us?" Murray asked.

Mackintosh shook his head slowly. He adjusted his tortoiseshell glasses and sighed.

"Sorry laddie. They don't provide us with crystal balls on the NHS. We've asked for them, but, apparently, the budget just won't stretch."

"Just your best guess," Speed cajoled. "We won't hold you to it if you're wrong."

Mackintosh pulled a face like a bulldog chewing a wasp. "You know, I'm not even supposed to be on-call until this afternoon," he complained. "But Dr Sadler is indisposed this morning and he somehow conned me into swapping shifts with him."

"I bet Dr Sadler would have been willing to give us a rough time of death," Murray said, raising an eyebrow and staring pointedly at the cantankerous FME.

The Scotsman snorted derisively. "Trust me, laddie, Dr Sadler wouldn't have given you the time of day."

"Which is why we're really glad we got you instead," Ray Speed said quickly.

Mackintosh gave each of the officers a long, hard, stare. They were persistent, he'd give them that, but he couldn't blame them for trying to do their job. *Perhaps a guess wouldn't hurt.*

"Sometime between midnight and three o'clock at a guess, and that's all it is, sorry." He shrugged, waved farewell, and turned to leave.

A devout Christian, this was one aspect of his work that Andrew Mackintosh didn't enjoy. Even after all the years he'd worked as a police Forensic Medical Examiner, he still felt shock and anger at the sight of such needless and brutal death, drained by the knowledge that his fellow man, made in God's own image, could inflict such terrible evil upon his own kind.

What a world we live in, he thought. The sooner he retired from his London practice and got away from this dreadful carnage, the better it would be.

"Your boys are gonna have their hands full with this one, I don't envy you," Speed said, as he and Murray walked back towards the site entrance.

"Thankfully my team won't be keeping this. The bosses are probably arguing over who gets it as we speak," Murray said.

At that point they noticed young Grier escorting a middle-aged man of medium height and build towards them. Grier looked distinctly nervous. He was clearly uncomfortable in the older man's presence.

The man, whose wavy fair hair was thinning on top, was a power dresser. His tailored grey suit, red braces, and gleaming Oxfords were very Gordon Gekko. Speed didn't recognise the man but he certainly recognised the type. Even before being told, he knew that this man was top brass. *Well, well, well,* Ray thought. *I guess bad news travels fast.*

He noticed a subtle change in Murray's demeanour as the senior officer approached. The detective had obviously recognised the newcomer. "Speak of the devil, that's DCS Holland, the head honcho at AMIP," he whispered to Speed. "What the fuck is he doing here?"

Speed was pretty sure he knew what Holland was doing here. A working girl had just been spectacularly butchered in Whitechapel, and the killer had left a gloating message for the police. Holland was here to make sure the organisation was fireproof before the media got wind of what had happened.

"Good morning sir," he said, accepting the hand that was offered. "I'm Inspector Ray Speed, the early turn Duty Officer." While speaking, Speed discretely nodded to Grier, letting him know that everything was okay, that he could go back outside.

"Inspector Speed, allow me to introduce myself. I'm Detective Chief Superintendent Holland from the Area Major Investigation Pool." The man held up his warrant card for inspection before continuing. "I've asked for the In-Frame team to be notified and I expect them to arrive shortly. Until then, no one is to touch anything inside the scene." Putting an arm around Speed, he steered him a few steps away from Murray. "Who on your team, apart from you, has seen the message on the Portakabin?" he asked.

"No one. The CSM and the crew of the HAT car didn't want anyone near the body or the porta-cabin while the evidence recovery is ongoing."

"Well, I'd like to see it for myself, if you don't mind. I'll clear it with the CSM first, of course."

CHAPTER FIVE

Jack Tyler was cocooned in a deep sleep when his bedside telephone rang. The harsh noise distorted the fabric of his dream; spreading outward, like the ripples from a stone that's been cast into the still waters of a pond. He instinctively rolled over and rammed his head under the pillow, but not in time to prevent the beautiful woman entwined in his arms, and the golden Caribbean beach on which they frolicked, from turning to dust and blowing away.

Ring-Ring.

Jack's eyes flickered open, and he cursed the telephone for dragging him away before he had even stolen a kiss.

Ring-Ring.

Bollocks! Tyler angrily threw the pillow onto the floor and sat up. He looked at his watch through bleary, half open, eyes. What was the world coming to when you couldn't even enjoy a dream in peace?

Christ! It was only seven o'clock! "This had better be good," he growled, reaching unsteadily for the phone. "Hello?" he snapped, his abrupt tone reflecting his mood.

"*Detective Chief Inspector Tyler?*" a voice at the other end of the line inquired after a moment's hesitation.

"Speaking." Tyler immediately recognised the caller's voice. It was Derek Peterson, George Holland's Staff Officer at AMIP.

As he rubbed the sleep from his eyes, he experienced that familiar sinking feeling in the pit of his stomach. In his line of business, things were generally bad when the office tried to contact you at home, and always worse when they succeeded.

"*It's DS Peterson, sir.*" Peterson was a crusty old detective on the brink of retirement.

"What is it Derek?" he asked without enthusiasm.

Peterson briefed Tyler on the day's gruesome discovery and explained that AMIP was taking on the investigation with immediate effect.

"What's that got to do with me, Derek?" Tyler pointed out irritably. "My team's not in the frame, DCI Quinlan's is."

"*Sorry sir, Mr Quinlan's team picked up a job in Hackney a few hours ago – two winos fell out over a can of Tennent's Super, so one killed the other and tried to hide his body in a wheelie bin. Luckily, the old biddy that lived opposite saw the whole thing and called it in. Locals got there just as chummy was trying to force the bid lid down on his dead mate's head. As your lot are second in the frame Mr Holland said to call you.*" Sensing Tyler's displeasure at not having been informed the moment his team moved into the frame, Peterson hurriedly explained that he hadn't put Jack on notice sooner because the chances of anything else happening overnight were so slim. "*I was going to call you bang on seven,*" he assured Tyler.

"I see," Jack sighed, knowing that Peterson had meant well. As angry as he was, there was nothing to be gained by biting Peterson's head off.

Then Peterson surprised him by saying that DCS Holland was attending the scene himself, going directly from his home in Epping. Something didn't add up. Why would Holland attend a scene in person? Against his will, Jack felt his interest piqued.

"*As per the instructions on the call-out sheet, I've already contacted DI Dillon, sir. He told me to tell you that he'd send out the group pager message. He should be with you in about twenty minutes.*"

Tyler thanked DS Peterson and replaced the receiver. Cursing under his breath, he made his way into the bathroom and turned on the shower. Jack detested early starts; always had, always would. The fact that he'd only had four hours of sleep made today particularly unpleasant.

How ironic, he thought. *The one night I let my hair down and this happens!* No one who knew Jack Tyler would have described him as a party animal. And yet he had partied with the best of them last night, celebrating a friend's fortieth birthday. It had been a crazy affair, and he had lingered to the very end, safe in the knowledge that today was his day off so he could sleep in until late morning, or early afternoon, if he wanted to – and he really wanted to.

That was clearly not meant to be.

As he stood in the shower cubicle, its powerful jet bombarding his tired limbs with steaming hot water, he gradually began to feel more human. He remained there for several minutes, allowing the scalding water to work its magic until he felt able to face the day ahead. As a token protest at being called in on his day off, he decided not to bother shaving, even though with two days' worth of growth already covering his face, he knew he really ought to have made the effort. Jack vigorously towelled himself dry, wondering how badly the call to duty would interfere with his plans for the day. Talk about bad timing! Today was his mother's sixtieth birthday, and his father had arranged a surprise dinner party to celebrate the event. The entire clan was under strict instruction to attend – come hell or high water. He didn't dare miss it; his absence would break her heart. And dad, who had gone to such efforts, not only to organise the get-together but also to keep it a secret, would never forgive him. Whatever else happened today, Jack promised himself, he would be there for his family.

Precisely twenty minutes after receiving the unwanted telephone call, Jack Tyler stood in the kitchen finishing off the last of his coffee and toast, which had been hurriedly prepared and hastily consumed. As he put the crockery in the dishwasher the doorbell rang half a dozen times in quick succession. Tyler opened the street door and scowled unwelcomingly, only to have a folded newspaper thrust in his face. "Aren't you a little old to have a paper round?" he asked, snatching the paper from his caller's outstretched hand.

"If my boss paid me more, I wouldn't need to," Detective Inspector Tony Dillon said.

"If I had my way, I wouldn't pay you at all," Tyler growled. "Ringing my doorbell like a bloody debt collector! What will my neighbours think?"

"Oh, I wouldn't worry," Dillon said lightly. "From what I hear, they don't like you much, anyway."

"Ha, ha," Tyler said, tossing the Sunday paper onto a kitchen worktop. He doubted that he'd get the chance to read that today. He returned to the hall, where he scooped up his warrant card, mobile phone, and keys from a small table.

"Bloody hell, Jack! You look rough," Dillon said. "What time did you get to bed last night?"

"The problem's not what time I went to bed last night, it's the ungodly time that I had to get up today!" Tyler complained.

Sometimes Dillon had to remind himself that Jack Tyler was not only one of the Metropolitan Police's youngest DCIs, he was also one of their most respected homicide detectives. Standing there, unshaven, with his short brown hair uncombed, his collar sticking up on one side and his shirt hanging out on the other, and looking as though he needed at least another four hours of sleep, Tyler more closely resembled a vagrant than a top-notch detective. "So, tell me. Are you deliberately trying to get yourself known as Britain's answer to *Columbo*?"

"What?"

"It's just that you're not wearing a tie today, and your suit is all creased like you haven't hung it up since the last time you wore it, and you haven't shaved or combed your hair. Oh – and your shoes could do with a polish," Dillon explained. "Apart from that, you look very presentable."

Tyler had five off the peg suits that he rotated, whereas Dillon was renowned for his immaculate appearance and his expensive taste in clothes. He had arrived at Jack's house looking resplendent in a charcoal two-piece Pierre Cardin suit, a crisp white T.M. Lewin shirt, and a red silk tie. The decorative silk hanky protruding from his top pocket was folded to perfection, despite the early morning call, and his gold cufflinks and diamond studded tiepin shined as though they had just been polished – as did his shoes.

"You're very observant. I can see why you chose to become a detective. So what if I'm not wearing a tie and my suit is a little creased. Who cares?" Jack had a tie in his pocket, which he planned to put on as soon as they got to work, but he was damned if he was going to tell Dillon that.

"I do," Dillon said, "You look scruffy, like *Columbo,* only worse."

"I look fine."

"I bet you haven't even looked in the mirror today," Dillon chided, shaking his head in disappointment. "You could've at least combed your hair. I'm sure you do it just to spite me. Well, I'm not being seen in public with you looking like that."

With a sigh that signalled defeat, Tyler briskly ran his fingers through his still wet hair, working it into something resembling order. "Have you arranged for an exhibits officer to go to the scene yet?" he asked, pulling out his tie.

"Of course," Dillon said.

"And the group pager message?"

"Sent. I've said there will be a briefing at HT at nine o'clock." HT was the phonetic code for Whitechapel police station.

"Good." Jack turned away from the hall mirror and faced Dillon. "Happy now?" he demanded somewhat petulantly.

"It's a bit better. Pity about the stubble though," Dillon said as he pulled Jack's collar down for him and straightened the knot of his tie. Unlike Tyler, Dillon wouldn't dream of going to work unshaven, unless he was on a stakeout and therefore forced to 'dress down'. This designer beard malarkey that was now becoming trendy was, in his not so humble opinion, for faggots and vagrants.

"Thank you for your care and concern, Mrs Dillon," Jack said, brushing his friend's hands away from his collar. "You'll make someone a fine wife one of these days."

"Is that an offer?"

"No. Now, if you're quite through picking on me, can I suggest that we make our way to the scene?" Tyler suggested, feeling a little like a henpecked husband.

Dillon obediently followed Tyler out of the house. "My, my," he goaded, "we did get out of the wrong side of the bed – *again*!"

Tyler glanced over his shoulder. "Bollocks," he growled.

Dillon smiled sweetly. "Next time you can make your own way in."

Jack paused in mid-stride. "Please, Dill, I'm feeling very delicate today so can we skip the usual pleasantries?"

"Bloody hell, Jack! Why are you always such an arse in the morning?"

"Because I hate getting up early, that's why."

"But the morning's the –"

"– best time of the day," Jack cut in, speaking over his friend. "How could I forget with you ramming it down my throat every five minutes?"

The bickering continued as they crossed the street to a battered dark green Vauxhall Omega, which had definitely seen better days. DS Steve Bull, another member of his team, was sitting behind the wheel, waiting to go. Jack raised a hand in greeting. "Morning Stevie."

"Morning guv. Rough night, was it?"

Did he really look that bad? Jack wondered, or had Dillon primed him to say that before getting out of the car?

"For fucks sake, don't you start, or I'll send you straight back to division."

Bull grinned. "Yes, boss."

"Right Steve," Jack said as he got in the car, "DCS Holland's already on his way, which can't be a good sign. I'd rather not keep him waiting, so let's blue light it," he instructed.

"You're the boss."

"It's a pity *he* doesn't realise that," Jack said, nodding at Dillon, who, having removed his jacket, was only now getting into the car.

"Oh, give it a rest. You don't want me to crease my jacket, do you?" Dillon replied belligerently.

"I don't know why you spend so much money on suits. With all those bulging muscles you look like a couple of sacks of potatoes wrapped in a tight-fitting cloth," Jack said, enjoying the look of hurt that appeared on his friends face.

"Yeah, well, at least it's quality cloth, unlike that cheap rubbish you wear," Dillon pointed out haughtily.

"Some of us are born with style, others have to buy it," Jack countered.

Not long after meeting them, Steve had made the mistake of remarking that they argued worse than an old married couple. The observation hadn't been well received by either of them, even though there was an awful lot of truth in it. After being told to mind his own business, Steve quickly learned to tune them out when they were having a go at each other. Now, he hardly even noticed the squabbling.

"Let's go then, Steve, before Sean Connery, here, starts making any more personal comments about me," Dillon said as he pulled his seatbelt on.

Grinning, Bull flipped on the switches that activated the concealed blue lights: one set fitted behind the front grill, the other mounted in the rear window of the unmarked police car. He dropped the automatic gearshift of the powerful car into sports mode and gunned the accelerator.

Steve Bull was a thin, athletic, man with greying hair. At forty-one years of age, he had been a policeman for more than two decades and had been 'around the block' a few times before joining the murder squad. He had been on the murder squad for six months now, and since joining Tyler's team they had taken on five murder investigations. A couple had been straightforward, but the rest had been challenging. It had been an interesting learning curve, to say the least.

Before transferring to AMIP, Bull had been a DS on a CIPP team in the main CID office at Stoke Newington, one of the busiest stations in the Met. The acronym, CIPP, stood for Crime Investigation Priority Project, but it was really just a fancy way of saying a small team of experienced detectives dealing with major crime on the borough. There were normally four, each being run by a DS and staffed by DCs.

The constant caseload of near-fatal shootings, abductions, stabbings, rapes and drug-related crime had left him feeling jaded and disillusioned with the job, or more accurately, with the people that stopped him from doing it properly.

He had spent too long working under the supervision of senior police officials who were so far removed from the real world that they couldn't differentiate between petty criminals and hardcore offenders who raped, murdered and pillaged without hesitation or remorse.

The job had become too political for his liking. He was sick of the never-ending power struggles within the Service, and continually frustrated by the interference of politicians and civil rights activists – the so-called 'do-gooders' brigade, who meant well but knew very little.

They seemed unable to understand one simple overriding fact: that the debased people he and his colleagues dealt with were extremely dangerous individuals who showed no remorse or guilt; they had no feelings of compassion towards those that had suffered, or their loved ones.

Working on the murder squad, with quality people like Tyler and Dillon, had been like a much-needed breath of fresh air to Bull, rekindling an excitement for the job he hadn't experienced in years.

He glanced at Tyler in the rear-view mirror. He looked younger than his thirty-one years. At six-foot-four, Tyler was a big man. He had a sharp mind and a quick wit. He had been married once, Bull knew, but his wife had been intolerant of his work, and unwilling to accept the risks that he sometimes took. Predictably, it hadn't worked out.

Steve Bull approved of the way that Tyler handled people. He was patient and fair but he refused to accept slackness from his staff. On his team, everyone pulled their weight or Tyler pulled them. Like Steve Bull, Jack Tyler was a product of the 'old school'. His 'do it to them before they do it to us' approach was surprisingly refreshing in an age where most senior officers had adopted a softly, softly, 'let`s all sit on bean bags and talk about this,' attitude towards crime.

As Case Officer, Bull had been the first member of the team Dillon had called. The news that his day was going to be disrupted hadn't pleased his wife. And he knew the boys would be annoyed when they woke up. They had made plans to visit the local park together for a Sunday morning kick around. Both of his sons played in a junior football league, and rumour had it that talent scouts for a big Premiership club were due to attend their next game. He had promised them they would fit in some extra practice before then.

Still, this was important work and someone had to do it. Besides, the extra money would come in handy. Having his weekly leave cancelled with less than eight days' notice meant he would be getting paid overtime at double time today. He knew his family understood his sudden abstractions, even if they didn't like them. Unlike Jack Tyler's ex, his wife and kids were behind him all the way.

As the speeding car hurtled towards London he glanced sideways at Dillon. Now here was a real character, someone that you either liked intensely or couldn't stand at all. With Dillon, there were no in-betweens. Detective Inspector Tony Dillon was a diamond in the rough; a down to earth person with simple, honest values. He would bend over backwards to help the needy, and he could be moved to tears by the suffering of others surprisingly easily. However, there was an aura of barely subdued violence about him, and when it came to a time for action Dillon was a man you definitely wanted on your side. He was six-foot-one-inches tall, with the impressive bulk of a power-lifter, and hands the size of shovels. Steve secretly thought that he resembled an overdeveloped gorilla. Dillon's jet-black hair was shaved to a number-one cut at the back and sides, and the tight French crop on top of his head was brushed forwards and gelled. Unlike Tyler, Dillon could never be described as shy. He was always outspoken, and he could be brutally blunt. You always knew exactly where you stood with him.

After a while, the pleasant greens and browns of the suburbs were replaced by the drab greys of urban concrete. Inside the car they discussed the case, oblivious to the gradual changes in the surrounding environment.

There didn't seem to be much to go on. The homicide sounded like the work of a 'crazy' to Dillon. Was that the case, or was it a skilful attempt to disguise the real motive for the murder, thus throwing them off the killer's trail?

Could it be a serial killer? Tyler asked. That was the worst-case scenario, they all agreed. It would transform the investigation from a Category B into a Category A case. It would also explain the unusual level of involvement from Holland.

Bull switched the siren on when they reached Leyton, a dense inner-city area within the London Borough of Waltham Forest, and the noise it made effectively killed any further conversation between them.

Steve Bull was enjoying himself as he negotiated the car skillfully through the early morning traffic that was already starting to congest Lea Bridge Road; he rarely got the chance to have a proper blat on blues and twos anymore, and he was determined to make the most of this opportunity. He barely slowed down as they approached the humpback bridge from which the road took its name, and Jack felt his stomach rise and fall in quick succession as they shot over it. He also felt his head hit the roof as they momentarily became airborne, and his spine compress as the wheels hit the ground again. "I want to get there in one piece if that's alright," he shouted irritably above the wail of the siren.

"Don't worry; you're in safe hands, boss. I'm an advanced driver," Bull assured him proudly.

"The only thing you're advanced in is age," Dillon observed, trying to keep his forefinger in the right place on the page of the battered map book that lay open on his lap.

Tyler, sitting back and rubbing his head, looked out of the window and kept his thoughts to himself.

The Omega powered past Hackney Police Station in Lower Clapton Road. They turned left when they reached Dalston junction, and drove the length of Kingsland Road, finally emerging into the one-way system at Shoreditch.

Jack glanced over at Shoreditch Church, seeing little more than a blur thanks to Steve's heavy right foot. For a moment, he was tempted to tell his colleagues that he had been christened there, but this didn't seem like the right time for trivia.

Big green signs appeared giving advance route information for the major junction ahead: Commercial Street and Aldgate were off to the left, the City lay straight ahead; Old Street, Holborn and Islington could be reached by turning right.

Dillon glanced back over his shoulder. "We're almost there now, Jack," he shouted.

On Tyler's instructions, the flashing lights and siren were turned off.

Following the map, Dillon directed Bull to turn left into Commercial Street. A few seconds later he ordered another left turn, this time into Quaker Street. And there, up ahead, were all the parked emergency vehicles and a foreboding looking police cordon.

"We're here," Bull said.

"Don't expect a tip," Jack replied, massaging the back of his neck.

The Omega pulled up next to the line of blue tape, which marked the perimeter of the police cordon, about ten yards from the site entrance. Tyler noticed several reporters lingering nearby, like vultures awaiting their next meal.

"Stay with the car, Steve," he instructed.

As he and Dillon got out of the car, a flustered looking young constable rushed over to them from behind the police line.

"I'm sorry, sir, you'll have to move your car. You can't stop here. We're trying to deal with an incident." Terry Grier was beginning to lose patience with all the reporters and other busybodies that had been arriving since this incident began. He was reaching the stage where it was fast becoming an effort to remain polite. He figured that these two were probably more media types, although the slightly shorter one looked more like a minder than a reporter. Whoever they were, they weren't staying there.

"It's alright son," Dillon said, producing his warrant card. "Murder squad. I'm DI Dillon. This is DCI Tyler. Who's in charge here?" The two detectives ducked under the outer cordon and continued towards the site entrance without waiting for a reply.

Grier, who was completely caught out by the unexpected move, had to rush to get back in front of them. He gave them a flustered account of the situation as they walked. "Sir, your Chief Superintendent is already here. He's just inside the entrance with Inspector Speed, the Incident Manager. The FME's been and gone, and the forensic people are well into their act. I think they were just waiting for you to arrive before removing the body."

He received a curt nod from Tyler in reply. Grier felt awkward and inadequate next to these men. Their quiet confidence, and the unspoken air of authority that they radiated was intimidating.

As they strode through the site entrance Tyler spotted Holland some way off to his left, already kitted out in a white paper suit. He was standing next to a uniformed Inspector who also wore a white paper suit, although he had slipped out of the upper half and wore it with the arms tied around his waist. What the effect lacked in style it made up for in terms of comfort and practicality. Both were drinking coffee. Holland waved to them and indicated that they should stay where they were.

It was highly likely that the perpetrator had gone directly from the gates to the body deposition site. As a precaution, the ground between the two points had been designated as the common approach route, and it would be kept sterile until it had been forensically examined. Hopefully, if the first responders hadn't already trampled it into oblivion, this would prevent any physical or forensic evidence that the killer had inadvertently left there from being obliterated or contaminated.

A strict log was being maintained of all persons entering the crime scene, their reason for doing so and the duration of their stay. Special entries would be made in a separate column for any person crossing the red tape into the inner cordon where the victim remained in situ.

Anyone entering the inner cordon, which was where Tyler and Dillon needed to go, would be required to wear white evidence gatherers suits like the ones currently worn by Holland and the lab team.

A few minutes later, Holland joined them. He shook Tyler's hand warmly. "Morning Jack, Dillon. Sorry to spoil your day off, but I think you'll both agree it was necessary," he said sombrely, nodding over towards the dead girl.

"It's okay, sir, we understand," Jack replied.

Tyler both liked and respected George Holland. He knew that the man was as smart as they came, and was famous for having a 'can do' attitude, even in the face of great adversity. Holland got the job done, whatever it took. Most of all, he was intensely protective of those who worked for him. Holland motioned for the uniformed officer to join them. The man quickly slipped his arms back into his suit and negotiated the common approach route.

"This is Inspector Speed, one of the first officers to arrive on scene. He's also the Incident Manager, and he's done everything that could be done to preserve the scene. Without a doubt, he is the best person to fill you two in on what has happened, thus far." Holland nodded to Speed.

"Thank you, sir," Ray acknowledged the senior man. He nodded to a SOCO standing near the outer cordon perimeter. The woman immediately came over with a bundle of paper suits, thin paper masks to cover mouth and nose, and plastic shoe covers. Without a word, she handed them to the two new arrivals. Tyler and Dillon began to slip them over their street clothes.

"Thank you," Holland said, dismissing her with a grateful nod.

"So, what can you tell us then?" Jack asked, zipping up his paper suit.

In clear, concise terms Ray Speed ran the two murder squad officers through the known chain of events. He gave a detailed account, omitting nothing of importance. His summary of events included the watchman's evidence, the doctor's findings, and his own observations.

Tyler was impressed. The two detectives had questions, lots of them, as Speed led them to the body.

"Who else has been near the body, and did they wear paper suits and overshoes?" Jack asked.

"Only me, Nick Bartholomew, DC Kevin Murray and the FME have been inside the yard. Nick and I did walk through the common approach route, but we didn't know what we had at that point and we were acutely conscious that there might be someone in need of urgent medical care. Only the doctor and I have come into physical contact with the body. I'm sorry; none of us were suited and booted. The paper suits and overshoes only arrived with the CSM There were none available at the nick."

Jack grimaced. He would have been happier if everyone who had entered the yard had worn the white coveralls and plastic overshoes, but it was done now and there was no point in crying over spilt milk.

"What about gloves?" Jack asked next, meaning white rubber gloves. Hopefully, no one had touched the body, or anything else within the scene, without first donning them.

"We all wore two pairs of latex gloves, sir," Speed informed him. At least there had been a plentiful supply of those readily available.

Jack nodded, impressed. A lot of uniform supervisors he knew would have only told their troops to put one pair on, not realising that moisture produced by the hands has a tendency to seep through the thin rubber after only a few minutes.

"Is it likely that she was murdered elsewhere and then dumped here?" Dillon asked.

"I don't think so. The blood patterns, and the sheer amount of it, make that unlikely in my opinion, but the forensic guys will have to confirm or disprove that in due course." Speed was slightly uncomfortable answering these rapid-fire questions. He felt like he was being put on the spot. Now he appreciated why Mack had been so reluctant to commit to a time of death earlier on.

Some arc lighting had been rigged up near the body to illuminate the scene for the forensic team. They were waiting patiently to begin a detailed search of the area in which the dead girl lay. They had been ordered not to start until Tyler had been able to conduct his own examination of the girl. After that, her head and hands would be bagged and the corpse would be protectively wrapped to preserve evidence, and then she would be removed to the local mortuary. The body would then be tagged and put in cold storage to await a special post-mortem the following morning.

As Jack looked down at the lifeless figure in front of him, he felt himself filling with anger. He absently wondered if his face reflected the shock that he felt inside. The injuries were utterly horrific. He studied her poor face. The skin looked waxy, almost translucent. The blue eyes had already lost their liquid and were flattening out. There was a look of pain and confusion on her once pretty features.

He wondered what she had felt, what she had thought, in her last moments. Had she known her killer? Had she been so drugged up and spaced out that she hadn't been aware of anything?

Tyler tried hard to concentrate on the scene, to take in every detail to be dissected later. He could almost sense the killer's presence here, like an unpleasant aura, a lingering residue from the earlier violence and mutilation.

Jack wished that he and Dillon could be left alone to absorb everything that the crime scene had to offer without interference or distraction. He needed to develop a feeling for what had happened here in the early hours of the morning, and that meant spending a few minutes alone with the corpse, just listening to what it had to tell him.

Knowing it couldn't be, Jack forced himself to ignore everyone else and take a closer look at her. After a moment or two, his eyes found themselves drawn to the marks on her jaw. Although not particularly obvious at first glance, due to the mask of blood that caked a large portion of her lower face, there was definitely something of interest there.

"What do you make of those blotches on the side of her jawline, Dill?" he asked his partner, eager for a second opinion.

Dillon reluctantly moved nearer. He hated getting too close to dead bodies. It wasn't so much the sight that bothered him. It was the smell. Death, he had learned a long time ago, had a particularly unpleasant smell all of its own. The whiff that drifted up from the poor girl's exposed innards, as he leaned over her, reminded him of the smell from his local butcher's shop.

The white mask he wore performed a dual purpose: first, it prevented the inhalation of airborne viruses. Dried blood containing Hepatitis or Tuberculosis could be reactivated if it came into contact with the wet mucous membranes in the nose. Second, it prevented him from accidentally leaving his DNA at the scene via a cough or sneeze. As useful as it was, though, the mask did nothing to lessen the reek of Tracey's innards.

"I don't know, Jack. Bruising, maybe?" he offered with a shrug.

"Yeah, that's what I think." He turned to face Inspector Speed. "Who's the Crime Scene Manager?" There was a trace of urgency in Tyler's voice as he asked the question.

"Um, CSM Calvin, sir," Speed informed him, quickly plucking the name from memory.

"Sam Calvin? Excellent! Get him for me, would you."

"Of course," Speed replied, quickly looking around the site for his quarry.

"What are you up to?" Dillon asked after Speed had left them alone.

"You'll see in a minute, but I wouldn't get too excited. It might just turn out to be nothing."

Sam Calvin materialised at their side a few moments later, a clipboard in one hand and an empty exhibits-bag in the other. His sombre expression betrayed his annoyance at being dragged away from a half-completed index of exhibits. His face relaxed as he recognised Tyler, and his expression changing to one of curiosity.

"Hello, Jack. What are you doing here? I thought you were with the anti-terrorist mob."

Tyler smiled, raised his hands and gave a carefree shrug as if to say: 'Nobody ever tells me anything, either'.

"I got myself promoted to DI a few years back. The Commander thought it would be good for my career to have a change. He was right, of course. Being a DI on the Branch wouldn't be anywhere near as much fun as being a DS was. More admin and less action, you see. So, I moved over to AMIP and I've been there ever since."

"I see," Calvin frowned. "So, what can I do for you? I'm a little tied up right now." He raised the clipboard and empty bag to illustrate his point.

"I'm sure you are, Sam. Tell me, have you examined the body yet?"

"I've had a brief look, why?" Calvin answered, a frown creasing his large forehead.

"Have you seen the bruises on her lower jawline?" Tyler asked.

"Yes, I did. I've got a pathologist on standby, but I didn't want to let my chaps disturb anything until you guys have had a proper look. What're you thinking Jack – I mean, sir?" he said, correcting himself to accommodate Tyler's higher rank.

"Jack will do fine, Sam. Look, about those marks. He obviously grabbed her from behind to leave marks in that position, right?" he asked, pausing to check that the other man was following.

"That sounds about right. Go on," Calvin encouraged.

"Well, the point is that he touched her. If he wasn't wearing gloves then he'll have left prints. Have you fingerprinted her skin yet, Sam?"

Calvin shook his head emphatically. He had a developed logical and very methodical routine which had taken years to perfect. He saw no reason to break with that tradition now.

"I know where you're coming from Jack. They bang on about this on the SIO course but there's no point in dusting her face." Calvin's tone was too dispassionate for Jack's liking, as if the girl lying before them was merely a lab specimen on which they were about to conduct an academic test.

"We should at least try," Jack said, forcefully.

"I'm not being awkward," Calvin explained, "but even in optimum conditions prints on skin only usually last about an hour or so. She's obviously been here a lot longer than that, you can tell from the livor mortis markings on the bottom of the body."

Livor mortis, or hypostasis, usually sets in about five or six hours after death. When the heart stops beating gravity takes effect and the blood, about eight pints of it, gradually settles in the lowest areas of the body, causing a distinctive dark reddening to appear there. However, if the body is moved soon after hypostasis has set in – up until about ten hours after death – the blood, which has not yet fully congealed, will relocate itself to the part of the body now nearest the ground. This results in a white blotching effect appearing amongst the lividity markings. When this telltale blotching is present it provides investigators with early evidence that the body has been moved since death and that there is at least one other crime scene that they should be searching for.

There were no such marks on this victim.

"Just humour me, okay," Tyler said.

"Well, you're the man running the show," Calvin said grudgingly. He could tell from the look on Tyler's face that there was no point in arguing. "I'll need my kit. Back in a jiffy," he said to no one in particular. Dillon watched his white-suited form as he marched back along the sterile path.

"Bit of a wet blanket, isn't he?" he said, wondering why Tyler had been so pleased to hear that Calvin was working the scene. So far, he hadn't said or done anything to impress Dillon.

Jack smiled. "Well, I wouldn't go out socialising with him, but I'll tell you this: there aren't many who can recover physical or forensic evidence at a crime scene like Sam Calvin."

"Really?" Dillon's voice was thick with doubt.

When Calvin reappeared, he was carrying a large metal case. Holland had tagged on behind, intrigued by the sudden flurry of activity around the victim.

"Sir," Tyler nodded respectfully.

Calvin knelt down and opened the case. He donned a pair of white fabric gloves, followed by two pairs of latex gloves before removing a brown envelope. It contained a stack of cards, similar in texture to standard photographic paper. He removed one and pressed it, glossy side down, against the side of the victim's face. He held it in place for three seconds exactly, looking stoically from Tyler to Dillon while he counted out loud. Then he lightly dusted the five-inch by seven-inch card with aluminium powder, which he applied with a thick brush.

"Well?" Tyler asked eagerly.

"I'm sorry Jack, it's not good news. Like I told you, it's been too long." He held up the card for them to see.

"I've got the shape of two fingers but none of the actual swirls or ridges that make up a print." Calvin bagged the card and slipped it into a pocket inside the case.

"Well, thanks for trying, Sam. We'll be out of your way soon. I'll speak to you later when you know exactly what you've got," Tyler said, making no attempt to conceal the disappointment in his voice.

"Sure thing," Calvin replied, pulling off the latex gloves. "Let me know when you're finished and I'll send the pathologist over." He shook their hands before retiring to his growing pile of evidence bags, all of which required indexing.

Tyler returned his attention to the victim, aware of Dillon beside him. *Tell me your secrets*, he implored her. Holland and Speed remained a step or two behind. No one spoke for a while.

When he had assimilated as much as he could, Tyler signalled for Calvin to send the pathologist over. Jack watched in silence as the boffin went through his usual routine. A chemical thermometer was inserted into the victim's rectum to take the internal body temperature. Next, the ambient temperature was taken. A corpse tends to lose body heat at one and a half degrees Fahrenheit an hour for the first twelve hours following death.

The pathologist then checked to see how advanced rigor and livor mortis was. Rigor is hastened by muscle mass, loss of blood and the prevailing temperature of the environment in which the body is found. Tracey, in her semi-naked condition, would have cooled faster and stiffened slower out here then she would have done had she been discovered laying in her bed inside a warm room.

An external examination was made of the body to note the injuries and state of her clothing. A search was then made of the body, the immediate area surrounding it, and underneath it. Photographs were taken and any obvious trace evidence was collected to prevent it being lost during transit.

Dillon turned to address Speed. "Just out of interest, where are her knickers?" he asked. The pathologist, who was just about to call the morticians over, hesitated.

"As far as we know she wasn't wearing any," Speed answered calmly.

"Either that or our ghoulish friend likes to keep souvenirs," Dillon suggested, glancing at Tyler.

Jack nodded his agreement but said nothing. He was too absorbed in his own thoughts to speak. He had the oddest feeling that he was being watched. He nodded for the removal to continue, and then carefully made his way over to the side of the Portakabin, where he began to examine the message. He read it several times, lost in thought. "Who's 'Jack'?" he asked at last.

"The obvious answer is 'Jack the Ripper' but that doesn't make much sense," Speed said.

"On the contrary," Jack Tyler said, miserably. "I hate to say it, but having seen the body I think it makes perfect sense."

Dillon frowned. He could see what Tyler was hinting at, but he wasn't convinced they were witnessing the dawn of a new Ripper style series. But if that were the case the investigation would quickly become a logistical nightmare, and unless it was properly handled right from the start it would cause widespread panic amongst large sections of the public. At least he now understood why Holland had felt obliged to attend the scene. "Bloody hell, Jack!" he whispered. "We need to catch this freak before he strikes again."

But Tyler wasn't listening. Studying the skyline, he swivelled in a three-hundred-and-sixty-degree arc until he found what he was looking for.

A few streets away stood a single tower block. It was undoubtedly high enough to give someone on the roof area a good view down into this yard. Maybe he was imagining things, but the spooky feeling just wouldn't go away. And then, just as he was about to turn away, sunlight suddenly glinted off something reflective on the roof, momentarily dazzling him. It was gone in an instant, but it was enough to alarm him. He turned to Ray Speed.

"I'm probably being a little paranoid, but I've had the eeriest feeling that we're being watched since we arrived here. That tower block over there is the only place high enough for someone to observe us from, and I thought I just saw something glinting up there, as if the sun was reflecting off the lenses of a pair of binoculars. Can you get someone to go over there, right now, to check out the roof?"

Speed looked up at the block and then at Tyler. Normally, if someone said something like that to him under circumstances like these, he would put it down to their having an overactive imagination, but he recalled Nick Bartholomew having exactly the same feeling about being watched when they first arrived. Speed didn't believe in coincidences. He raised his radio and began to issue orders.

CHAPTER SIX

The Disciple sat on the roof of Richmond Point watching the drama unfold down below. He had been there since five-thirty and had thoroughly enjoyed the show so far.

After carefully arranging the body and writing the message, he had fled up here to await the arrival of the watchman. One of the unexpected highlights of the overall experience was the elderly man's reaction when he unwittingly stumbled across her dissected remains. Clutching his chest in shock, the old fool had nearly keeled over, and it had given The Disciple such a buzz to watch.

So far, the experience had surpassed all his expectations. The pleasure he'd derived from his time with the girl was nothing short of exquisite. Just thinking about the things he had done to her produced a warm, tingly feeling in the pit of his stomach.

He reached down into his rucksack and removed the lace underwear he had taken from her lifeless shell. Slowly, almost reverently, he raised the keepsake to his face and gently breathed in her scent. He could smell her cheap perfume, her body odour and, best of all, her fear.

After gutting her like a fish, he'd extracted samples from the whore's Duodenum, Jejunum, and Ileum, and he planned to eat a mouthful of each immediately after sunset this evening – when the veil that separated this world from the Otherworld was at its thinnest – while chanting the specific words of power that accompanied the cannibalistic stage of the ritual.

All in all, he was feeling mightily pleased with himself, and although he still had another four whores to kill, he felt that he was entitled to give himself a little pat on the back for the way things had turned out so far.

Tenderly, almost lovingly, he lowered the dead girl's undergarment to the floor and reached back into his rucksack for the powerful Zeiss binoculars. Lifting them to his eyes the killer studied the cyclone of activity below. Nothing had changed; the police were still running around like headless chickens.

He scanned the crowd gathered along the outside of the cordon through the binoculars, and smiled. They really were like sheep; if one went to look, the others all followed; if one waited to see what was happening, they all waited, even though none of them had the faintest idea what was going on.

They would find out soon enough.

Soon the mere mention of his stage name, *'Jack'*, would be enough to send spasms of terror through the heart of every whore in London. He could picture it all so clearly in his mind's eye.

The sudden radio transmission startled him, and he swung the binoculars back towards the centre of the yard. To his horror, one of the detectives was pointing up at the tower block. He quickly ducked his head down beneath the overhang, wondering if they had spotted him. The Disciple listened attentively to the increased radio chatter, and within moments his fears were confirmed: they were sending people up here. "Son of a bitch!" he growled, as surprise and then panic set in.

He had to move quickly. If he didn't, the game would be over before it had properly begun. Jumping to his feet, his joints stiff from having sat still for so long, he scooped up his bottle of mineral water and hurriedly wedged it into his rucksack between the carefully wrapped selection of knives and scalpels and the cool bag that contained the dead girl's intestines. The binoculars went in next. When he tried to ram the Storno radio into the bag, its wire immediately snagged on the blade of the hacksaw he had used to remove the fire escape's padlock when he'd climbed up onto the roof earlier.

"Fuck," he exclaimed, trying to untangle it.

Crouching so that they wouldn't be able to see him from street level, he began to scuttle crab-like towards the fire escape door, still trying to jiggle the radio's wire free of the hacksaw blade so that he could close the blasted rucksack.

As he reached the metal door, he checked over his shoulder to make sure he hadn't inadvertently left anything incriminating behind, and what he saw caused him to stop dead in his tracks. Somehow, the girl's underwear must have fallen out of his rucksack as he'd stood up. He knew there was no time to retrieve the item, not if he wanted to guarantee his escape, but he couldn't leave without his trophy, not after going through so much to get it.

"Fuck, fuck, fuck," he screamed. Dropping the cumbersome rucksack, he sprinted back to the spot he had just vacated, trying to keep as low as possible. Skidding to a halt, The Disciple stooped down and snatched the panties up like a relay runner collecting a baton. Spinning on the spot, he charged back to the fire escape, colliding painfully with the edge of the metal door. Scooping up the rucksack, the killer darted through the outer fire escape door and descended the narrow flight of stairs that led back inside.

The radio continued to blare inside his bag. Somehow the volume had been turned up to the maximum as he put it away. A tinny voice informed him that two officers had just entered the lift and were on their way up to the top floor. He had to get into the main stairwell before they emerged from the lift or he'd be trapped. His heart felt as though it had swollen to the size of a football and was pounding fiercely against his ribcage, trying to break free.

He wasn't going to make it.

He stumbled and almost fell down the last step. He slammed the heavy inner fire door shut and began fumbling desperately inside his jacket pocket. Where was the new padlock he had purchased to replace the one he had sawn through this morning?

He glanced at the lift. The floor counter above indicated that it was nearly at the top.

"Come on, come on!" he hissed, pulling the padlock from his pocket at last.

With trembling fingers, he threaded the clasp through the hole and snapped it shut.

The killer darted into the stairwell just as the lift door started to open.

Had they seen him?

He lingered long enough to catch a fleeting glimpse of the two uniformed officers through a crack in the door, and then he was gone, taking the stairs three at a time. He descended the upper floors as fast as he could, cannoning into walls as he negotiated one right angle after the next. When he got halfway down, and there was still no sign of pursuit, he began to feel a bit more confident, but he increased his pace anyway, just in case the clever bastards had gone back down in the lift. By the time he reached the bottom he was exhausted by his exertions and struggling for breath. Despite this, The Disciple began to giggle; the lift was still on the top floor. He had made it.

If they only knew how near they had come to catching him.

But how had it happened?

He racked his mind for answers, finally concluding that it must have been pure luck; there was no conceivable way that they could have known he'd be up there. But did it really matter? He had outsmarted them and he was still ahead in the game, and that was the way it was going to stay. As he left the block, his face bright red and dripping with sweat, and his makeup running, he started laughing uncontrollably. A police car, the blue lights on its roof bar still flashing brightly, was parked right next to his van. He patted the patrol car's roof as he slipped past it to reach his van.

The killer climbed into the beat-up old Sherpa and started the engine, then reversed out of the parking space. It was time to go, but not before he took one last look at his work. He knew it was reckless to return to the scene of the crime, but the impulse was too strong to resist.

He whistled merrily as he guided the ancient van back along Quaker Street, driving slowly past the length of the police cordon, just another motorist caught in traffic and following the queue of vehicles in front.

As he drew level with the site entrance, he spotted two men coming out of it. He recognised the taller of the two as the one who had pointed up at the tower block. Frowning, The Disciple eased off the gas pedal to give himself a better view of the man. He sensed that this man was determined and resourceful and that he would make a dangerous opponent. He would remember that face; store it away for future reference. The other man looked dangerous in a different way, like a bare-knuckle fighter.

The two detectives – he didn't recognise them so, presumably, they were from the murder squad and not locals – were engaged in conversation as they crossed to the big green saloon on the other side of the road. As they climbed inside, he wondered what they were talking about. While the killer covertly studied them in his side mirror, he became aware that a constable on the opposite pavement was shouting at him to move on. "Alright, alright," he griped. Placating the hot-headed officer with an apologetic wave, The Disciple gunned the accelerator and drove away.

As he entered Commercial Street he glanced down at his watch and saw that it was nearly ten o'clock; time to conceal the van and get some sleep. He wished the old heap's radio still worked so that he could catch the hourly news bulletin. Still, there wouldn't be much to report yet.

He suddenly felt inexplicably tired, as though he had hit a wall of fatigue. For a moment he wondered if he would have the energy to make the journey back, so urgent was the need to rest. Despite the exhaustion, The Disciple was feeling pretty good. He grinned contentedly as he patted the dead girl's panties, which were still safe in his jacket pocket. It would have been unthinkable to leave these behind.

Now that the first killing had occurred the authorities would be looking for him, and he would have to hide under the mask of his *other*, weaker, persona for a little while. It wouldn't be easy after the freedom he'd enjoyed these last few hours, but he'd just have to grit his teeth and get on with it. He understood that the disguise was a necessary inconvenience. Anyway, his return to anonymity wouldn't last very long, he promised himself. The reign of Jack, the new improved 'Ripper', had finally begun.

Long live the Ripper!

The two officers dispatched to check the top floor and roof area of the tower block reported back with a negative result. There was no sign of activity on the top floor stairwell and the entrance to the roof area was safely padlocked. There was no other way up onto it.

Tyler thanked Ray Speed for his assistance and allowed the forensic technicians to get on with the scene examination. The victim's head and hands were forensically wrapped by Sam Calvin, then she was placed in the black body bag and the zip was done up and security tagged.

"I think I've seen enough for now," Tyler said, nodding for the others to follow him. "Have we managed to identify her yet?" he asked as they walked back towards the site gate, Speed at his side, Dillon and Holland following behind.

"She had a small bag, a purse with thirty pounds in it, plenty of condoms and a Social Security book. The name on the book is Tracey Phillips," Speed informed him. "She's a South London girl, from the look of it. We've arranged for someone from the local nick to call on the home address. We should have a result on that fairly soon."

"Let me know as soon as you hear anything, Ray. And as soon as you can, get your troops relieved and bring them back to Whitechapel for the hot debrief."

"I'll get it organised right away," Speed said, and promptly peeled off to make the arrangements.

When they reached the gate the three detectives removed their paper suits and overshoes.

Jack noticed a look of misery darken Holland's craggy face. "Alright

Jack, let's get down to business," he said. "I've got a nasty feeling about this one. If the media gets hold of this, which it will, you'll be under a lot of pressure to get a quick result, so you'll need to move fast. I know you've only had the rank for a few months but I've every confidence in you."

"So I'll definitely keep it, even if it becomes a Cat. A?" Tyler asked, excited and scared at the same time. The Macpherson report, published back in February, had focused on the Met's handling of the 1993 murder of South London teenager, Stephen Lawrence. The report didn't make for fun reading, and the organisation had been heavily criticised for, amongst other things, failing to recognise that this was a racially motivated crime and failing to react accordingly.

Apart from being branded insensitive and institutionally racist, the organisation's ability to investigate murder and other serious crime had come under close scrutiny, and a number of serious failings had been highlighted. The report concluded that a lack of proper training was being provided to senior investigating officers to enable them to make informed investigative decisions, and a lack of training was given to officers carrying out specialised roles. It also bemoaned the lack of resources provided to effectively conduct murder investigations and talked about failures to document decision making and conduct evidential procedures in a manner that would stand up to close inspection.

The Commissioner had been hauled over the coals, and the backlash from his political masters and the media had prompted an urgent review of the Murder Manual, resulting in the new Gold Standard for murder investigation being promptly published in Police Order 6/99, which had come out in March.

The rumour coming out of the corridors of power at The Yard was that the days of the Area Major Investigation Pools were over and that a new centralised command would be formed within the Serious Crime Group to replace them. Jack wanted to be a part of that, and while he recognised that leading this case to a successful conclusion would pretty much guarantee him a spot in the new Homicide Command, anything less could pretty much ruin his future career prospects.

"Unless you fuck up, which you won't," Holland said. "Don't worry,

I'll be watching over you. Pull out all the stops and keep me updated as it develops." Holland shook Tyler's hand again and gave him an affectionate pat on the shoulder. With a final nod to Dillon, he left them.

As they crossed the road towards Steve and the car, Tyler turned to Tony Dillon.

"I think this killer is in a different class to anyone we've ever come up against before, Tony," he said.

Dillon stopped in mid-stride and turned to face his friend. Jack hardly ever called him by his first name, never had in all of the years that they had worked together. It was a sign that he was worried. "Why do you say that?"

"It's the message," Jack explained as they resumed walking. "He's proud of what he did and he wants us to know that it was just the start. He's going to strike again. The only question is when? We're racing against the clock with this lunatic, playing a game that only he knows the rules to."

"So, we do what we're good at, Jack. We go out on the streets and crack a few heads together until we get a lead. And who cares if we don't know the rules to his game. We make our own rules, remember?"

As the two detectives climbed back into the dark green Omega, Steve Bull glanced expectantly from one to the other. "How bad was it?" he asked.

"As bad as it gets, Steve," Tyler answered.

Shouting from across the street interrupted their conversation, and Tyler glanced out of his window to see young Constable Grier gesturing angrily at a beat-up van whose driver had stopped to gawk at the scene. He wondered why people had such a morbid fascination for death and gore. A large cloud of grey smoke spewed out of the van's blowing exhaust as it drove off noisily.

When it had quietened down outside, Tyler gave Bull the full rundown on what they had discovered at the murder scene. Steve was shocked. As Case Officer, he had been itching to go inside with them. Now, having heard the gory details, he was glad he'd remained with the car.

"Where to now, boss?" he asked, keying the ignition.

"Whitechapel nick, please Steve," Tyler Instructed. "We've got a lot to do." At this rate, he wasn't sure that he would make his mother's birthday dinner this evening after all. "What a day," he sighed, rubbing his eyes with the heels of his hands.

As the Omega pulled into the cluttered rear yard at Whitechapel, Steve Bull spotted six murder squad colleagues waiting for them by the entrance to the custody suite. "Looks like the cavalry's already here," he grinned, pulling up next to them.

A few minutes later, Jack Tyler and his staff were shown into an open plan office by the Station Reception Officer. "You can use this room all day, sir," she said. "It doesn't officially become operational until next week."

Jack smiled his thanks. Everything in the room looked brand new; from the dark blue heavy-duty carpets to the four rows of rectangular beech desks that ran along the left-hand wall; from the high-backed chairs, still neatly wrapped in the manufacturer's cellophane, to the shiny silver filing cabinets. Even the walls were newly plastered and freshly painted.

There were no grubby handprints or scuff marks from dirty shoes, no ugly gouges where people carrying heavy items or awkwardly shaped exhibits had dented the walls as they rushed down to the custody suite or out to the lab.

On the downside, because it was so new the room was completely devoid of all the clutter that gave it personality; there were no photographs of loved ones; no pin-up posters, not even the odd jokey cartoon or topless calendar.

But that would all soon change; nothing was policeman proof and within a couple of months the desks would be overflowing with case files and riddled with etchings and doodles, the walls would be dented and dirty; the velvety smooth swivel chairs would have squeaking casters and dodgy backs; the carpet would be covered in coffee stains and the incessant scatterings of little white dots that spill from leaky hole punches and make a cleaner's life hell.

"Pull up a chair and make sure you've got something to write on, and we'll start the briefing," Dillon told the six newcomers.

"Wait," Tyler said, signalling for his team to hold fire. "Before we get started can someone please organise some teas and coffees?"

Exactly fifteen minutes later, after Bull had managed to scrounge some hot drinks from the canteen, Tyler started the briefing. It was pretty basic because the information they had was so scant, but it was enough to get the wheels rolling.

With only six people available, Tyler had to prioritise the taskings. DC Kelly Flowers, the dedicated Family Liaison Officer for this investigation, was told to contact the CAD room and find out how the call-on had gone in South London. If the victim was confirmed as the Phillips girl she was to get straight over there, update the family regarding what had happened and how the investigation would be carried out, and to obtain as much background information about the victim as she could.

DC George Copeland, the exhibits officer, was dispatched to the scene to liaise with Sam Calvin.

The house-to-house enquiries would have to wait until he had more staff at his disposal.

DC Paul Evans was told to get his arse straight over to the local authority base and establish what CCTV coverage the borough had in the vicinity of the scene. He wanted last night's footage from any camera covering the scene, and any that covered the various approach and exit routes, downloaded and viewed immediately.

That left three detectives: DCs Colin Franklin, Reg Parker, and Richard Jarvis.

He dispatched these to Commercial Street with specific instructions to look for any hookers, pimps, dealers and homeless types still floating about, and to see if any of them could shed some light on the victim's last movements. He also wanted to know if any of the working girls could tell them who her friends and associates were and if she had any regular punters who might be weird enough to do something like this. They could say that a working girl had been found dead in suspicious circumstances, but they were not to reveal the nature of her death or the extent of her injuries. As soon as the local Safer Neighbourhood officers and anyone from the division's small vice team came on duty, Jack promised he would get them to make contact and join up with his own people.

Bull went down to the briefing room, where he gathered up the early turn officers who were arriving back at the station in dribs and drabs. When he finally had them all assembled he commenced the hot debrief. That took him the best part of an hour.

By four o'clock that afternoon very little progress had been made. The detectives who had been dispatched to Commercial Street had quickly reported back that, thanks to the ongoing police activity, it had become a 'dross free zone' by the time they arrived. They had promptly been redirected to commence preliminary house-to-house enquiries, but so far all they had to show for their efforts were sore feet.

Not long after the briefing, a few more staff had arrived, and Tyler had dispatched two detectives to see the old watchman at the hospital. That hadn't yielded anything significant either.

DC Dean Fletcher and DC Wendy Blake, the two researchers from his Intel cell had been sent back to Arbour Square to start researching the victim and her known associates, but nothing was jumping out at them yet, much to Tyler's displeasure.

South London officers had conducted a call on at the address on the benefit book found in the victim's purse, and they had spoken to Tracey Phillips's mother, who described the clothing her daughter had been wearing when last seen; it matched their victim exactly. She had also given the officers a recent photo, which had been brought over to Whitechapel and shown to the continuity officer when he returned from escorting the victim's body to the mortuary. Although a formal identification would still have to be made when the victim was cleaned up, there was no doubt that their victim was Tracey Phillips. DC Flowers, the FLO, was with the family now, but they had no idea who might have done this to her.

After the hot debrief, Inspector Speed popped his head around the door and asked if there was anything else he or his team could do before they left for the day. Tyler said no, thanked them for their hard work, and told the Inspector to go home and get some much-earned rest.

"Oh, one last thing," Tyler said. "I'll need a leg up for a week or two from someone who knows the area and the local working girls. Have you got any idea where I might find a suitable candidate?"

Speed smiled. "Well, funnily enough, I think I have the perfect person for you in Nick Bartholomew. He was on the Safer Neighbourhood Team covering Commercial Street for a year and knows all the main faces fairly well. Also, he has expressed an interest in applying for the TDC scheme next time it comes out, so this would be a good chance to gather some evidence, I suppose." The Trainee Detective Constable scheme came out once a year, and it was the only route into the Criminal Investigation Department. Successful candidates were required to sit various exams and undertake a comprehensive training syllabus before becoming substantial detectives and pursuing a career within the CID.

"What's he like as a copper?" Jack asked.

"He's very good. He's switched on and he's been involved in this right from the start, which is a bonus, I suppose."

"Would my borrowing him cause you any hassle?"

"Nothing I can't handle. We go off core shifts for a few days now anyway so he would only be walking around doing Sector based stuff. You might want to consider taking Grier as well. They're currently partnered, and the kid has a lot of potential."

Tyler nodded thoughtfully. "Okay," he told Speed. "Tell them to be at Arbour Square for an 8 a.m. meeting tomorrow, and to dress smartly."

Tyler was lost in thought as he sat in the back of the car during the journey back to Arbour Square. The first few days of a murder investigation were always the most crucial.

George Copeland and Dillon would have to attend the special post mortem. Sam Calvin had called him to say it was being carried out at Poplar Mortuary in the morning.

Other than that, tomorrow's main thrust would be to push on with the CCTV. They would have to identify and seize all CCTV in the area, private systems as well as the local authority ones. So far, there was no news from the Paul Evans, the feisty Welshman he'd put on CCTV duties earlier today.

House-to-house would have to start in earnest, but he'd been promised additional resources for that.

His team would have to go out on the streets again tonight, canvassing the local prostitutes. He suspected it would be hard to gain the girls' confidence and he anticipated that they might have to go back several nights on the trot before anyone started to talk to them. Perhaps Bartholomew would be able to help with that if he was the known and trusted face of the local plod. He would also speak to the people on 'Clubs and Vice', see if they had any ideas on how to break down the barriers between his team and the working girls. A sudden thought occurred to him. "I wonder if she was freelance or if she had a pimp?" he said.

"Maybe we'll find out later," Dillon suggested. Hopefully, Kelly would get detailed background information about the victim from her family.

Tyler had telephoned Chief Superintendent Holland with an update before leaving. They would talk further in the morning.

As Bull glided the car to a halt outside the gate at Arbour Square, Dillon leaned into the back.

"You shoot straight off; go to your mum's birthday party for a few hours. I'll hold the fort here."

"Thanks, Dill."

"There's no need for you to come back in later, either, Jack. I'll be there and if we get anything, I'll call you on your mobile."

"We'll see." Tyler was tempted to accept the offer, but he knew he should be there with them. "I'll phone you in a couple of hours. I can delay any decision about coming back in until then," he said, getting out of the car.

"You're the boss," Dillon sighed.

As soon as they got to the office, Tyler grabbed a log book and set of keys for a pool car and waved goodbye. He would try to put this case out of his mind for a few hours and concentrate on his family, but something told him it would be easier said than done.

CHAPTER SEVEN

Claude Winston was in a foul mood when he awoke, just after six that evening. The side of his face hurt like hell, and when he glanced down at the pillow, it was smeared with dried blood. "Bitch!" he cursed, tentatively reaching a large hand up to explore the inflamed skin around the scratches.

Wrapping a bathrobe around his great bulk, he stumbled into the toilet, bladder full. He caught sight of himself in the bathroom mirror, and his hatred flared, "She'll pay for this," he promised as he relieved himself.

Winston had returned to Quaker Street just before six this morning, looking for Tracey. His plan was to lure her into the car by pretending to have a client for her to service nearby. He knew the crazy mixed up bitch was stupid enough to believe him, and it would have been easy to take her somewhere quiet and give her a severe beating.

He had checked all her usual haunts, but she seemed to have disappeared off the face of the earth. Even her bosom buddy, Fat Sandra, had denied knowing where Tracey was. Then again, she wouldn't tell him Jack shit if her life depended on it.

Winston knew exactly what Tracey was up to; the little slag was lying low to avoid being punished. Well, she could hide all she wanted. Sooner or later, he would find her, and when he did, she would pay dearly for her disrespectful behaviour.

Claude dressed hurriedly as he was running late. A consignment of cocaine was ready for collection from the safe house on the Isle of Dogs. A mule had brought the stuff in a couple of days ago, but he'd had to wait for her to shit it all out. Now it was ready to be moved to the washhouse in Limehouse, where his 'chemist' would cut it up. Then he could start to distribute the finished product through his small network of runners.

He didn't sell the merchandise himself anymore, preferring to make use of the tough young bucks that roamed the estate on which he still lived. They were well paid for their time, and the risks that they ran were small compared to the rewards they reaped. A lot of Winston's runners were under the misapprehension that being in his posse gave them enhanced status on the street, and he was happy to encourage this myth.

As he climbed into the BMW, he caught sight of his scarred face in the rear-view mirror.

"Damn!" As soon as he'd taken care of business on the Isle of Dogs, he would hunt that bitch down.

Just after eight that evening Dillon took six murder squad detectives back to Commercial Street, where they met up with half a dozen uniform officers that the division had provided. Working together, they began the thankless job of canvassing for witnesses.

During the next few hours, the officers spoke to numerous girls. The reaction they received was consistent; the hookers were all shocked and upset by what had happened, but none of them were willing to speak to the police, although one girl did offer a discount to the detectives for group bookings. "How times have changed," remarked DS Charlie White, a diminutive Scotsman whose nose had been broken so badly in his youth that it was now almost forty-five degrees out of alignment with the rest of his face. His naturally bowed legs were wickedly accentuated by the drainpipe trousers of his suit and the winkle pickers on his feet. "When I joined the Job, we used to get offered freebies, now all we get is a poxy discount. There's just no respect anymore."

Tyler joined them just before eleven o'clock to find his team showing signs of annoyance and frustration.

"This is pointless," Dillon exclaimed after summarising their lack of progress. "We'll never get anywhere at this rate." It was obvious that the girls feared and distrusted the authorities as much as they did the murderer.

It was a sad state of affairs.

"Someone must know something!" Kelly Flowers, who was feeling somewhat drained after an afternoon comforting the grieving family, complained. "What's wrong with them?"

Jack's face softened. "These people live a complicated and dangerous lifestyle, Kelly," he explained. "Traditionally, we've always been their enemy, and because they're scared of us, they won't open up, in case it drops them or their friends in the shit. We've got to gain their confidence somehow." He had been giving this a lot of thought on the journey back in but was no closer to finding an answer.

Having spent a few hours of quality time with his family, Jack's spirits were much higher than they had been earlier in the day. The surprise dinner party had been a roaring success, and it had been simply wonderful to see the surviving generations of his family united under one roof again, for what felt like the first time in ages.

How strange, he had thought, that even the closest families could drift apart without realising it was happening. It was understandable, of course. Life in the twilight of the twentieth century was complicated and hectic, and if you lived your life in the fast lane something had to give. Quite often, Jack felt totally drained by the end of the week, and it took him the entire weekend to recover, just so that he could start the whole process all over again on Monday morning.

Back in the seventies, when Jack was a kid growing up in the East End, it had been different. His parents had drummed it into him that family was all-important. His grandparents, aunts, uncles, and cousins all lived within walking distance. His relatives were always popping in unannounced, and he spent as much time in their houses as they did in his. More importantly, there was a real emotional bond; the adults relied upon each other to get by, to survive.

During the eighties and the nineties, city life had changed for the worse, and many of his relatives had moved away from their London roots. Nowadays the family only came together for special occasions such as christenings, milestone birthday and anniversary celebrations, weddings and, increasingly as the elder generation dwindled, funerals.

The continued presence of uniformed officers in high visibility jackets was bad for business, and it was hardly surprising that the working girls who had shown up in this part of Commercial Street had all buggered off pretty sharpish once they'd been spoken to. After all, drug habits didn't pay for themselves. Word had obviously got out that plod was there for the night because no new faces had turned up in ages.

Steve Bull and Charlie White decided to go for a little wander. They headed south-east along Commercial Street for a while and then branched off into the side streets. They had just discovered a narrow lane that looked like it might be a cut through to Spittalfields and were debating whether or not to take it when they spotted Sandra Dawson, who was leaning against a wall at the far end, smoking a cigarette.

"Is she one we've already spoken to?" White asked.

"No, she's fresh meat, if you'll excuse the pun," Bull replied.

"Aye, well, we'd better go and have a word in her shell-like," White said.

Sandra looked up when she heard the echo of approaching footsteps, and immediately clocked the two men walking purposefully towards her as police officers – they couldn't have been more obvious if they had flashing blue lights strapped to their heads and were shouting, *'nick, nick, nick...'* à la Jim Davidson. Under normal circumstances, their presence wouldn't have bothered her in the slightest. After all, she was just having a quiet fag and minding her own business so they couldn't even do her for soliciting. However, because she still had the two rocks of crack in her coat pocket, Sandra panicked. Being arrested for prostitution was one thing, it went with the territory, but a drug bust was something else.

And so, as the two detectives strolled amiably towards her, Sandra did something very stupid. Making no attempt at subtlety, she tossed the wrap containing the two rocks into the gutter and ran off. They were slow to react, which gave her a few seconds head start, but when Bull finally sprang into action it didn't require much of an effort to catch her up. In the meantime, White stooped to retrieve the evidence.

"What was the point in running? You're bloody old enough to know better," Steve said, taking a firm grip on her arm as she reached the other side of the road.

Sandra Dawson was thinking the same thing herself. One of her stilettos had caught in the grill of a drain cover as she negotiated the road. It had snapped off, and she now stood lopsided. Sandra shrugged her shoulders, feeling extremely silly. "Gawd knows love. I don't suppose you'll believe me but it's not mine. I was just looking after it for a mate."

"What's not yours?" Steve asked.

White dangled the wrap in front of Bull's face. "Crack," was all he said.

The two detectives exchanged troubled glances. Tyler wasn't going to like this. They were supposed to be coming across as non-threatening, trying to gain the working girls trust. This incident wasn't going to help their cause.

"What happens now?" Sandra asked, racking her brains for a way to explain the drugs without grassing her friend up. She was unaware that Tracey no longer needed her protection.

"It's simple, love," Bull informed her miserably. "You're nicked and we're going to get our backsides kicked."

"Less of the *'we'* if you don't mind, Stevie," White was quick to point out. "*You* nicked her, old son, not me."

"Thanks a lot, Whitey," Bull said as they marched her back to their car.

By eleven-thirty, a low ceiling of cloud had completely blocked out the moon. Luckily, the neon vapour of a hundred streetlights was more than capable of compensating for its absence. Plenty of cars were still whizzing up and down Commercial Street, but all pedestrian activity had dried up ages ago, and with nothing to do the uniformed officers had huddled together by their carrier waiting for further direction.

It had been a long and extremely tiring day, and Tyler was painfully aware that this was probably just the first of many to come. As he needed the team back at the office for an eight o'clock meeting, he reluctantly decided to call it a night.

A Shamrock green Ford Transit mini-bus drove past the police carrier, catching Tyler's eye. It had the logo *'The Sutton Mission'* stencilled along the side. The driver was a middle-aged man with greying hair. Several dishevelled looking men were dotted amongst the rear seats, all looking back at Tyler with the vacant stares of the downtrodden. A thought occurred to him as the mini-bus receded from view. Winning the street workers over was going to be a slow, laborious, task. Sure, local sector and divisional vice officers would be able to point them in the right direction, but what they really needed was someone who the street workers knew and trusted to act as a go-between. The Sutton Mission was probably a local charity. There would be others like it. Perhaps he should explore the merits of using one of these charities as an intermediary.

As he slid into the rear of the Omega, Jack noticed a black BMW slowly cruising towards them. The driver, an enormous black man with dreads, appeared to be looking for someone in the various recesses that dotted the sidewalk. As the car drew level Jack noticed the tight cluster of vertical scratches on the driver's face.

Even if the uniforms hadn't been out there with him, Jack knew he stuck out like a sore thumb, but the stranger slowed long enough to give him a cold, arrogant stare nonetheless.

The BMW then increased speed and within seconds it vanished from view, but not before Tyler noted the registration number. He would run a check on it later.

Was the man a pimp or a punter? Either way, Jack doubted that he had anything illegal on him; he had been far too cocky, almost seeking confrontation.

"Did you see that ugly bugger in the BMW?" Dillon asked, popping his head into the car.

"I did," Tyler confirmed.

"Well worth a stop, that one." Sometimes Dillon longed for the good old days when they had been free to act on impulse and get involved with anything they came across.

Tyler smiled nostalgically. He knew exactly what his friend meant. It was at this instant that he spotted Bull and White escorting the limping form of Sandra Dawson towards their car. The smile vanished instantly, and he got out of the car to meet them.

One of his staff joked that her legs were almost as bandy as Whitey's, and there was laughter, which Jack silenced with a stare.

"What the bloody hell's going on here?" Dillon demanded, guessing the answer and not liking it one bit.

"Tell me this isn't what I think it is, Steve," Tyler asked. The calmness of his voice belied the anger he felt inside.

Bull glanced at White for support, but his colleague's gaze was riveted on the floor.

"Excuse me, how long till we get to the cop shop?" Sandra inquired, breaking the awkward silence. "Only I'm desperate for a wee."

"Well?" Tyler said, irritation creeping into his voice.

Bull shrugged apologetically. "It's a long story, sir."

Unexpectedly, the arrest of Sandra Dawson gave the Murder Squad its first break, although by the time this became apparent Tyler, along with the rest of the team, was at home fast asleep.

As an unspoken punishment Bull and White had been left to process Dawson and make their own way back to Arbour Square, and Tyler had made it clear that whatever time they finished he expected them to be there for the meeting.

The tape-recorded interview was to be conducted in a small,

windowless and sparsely furnished room in the custody suite at Whitechapel police station.

They waited impatiently for their turn, and even though they managed to pull some strings, there was still two hours between arrival and interview.

Bull wrinkled his nose as he ushered Dawson inside. The room was a disgrace: rubbish on the floor, paper strewn across the small table, a crushed *Seven-Up* can lying on the floor right next to the overflowing trash basket. To add insult to injury, the previous prisoner – at least they assumed it was the prisoner and not the interviewing officers – had left a pungent legacy of stale body odour and rancid farts.

Steve indicated that Sandra should sit down across the table from him. He let Charlie deliver the usual pre-interview spiel about what the process entailed, wondering if she could understand a single word he was saying; it wasn't always easy to follow Charlie with his broken nose induced nasal problems and thick Glaswegian accent.

As he unpacked the cellophane wrapped audiocassettes, Steve reflected that he was probably in for a roasting next time he saw the boss. Well, sometimes shit happened. All he could do was explain how circumstances beyond his control had forced his hand and hope that Tyler would understand.

In truth, neither officer expected the interview to yield anything productive in relation to the murder. They just wanted to ask her about the Class 'A' drugs she'd thrown away and get her bailed as quickly as possible pending the lab results. Dawson waived her right to have a solicitor present, which they were grateful for because it would speed the whole process up.

Steve opened the interview by explaining that he and White were part of an enquiry team who had been canvassing working girls in the area in relation to a murder investigation, and that was why they had approached her.

"Hang on a minute, love. Murder? What murder? What are you talking about? I thought this was just about drugs."

"A working girl was murdered last night." Charlie White explained impatiently. He was annoyed that she'd interrupted; the interview would only take five minutes if she'd refrain from speaking other than to answer a direct question.

"What did he say?" Dawson asked, looking at Bull for help.

"A working girl was murdered last night," Bull translated.

"Oh, my gawd. That's terrible," Sandra said, clearly shocked by the news. "But what's it got to do with me?"

"Her name was Tracey Phillips," Steve said, watching carefully for any sign of a reaction. "Did you know her?"

Sandra gasped as though she had just been punched, and the colour drained from her chubby face. "Oh gawd, no," she said, shaking her head in disbelief. "Please tell me it's not true. Not poor little Tracey."

As the murder squad detectives shared a look of surprise, Sandra buried her head in her hands and began to cry uncontrollably. After a pregnant pause, Steve fumbled inside his pocket for a clean tissue, which he handed over awkwardly. Charlie White looked down at his watch and grimaced as he realised any hope they had of grabbing some kip before the meeting had just evaporated.

Suddenly, Sandra looked up, her moist eyes wide with horror. "Oh, my gawd, I think I know who did it," she exclaimed.

"Who did what?" Charlie demanded impatiently, convinced she was still away with the fairies after smoking too much crack.

Steve Bull placed a restraining hand on his arm. "What do you mean, Sandra?"

Sandra Dawson didn't respond. Tracey's failure to come back and collect the crack she had been so desperate to get her hands on was completely out of character, and it had worried Sandra. So much so that she had popped over to the squat Tracey usually dossed down in this afternoon to make sure she was okay. No one there had seen her for a couple of days. The fact that this was not unusual did nothing to ease the fear gnawing at Sandra's insides like a bad case of indigestion. Now, a disturbing chain of thoughts exploded inside her head, creating a graphic menagerie, through which she pictured the tragic sequence of events that had led up to her friend's death, with astounding clarity.

"Sandra..." Steve said, placing his hand on her arm. When she didn't respond he looked at Charlie and shrugged, as though to say: *what do we do now?*

Sandra was having an epiphany. It was as if someone had placed the last remaining piece into a complex jigsaw puzzle, enabling her to see the full picture for the very first time. Her head was spinning from the process, but she realised that everything suddenly made perfect sense.

"Sandra," Steve said, clicking his fingers in front of her face to get her attention.

When she didn't respond, Charlie White leaned forward and shook her arm impatiently. "SANDRA!" He shouted.

This seemed to do the trick. With a gasp, she jolted forward. "Sorry, love," she said, smiling apologetically. "I'm just a little shocked."

"Is there something you want to tell us?" Steve asked, trying not to sound too hopeful.

"Yes. There is something," she whispered as her eyes focused on her surroundings for the first time since hearing the news. "But I'd like a drink of water first if that's alright."

They had a short break while Sandra tidied her face up. A female PC accompanied her to the toilet, and she was given a drink.

"Do you think the daft cow's trying to string us along to get out of the drug charge?" Charlie asked when she had left the room.

"I don't know, mate, but we'll find out soon enough," Steve said with his usual stoicism.

While they waited for Sandra to sort herself out, Charlie White popped out to see the custody sergeant, a middle-aged man with greying hair and a world-weary face, who was scribbling away on a custody record that needed updating.

"Don't suppose you've got any paracetamols handy, have you?" White asked. "Only I've got a splitting headache."

"Sorry, we don't keep anything like that in here," the custody sergeant said without looking up. "Pity really," he added as an afterthought. "I reckon I'll be in need of a couple before too long, the way this bloody shift is panning out."

As White turned to walk away, the custody sergeant looked up. "You could ask the FME," he suggested. "Dr Sadler's in his room examining a probationer PC who managed to get himself head-butted while restraining a drunk. I'm sure he'll be happy to oblige."

"Aye, cheers," White said, smiling gratefully. "I'll do that."

When the battered PC emerged from the FME's room a few moments later, nursing a black eye that was going to turn into a real shiner before it faded, and looking mightily embarrassed about it, White popped straight in.

Dr James Sadler was a slender man in his early to mid-forties, with short brown hair and a high forehead that seemed set in a permanent frown. He was clad in the leathers of a motorcyclist, and a shiny black crash helmet sat on the desk next to him.

"Yes," Sadler demanded, eyeing Charlie White suspiciously.

White smiled apologetically. "Hello doctor, sorry to disturb you but I'm just about to interview a prisoner and my poor head feels like some bugger's playing the drums in it, so I was wondering if you had any painkillers you could spare?"

"You're not a local officer, are you?" Sadler asked, running his eyes over the newcomer.

"No, I'm one of the murder squad officers investigating the death of the prostitute who was found in Quaker Street this morning."

Sadler tilted his head. "Are you now?" he said, looking at White with interest. "And how is your investigation coming along?"

White shrugged. "Too early to say, really," he said.

The doctor's medical bag was sitting on the floor beside the examination table, and White noticed the corner of a thick book protruding from it. The title, written along the length of the spine, started with the words 'Jack the Ripper', but he couldn't make out the rest as it was concealed by the bag.

"Bit of an amateur Ripperologist, are you?" White enquired light heartedly.

Sadler scowled at him. "What do you mean?"

"Nothing at all," White said, hoping he hadn't caused any offence. "I just noticed that you had a book on the Ripper sticking out of your bag."

Sadler seemed impressed. "You're very observant," he said, bending down to tuck the book into his bag.

White shrugged disarmingly. "Nosey is the word you're looking for," he said, "but I can't help it. It comes with the job."

Sadler smiled. "I do find the subject rather interesting," he said, straightening up. "In fact, I had one of those Ripper tours booked for later in the week, but I'm not sure if it's appropriate now, given what's just happened."

"I don't see why not," White said. "What happened is very sad, but life goes on."

Sadler bent down again and rummaged around inside his bag for a moment, producing a small bottle of pills. "Yes, it does," he agreed. "Now, about those tablets, you're not allergic to anything are you?"

"Only hard work," White replied with a lame grin.

When the interview with Dawson recommenced, ten minutes later, Sandra proceeded to disclose information that, to put it mildly, astonished her captors. She told them how upset and afraid Tracey had seemed the night before, as they stood together on the street corner. She described the fresh scratch marks on Winston's face when he came looking for poor Tracey in the early hours. She confessed her belief that Winston had eventually found her and killed her because of the incident in the car. He was, she explained, an evil bastard. Finally, she went on to explain how, to help Tracey, she had come to be in possession of the crack. Crying unashamedly, Sandra agreed to make a full statement for them, despite being scared shitless about reprisals from Winston and his lackeys.

When Steve Bull asked her if she was really sure that she wanted to do it: to put pen to paper, she nodded once, saying tearfully, "Tracey was my friend. I owe it to her memory."

Charlie gave him a stern look out of the corner of his eye that seemed to say: *don't ask her questions like that in case she changes her mind.*

Charlie needn't have worried. True to her word, Sandra co-operated fully, telling them everything she knew and everything that she suspected about Claude Winston and his illegal activities. She gave them a detailed description of his car, of the various places he frequented and the people he mixed with. Unfortunately, she didn't know where he lived, which was a minor disappointment but not an insurmountable hurdle. They were confident that a man like Winston would be in the system somewhere. At least they had a name and a description to work with.

Having obtained the Duty Officer's authority to deal with the drugs by way of an adult caution, they escorted Sandra Dawson out of the station just as dawn was breaking.

The sky was battleship grey, which didn't bode well for the coming day. Despite a biting wind, the birds in the park opposite were chirping away happily.

With nothing left to say, the three endured an awkward silence together until Dawson's mini-cab arrived and they waved her off.

As they crossed the rear yard to their car a few minutes later, Charlie White turned to Bull, a satisfied look on his bent-nosed face. "You do realise that when the boss finds out what we've achieved by nicking her we'll both be heroes. Less than a day into the job and we've already identified the killer. Not bad going, eh, Stevie?" Charlie was feeling immensely pleased with himself.

"We?" Steve said icily. "Let's have less of the *'we'* if you don't mind, Whitey. *I* nicked her, not *'we'*. You said so yourself, remember?" Steve Bull gave him a bittersweet smile while thinking, *up yours an' all mate!*

"Cheers very much," Charlie said as his shoulders sagged. "I guess I had that coming."

"Yep. Felt good too."

CHAPTER EIGHT

Monday 1st November 1999

The sky above Arbour Square was grey and foreboding and heavy showers were forecast to arrive by mid-morning as an easterly wind blew the storm front ever closer.

It was day two of the enquiry, and the office was already buzzing when Tyler and Dillon walked in, just after half seven that morning. Jack, clean shaven today, felt like shit, but five hours of sleep had fully recharged Dillon, and he was being annoyingly loud.

Tyler nodded at a steady stream of familiar faces as they passed through the main office.

Staff from his Major Incident Room staff fussed over an untidy assortment of statements, messages, and actions that had been brought back the day before, trying to put them into some semblance of order so that they could be inputted onto HOLMES – the Home Office Large Major Enquiry System that was used nationally to run all murders – after the meeting. DC Evans was booking in the CCTV he had seized the previous day. Kelly Flowers sat alone, frantically writing up her FLO log. Charlie White looked dog tired; he had managed to doze at his desk for an hour or so after getting back from Whitechapel, and his shirt – the same one he'd had on yesterday – was now criss-crossed with creases.

Nick Bartholomew and Terry Grier were also there, the latter looking uncomfortable in plain clothes. The two local officers stood up respectfully as he approached. Jack nodded a tired acknowledgement and told them to help themselves to coffee.

Dillon glared malevolently at Kevin Murray, who did his best to avoid eye contact.

"What the fuck is he doing here?" he asked as soon as they were out of earshot. There was bad blood between the two, stemming from an investigation that had gone sour when Dillon had been Murray's supervisor back on division. Papers relating to a six-figure fraud that potentially implicated a prominent local businessman and several councillors had mysteriously disappeared, and although he had never been able to prove it, Dillon suspected that Murray had been offered a financial incentive to misplace them. Complaints had tried their hardest to find someone – anyone – to blame, but nothing had ever been proven.

Jack shrugged. "He was on the HAT car when it responded to the call. He's here for the formal handover, I guess," he said as they entered his office.

"Jack, I know you've asked Holland for some troops from other teams, but please tell me you didn't ask for *him*," Dillon said.

"No way," Tyler reassured his friend. But it occurred to him that he hadn't specifically said he *didn't* want Murray either.

There was a rap on the glass door, and Bull stepped in without waiting to be invited. "I've got an important update from last night," he told them, but, before he could give it, Tyler's phone went. He held up his hand, indicating for Steve to be quiet while he answered it. After a brief conversation, which from the tone of his voice the other two realised was with Holland, Jack hung up, looking thoughtful. "It'll have to wait a little while, Steve. I've just been summoned to the boss's office. Spread the word that the meeting will have to be put back half hour or so."

Although DCS Holland was primarily based at the Yard, he also kept an office at Arbour Square.

Jack knocked on the door, which was ajar, and waited to be called in. Holland was standing behind his desk putting his tie on as Jack entered. He indicated a percolator on the window ledge. "Pour me a brew while I sort myself out, please, Jack. Have one yourself if you want."

Tyler declined the offer, but poured one for his boss and then sat quietly while the older man scribbled a few notes in a day book.

When Holland finished writing he took a sip of the fresh Columbian coffee. "I've had the Assistant Commissioner on the phone this morning. Needless to say, he wants a quick result. Have you seen the papers yet?"

"No, not yet."

"They haven't made too much out of it yet, but they will, you mark my words." Holland glanced at his watch. "I've got to be at the Yard at ten for a meeting, and then I'm off to the Bailey for the afternoon, so you won't see me anymore today."

"That's okay, I haven't needed anyone to hold my hand since junior school," Jack said.

Holland swilled his cup for a few seconds, and then drank more coffee. "I'm not trying to mollycoddle you; I'm just making sure you have the support structure you need to run a Cat A investigation"

"Is that what this is now?"

"I suspect it will be before the day is out."

"Don't worry, I'll call you if I need anything," Jack assured him.

"You'll call me *immediately* if anything significant happens. I don't want to find myself in a position where the AC asks me what's happening and I don't know. If nothing too exciting happens during the day I still want a call at home tonight giving me a general update."

"Yes, sir," Jack said, obediently.

Holland smiled at the pained expression on Jack's face. "You're going to get a lot of unwanted attention with this case, Jack. It goes with the territory, so get used to it. On the bright side, powerful people are watching. Get this one right and it will do wonders for your career."

What he means, Tyler thought, *is get it wrong and I'm fucked.*

"We need to crack this one quickly, Jack, so I would appreciate some good news next time we speak."

It was an unrealistic request and Jack was tempted to tell him so, but there was no point. Shit cascades downward; Holland was only passing on the demands from above. Besides, complaining would only make him look weak, so Tyler simply nodded and said he would do his best.

They moved onto staffing issues; Jack pointed out that his team was drastically under strength and would need considerable bolstering if they were to do justice to the enquiry. Holland raised a hand to silence the protest. "Jack, everyone's in the same boat. We've been fielding scratch teams across London all year long. If it's any consolation I've already found you some extra people to make the numbers up."

Jack waved this aside impatiently. "It's not just about numbers; it's about having the right blend of skill and experience."

Holland's face darkened. "I'm not blind to that Jack, but sometimes you just have to do the best job you can with the tools at your disposal." He handed a sheet of paper over.

"Here's a list of the personnel you'll be getting. Every AMIP team will supply two DCs, except Andy Quinlan's. As you know they took a new job at the same time as you, so Andy can only spare one, a chap called DC Murray. You're getting an extra ten people in total, which should be more than enough. Most of them have been warned to parade in your office at eight, but a couple can't make it till mid-morning. It's all on that sheet. "Right, I'll let you crack on." Holland gulped down the last of his coffee and nodded at the door, indicating the meeting was over.

Tyler was not in a good mood when he made his way back upstairs. This case was going to be hard enough to crack without Holland and the AC putting undue pressure on him. The staffing situation hadn't been resolved to his satisfaction either. He'd been hoping to cherry-pick half a dozen names from the other teams, but instead, he'd had to settle for whoever the various DCIs could spare. They were unlikely to release their best assets, but hopefully, none of them would be quite as useless as that plonker, Murray.

There were an extra seven people in the office by the time he returned; he recognised a couple, although most were unknown to him. He signalled for Bull to call the office meeting to order and nipped into his office to collect his notes.

Dillon sidled up next to him as he came out of his office. "What about that wanker?" He indicated Murray with his chin. "Shall I tell him to piss off?"

Jack winced. "I've got some bad news on that front," he said.

Dillon looked as though he had developed indigestion. "Oh no, you're not going to say what I think you are – are you?"

"Sorry, Dill," Jack said, handing him the list of names he'd been given downstairs. "DCS Holland has sorted us some assistance from the other teams."

"And he's on it?"

"And he's on it, unfortunately."

"First things first," Tyler began. He was sitting with his back to the tea urn, just to the side of the main door, and everyone else had gathered into a semi-circle around him.

"This is going to be a bit of a scratch team; the core roles will be performed by my staff, but we have back up from other teams and a couple of lads from the host division. DS Deakin from team six will be covering the Office Manager's post until Matt Blake returns." Blake, his regular OM, was currently bumming around Australia and New Zealand on a three-month career break. Chris Deakin raised a hand to let everyone know who he was. "Be patient with me," he said. "I've done the course but I've never performed the role outside of a classroom." Tyler was distinctly pissed off to hear that. He didn't want his Major Incident Room run by a rookie; he needed someone who could hit the ground running. No disrespect to Chris Deakin, but as the person responsible for ensuring the MIR ran smoothly, the OM was one of the most important people on a major enquiry. This was hardly the time to blood a novice. What was Holland playing at?

"To assist Chris, I've got to nominate a receiver to cover for Todd Dervish, who's still off with a broken ankle." Dervish had injured himself at an artificial ski slope three weeks back. Ironically, his wife had booked him four 'beginners' lessons in preparation for the trip they were hoping to take next February. The accident had occurred ten minutes into the first lesson.

"Sorry, Tim," Jack gave Tim Barton a sympathetic smile, "I know you only came out of the MIR two months ago but you're going to have to return for a little while." He needed to compensate for having a novice OM in charge by supplying an ultra-efficient Receiver, and Tim was definitely that

Barton stood up. "I guess I'd better grab a pen and pad and start taking notes of the meeting," he said.

"Sorry, Tim," Kelly whispered as he moved past her to collect his writing materials. She had recently completed the three-week HOLMES user's course at Farrow House but was not yet ready to go in the MIR unsupervised.

Barton winked conspiratorially at her. "Don't fret. If Todd's not back in time for the next one you can do it," he promised.

Tyler waited until Barton returned before continuing. "While I'm on the subject of MIR personnel, the four ladies sitting at the back of the room are our HOLMES inputters and typists." He nodded to them and was rewarded by smiles. One of the girls giggled nervously as other heads in the room followed Tyler's gaze. "I'd also like to welcome Brian Johnson, who recently transferred into the Command from Whitechapel. Brian is an analyst and he'll be working with us during this investigation. Hopefully, his past association with the borough will prove very useful."

All heads turned towards a dumpy looking, middle-aged man, whose comb-over was failing miserably in its attempts to conceal his receding hairline. He sat at the rear, and was noticeably detached from the rest of the group.

"For those of you who don't know me, I'm DCI Jack Tyler, the SIO. This," he indicated Dillon, who was sitting to his left, "is DI Tony Dillon, the IO." The IO – or Investigating Officer – was the deputy SIO. Dillon saluted them Benny Hill style.

"And this," Jack said, pointing to the man sitting to his right, "is DS Steve Bull, the Case Officer."

With the introductions over, Tyler gave an overview of the case, which took about twenty minutes. Five minutes in, Sam Calvin burst through the room's swing doors looking tired and dishevelled. He smiled sheepishly, apologised for being late, and sat down next to George Copeland.

Jack had noticed that a few of the seconded detectives, obviously peeved at being torn away from their own heavy caseloads, had looked somewhat disgruntled when the briefing had started, but by the time he had finished outlining the case he was pleased to see that they were all sitting up and paying attention.

Jack played them the scene video as he talked them through the initial police response. He occasionally paused the tape to fire questions relating to the initial response at Bartholomew, who without exception consulted his notebook before answering. Then, Tyler directed a barrage of forensic-related questions at Calvin, who had all the relevant information stored inside his head.

"George," Tyler said, turning his attention to Copeland.

"Guv?"

"The money found on the victim, thirty quid, wasn't it?"

"That's right, three crisp new tenners if memory serves."

"Yes," Calvin confirmed. "They were in pristine condition and could have come straight from a cash machine."

"That's interesting," Tyler said. "What are your views on sending them off to the lab to be treated for fingerprints, Sam?"

Calvin nodded thoughtfully. "Might be worth a shot," he said. "Especially as they are new notes and won't have been handled by all and sundry. Are you thinking the killer might have given the money to her for sex?"

"Don't know," Jack admitted, "but it's a distinct possibility, and one we should look into." A thought struck him. "Who here has been involved in financial investigations?" he asked, looking around the room hopefully. After a few moments passed, during which there was much shaking of heads, Deakin raised a reluctant hand, hoping his honesty wasn't going to result in him being saddled with extra work.

Reading his mind, Tyler smiled. "Chris, I know you've got more than enough to do without this, but in light of your being the only person in the room with the necessary experience, I need you to get the serial numbers from the notes and make some enquiries to see if we can locate when and where they were issued. I'm guessing the answer will be a local hole in the wall."

Deakin nodded. "Very probably," he agreed. Forcing a smile, he tried to sound enthusiastic. "Leave it to me. I'll get the details from George and start making some enquiries."

Jack winked at him. "Thanks, mate. Okay, on to the family. Kelly's our FLO. What have you got for us?"

Kelly explained that although the family was devastated, they were holding up as well as could be expected. She had obtained some sketchy background information, but nothing to influence the direction of the enquiry. Tracey's mum knew she was taking drugs and, on the game, but she didn't know where she bought her gear or where she sold her body. "Apparently, Tracey went completely off the rails a few years ago, after her father died, and since then her mother has never been able to break down the barrier she put up between them," Kelly told the assembled detectives. "Her relationship with the kid, April, was more like that of a big sister than a mum. Rita has always performed the maternal role. The only other thing of note is that for the last few months Tracey has spent most of her time living in a squat on this side of the river. Rita doesn't know where, just that it's in the East End."

Tyler looked at the analyst. "Brian, can you see what you can dig up for us. It might be important, it might not, but we need to know where she was putting her head down at night, and who with."

"Leave it to me," Johnson said, making a note in his daybook to allocate that task to one of the researchers after the meeting.

"Right, CCTV and house-to-house enquiries," Jack said, nodding at Paul Evans and Colin Franklin respectively.

Evans said he had viewed what they could at the local authority office yesterday, but it hadn't been easy, and as far as he could tell there was no sign of Tracey on it. He would be returning later today to collect all the footage Tyler had requested. "It may be that once I get the footage back here and view it on our equipment, we'll have more luck," Evans said.

"Yeah, especially if the Geek can work his magic," Franklin chimed in.

The Geek was DC Reg Parker. A rotund man in his mid-thirties, Reggie had a cherubic face that belied a wicked – some would say irreverent – sense of humour. No one in the office was safe from his pranks.

"Good," Tyler said. "What about house-to-house? Where are we with that?"

"It was all very hit and miss yesterday," Franklin admitted, "but I'll scope it properly this morning and then get the dockets put together,"

"I want you and Paul to sit down with me after this meeting and I'll define the parameters for both CCTV and house-to-house," Dillon said.

Then Jack asked Steve to talk them through Dawson's arrest. This drew sniggers from the back of the room, which Jack silenced with a severe stare.

By this stage, everyone in the room, even the people on secondment from other teams, had heard about 'the failed public relations exercise'. The general feeling was that they had scored an own goal by arresting Dawson, as it would be twice as hard to get any of the girls to trust them now.

Tim Barton had voiced the words that many of them had thought: Not even Steve Bull, who had more lives than a cat, could wriggle out of this one without getting his balls chewed off.

As Bull cleared his throat the room went quiet. "Although it was the last thing I'd intended to happen," he said, staring directly at Jack, "arresting Sandra Dawson turned out to be a blessing in disguise." He let his gaze wander around the assembled faces before continuing.

"Because during the interview she told us who killed her friend, Tracey."

The room erupted with noise. Just about everybody had something to say about this revelation, and they all wanted to say it at the same time.

"Quiet!" Dillon barked, and the room became hushed once more.

All eyes were riveted on Bull.

"Carry on, Steve," Tyler told him. "Tell this lot what you told me and Mr Dillon just before the meeting."

Taking a deep breath, Bull recanted Sandra's story. As he shared her revelations a few of his colleagues grinned at each other; Steve 'Teflon man' Bull had come out smelling of roses yet again.

When Steve had described Winston's facial injuries to his bosses, just before the meeting started, it had immediately dawned on Tyler that he'd already seen the man. Dillon had obviously been thinking the same thing because he'd nudged Tyler's arm and whispered, "I knew that bugger was worth a stop. I told you so last night."

"This information is crucial," Tyler said. "Now we've got a clear direction to go in, so let's get cracking."

Jack handed Dean Fletcher, his lead researcher, the piece of paper with Winston's registration number written on it and asked him to check it out. He also told him to run Winston through every database they had access to and then phone the Regional Crime Squad offices in Hainault and the Customs and Excise people over at Customs House; if Winston was involved in smuggling contraband, they were likely to have a file on him. Lastly, they were to check with the Met's drug squad. Winston was bound to be known to them.

"One last thing," Tyler said, "Can you have a gander at the various charities working in and around Whitechapel, preferably ones that have good interaction with the street workers. I saw a mini-bus from an outfit called The Sutton Mission last night, and it got me wondering if we ought to get one of these charities on board, to act as an intermediary between us and the working girls."

Brian Johnson appeared at Tyler's side. "I might be able to save you some time on that front," he said. "There are a few very good charities in the area, all doing sterling work. However, The Sutton Mission is probably as good a starting place as any. They mainly work with the homeless, but they also do a lot for local prostitutes and drug addicts. They're based in Old Montague Street, and their Director, Simon Pritchard, is a golfing buddy of Chief Superintendent Porter. In fact, Pritchard is one of the borough's Lay Advisors, so he would probably be a good person to speak to. Even if The Sutton Mission can't provide the help we need, they will definitely be able to steer us in the right direction."

Tyler nodded, impressed. "Thank you, Brian. Deano, you can cancel my last. We'll start with a visit to The Sutton Mission and see where we go from there." He glanced around the room, trying to decide who was best suited to make the approach. He needed someone who was personable, which eliminated Dillon. He was too busy to go himself, but it really ought to be a supervisor, to demonstrate the urgency of the request. After a few fruitless seconds scanning the room, his eyes settled on Steve Bull, and a smile crept onto his face. Stevie was the perfect choice: polite, professional and non-judgmental.

After giving his Case Officer the good news, Jack left Dillon to task the rest of the detectives and headed for the office to call Holland. He sat down and momentarily closed his eyes, picturing the expression on Winston's face as he'd driven by the previous night, thinking about the arrogance and malice that had been etched into his features. He instinctively knew one thing for sure: he wouldn't come quietly.

He picked up the phone, hesitated a few moments and then slowly lowered it back into its cradle. As promising as this tip-off sounded, there was no actual evidence to back up what the hooker had said, and his instinct was telling him to hold fire on calling Holland until he had more. After all, he was under enough pressure already, without piling more on himself over a lead that might pan out to be nothing at all.

Jack blew out his cheeks and turned his attention to the mound of paperwork sprawled across his desk. Like the furry little Tribbles in Star Trek, the pages seemed to be self-replicating at an alarming rate.

CHAPTER NINE

The Sutton Mission was located in Old Montague Street, just east of the junction with Brick Lane, a few doors along from The Archers Public House. The double fronted shop had a green façade with the words: 'The Sutton Mission' printed in bold white capitals above the entrance. It was nearly ten-thirty by the time Steve Bull pushed open the door, triggering a very loud and very annoying entry buzzer.

Biiiiiinnnng-boooooonnng.

He had the hump; partly because it had taken the best part of ten minutes to find a parking space, and partly because, despite all the flannel the boss had given him about him being the right man for the job, Steve couldn't help but feel he had been lumbered.

A small glass partition in the wall, like the serving hatches he'd seen in houses built in the 1970s, separated the receptionist's office from the waiting area, which contained half a dozen worn fabric chairs and a battered coffee table laden with out of date health magazines. A sprinkling of watercolours broke up the obligatory plethora of posters promoting local self-help groups, walk-in medical centres, and soup kitchens. The walls themselves were in desperate need of a fresh lick of paint, and the grey industrial carpet that covered the floor had obviously seen plenty of wear during its long lifetime. While the décor was a little shabby, at least the Sutton Mission was clean and odour free.

"Help you?" a bored voice enquired from within the serving hatch. It emanated from a twenty-something Asian girl in baggy blue jeans and a red woolly jumper, who was sitting at a cluttered desk inside the tiny office, filing her fingernails. Her jet-black hair was swept back and tied into a ponytail that reached just below her shoulders. The face, while undeniably pretty, was every bit as bored as the voice. A radio was playing quietly on a shelf just above and behind her head, and Bull could just about make out some of the words from Elton John's 1973 ballad, *Daniel*.

"Hello," he said, leaning into the small opening to show his warrant card. "My name's Steve Bull. I'm a Detective Sergeant from the murder squad. I wonder if I might have a word with whoever is in charge."

The receptionist regarded Bull with interest. "That sounds exciting," she said. "Is it to do with the girl who was murdered in Quaker Street? I heard about that on the radio."

Before he could answer, the telephone rang and she immediately picked it up, motioning Bull to wait with an upraised index finger. "Hello, The Sutton Mission, Charise speaking, how can I help you?" Her features reverted to 'bored' while she listened to the caller speaking. "Okay, thanks for letting us know. I'll let Mrs Pritchard know you're running late." She hung up and scribbled a note on the pad in front of her.

"As I was saying –" Steve said.

Charise held up her finger again. "Sorry, hon," she said. "Just gotta let the boss know her ten-thirty is gonna be late." She dialled an internal four-digit number, which was picked up almost instantly. "Oh, hello, Sarah. Just to let you and Dr Pritchard know, Jim Sellers has phoned to say he's going to be delayed by about thirty minutes due to bad traffic. He sends his apologies and promises he'll be as quick as he can."

As soon as she hung up, Steve tried again. "As I was saying..."

"Oh yes," she smiled at him conspiratorially. "You were just about to tell me all about that grisly murder."

"Actually, Miss, I was going to ask if I can speak to your boss. Sarah, was it?"

The look Charise gave him implied that he'd just deprived her of the only excitement her otherwise boring day would contain, but she redialed the extension she'd rung a few seconds earlier without protesting. "Hi, Sarah – me again. I've got a police officer here who wants to talk to you about that murdered prostitute." She looked up at Bull and said, "Yes, very important from the sound of it, and very hush-hush, too". She shook her head in response to something her boss had just said and gave him a sad pout. "No, he won't tell me anything more, says he needs to speak to you in person."

Bull shrugged apologetically. *Sorry*, he mouthed.

Charise cradled the phone. "Sarah will be right out," she said.

"Thank you."

"For the record," Charise said, smiling knowingly, "I would have cracked you, given a few more minutes. Not that it really matters. Sarah will tell me all about it when you've gone."

Bull grinned back at her. "I'm sure she will," he said.

A door at the far end of the waiting area opened and a slender, middle-aged woman with silvery blond hair, sparkling blue eyes and a radiant smile emerged. She wore faded jeans and a blue V-neck sweater over a white cotton blouse. A worn pair of Timberlands completed the outfit.

"Detective Sergeant Bull?" she enquired.

"Yes, ma'am," Bull replied, guessing that this must be Sarah. The woman stepped forward to shake his hand warmly. "I'm Sarah Pritchard. I run The Sutton Mission. Let's go to my office where we can talk in private. Please come this way," she said, retreating through the door she'd appeared from.

As he followed, Bull glanced back over his shoulder at the receptionist. "Nice to have met you, Charise," he said.

Charise gave him an impish wink and resumed filling her nails.

Sarah Pritchard led Bull along a narrow corridor lined with rooms to a large office at the far end. She opened the door and waved him inside. "Take a seat," she said, gesturing towards a brown leather sofa by the far wall. Apart from the sofa, the office contained an old mahogany desk, a couple of dented filing cabinets and a small fridge.

As he sat down, Steve's eye was drawn to a large colourful painting that hung on the wall behind the desk. It featured a pair of carefree teenagers, siblings judging by the striking similarity of their facial features, standing side by side in a farmyard. Both had wavy blond hair, with the boy's being only marginally shorter than his sister's. Both were clad in well-worn dungarees and mud-stained work boots. One held a rake, the other a hoe. Both were smiling contentedly, and the boy had an arm draped protectively around the girl's shoulders. The girl looked vaguely familiar.

"That's me and my twin brother, Edward Sutton," Sarah said, following his gaze. "We were inseparable in our youth. I founded this Mission five years ago to honour his memory."

"What happened to him?" Steve asked.

"He died in his mid-twenties from a heroin overdose. Actually, his body was found in a squat not too far from here."

Bull could see that the pain of her loss was still raw, even after all these years. "I'm sorry to hear that," he said softly.

"Was he living rough?"

She gave him a sad smile. "Eddie and I came from what you might call a very privileged background. Unfortunately, after Eddie moved to London he started mixing with the wrong people and they got him hooked on drugs."

"I see," Bull told her, not knowing what else to say.

"When my father passed and I inherited his wealth, I decided to put some of the money to good use. It was too late to help my brother, of course, but at least I could do something to help the many others like him." Sarah Pritchard sat down next to Steve Bull, closed her eyes for a moment and took a deep breath. "But that's enough about me and my family. Why don't you tell me what brings you to the Mission?"

"Well," Steve began, "a young sex worker called Tracey Phillips was found murdered at a building site in Quaker Street in the early hours of yesterday morning." He removed the photograph that Rita had supplied from his inside jacket pocket and showed it to her. "Do you know her?" he asked.

Sarah studied the photograph carefully for a few moments and then shook her head. "No, she's not one of ours," she said with certainty.

Steve pocketed the photograph. "It's possible that some of the other working girls have information that would help us identify and catch her killer, but none of them are willing to talk to us."

Sarah Pritchard understood where he was going with this immediately. "I see," she said. "I'm guessing you're hoping that we might be able to persuade them to speak to you?"

Steve nodded. "Basically, yes."

"Why us? There are a lot of local charities that might be better placed to do this sort of thing than we are. After all, we mainly work with the homeless."

"One of our colleagues recommended you. Besides, isn't your husband on the Lay Advisory Group for the borough?"

She nodded. "Simon does sit on the LAG. Did Charles Porter recommend us?"

"Actually, it wasn't Chief Superintendent Porter, it was a civilian analyst called Brian Johnson, who used to work in the Borough Intelligence Unit but recently joined us at AMIP."

Sarah shook her head. "It's not a name that I'm familiar with, but I'm flattered your colleague thinks that highly of us." Sitting with her hands clasped on her lap, she studied him carefully. "So, what do you know about the work we do here?" she asked.

Bull smiled guiltily. "To be honest, I know absolutely nothing."

"Let me enlighten you, then," she offered.

Inwardly, Steve Bull groaned. He didn't care what they did. He just wanted their help to win over the sex workers so that he could get justice for Tracey Philips. "Please do," he said, trying to sound interested.

"At the Sutton Mission, we firmly believe that everyone who comes through our doors deserves a second chance, regardless of their background or offending history," Sarah Pritchard said with the pride and passion of a zealot.

Bull smiled diplomatically. Experience had taught him that some people were rotten to the core and really didn't deserve a second chance, but, as he was trying to get her onboard, he refrained from saying so.

"We hold wellbeing classes and provide basic office skills training and career advice for those trying to re-enter the workforce. We've developed a specialist support scheme for individuals with complex needs, encouraging them to address the issues that caused their homelessness, prostitution or addiction. We're helping them to acquire the skills and confidence necessary to make life-changing decisions and re-integrate into society."

Bull gave an appreciative nod to demonstrate that he was paying attention, but in truth, he was only half listening. Tyler had certainly been right when he'd said it wasn't a good idea to send Tony Dillon along.

"The Mission has several full-time members of staff and a wonderful team of volunteers who are all dedicated to eradicating the root cause of homelessness in Whitechapel. Our volunteers don't just distribute clothing and other donated items; they work one-on-one with people who are homeless or trying to cope with addiction. Every morning we lay on a breakfast club for the homeless, and every evening we send out a mini-bus to round up those most in need of support and find overnight placements for them in local hostels."

"You clearly do a lot of very good work," Steve said," hoping she had finished and they could get back on topic.

She hadn't.

"This Mission is open three-hundred-sixty-five days a year," Sarah continued. "It's not unheard of for as many as one-hundred people to pass through our doors in a single day. We provide help and support without judgment or ridicule."

"Very commendable," Bull said, resisting the urge to glance down at his watch. "How do you survive without public funding?" He didn't actually care, but he sensed she expected him to ask the question.

She shrugged. "We rely on donations and volunteers; just as most other charities do. My husband, Simon, acts as our finance manager and chief fundraiser. My inheritance left me rather wealthy, so neither of us needs to draw a wage."

"I'm very impressed," Steve said, hoping he sounded sincere. "I really hope that we can rely on your support in this matter."

Sarah Pritchard nodded. "I'll speak to my husband and some of our senior volunteers at the team meeting this afternoon. Hopefully, we can allocate some resources to accompany you the next time you canvas the girls."

"That would be marvellous."

"Don't get your hopes up," she warned. "I can't promise anything."

"I understand."

"And you also have to understand that our priority will always be to act in the best interest of the girls. We won't encourage them to say or do anything they are uncomfortable with. After all, we have to continue working with these people long after you have moved on to the next case."

Steve nodded. "I get that," he said, and he genuinely did. "All we want your people to do is introduce us and explain that we are not looking to cause them any trouble. We just need their help to get justice for Tracey. Even if they won't talk to us in person, it might be a case that they will be willing to pass information to us via your volunteers."

"That might work," Sarah said, "but you have to accept that, if a girl tells us she wants you to have information but not know who provided it, we won't disclose that person's identity to you."

Bull frowned. He had half expected her to stipulate a condition of this nature. "Okay," he said, guardedly. If any of the street workers provided general information or intelligence there would be no issue with them withholding their personal details. It wouldn't be that simple if any of them turned out to have direct evidence relating to the murder. If that happened, there would be an expectation that the girl's details would be disclosed. He hoped Sarah realised this. "I'm sure you can appreciate how time critical this is," he said. "We were hoping to get something in place within a day or two if at all possible."

"Leave it with me," she said. "I'll see what I can do."

As Bull was standing up to leave, the office door opened and a stylish looking man in his mid-forties breezed in. He had a full head of brown hair, which was greying at the temples. Intelligent hazel eyes, an aquiline nose, and paper-thin lips combined to give him a distinguished countenance. The newcomer stopped in his tracks and glanced from Bull to Sarah, startled. "Oh, I'm terribly sorry, Sarah, I didn't realise you had company." The voice was public school posh.

"It's quite alright," she said. "DS Bull, allow me to introduce my husband, Simon."

"How do you do, Mr Pritchard," Steve said, moving towards the other man and extending his hand.

"It's Dr Pritchard," the newcomer corrected him with a smile. Simon Pritchard had soft skin and a handshake like a wet lettuce, Bull thought, resisting the urge to wipe his hand on his trouser leg after it was released.

"To what do we owe the pleasure of your visit?" Dr Pritchard asked.

Bull opened his mouth to formulate an answer, but Sarah got in first.

"The police need our help."

"Do they?" her husband said, suspicion creeping into his voice. *Marvellous!* Bull thought, picking up on Pritchard's tone. *This bloke is a Lay Advisor and he doesn't even trust our intentions.*

"Yes, they're hoping our relationship with the area's street workers might persuade a few of the girls to come forward if they have any information about the young girl who was murdered yesterday."

Dr Pritchard frowned. "Well, dealing with the working girls is your area of expertise, not mine." Something about the way this was said made Bull wonder if Simon Pritchard didn't fully approve of the Mission devoting its precious time and resources to that particular brand of clientele.

"I heard about the murder, of course," the doctor said, turning to face Bull. "Terrible. Quite terrible. How's the investigation going? Do you have any leads yet?"

"We're pursuing a number of lines of enquiry," Bull said, giving a stock in trade answer that roughly translated to: *'I'm not telling you anything.'*

Dr Pritchard raised an amused eyebrow. "I see," he said.

"I'll see myself out," Bull told Sarah Pritchard. "Thank you for your time. I hope to hear from you soon."

"I'll be in touch once we've discussed the matter further," she told him.

Charise was still filing her nails when Steve Bull passed back through reception. He gave her a little wave. "Bye Charise."

"Bye, hon," she called back.

He left the shop as he'd arrived; to the accompaniment of the most irritating 'Bing-bong' he had ever heard.

The refrigerated drawers at Poplar mortuary were kept at a constant temperature of 2 degrees centigrade to ward off decomposition in the bodies, some of which were retained for weeks on end until they were properly identified and the cause of death was established, allowing the Coroner to release them for burial or cremation.

The pathologist's assistant, or the Anatomical Pathology Technician to use her full grandiose title, was a pretty woman in her mid-twenties called Emma Drew. When everyone was ready, she removed the drawer containing Tracey Phillips, and they all crowded around it, Dillon, Copeland, Sam Calvin, a nerdy looking photographer called Ned, and the Home Office Forensic Pathologist assigned to carry out the SPM. The visitors all wore compulsory green gowns and overshoes, but Emma and the pathologist wore surgical pyjamas and wellington boots. Both wore surgical caps, and they had masks hanging loosely under their chins.

Dillon stared down at the cadaver, which was still in the plastic body bag it had been wrapped in at the scene, and wondered why a good-looking, bubbly girl like Emma would want to spend her working day surrounded by death.

"I hear this girl was pretty badly cut up," Emma said.

Dillon nodded. "You could say that." Under normal circumstances, he might have asked Emma out for a drink, but the idea of getting intimate with someone who spent her days cutting open corpses and handling dismembered or decaying body parts was a total turn off.

When the Home Office Pathologist, Dr Ben Claxton, signalled that he was ready to begin the procedure, Tracey's body was hoisted onto a sterile metal trolley and wheeled over to an autopsy table connected to a large drainage sink. George Copeland helped Emma to remove the body bag. It would be sent off to the lab with all the other samples, to be checked for microscopic traces of skin, and for soil and fibres.

Tracey was weighed and measured and then photographed front and back. Ned took a few frames of Tracey in her clothing.

Calvin then removed Tracey's clothing and passed it all to Copeland, who bagged and sealed each garment methodically.

Next, Calvin carefully removed the head and hand bags and passed them to Copeland. Like the body bag, they were destined for the lab.

Before handing over to the pathologist, Calvin swabbed her lips, it was not uncommon in cases like this to find the killer's DNA on them. When he had finished, he stepped back and made a 'she's all yours' gesture to Claxton.

Claxton turned on a small recording device and stated the date and time, the location and persons present, and the details of the deceased. He announced that he would be making verbal notes from which he would compile his final report at a later date, and asked that there be no unnecessary talking as this was likely to interfere with the recording and distract him.

Claxton started with a superficial check of the skull for indentations and lacerations, but found none. "I'll come back to the head when it's time to examine the brain," he promised.

"I can't wait," Dillon muttered under his breath. When he had first walked through the mortuary door twenty minutes earlier, the bittersweet blend of death and Trigene had struck him as overpowering; now it barely seemed noticeable.

Dillon had made his first visit to a mortuary as a fresh-faced probationer, two weeks into his street duties course. He had thrown up as the mortician prepped an old lady – who had died in a road traffic accident – for the pathologist, and had spent the rest of the procedure with his head tucked between his knees trying to stop the world from spinning.

He didn't throw up anymore, but the smell still affected him just as badly as it always had, and he knew that by the time he left the mortuary every pore of his skin, every follicle of his hair and every fibre of his clothes would be impregnated by the foul stench. Another very sound reason not to ask Emma out, he decided. He knew that every time he put an arm around her, he would find himself surreptitiously sniffing her, to see if she still reeked of death. He could imagine them being locked in the throes of passion and catching a sudden unexpected whiff of Trigene in her hair. Well, it would be an incredibly effective method of birth control, if nothing else.

As the others clustered around the pathologist to watch him work, Dillon kept as far away as he could, wishing he could wait outside and avoid the unpleasantness altogether.

The photographer was asked to take some preliminary record photography of the victim before the special post mortem commenced. He would then take further photographs as directed by the pathologist at various stages of the autopsy. "Sure thing," Ned said, clicking away enthusiastically.

The SPM began in earnest with the pathologist logging the dimensions of the bruising around Tracey's jawline. Apart from that, her face was completely untouched. By the time the mortician applied a dab of makeup and tidied up her hair, she would look quite presentable when her family came to make the formal identification; as long as they didn't look at the carnage being concealed by the clean white sheet that would be drawn right up to her chin.

The pathologist moved down to the neck injury. He carefully examined and measured the gaping wound, and then called the photographer forward to take shots from different angles. A ruler was incorporated into each frame to show the angle and depth of the cut.

Claxton dissected and removed some layers of tissue from the neck, which Copeland packaged for him. He left the tongue in place as there was no specific reason for doing otherwise. The voice box and trachea injuries were noted, as was the damage to the carotid and jugular arteries, and the grooves the killer's knife had made on the vertebrae.

Much of what the pathologist said into his little recording device was technical mumbo jumbo to Dillon, but in between all the medical terms, he basically stated that the killer, who had held the blade in his left hand, had grabbed Tracey from behind. He had slit her throat in one powerful and fluid motion, cutting from right to left. The marks on her face, which Jack had noticed at the scene, were grip marks from his right hand. She fell to the floor – there were impact marks on her knees – and rapidly bled out. Although she would have lost consciousness fairly quickly, it could have taken several minutes for her to die.

Claxton carried out a visual examination of the torso, concluding that the killer had probably used a surgical scalpel to make the incisions.

"So, he slit her throat with a knife but opened her torso up using a scalpel?" Copeland asked.

"That's correct," Claxton said.

He explained that a midline laparotomy – a vertical incision that follows the linea alba – had been made, extending from the xiphoid process to the pubic symphysis. Claxton drew their attention to the smooth curve around the umbilicus and noted the precision used to cut through the skin and subcutaneous tissue. "I hate to say this, but in my opinion, the killer's technique suggests that he – or she – has some rudimental surgical knowledge," he said.

"Under what circumstances would a surgeon normally make an incision like that, Ben?" Calvin asked.

"In my experience, incisions like this are most often seen in trauma cases, where the site of the internal injuries is unclear and immediate access is required to the whole abdominal cavity."

In addition to the main midline incision, there were three transverse incisions, each differing in length and depth. These were measured and photographed. As with the other incisions, a ruler was used to demonstrate the angle of the blade's entry.

"I think," Claxton said, and Dillon was unsure if he was addressing them or merely thinking out loud, "that the blighter made these transverse incisions for his own convenience so that he could peel her skin back and make it easier for himself to rummage around inside."

"Why would he want to do that?" Dillon asked, knowing that he was not going to like the answer.

"Well, I should be able to confirm what he was looking for when I start cutting her open, but even at this early stage I can see that our killer has cut out sections of her upper and lower intestines."

"Good God," Dillon said, starting to feel sick. "Why would anyone do that?"

"My dear Inspector," Claxton said, looking up from the corpse, and reminding Dillon of Peter Cushing's maniacal portrayal of Victor Frankenstein in the Hammer Horror films, "while I can tell you what he did, from a pathological point of view, I'm afraid I'm as baffled as you are as to why anyone would ever want or need to do something like this."

As the examination continued, the pathologist formed the opinion that the girl was already dead by the time these incisions were made, and he highlighted a lack of blood loss and an absence of bruising as supporting indicators.

Claxton commentated on the loops of bowel that were sticking out, speculating that the killer had deliberately arranged them like that for effect; he could offer no other logical explanation. He asked if the missing intestinal segments had been found at the scene, and was told that they had not.

"There are elasticised marks around her waist but I note she wasn't wearing underwear. Was this recovered at the scene?"

Sam Calvin shook his head." No. It remains unaccounted for."

"So, he's a trophy taker?" Claxton asked, raising an eyebrow.

Calvin nodded. "It certainly looks that way."

Claxton found traces of nylon in the pubic area, and these were carefully removed, bagged and exhibited. If her underwear was ever recovered, ideally in the killer's possession, fibre comparisons would be carried out. Her pubic hair was then combed and swabbed for semen.

The pathologist peered down at Tracey's exposed genitals and winced. "There's probably no point in taking vaginal swabs, but we'll do them anyway, just for the sake of being thorough. Even without opening her up I can see that a large and very sharp instrument has been forcibly inserted into her vagina. There is severe bruising around her crotch, and her inner thighs have been flayed as the blade was repeatedly rammed in with considerable force. When I open her up, the internal damage will be catastrophic."

Claxton decided to examine her limbs next, pausing to ask for a magnifying glass when he reached Tracey's forearms. "This is interesting," Claxton said, waving for Dillon to come over. "I've found track marks on her arms, which is hardly surprising considering her lifestyle, but there are also what I believe are faint handcuff marks on both wrists. Had she been arrested recently?"

"Yes. They had her in for fraud or something yesterday. She was only released from custody a few hours before she died," Dillon said.

"Ah that probably explains it then," Claxton said, losing interest.

"Actually," Dillon said, taking a step closer despite the revulsion he felt inside. "I've read the custody sheet. She wasn't handcuffed when she was arrested. Whoever did that to her, it wasn't the police."

"Maybe she wore them during a kinky sex session with a client before the killer got to her?" Emma suggested.

"I don't think so," Dillon said. "This was a girl who had rough sex on street corners to fund an all-consuming drug habit. She wasn't into anything as refined as games."

"Which means the killer must have handcuffed her when he abducted her," Copeland said, stating the obvious.

"Perhaps," Claxton allowed, "but I don't understand why the marks aren't more pronounced. If you apply handcuffs tight enough to stop someone from wiggling free, they leave defined marks. If a person in handcuffs struggled, say to resist being kidnapped, it would result in chaffing or bruising; a serious struggle would have caused them to bite deep into the skin, even if they were double locked. These marks are so faint that they are hardly visible; you have to really look to find them. It is almost as if the handcuffs were heavily padded."

"Why would a killer who viciously mutilates his victim pad the cuffs? He's hardly going to worry about her bruising her wrists," Dillon said.

"Maybe what he was worried about was leaving telltale marks," Claxton surmised.

"You mean he didn't want us to know that he had used handcuffs?" Dillon said.

"That's exactly what I mean," Claxton confirmed.

"It's an interesting supposition," Dillon admitted, "but it's very bizarre."

Claxton examined her arms and hands for defence wounds, and then took nail clippings and scrapings, starting with the right hand and then moving on to the left. "Well, well, look what we have here," he said, holding the fingers of her left hand out for the others to see. Calvin, Emma, and Copeland all crowded in for a closer look. Dillon stayed where he was.

"There's some debris under her nails," Claxton told them, scraping it out. "At a guess, I'd say it was human tissue. It looks like she tried to fight her attacker off."

"Result!" Copeland said, triumphantly punching the air. If that was the case, they had his DNA, and it was no longer a case of if they solved the murder, but when.

Claxton examined the dead girl's legs and feet next, and to no one's surprise found more track lines along her inner thighs and between her toes.

"Right," Claxton said, "Let's turn her onto her front. Unlike a standard post-mortem, which begins with a Y shape incision being made on the front of the torso, the start of a special post-mortem generally involves the deceased being placed face down. The initial incision is made across the shoulders, and the skin is then peeled back so that the pathologist can begin his internal examination of the body. Dillon stepped back to the very edge of the room, feeling sick. The others were so engrossed in the procedure that they didn't even notice his abrupt withdrawal, or the greenish pallor of his skin.

When Tracey was eventually placed on her back and cut open from the front, Claxton picked up an instrument that reminded Dillon of a pair of gardening shears and cut out the chest plate, exposing the heart and lungs. Because the victim had suffered an arterial bleed out there was hardly any blood left in the chest cavity. He called the photographer forward and directed him to take shots of all the internal injuries, which he described in great detail on his little recording device.

When the photographer had finished, he took blood samples, which would be sent to the lab for toxicology. When that task was completed, the pathologist used a small knife to expertly remove all the internal organs: heart, lungs, pancreas, spleen, and what remained of the intestinal tract, liver and kidneys. Claxton inspected each one and weighed it. Histology samples were taken and passed to Copeland.

Lastly, the bladder, uterus and ovaries, or rather what was left of them after the genital attack, were removed, exposing the full horror of the killer's onslaught. Claxton sawed through the pubic bone, unfolded her vagina and called the photographer forward to record the terrible injuries. Dillon turned away, thinking that even a whore deserved a little dignity in death.

"I can honestly say I have never seen anything like this," he heard Claxton say. "It is quite astonishing."

"Talk us through it, please, doctor," Dillon asked, turning to face them again.

"In my opinion, the killer probably used a hunting knife in the genital attack. The blade would have been pointed, extremely sharp along the cutting edge and serrated along the other. It penetrated almost thirteen inches inside her. I can't tell how many times because her insides were decimated by him twisting the blade backwards and forwards inside her." He mimed the action, twisting his wrist like he was revving a motorcycle, several times to demonstrate.

"Sweat Jesus," Copeland whispered.

Even bubbly little Emma, who spent more time with the mutilated and putrefying corpses that populated her morgue than she did with the living, and who firmly believed that she had become immune to anything that her job could throw at her, visibly blanched.

"The angle of insertion suggests that she was lying down at the time of the attack; the blows were powerful, the movement frenzied. Her fallopian tubes and cervix are, to put it in layman's terms, shredded like mincemeat. Even though she would have bled out pretty quickly from the arterial haemorrhaging in her neck, it is quite possible that she was still alive when the knife was inserted into her vagina, and I base this on the degree of bleeding and bruising both within and around the attack site. The stomach wounds, on the other hand, were almost certainly administered at his leisure after she had expired."

Dillon could feel the room starting to spin, and he leaned against the wall and forced himself to take slow deep breaths until everything returned to normal. He wondered how people like Claxton and Emma slept at night. Perhaps, instead of counting sheep, they counted bodies on cold metal slabs. They were so matter of fact about the whole thing; cutting up human beings as routinely and casually as teenagers dissecting frogs in the school lab.

Copeland and Calvin weren't much better; they were perfectly comfortable in this depressing environment and seemed to find the whole process fascinating. Even Ned, the photographer seemed pretty chilled out.

All he felt was revulsion. And that, he told himself, was a good thing.

"Was there any sign of the missing bits of intestine inside her abdominal cavity?" Calvin asked as Claxton moved towards the top of the table.

Claxton shook his head. "No. Are you sure they weren't left at the scene?"

"I processed the scene myself," Calvin said. "There was nothing like that there."

"We know he's a trophy taker," Dillon said. "Maybe he took it home and is keeping it in a jar of formaldehyde."

"Why would anyone want to keep human flesh?" Copeland asked, and then grinned wickedly. "Perhaps he just hadn't had time to go to the butcher's and needed some offal to feed his dog."

"I said we'd come back to the head," Claxton said as he placed the point of his knife against the skin behind the right ear and pressed down sharply. He drew the blade along the top of the head to the skin behind the other ear. Dillon was appalled to realise that he was humming while he worked. He couldn't suppress the shudder that passed through him; this part of the autopsy always turned his knees to jelly.

With the scalp split, the pathologist pulled on the skin at the top and peeled it down to the level of the eyebrows, folding it over like a grotesque Halloween mask. Dillon tried to ignore the sickly slimy noise that accompanied the movement. Claxton peeled the rest of the skin back the other way, exposing the remainder of the skull as Emma stepped forward wielding a big electrical saw.

"You gentlemen might want to step back beyond the yellow line," the pathologist suggested, indicating a line on the floor by the entrance to the washroom area.

"Good idea," Dillon said, dragging a protesting Copeland back with him. Although there was nothing to indicate that Tracey had any conditions that might make her a health hazard, they were not wearing masks and there was a risk of unwittingly breathing in airborne blood in the fine spray the saw generated.

"I find this the most interesting part," Copeland said from behind the line.

"You're sick in the head, you know that?" Dillon told him.

"I agree with George," Ned said. "This is all so fascinating."

"You should seek professional help," Dillon advised him.

The buzz of the saw was uncomfortably loud in the tight confines of the mortuary, and it seemed to go on forever. Eventually, her task completed, Emma stood aside and the pathologist pulled off the cap of the skull in preparation for removing the brain.

"You can come back over now," Emma told them, smiling happily.

Anyone would think she was doing us a favour, Dillon thought, noting with some disgust that George Copeland and his buddy, nerdy Ned, were heading back to the body before she had even finished speaking.

"I suppose we had better take a look, too," Sam Calvin said.

"I suppose so," Dillon agreed, forcing himself to take a step closer, and then another, and then another, until he was near enough to see the dura matter, the tissue covering the dead girl's brain. He watched the pathologist cut that away and lift the brain out of the cranial cavity. Claxton weighed and inspected it, and recorded his findings.

Save for the various tissues that Sam and George had packaged as samples, the extracted organs were placed together in a single plastic bag and deposited back inside the body cavity, which was sewn up by Emma.

The autopsy was finally over and the pathologist confirmed that the cause of death was a single cut to the neck, which was carried out anti-mortem. This had severed the windpipe and led to arterial bleed out or exsanguination. The vaginal injuries were inflicted peri-mortem and would have proved fatal had she not already received the terminal neck injuries. The incisions to her abdomen and the partial extraction of her intestine were all done post-mortem. "An interesting piece de resistance, wouldn't you say?" Claxton said.

"I'm sure the Psychobabble people would think so," Dillon agreed.

Four long hours after it started, the SPM was finally over, and Dillon had hated every painful minute of it.

After collecting the exhibits and exchanging the usual pleasantries they made their way out to the front of the building as quickly as they could. It was raining heavily and the air was thick with diesel fumes, but compared to the oppressive atmosphere inside the mortuary it was pure heaven.

"Those places always give me the creeps," Dillon said, dodging puddles as they walked towards the Vauxhall Astra pool car.

"You shouldn't let it get to you, guv," Copeland said. "You have to be completely detached and think of the body as a machine we're examining for mechanical defects. You can't let yourself be drawn in by who the person was or anything like that."

Dillon failed to see how anyone could avoid being drawn in, especially when the victim was young, like this one. Even after having seen it with his own eyes, he still couldn't quite believe the extent to which this woman had been defiled. How could anyone not be disturbed by seeing a sight like that?

"What do you think about the pathologist's suggestion to revisit the body in a few days to see if any further evidential bruising comes out?" Copeland asked. These had been Claxton's parting words. He'd pointed out that bruising isn't always apparent on fresh cadavers. Sometimes it takes several days for marks to appear and even longer for them to become fully developed.

"Not sure if it's going to give us anything more than we've already got, to be honest, George. We know how she died. Logging some additional bruises won't take us any closer to her killer."

"Suppose so," Copeland said, wondering if Dillon really believed that or was just trying to avoid a return trip to the mortuary.

"Anyway," Dillon said, "it can always be checked during the second

PM." If someone was arrested and charged, their defence team would be able to instruct an independent pathologist to carry out a second PM to verify the findings of Dr Claxton. If no one was charged by the time the Coroner was ready to release the body to the family, the Coroner's Office would have to arrange a second PM anyway. And the good thing about second PMs, they both knew, was that they didn't require a DI to attend.

Dillon checked his watch and was surprised to see it was gone four already. "George, I want you to complete a lab form tonight and get the nail scrapings up to the FSS at Lambeth first thing tomorrow morning. There's a good chance that whatever trace material was recovered from under her nails belongs to our killer." He pictured Winston's badly gouged face from last night and thought about the flesh under Tracey's nails. What were the odds that these two events were unconnected?

A simple comparison of two samples – the DNA profile recorded on Winston's file and the findings from the skin found under the victim's nails – would provide all the answers they needed, but the results would take the best part of two days to come back, even though the Forensic Science Service would fast track the submission.

It was definitely looking like Winston had killed her, but why had he left the message? And what had driven him to mutilate her body like that? He was still trying to fathom that last one out when the telephone rang.

It was Jack.

"The drug squad has housed Winston for us. I need you to get back to the office as quickly as possible!"

CHAPTER TEN

It was almost five p.m. by the time they got back to Arbour Square. While George booked all the exhibits into storage, Dillon gave Jack a breakdown on what the autopsy had revealed.

"Is he sure about the killer having medical knowledge?" Jack asked. He didn't like that idea one little bit, and neither would Holland. He could already picture the headline if the tabloids got hold of that information: '*DOCTOR DEATH STALKS THE STREETS OF LONDON*'.

"I'm afraid so, Jack," Dillon confirmed. "And it makes sense. He cut her open like he knew what he was doing."

"Fuck," Jack said, gloomily. "That's all we need – a psychotic doctor."

"To be fair," Dillon said, putting things into context, "Claxton did only say rudimentary medical knowledge."

"So, it could theoretically be a mortuary assistant, a paramedic or even a hospital porter?"

Dillon nodded. "Or just someone who's worked in a funeral parlour, embalming bodies. It could even be a weirdo who's been reading too many medical books."

"Well, that's as clear as mud," Tyler said, deciding that there was no point in speculating further. It would all come out in the wash, as his mum was fond of saying.

Dillon sniffed his lapel and wrinkled his nose. "I think I need a shower. I've got the smell of death all over me,"

"I thought it was just that ropey aftershave you wear kicking up," Jack teased.

"Funny," Dillon said, giving him the finger. "So, what's been happening here while I've been gone?"

Jack explained that Reg had managed to fast-track subscriber information on mobile phones belonging to Tracey Phillips, Sandra Dawson, and Claude Winston.

"The call data shows that Tracey rang Winston once during the early hours of yesterday morning, a call that lasted approximately two minutes. Between five and six-fifteen a.m. Winston made a number of calls to Tracey's mobile, none of which were answered. He also made one short call to Sandra Dawson just before six a.m."

"What about cell site, have we got that?"

"We have, and the cell site data is even more interesting. It places Winston in the vicinity of Commercial Street around the time we think Tracey was killed."

"So, things aren't looking too good for Claude?"

"No, they're not. Dawson's testimony, combined with the phone data, put him squarely in the frame for this. If the DNA from under Tracey's nails turns out to be his, which I suspect it will, I think we'll have enough to charge him."

"So, how did we find him?"

"The drug squad boys have been watching a wash house in Limehouse, run by a little oik called Clifford Mullings. They followed Mullings to another flat on a dodgy estate in Canning Town last week, and guess who opened the door to let him in?"

"Winston?"

"None other."

"It doesn't mean he lives there, though. He could just have been visiting."

"I pointed that out to the drug squad, but they assured me it was

Winston's flat; said their information was one hundred percent reliable."

"Have you told Holland?" Dillon asked.

"I've updated him with what we've got, but I've made a point of telling him not to get too excited just yet. I don't want him telling the AC we've got this case cracked, only to find that Winston's not our man after all."

Dillon frowned. "He ticks all the boxes for me," he said.

Jack shrugged. "'He would tick all the boxes for me, too, if it wasn't for that message. I just don't see what he could gain from writing something like that."

"Maybe he's trying to deflect us away from the real motive, hoping we'll think we've got a serial killer on the loose when it's nothing more than a simple revenge killing by an angry pimp."

"Do you honestly think that's why he went to town on her genitals or pulled half her intestines out – just to throw us off the trail?"

Dillon thought back to the SPM and shuddered. "She's a sex worker. Maybe she was shortchanging him and this is a message to the other girls."

"Do you really buy that?" Jack asked.

Dillon sighed, "How many times in the past have we been surprised by the senseless brutality of murder? How many times do we hear people say, 'I never thought he would be capable of something like that?' Maybe Winston was high when he killed her, or maybe he's just an old-fashioned psychopath."

"Yes, but is he an old-fashioned psychopath with rudimentary medical knowledge?" Jack asked.

Dillon considered this. "That's a good point," he admitted. "I can't imagine Winston having any medical knowledge, but I could be wrong."

"So, that makes two reasons why he doesn't tick all the boxes for me," Jack said.

Steve Bull shuffled into the office looking fit to collapse. He stopped, sniffed and recoiled. "Phwoor, it smells like something died in here. Where's that pong coming from?"

"Me, I'm afraid," Dillon admitted.

"How are you getting on organising a surveillance team?" Jack asked him.

Bull shook his head. "I'm not. I've spoken to C11. Every team in the Met is already deployed tonight. All they could advise was to phone back in the morning and they'll try to accommodate us then. The one thing they did say, though, was that they won't deploy unless we have a definite pick-up point. They just don't have the resources to let a team sit on a dead plot all day."

"Okay, put a briefing package together, Steve. If they aren't willing to deploy unless they know he's there, we'd better house him for them."

"But we don't even have a 'nondy' van," Steve pointed out.

Tyler turned to Dillon. "Any chance you could blag the observation van from those Flying Squad mates of yours at Rigg Approach?"

Dillon shrugged. "I suppose I could phone over and see if they're using it tonight," he said.

"You might want to shower first," Bull suggested, fanning his nose.

The observations on Claude Winston's address began at seven p.m. Despite their tiredness a sense of expectation now buzzed through the team, reinvigorating them.

While the aim on paper was purely to confirm that Winston was using the flat, Tyler had made it clear during the briefing that if Winston came out, they would try and follow him away from the estate. If the chance presented itself, once they were far enough away to protect the drug squad's source, they would jump the bastard and make an arrest.

A battered nondescript van was driven into the estate and parked up at the base of Winston's block, and the rest of the team strategically positioned themselves to cover the estate's three exits. They communicated via Cougar radios, using an encrypted radio channel specially designated to their team.

Kelly Flowers had drawn the short straw, and from her cramped position in the back of the 'nondy' she was watching the communal entrance to the block like a hawk. The first-floor balcony had a large overhang, making it virtually impossible to see Winston's door, but it didn't really matter; the communal entrance was the only way out. As long as they kept eyeball on that, they should pick him up, sooner or later.

At least the torrential rain that had been lashing the capital for most of the afternoon had subsided; now there was nothing more than a minor drizzle to contend with, and even that was clearing. As long as the van's blacked out rear windows didn't steam up too much, she would be fine. "Control from Kelly," she whispered into her Cougar, "I'm in position and have eyeball on the stairwell leading to the target address. For your info, there's no sign of the subject's vehicle outside the block."

"*Received, Kelly. We'll get someone to have a gander.*" Dillon's voice came back.

Colin Franklin was one of several P9 surveillance trained DC's on Tyler's team. Wearing a pair of dirty coveralls and a dark bandanna, he sauntered through the estate in search of the BMW.

A few minutes later he reported back that it was nowhere to be seen. Furthermore, there were no lights on inside the address, which was sealed up tighter then Fort Knox: The street door itself was made of solid metal. There was a heavy-duty iron grill covering it and another one over the kitchen window. Even a door-busters team, equipped with thermal lances and other high-tech cutting tools, would take time to gain entry. To make matters worse, a group of black teenagers, looking sinister in their Echo and McKenzie hoodies, were congregating in the stairwell that led up to Winston's flat. Some of them would undoubtedly be on Winston's payroll.

Franklin had drawn hostile stares as he wandered around the estate, and he had promptly been ordered to withdraw. Under the circumstances, they could do no more without the risk of showing out. Hoping it wouldn't take too long, but knowing that it probably would, the team settled down and prepared to play the waiting game.

By nine-thirty the initial excitement had long since turned to boredom. Fatigue was setting in as the effects of working two ridiculously long days started to take their toll.

The Omega was tucked away in the corner of a small car park at the side of a Presbyterian Church opposite the estate. Traffic was light, and their position provided a good, albeit angled, view of the estate's main entrance.

Dillon had just returned from a nearby McDonald's. His arms were laden with an assortment of burgers, fries, and shakes, which he quickly shared out.

He had showered and changed into his spare suit before leaving Arbour Square, and now that he no longer smelled like a rotting corpse his mood had improved.

"*No change.*" Kelly's voice crackled over the radio, giving the latest update.

"Poor cow," Dillon said, unwrapping the first of his two burgers. "She must be breaking her neck for a leak by now."

"She's got a plastic container and a funnel for emergencies," Jack said.

Steve Bull grimaced. "That's really not an image I wanted to have of Kelly."

"How long are you going to give it, Jack?" Dillon asked; at least Jack thought that was what he said, but with so much food in his mouth it was hard to be sure.

"If there's no activity by midnight I'll knock it on the head."

"Do we even know if he's in there?" Steve asked. "The lights were off when Colin did the walkthrough."

"The lights could have been off because he was sleeping, or maybe the lights were actually on but he's got heavy blackout drapes up," Jack said.

Bull fidgeted in his seat. "We could do a quick drive through the estate to see if the car's turned up," he suggested. Having dozed for nearly two hours, his batteries had recharged a little and he was ready for action again.

"Let's just hold our position and wait for him to come out," Jack said.

"If he doesn't show his face tonight, are we going to get a warrant and do the flat in the morning?"

"I think we should get a warrant, but we'll keep it in our back pocket for now. It'll be better if we nick him on the street. That way, he won't realise that we know where he lives, and I won't get a hard time from the drug squad for burning their snout."

"Logical," Dillon said, like he was Spock, except that Spock didn't normally talk with his mouth full.

"But he's not likely to give his real address once he's in custody, so when we go and search his flat it'll be pretty obvious that someone's tipped us off."

"Also logical," Dillon allowed, slurping noisily from his strawberry milkshake.

"I'm sure we can come up with some plausible bullshit to hoodwink him once he's in the bin," Jack said, "but even if we don't, at least any evidence inside the flat will be saved." The murder weapon and the victim's underwear were still adrift. Retrieving them would provide irrefutable proof of Winston's guilt. "If he doesn't appear by midnight, I think it's safe to assume he isn't coming out tonight. If we reach that point, I'll arrange for the night duty HAT to cover the address for a few hours, and we can be back in place first thing in the morning."

"God, we're gonna be so fucked by the end of the week," Steve said.

"Which is why I'm going to catch forty winks now," Tyler said. "Wake me in an hour and I'll relieve you." With that, he slouched down in the back seat and closed his eyes.

Dillon gave Steve a friendly pat on the arm, burped loudly and then followed Jack's lead.

The radio squawked into life unexpectedly, jarring Tyler awake. He sat bolt upright in the back of the car, blinking rapidly.

His watch said 10.15 p.m.

Another transmission came through with heavy background noise. "...ject....out of block......wards mai......foot...." The voice belonged to Kelly Flowers, but what was she trying to say?

"This is really not the time for her radio to pack up on her," Tyler said, leaning forward. There was a sense of urgency as the atmosphere inside the car became charged with adrenalin.

Bull started the engine just in case.

"*...Repeat Subject has come out of the block, going towards the main road on foot.*" Flower's voice came through on the speaker again, crystal clear this time, but was the warning too late?

"He's coming towards us!" Jack said. "Keep your eyes open, boys."

The first few seconds after a contact is established are always the most dangerous, and when Winston didn't appear Jack started to fret. Surely, they hadn't lost him already?

Jack was staring at the entrance so hard that his eyes were hurting, but he was afraid to blink in case he missed something. Seconds passed with excruciating slowness.

"Where the fuck is he?" Bull asked; his voice strained.

"Be quiet Stevie," Dillon soothed. Like the others, he was painfully aware that Winston should have reached them by now. Had he somehow managed to slip out of the estate while Kelly was transmitting? Dillon bit his lip and thought hard. Pace, time and distance, that's what it all came down to in the end: at the pace Winston was walking, how far could he have travelled in the time that had elapsed since he was last seen?

Steve Bull snatched up a map the Intel Cell had printed of the estate. Had he missed something when he was preparing the briefing? Not according to the map. Whatever route Winston took out of the estate, someone should pick him up.

So, where the hell was he?

"There he is, over there," Bull suddenly exclaimed, pointing into the darkness.

Tyler froze, conscious that sudden movement draws the human eye like nothing else, even from a distance. He allowed his eyes to follow the line indicated by Bull's extended finger, and sure enough, there he was, strutting through the estate like he owned the place.

"Fuck me, look at that leather jacket? It's that Lawrence Fishface bloke from *The Matrix,* only with dreadlocks," Steve whispered.

Tyler let out his breath and sagged back into his seat, relieved.

A slow smile spread across Dillon's dark features. "Got you now, you bastard," he purred.

Dillon took the radio back from Jack and began issuing instructions to the others, telling them to be ready to move off in case he got into a vehicle.

Claude Winston paused at the edge of the road and had a good look around before crossing.

"He's eyes about," Tyler warned.

"Bloody hell, if he turns right, he'll walk right past us," Steve said, looking around to see what options they had.

"It's alright, he's not coming this way," Dillon said as Winston veered off to the left.

"C'mon Dill," Jack said, as he killed the internal light and slid out of the car.

On his way out, Dillon turned to Steve Bull. "Try and shadow us if you can, and be ready for a quick off. If he gets in a car, you'll only have seconds to pick us up and get behind him."

"No pressure there, then," Bull said.

Dillon winked. "We live for pressure," he said as he closed the passenger door.

"Not me. I just want a quiet life," Bull told the empty car.

Tyler crossed the road and began following Winston at a discrete distance, hands in pockets and head down. Dillon stayed on the same side, but he dropped much further back, adopting the classic surveillance 'back-up' position. He found himself wondering where the hell Winston was heading.

―――

Winston had collected the drugs from the safe house without incident, and they were now safely hidden in his flat, ready for him to drop off at the washhouse first thing tomorrow. Their presence made him uneasy. He wasn't worried about break-ins; the iron gates that he had fitted would foil any burglar. Besides, he was 'The Man' and his reputation was known, respected and feared. What concerned him was the drug squad's growing interest in his operation. They had been carrying out sporadic surveillance on his people over the last couple of months, not that it had got them anywhere.

Walking briskly, he passed several turnings before reaching the one he wanted. Checking to make sure that he wasn't being followed, he ducked into the narrow street.

The BMW was parked about twenty yards in from the junction. Since the drug squad had started taking an unhealthy interest in him, he had made a point of not parking outside his address anymore. In fact, he had made a point of not parking in the same street on any two consecutive nights. If they were watching him, the last thing he wanted to do was make it easy for them to predict his movements. Predictability was a death sentence to someone in his profession.

He slid into the driver's seat, started the engine and cranked the sound system up to full blast. Barry White sounded as cool as ever as he sang *'Don't make me wait too long'*.

Winston reached into the inner pocket of his leather jacket and removed a bulky object wrapped in a leather shammy. Placing it on the passenger seat, he carefully unfolded it, reached down and cupped the gun in his hand. It felt good. Winston often wished that his parents had chosen to immigrate to America back in the sixties, instead of Britain. He had grown up watching programmes like *Miami Vice* and *Hawaii Five-O*, and he longed to live in a subtropical climate, surrounded by fast cars and even faster women. A man with his talents could become a serious player over there.

The gun was a Smith and Wesson snub-nosed .38 revolver, often referred to as a 'Saturday night special'. The five-round cylinder was fully loaded. Claude had obtained the gun as payment in lieu of a drug debt. Pointing the gun at an imaginary front seat passenger he adopted a Gangsta pose. "BANG! You're dead mutherfucka!"

He slowly raised the barrel to his lips and blew on it, and then threw back his head and laughed. It was a loud humourless sound. Placing the gun back in its protective cloth, he set off towards the East End. He had business to attend to.

CHAPTER ELEVEN

The rear wheels spun impressively as the BMW accelerated away, leaving the air thick with the cloying smell of burning rubber.

Tyler stepped out of the shadows, followed closely by Dillon, whose face was grim as he spoke into the handset. "The subject just got into a black BMW and is heading north along Kimberley Road." He broadcast the registration number and told the team to fan out and try to pick it up.

The Omega appeared at the top of the road, engine roaring, before he had even finished speaking. A few seconds later it screeched to a halt beside them and both men dived in. Bull was pulling away before the doors had closed, but the BMW was already out of sight, and Jack was forced to face the ugly possibility that they might have lost him. The thought left a bad taste in his mouth. Suddenly, up in the distance, he caught a brief glimpse of bright red.

Red for brake lights.

Red for danger.

A frisson of hope stirred in his chest, only to be dashed as an old red Mini pulled out of a side road straight in front of them, blocking their path and forcing Bull to brake heavily. Oblivious to the urgency of the situation, the Mini's elderly driver seemed content to pootle along at twenty miles per hour.

"Shall I put the blues and twos on?" Bull asked.

Jack shook his head glumly. He was trying to blot out the noise that Dillon was making as he screamed non-stop abuse at the Mini's driver, but it really wasn't easy. "No, we can't do anything that might tip him off that we know where he lives."

"We'll lose him if we don't," Bull warned, shouting to be heard over the cacophony that Dillon was making.

"I know," Tyler said, miserably. "We'll just have to try and reacquire him once we get past this old fogey." As he spoke, the BMW's tail lights dwindled into tiny pinpricks and then disappeared altogether. Dillon nudged Steve's arm so hard that the car swerved. "Ram the dozy fucker out of the way," he demanded.

"Not helping, guv," Steve snapped, shrugging Dillon's massive hand off his arm.

As soon as the road opened up, Steve Bull buried the accelerator pedal into the floor and the Omega powered past the Mini, but it was far too late by then; the trail had gone cold.

"Right or left?" Steve demanded as they skidded to a halt at a T-Junction a few moments later.

Jack shrugged. "No idea," he said, feeling totally depressed.

"I'll plot a route for the City," Dillon said, frantically pawing through the Met issue Geographia to work out how to get to the A13 from their current location. "Chances are he's heading into town to go pimping."

A car behind them sounded its horn aggressively. Looking in the rearview, Bull was surprised to see it was the red Mini that had unwittingly run interference for Winston, its driver impatiently gesturing for him to move off.

"What's that racket about?" Dillon demanded without looking up.

"Nothing," Bull said quickly. If Dillon realised who was behind them things were likely to get ugly.

Tyler had also seen the Mini. "Just go with your instinct, Steve," he instructed.

Bull nodded. He pulled the selector into Drive and glanced in both directions, knowing that sod's law dictated whichever way he went was bound to be wrong.

Right or left?

"Fuck it," he said, initiating a left turn just as the Mini honked again. This time the old codger flashed his headlights as well.

Dillon put the map down and spoke into the radio. "We've lost him," he told the team, "but the chances are he'll head back towards Tower Hamlets." He directed the team to starburst, dispatching cars in various directions to hedge his bets. Putting the radio down, he glanced back at Tyler, lips compressed into a tight, thin line. "It's gonna be bloody embarrassing if we lose him."

"Hopefully, we won't," Tyler said, but his voice lacked conviction.

The silence was unbearable as they waited for someone to spot Winston, knowing that the odds of doing so diminished disproportionately with every passing moment. As the seconds stretched into minutes, the mood inside the car became increasingly sombre.

"It's been too long," Bull finally said, breaking the silence.

"Contact! Contact! Control from DC Murray, we've spotted the Target. We're two behind and he's just taken the A13 slip road at Canning Town. He's heading along East India Dock Road towards the Blackwell Tunnel, and he's not hanging about either."

Bull sat up ramrod straight and began driving with renewed purpose. When he caught Tyler's eye in the rear-view mirror, the boss winked at him. Despite the evening's tribulations, he found himself smiling as relief flooded through him. Somehow, they were back in the game.

"I never thought the day would come when I'd be grateful to that little twat for anything," Dillon admitted, "and if either of you ever tells that scrawny little prat what I said, I swear I will put dog excrement in your exhaust pipes."

"Don't worry, your secret is safe with us," Tyler assured him.

"Guv, do you want us to try and stop him?" Murray was asking excitedly.

"No Kevin, just keep your distance and wait for everyone else to catch you up," Dillon advised, trying to keep the dislike he felt from his voice.

One by one, the other cars called in their locations. The nearest was the one containing Charlie White and George Copeland, which had just turned onto the A13 from Prince Regent Lane and was a mile or so behind the eyeball car.

―――

When Winston drove straight past the Blackwell Tunnel Southern Approach, they became increasingly confident that he was heading towards his usual pimping ground to start his rounds.

"Passing Burdett Road on our right," Murray said, giving the latest update.

Grier was becoming worried. "I think we're on our own," he said, looking out of the rear window for signs of reinforcements.

"Don't worry, Terry," Bartholomew reassured him. "They'll catch us up soon."

―――

"I still can't see anyone yet," Grier fretted as they left the A13, fifteen minutes later.

Murray raised the radio to his lips. "We're turning into Whitechapel High Street," he informed the team.

"*We're nearly with you*," Charlie White's voice came back.

"He's been saying that for the last ten minutes," Grier complained.

"He's indicating to turn right into Commercial Street," Murray said, keeping the commentary going.

As Bartholomew followed the BMW into Commercial Street, the radio slipped off Murray's knee and fell to the floor. He immediately started fumbling around in the footwell, cursing his driver for taking the corner too fast. Bartholomew was so distracted by the unexpected commotion that he was caught off guard when Winston abruptly jammed his brakes on and pulled over sharply, tucking into a bus stop without signalling. Bartholomew hesitated, stabbing at the brakes indecisively as he debated whether to pull in behind Winston, but then professional instinct kicked back in and he knew they would be blown if he did.

"He's pulled into the bus stop," Grier shouted as Murray resurfaced clutching the Cougar radio upside down. "Quick, you've got to tell the others."

"I'm trying, I'm trying," Murray screamed, almost dropping the radio again. With a shaking hand, he pressed the transmit button. "Murray to all units, he's stopped suddenly in Commercial Street. We've had to drive past or we'd have been blown."

Bartholomew pulled over further down the road and shot Murray a look of disgust. If this went belly up because Murray had dropped the radio and not warned the others quickly enough, he and Terry would be found guilty by association.

"Don't worry, we were right behind you and we've got him," Copeland's calm voice informed them over the radio. George had pulled into the kerb a safe distance behind the BMW. *"What do you want us to do, boss?"* Copeland asked. *"There are five of us here in two cars. Do you want us to try and take him?"*

"No, George. Wait till at least one more car joins you," Dillon ordered. Although five officers should be more than enough to arrest one suspect, Winston was a huge man, and his research docket had revealed that he had warning signals on the Police National Computer for violence and carrying offensive weapons.

The Omega was now speeding through Stepney on blues and twos, trying to catch up. The remaining two cars were still a little way behind, but neither had lights or sirens fitted, so it was much harder for them to make progress.

Jack's impatience was getting the better of him "What's our ETA, Steve?" he shouted in order to be heard above the siren.

"We're still a few minutes away, boss," Bull responded, pulling onto the wrong side of the road to overtake a line of slow-moving traffic that was blocking his path.

Dillon turned around to face Tyler, concern plastered across his broad face. "You're not thinking of telling them to move in before we get there, are you?" he asked.

"No," Jack said, shaking his head emphatically. "I agree with you. Having read his form, I think we need to have more people there before making our move."

Dillon seemed relieved to hear that. Facing the front again, he raised the transmitter to his lips. "What's he doing now, George?" he asked.

"*Nothing,*" the Yorkshire man replied almost immediately. "*He's just sitting in his car.*"

"Do you think he's stopped to pick someone up?" Jack asked, wondering why Winston had pulled over so randomly.

Dillon shrugged. "Possibly," he said, raising the radio to his lips again. "We're just passing Whitechapel hospital, George," he said into the handset. "We'll be with you very shortly."

―――

In Copeland's car, neither occupant spoke. All eyes were glued on Winston, who just sat there, twenty yards ahead of them, making no effort to get out of his car. Could he have spotted them tailing him, or was he just performing anti-surveillance techniques out of habit?

In fact, Winston hadn't spotted them. Nor was he carrying out anti-surveillance techniques. He had stopped so suddenly because he mistakenly thought he'd spotted Fat Sandra going into the Tesco store across the road. When she emerged a few minutes later, he immediately realised that the woman he was looking at was an equally fat, and equally ugly, doppelganger. Cursing her for wasting his precious time, he pulled back out into traffic, cutting up the car behind him, which braked hard and was rear-ended by a van.

With their view initially blocked by the back of the van, and their attention then drawn to the fracas developing between the car owner and van driver as they started blaming each other for the prang, neither Copeland nor White realised that Winston had pulled away.

Winston quickly spotted a couple of girls plying their trade on a street corner, and another one lingering in a shop doorway. Generally, though, it looked like a very quiet night for the sex trade. "Must be a whore's convention going on somewhere," he mused to himself, wondering where all the regulars were. There was no sign of either Tracey or Fat Sandra outside the used car sales lot in Quaker Street. Of course, they could both be off with punters; or maybe Tracey had got herself arrested again and was banged up in a cell, clucking.

Winston checked out the surrounding roads, but they were equally deserted. *Where the hell is everyone?* He was on the brink of giving up when he remembered an underground car park that some of the girls used, not far from Brick Lane. He recalled Tracey telling Sandra that in bad weather she occasionally took clients there for a quick knee-trembler or a blow job in the darkness.

Winston gunned the car along Jerome Street, swung right into Calvin Street and then left into Grey Eagle Street. Within moments he spotted the place that she had been talking about and turned in, driving down the ramp at a crawl. At the bottom, he paused to take in his surroundings.

The underground car park was seven feet tall, fifty feet wide and one hundred and fifty feet long. Almost all the overhead lighting was out; the lights that did work were set to dim, making the cavernous space seem dark and foreboding. A few cars were randomly parked near the up ramp on the other side, but most of the spaces were empty. At first glance, the place appeared deserted, but Winston decided to do a slow drive through and check behind the evenly spaced lines of concrete support pillars. He wound down his front windows and nudged the car forward slowly.

He spotted a sudden movement up ahead as two figures slid behind a pillar on the other side of the car park by the exit ramp. Adrenalin kicked in and Winston floored the gas pedal, making the car rocket forward. He flipped the main beam on and the car park was bathed in harsh white light. The two figures locked in an embrace disengaged violently. The larger of the two, hitching his trousers up as he went, took off up the exit ramp like an Olympic sprinter. The smaller of the two stepped into the light, shielding her eyes with one hand and pulling her skirt down with the other.

It wasn't Tracey.

―――

The control car was secreted in a tiny cul-de-sac behind the multi-level car park in Whites Row. It had been parked there for several minutes now, its frustrated occupants animatedly discussing what they could do to recover the situation.

When Copeland had initially announced the loss over the radio, five-minutes ago, the bad news had hit Tyler like a kick in the proverbials. Trying not to let his disappointment get the better of him, he had immediately ordered everyone to do a quick sweep of the area on the off chance that Claude Winston was still nearby. If that failed – and it had – they were all to regroup in Whites Row.

Predictably, the last car to arrive was Copeland and White's, and as the two men got out and approached the control car on foot, it was clear that they were both acutely embarrassed. Charlie White, who had been driving, displayed all the enthusiasm of a man walking to the gallows. "It's no' fair, boss," he whined as soon as Tyler opened his door to get out. "We were watching like hawks, but we didnae stand a chance of seeing him move off after that accident happened right in front of us, especially as the two wee blockheads involved got out and started punching shite out of each other."

"It's alright," Jack said, cutting White's tale of woe off before the violins and hankies came out. "We lost him ourselves earlier, but luckily Kevin's car picked him up."

That made Copeland and White feel marginally less like abject failures, but it did nothing to ease their guilt, and every few seconds one or the other would mutter another apology to someone in the team until Dillon became bored with it and told them to shut up and stop trying to out-apologise each other.

"Sorry," they said in unison.

"I'm gonna punch the next fucker who says sorry," Dillon warned, waving a ham-sized fist at them.

With everyone gathered around him, Tyler spread a map out on the bonnet of the Omega and asked Bartholomew to indicate the local hot spot for sex workers. Using a pen, he quartered the area Nick highlighted and dispatched one car to each sector with orders to patrol it for the next hour. In response to their disgruntled groans, he promised that if they hadn't reacquired Winston by then he would accept defeat. If nothing else, he told them, they had confirmed Winston was still using the flat, and while he would have preferred to make an arrest tonight, at least he now had grounds for getting a properly resourced surveillance operation up and running.

Despite his sterling pep talk, the troops looked demoralised as they returned to their respective cars, and Jack could hardly blame them; reacquiring Winston earlier had used up a shed load of luck, and they all knew it. Surely, they couldn't hope to be that lucky again?

Could they?

A few streets away, Winston pulled up outside Christ Church of Spitalfields. Built by Nicholas Hawksmore in 1714, the old church was steeped in local history. Its cramped cemetery was full of decaying tombstones bearing the faded names of the French Huguenots who populated the area at the time. During daylight hours the site was popular with aspiring scholars. At night, junkies and whores held the monopoly. Perhaps Tracey was in there right now, bent over a headstone while some city gent shafted her from behind. He decided to give it a few minutes and see if she came out.

While he waited, he studied the motley collection of undesirables gathered outside the crypt, brandishing their cans of extra strong as though they were the latest fashion accessories. With his customary cynicism, Winston surmised there must be a free soup kitchen inside;

there was no way this lot had gathered to pray. He snorted in disgust; these wasters really knew how to milk the system. What incentive was there for them to work while they could scavenge all the handouts they needed from the nanny State?

He sometimes wondered if he was the only one who could see that this whole poverty thing was just a scam. They didn't beg because they were desperate, living hand to mouth, as they would have people believe. They did it because it was such an easy way to make money.

He hated them; they were pathetic wannabes who spent their time wallowing in self-pity. They complained bitterly to anyone willing to listen that life had dealt them a bad hand, but what did they ever do to try and better themselves?

He finished his silent vitriol and glanced at the clock on the dash. Tracey obviously wasn't in the graveyard; she could have serviced three customers in the time he had been waiting. He tried her mobile, but it was switched off. He considered leaving a voicemail telling her to call him back but didn't trust himself not to rant. Winston was fast running out of ideas. As he pulled back into traffic, he decided to do one more circuit of the area and then call it a night.

Five minutes later, as Winston was about to make a right turn into Wheler Street from Quaker Street, the car in front of him suddenly stopped. He was about to pound his fist on the horn and shout at the driver, but then the passenger door opened and a peroxide blond head poked out. "Well, well, well, look who it ain't," he said, reaching down to access the revolver in his pocket.

As the old Mercedes E Class drove away, Fat Sandra gave it a bon voyage wave, pulled a compact mirror from her purse and began fussing at her hair. Winston drove past her and pulled over to the kerb to let the car behind him get by. The black man in the Astra's front passenger seat gave him a funny look. "Fuck you looking at?" he wondered aloud. Normally, he would have wound his window down and told the fool to avert his eyes if he wanted to keep them. Right now, he had more pressing matters on his mind.

Looking in his rear-view mirror, Winston watched Fat Sandra waddle back towards Quaker Street, presumably in search of a new punter. He waited until she took up her usual station outside the used car lot and then quickly drove around the block. Moments later, he drew level with her and honked his horn. Sandra turned around with all the elegance of a hippo in a tutu, expecting to see a customer. Her demeanour changed the moment she saw him, and he was pleased to see the smile on her chubby face replaced by an expression of deep-rooted fear.

Paul Evans and Colin Franklin had driven around the same boring circuit, checking out the same boring streets, so many times in the last forty-five minutes that they had stopped paying attention. Convinced that Winston was long gone, Franklin decided that enough was enough. He wound his seat as far back as it would go and wriggled himself down until he was relatively comfortable. Clasping his hands behind his neck, he let out a long yawn and closed his eyes. "Wake me up when the boss calls it a night," he told his driver, who was listening to a very boring discussion about international football on Talk Sport.

"Will do, mate," Evans promised, smiling affectionately at his friend.

As they were just driving around aimlessly, killing time until Tyler decided to dismiss them, Evans decided to do the decent thing when he spotted a black car in a side road on his left waiting to be let out. He slowed and flashed the driver, who pulled out without bothering to acknowledge his kindness. "Ungrateful bastard," Evans muttered, wishing he hadn't bothered. It was only at this point that it registered with Evans that the car was a BMW. He felt his pulse quicken. "What's the registration number of Winston's car?" he asked.

Franklin opened puffy eyes and squinted at the clipboard resting on his lap. Fighting back a yawn, he recited the number he had written down in big bold letters.

"Blimey!" Evans exclaimed when the digits Colin read out matched those on the car directly in front of them. "Colin, be a good lad and get on the radio, would you. That's our target in front of us." He was so matter of fact about it that it took a second or two for Franklin to register what he'd said.

Tyler could scarcely believe his ears when the 'contact' transmission was received inside the control car. To his great surprise – and even greater relief – Evans and Franklin had stumbled across Winston and were now following him along Commercial Street, where he seemed to be checking out every corner and recess he passed. Thankfully, despite his earlier use of anti-surveillance techniques, Winston now seemed completely oblivious to the Astra that was stalking him from a distance; a predator waiting for the rest of its pack to arrive before moving in for the kill.

The other cars had immediately hot-tailed it over and had taken up station around him.

"What do you think he's up to?" Tyler's asked. His brow was creased with thick worry lines.

"What do you mean?" Dillon asked.

"He was doing exactly the same thing the first time we saw him," Jack explained. "It's almost as though he's searching for someone."

Dillon shrugged. "He's a pimp. Maybe he's checking up on his girls to make sure they aren't slacking."

"Maybe," Jack allowed, but something about that felt wrong.

"Maybe he's just making his presence felt," Bull offered. "Letting people on the street know he's out there watching them in case anyone starts getting daft ideas about talking to us,"

"Makes sense," Dillon agreed.

"What if..." Jack's voice petered out as he searched for the right words. "Okay, how's this for a theory: what would a man like Winston do if he suspected that someone knew he'd killed Tracey?"

"That's easy," Dillon said. "He'd hunt them down and do whatever it took to shut them up."

"Of course he would," Jack said. "And if he's been looking for that someone but hasn't found them yet?"

"He'll keep on looking until he finds them, and the longer it takes the more desperate he'll become," Dillon said. "I take it you think he's looking for Sandra Dawson?"

Jack nodded, thoughtfully. "I do. I think he was actively looking for her when we first saw him, but luckily Steve found her before Winston could get his grubby paws on her. He doesn't know that, so he still out there looking for her."

"Surely, she's not stupid enough to go back out on the streets?" Dillon said. "Not after making a statement to us." He turned to face Bull, seeking confirmation.

"I've warned her not to," Steve said quickly. "She promised me she would lay low, but she was obviously very worried about losing her income."

Dillon shook his head in frustration. What was wrong with these people? They had their priorities all wrong. "She should be more worried about losing her life," he said, thinking that if anything happened to her it would be entirely her own fault.

CHAPTER TWELVE

DC Franklin's voice came over the speaker, interrupting their conversation. The disembodied voice was crystal clear as it gave its message.

"...*Subject has just turned into Quaker Street...Stand by. He's just pulling up behind a manky looking old Tom outside the used car lot...*"

The three men inside the Omega stared at each other uneasily, each wondering the same thing.

Dillon quickly squeezed the Press-To-Talk button. "Describe her, please," he demanded in a voice full of urgency.

"*She's really fat, and she's ugly, and she's got peroxide hair,*" Franklin informed him, "*All in all, she's just your type, guv.*"

"Shit! That's got to be Sandra!" Bull exclaimed. None of the other working girls they had seen had hair like that.

"Take him out, now," Tyler ordered.

"All units from control," Dillon announced. "We think that Tom's our star witness, and we think he's out to knobble her. Move in now. Effect an immediate arrest."

The team was startled by the unexpected order but they nonetheless reacted quickly. In accordance with their training, they moved as a cohesive unit. Three murder squad cars converged on Winston's black BMW in a matter of seconds, blocking it in.

Franklin and Evans, who were already on scene, were already half out of their car as the others arrived.

As Bull threw the Omega, its tyres squealing, into Quaker Street, a frenzy of activity was unfolding in front of them. Squad cars were being abandoned in the middle of the road as officers sprinted towards Winston, each one eager to lay hands on him and claim the arrest. Shouts of "POLICE!" and "STAY STILL AND SHOW ME YOUR HANDS!" filled the air. Winston sat there in stunned silence inside the car as they rushed towards him.

In his peripheral position, Bull spotted a single prostate form beside the BMW. Slumped forward, it remained supine and unmoving. Although it was too dark to be positive, he instinctively knew it was Sandra Dawson. The burning question inside his mind was what condition would they find her in?

Had they moved too late?

At that moment, from deep within the heart of the chaos, there came a loud boom. As the explosion filled the air Franklin, a twenty-five-year-old detective who Tyler had recently encouraged to apply for the accelerated promotion scheme, went down hard. A strong sprinter, he had rapidly closed the gap on Winston and was still running as he fell, arms stretched out and flailing.

Tyler was still only half out of the Omega when the shot was fired, and the unfolding scene registered on his shocked mind in slow motion, a frame at a time. There was nothing he could do but watch on in horror. As Franklin lay on the floor, legs wide apart, Jack saw that he was terribly still. "Oh my God!" he breathed.

"GUN!" one of the officers nearest to Winston shouted, breaking the spell.

"GET DOWN, GET DOWN!" Someone else screamed.

Another shot rang out, but Jack couldn't tell if anyone else had been hit in the pandemonium that ensued. At least one officer was down, the extent of his injuries unknown; the others were all unarmed and dangerously exposed.

As the detectives scattered – diving behind whatever meagre cover they could find – Winston seized the moment. He floored the accelerator, and his car surged forward to ram a Squad Vectra blocking his path.

DC Evans, in a cold rage and completely oblivious to the danger he was placing himself in, had drawn his extendable metal baton and was repeatedly striking the BMW's windscreen. He ignored calls from the rest of the team to take cover. This low life had shot and possibly killed his friend and partner. Evans wasn't letting him go without one hell of a fight.

Winston rammed the Vectra again. Another shunt and he would be able to squeeze the BMW through the gap he was creating. Seeing this, Tyler, Dillon, and Bull all dived back into the Omega, intent on giving chase when it happened.

"Don't you dare let this asshole get away," Jack thundered. "Do you hear me, Steve? I want this bastard,"

"Then you'd better get in line, guv," Bull snapped back through gritted teeth. "Colin and his wife are expecting their first baby in a couple of weeks."

This was personal now, for all three of them.

Dillon was already on the Main-Set to the Central Command Complex at New Scotland Yard, requesting urgent armed assistance and an ambulance for Colin Franklin.

The sound of metal scraping against metal was horrendous as Winston shunted the unmarked police car yet again, this time forcing it completely out of the way.

After being used as a battering ram, the front of the BMW was badly damaged. The grill, bonnet and one wing had all crumpled, and the nearside fender protruded at a dangerous angle, but the wheels still turned freely and smoke billowed from his tyres as he fled the scene, desperate to escape at any cost.

The acrid stench of burning rubber filled the night air as the Omega gave chase. It was, Jack thought grimly, a trail of carnage that even a blind man could follow. Looking back out of the rear window, Tyler was aware of his officers getting up and running towards Colin Franklin. The scene appeared surreal to him. He knew that they would perform whatever Emergency Life Support they could until the experts arrived, but would it be enough?

Jack was furious with himself for not having anticipated this. His lack of foresight had endangered one of his best men. He shook his head, attempting to dispel his anger and focus his thoughts. There would be plenty of time for recrimination later. Right now, all that mattered was catching Winston before he escaped or, worse, harmed someone else.

The BMW skidded through the stop line at the junction with Commercial Street, colliding heavily with the side of a London taxicab. The shocked cabby, screaming obscenities at Winston, was forced onto the pavement by the impact, scattering a small group of horrified pedestrians unfortunate enough to be in his path.

Winston's gaze darted nervously towards the rear-view mirror as he struggled to control the rear end of his car, which was still fishtailing violently. As the BMW settled, he slapped the steering wheel in frustration. "Shit, shit, shit! What the fuck have I done?" he screamed, breathlessly.

He didn't fully understand what had happened back there. All he knew was that one moment everything was going according to plan and then, without the slightest warning, he was being raided. They had materialised out of thin air as if by magic, and it had taken him by complete surprise. He doubted that David Copperfield could have done a better job.

Surrounding him quickly, their triumphant smirks openly mocked him as they advanced on the stationary BMW like a pack of starving hounds baying for his blood.

He had weighed up his options in an instant. Carrying a loaded firearm would automatically guarantee him a five stretch at one of Her Majesties less salubrious establishments, maybe more given his form. And he could expect his sentence to be increased considerably when they found the drug stash in his flat, if they hadn't already.

Those drug squad bastards had been trying to cultivate a snitch inside his network for ages, and it looked like they had finally succeeded. It was too much of a coincidence to believe they had randomly chosen tonight of all nights, when he had a small fortune in raw cocaine hidden inside his flat, to come after him in earnest. Well, they had caught him with his pants down, he'd give them that, but they had severely underestimated him if they expected him to come quietly. Surrender was not in his nature; he would escape or die trying.

Shooting the damn cop had been stupid, but he just hadn't been able to stop himself. His hatred for them was so deep-rooted and malignant, like a living thing eating away at his insides. It had completely overwhelmed him as they surged forward to effect the arrest.

And he didn't regret it, even though he was now potentially facing a murder charge. No matter what the personal cost, he had shown them that messing with him was a fucking big mistake.

An unmarked police car appeared behind him; blue lights flashing, siren wailing. Winston dropped a gear and floored the accelerator. Ignoring the protests from his screaming engine, he overtook two cars on a straight section of road, but just as he started to put some distance between himself and the cop car, he found himself stuck behind a double-decker that was only doing thirty. Cursing profusely, he gunned the gas pedal and went for the blind overtake.

As he pulled out, he was dazzled by the flashing headlights of a large Ford van coming the other way.

There was nowhere for Winston to go; he was already level with the bus and he was travelling way too fast to stop. Convinced he was about to die, he instinctively swerved to his left, crashing into the side of the Route Master. The driver of the Ford Transit, reaching the same conclusion, also swerved to his left, scrapping the nearside of his vehicle along a row of parked cars. Somehow, the seemingly inevitable head-on collision was avoided, but Winston's car suffered terribly as it was violently buffeted between the side of the bus and the van. Sparks flew everywhere. Both of his wing mirrors were ripped off. The sound of metal distorting and shearing was horrific.

And then the BMW had torn itself free. Marvelling that the Beamer was still drivable after what it had just been through, Winston lost no time in building up speed. He had left a trail of destruction behind, and with any luck, this would prevent the pursuing police vehicle from getting through.

The Omega had indeed been forced to stop, but only for as long as it took to make sure that no one was seriously injured and to tell everyone to stay exactly where they were as help was on the way. The BMW was still in their sights as Bull carefully manoeuvred his way through the debris. "Some poor sod's going to be doing paperwork for a week, writing this mess up," he told his passengers.

"Never mind that," Dillon told him. "You just concentrate on getting us back in the chase."

"Consider it done," Bull promised.

Winston glanced down at the speedometer and saw he was touching seventy. A major intersection was looming towards him, and to his horror the lights were red. Braking heavily, he swerved onto the wrong side of the road and zoomed past a line of vehicles that were waiting for the lights to turn green. He was still doing fifty when he launched the car into the four-lane junction, cutting through a stream of cars, trucks, and buses criss-crossing his path. Claude Winston screwed his eyes tightly shut and waited for the terrible impact that must surely come, repeating the mantra that it was better to die than to be caught.

The BMW bounced madly across the uneven road surface, losing the rear bumper in the process. He was vaguely aware of cars around him locking up and skidding. He ignored the cacophony of horns blaring at him in anger and fear.

After clearing the junction, Winston let out a loud whoop. His heart was beating like a jack-hammer as he ran a large forearm across his brow and blinked the sweat away from his eyes. Somehow, he had survived, and there was no sign of his pursuers in the mirror.

The badly cracked windscreen was severely affecting his view, and he suddenly realised that the right-hand bend he was entering was much tighter than anticipated. He slammed on the brakes to reduce the car's frightening momentum, and the tyres screamed as they fought a losing battle to maintain traction. Turning broadside, the BMW eventually skidded to a halt, its engine stalling. Hands shaking, Winston was frantically turning the key in the ignition, trying to get the car running again when he became aware of the damned siren. His eyes immediately darted in the direction of the dreaded sound. "What the hell...!"

Brian Johnson turned off the fluorescent lights in the divisional BIU at Whitechapel police station. He closed the door and trudged along the deserted corridor towards the lift. Everyone else was long gone. It had been a stressful day, and his head was throbbing. The two extra strong painkillers he'd taken an hour ago hadn't helped in the slightest.

He waited impatiently by the elevators, massaging his neck to ease the dull pain that had formed there.

"Hello, Johnson."

Johnson spun around, startled. He recognised the speaker at once and relaxed. "Oh, it's you, sir. I didn't realise you were still in the building."

If Chief Superintendent Porter registered Johnson's edginess he chose to ignore it. Instead, he made a sweeping gesture and smiled benignly.

Charles Porter was the Divisional Commander for Whitechapel. He was a short man, overweight but not badly so, with a politician's charm and the watchful eyes of a hawk. A pair of metal framed spectacles perched precariously on the end of his beak-like nose. "You know, contrary to what most people around here seem to think, even the boss has to work late sometimes," he said, wearily removing his flat cap to reveal a thick thatch of salt and pepper hair.

"Of course, sir," Brian said quickly. "I didn't mean to imply otherwise." Experience had taught him that it always paid to suck up to senior management, even when you didn't really give a fuck.

"So, how's it going?" Porter asked.

Johnson frowned. What was the old fool on about now? "Sir?"

"Your first murder enquiry: how's it going?"

Johnson shrugged. "It's early days, yet," he said.

At that moment the elevator arrived and both men stepped in.

Station Reception Officer Henry Boyden had just finished his tour of duty and was donning his coat when Johnson came into the front office. "Brian? What are you doing here?" he called. "Hang on a minute. I'll walk out with you."

Johnson grunted a surly acknowledgement and waited impatiently for the other man to join him.

"You only transferred out of here a few days ago, and you're back already. Are you here on official AMIP business?"

"Yep, I'm working on that prostitute murder that happened yesterday."

"Sounds nasty, have you got much to go on?"

"Nope, not yet."

"Poor girl. Is it right she was sliced up?"

"Yep, he gutted her like a fish. Serves her right for being a slut."

"That's a terrible thing to say," Boyden admonished.

Johnson shrugged, and then sneered nastily. "I seem to remember that you were a bit partial to the odd hooker back in the old days, though I never understood why a good-looking bloke like you would want to pay for it."

Boyden cringed. "Every squaddie in our unit occasionally went with prostitutes when we were stationed over in Germany," he said defensively, "especially you. Anyway, that was years ago, when I was young, free and single. I'll have you know I'm a happily married man now."

"Whatever," Johnson sneered.

They crossed the main road in silence. When they reached the council estate opposite, they stopped. "Need a lift?" Boyden asked. "My car's only a few streets away."

"I'm parked in there," Johnson said, nodding into the estate.

"Are you mad? You know you'll get it clamped if you leave it there,"

"I know," Johnson snapped, "but as a civilian analyst I don't get to drive police cars, so I've had to use my own vehicle to come over here just to spend a fruitless afternoon in your rubbish BIU, going through a load of out of date intelligence that has got me absolutely nowhere."

Boyden seemed disappointed. "Why do you have to behave like such a wanker? You really ought to change your attitude, mate. You used to work in that BIU. A little loyalty wouldn't go amiss."

"Oh, I'm a wanker now, am I? You didn't think I was a wanker when I got you a job, did you?" Johnson said, haughtily.

All Johnson had done was mention to him that the station was recruiting and he should consider speaking to HR if he fancied a change in career. Anyone listening to Johnson telling the story would be forgiven for thinking he had personally gone cap in hand to the Chief Superintendent, begging for a job on Boyden's behalf.

Boyden rolled his eyes. "I'm very grateful," he said patiently, "but that doesn't mean I approve of you running your former colleagues down."

"I should hope you are grateful. I went to a lot of trouble to get you in."

"I said I'm grateful, Brian."

Johnson nodded. Without saying goodbye, he hurried over to the old Vauxhall that was parked out of sight at the base of the flats. A sign on the wall said: '*Residents only. Unauthorised vehicles will be clamped or removed. Fine £50'*. He doubted anyone would pay attention to the old car. It blended into its surroundings too perfectly. He started the engine and manoeuvred the Cavalier around the little courtyard until it finally faced the exit gates. Checking to make sure no one from the station was around, he pulled into the main road and turned left.

After flooding the stalled BMW, it had taken Winston so long to get it going again that Steve Bull had made up all the lost ground, and now the pursuit car sat right on the bandit's tail as it motored towards the City. Armed support was on its way, but typically wouldn't be with them for several minutes. The helicopter was refuelling and couldn't get airborne for another ten minutes minimum. The controller at NSY had just ordered them to abandon the pursuit, insisting that it was far too dangerous to continue. Dillon immediately declared that their radio had developed a malfunction and was not receiving properly. They might suspect that he was lying, which of course he was, but they would never be able to prove it. The Chief Inspector at the Yard came on the air, screaming at them to stop playing 'clever buggers' and drop back. *"End this pursuit right now,"* he demanded. In a voice oozing sarcasm, Dillon told him that it was pointless to shout because they couldn't hear him.

The chase hurtled along Shoreditch High Street towards the Met's boundary with the City of London Police. Unless Winston changed course soon, he would have to negotiate the chicanes that formed part of the famed 'Ring of Steel', the security and surveillance cordon consisting of barriers and manned checkpoints that was erected in 1993 to deter terrorism and other threats following the PIRA bombing campaign of the late 1980s and early 1990s.

The Nat West Tower dominated the skyline ahead of them as they entered London's financial district. "I think the bastard's looking to decamp, boys," Tyler shouted over the wail of the siren.

Brake lights suddenly bloomed, and a thick cloud of smoke mushroomed from the rear of the BMW as its wheels locked up. "Watch out, he's stopping!" Dillon yelled.

"Thanks, I hadn't noticed," Bull replied sarcastically.

Winston's furious braking had been caused by a stationary line of vehicles waiting to go through a City Police checkpoint. Jack wondered if the City cops had been notified of the pursuit and had decided to stop all traffic and use the backlog to block Winston's path.

Ahead of them Winston's car suddenly veered sharply across the road, screeching onto the opposite carriageway as it accelerated past the checkpoint. A City officer rushed into the road with his right hand raised, palm outwards, waving for it to pull over and stop. He stood defiantly in front of the speeding car, determined to engage the renegade driver in a battle of wills.

"Get out of the way, you damn fool!" Dillon said quietly, willing the idiot to move before it was too late.

A look of terror appeared on the young officer's face as he realised the enormity of his mistake and dived for cover.

"Arsehole!" Dillon mouthed the word at the astonished policeman, who lay on the floor looking up at him as they shot by. There was an audible clunk as Bull squashed the City officer's headgear beneath the wheels of the Omega. "Tosser!" he growled, glancing in the rear-view mirror to see the flattened helmet in the middle of the road.

"That'll make us popular with the City plod," Tyler said.

"Who gives a fuck?" Dillon said grimly. All he could think about was Franklin. The image of him tumbling to the floor kept repeating itself in his head, like a tape on a loop.

"Not me," Bull admitted. He was determined to stay behind the BMW at any cost.

Bull suddenly slammed on the brakes as a large white van turned out of a side street on their right and almost drove straight into them. The two vehicles stopped with their front bumpers inches apart.

"Come on, move it back you idiot!" Dillon screamed at the man through his open window. Rage and frustration welled up inside him as he tried to wave the vehicle aside. Flustered, the driver stalled his van. In desperation, Bull reversed back a short distance, then shifted back into drive and mounted the high pavement of the central reservation, scrapping the underside of the car. He ignored the grinding noise that followed, hoping that no real harm was being done. He had to stay with the BMW, which was scything a path through the traffic ahead.

"Well done, Steve." Tyler cheered, relieved that they were moving again.

"I hope the traffic skipper sees it that way if I've fucked the sump up," Steve said as they re-joined the road.

"You leave him to me," Tyler told him.

Dillon pointed to a large sign on the pavement that read: *'MAJOR ROADWORKS AHEAD – EXPECT LONG DELAYS'*.

"That ought to slow the bastard down," he yelled, slapping the dashboard triumphantly.

And he was right. Winston had given himself a hundred-yard lead, but further progress was prevented by a solid line of cars that were waiting at temporary traffic lights to be funnelled through a single lane contraflow around a massive excavation in the road. Traffic could only move in one direction at any given time, and right now a stream of cars was spewing out of the contraflow towards the BMW.

"I never thought I'd be pleased to see a traffic jam," Bull observed.

"We've got you now, you bastard," Dillon growled.

Unfortunately, Winston wasn't ready to throw in the towel just yet. Without hesitation, he drove onto the pavement and continued for another fifty yards, scattering pedestrians like tenpins. Steve Bull followed, but much slower. "He's bailing out," Bull shouted, automatically unclipping his seatbelt in readiness to follow suit.

Before the BMW came to a complete stop, the driver's door flew open and Winston clambered out. With a harried glance back in the direction of his pursuers, he abandoned the car, which was still rolling, and began to run up the steps leading into Liverpool Street station's main concourse. The Omega screeched to a halt beside the abandoned BMW. "If we lose him in there, boys, he'll be gone for good," Dillon said, his voice filled with urgency.

The three detectives sprung out of the Omega as one, just in time to catch a last fleeting glimpse of Claude Winston's giant bulk as he disappeared into the station.

"Don't take any chances, you two. Remember, he's got a gun and he likes shooting policemen," Jack warned them as they sprinted up the steps after him.

CHAPTER THIRTEEN

All three detectives were acutely aware of how vulnerable they were as they entered the station. Jack paused in the foyer to scan the massive concourse below, his mind in overdrive as he tried to cobble together a cohesive plan of attack.

Below, the concourse's perimeter was littered with various shops and eateries including *WH Smith*, *Tie Rack,* and the *Upper Crust* bakery. Winston could have ducked into any of them. He could also be hiding in the photo booth that stood next to a small cluster of ATMs. Jack scanned a long line of main platforms spanning virtually the entire length of the concourse. These all had ticket collectors stationed at the entrances, and Jack doubted Winston could have got in there unchallenged. At the other end of the concourse, a wide metal staircase ascended to street level. If Winston could reach that, or the London Underground entrance located at its base, he would have a very good chance of evading capture. There were probably other exits, too, that he couldn't see from where he was standing.

Despite the lateness of the hour, the concourse was still relatively busy, with plenty of people milling around.

Winston was nowhere to be seen.

"Where the hell has he gone?" Jack demanded.

"Dunno," Dillon said, his eyes darting in every direction.

"Should we split up?" Bull asked.

"No, we stay together," Jack replied without hesitation. Under the circumstances, he felt there was greater safety in numbers. As he spoke, Steve tugged sharply at his sleeve and pointed off to their right, towards a small scattering of shops on the upper level. "I think I just caught a glimpse of him over there," he said, breathlessly.

Jack scanned the area Steve had just indicated, but there was no sign of their quarry. He now had to make a very difficult choice: hold his current position on the high ground, where he had a good all-round view, or check out the possible that Steve had put up? Nodding for his colleagues to follow him, he set off at a brisk pace. "Keep your eyes peeled," he warned.

A garbled announcement over the public speaker system advised stragglers that the next Stansted Express was about to depart from platform seven. Down below, people started moving in that direction.

"Are you sure you saw him, Stevie?" Dillon asked, studying the people heading for platform seven in case Winston was among them.

"I think so," Bull replied, but there was an element of doubt in his voice now. Suddenly, no more than ten yards ahead of them, Winston's great bulk emerged from behind a pillar. He had his back towards them and was heading for the far staircase, which led down to the concourse below. Jack signalled for Dillon and Steve to fan out, so they could take him in a pincer movement.

As he reached Ponti's restaurant, three males emerged, blocking Jack's path. All had dirty, braided hair, CND badges, and identical Green Peace T-shirts. One had a stack of protest posters crammed under his arm. They reeked of alcohol. "Excuse me, lads," he said, as he tried to squeeze past them.

Dillon was less polite. "Move it," he demanded, manhandling their leader out of the way.

As the detectives continued along the upper landing, one of the Soapy types called out, "Fascist pig! That was police brutality!" His comrades slapped him on the back and cheered his stand against the government bullyboys. Winston must have heard this because he immediately broke into a run.

"Shit!" Jack growled, following suit.

As he reached the staircase, Winston cannoned into a drunk coming the other way. The inebriated man staggered backwards, reeling from the impact. His half-eaten cheeseburger fell to the floor; his milkshake exploded over his chest. With a vicious snarl, Winston shoved him aside and descended the stairs towards the main concourse.

"He's heading towards the underground system," Tyler shouted.

The drunk was ineffectually dabbing his shirt with a napkin as they filed past him.

As Tyler descended the steps, he tried not to contemplate the consequences of Winston opening fire inside the station.

They ran the length of the concourse, zigzagging through a scattering of bored looking commuters who were patiently awaiting boarding calls for their trains.

"Winston, stop!" Jack shouted in vain.

There was no sign of him when they reached the barrier a few seconds later. "Okay, we'll have to spread out inside," Jack said, breathing heavily. It went against the grain, but they had no choice now. "You two check out the Circle line platforms, I'll try the Central Line, but don't approach him on your own if you see him. I don't want any dead heroes on my hands." He'd almost made the mistake of saying, 'any *more* dead heroes.'

Once they cleared the turnstiles, Dillon headed straight for the Circle line's eastbound platform, thinking that this was the most likely route the drug dealer would have taken. When he drew a blank, he swore in frustration and doubled back to find Tyler.

Bull made his way over the bridge that to the Circle's westbound platform and the exit into Old Broad Street. He felt isolated and vulnerable without a weapon of his own, and while he desperately wanted to find Winston, a part of him was hoping that he wouldn't.

Jack paused when he reached the top of the escalators that led down to the Central Line and cocked his head, trying to analyse the muffled sounds drifting up from below. Was the faint commotion he could hear a fight, or simply some boisterous late-night revellers enjoying themselves? He was still trying to decide when Dillon appeared beside him, breathing hard. "No sign of him back there," he said.

Just then, the unmistakable explosion of a gunshot erupted from below, sparking a series of screams from late night commuters caught up in the gunfire.

"Bloody hell!" Dillon spluttered, ducking instinctively. The two detectives exchanged tense looks, and then, as one, they moved towards the down escalator. Almost immediately, another shot rang out, stopping them in their tracks.

Jack was horrified. "Who the hell is he shooting at now?" he asked.

Dillon shrugged. "Perhaps someone asked to see his ticket," he suggested as the first fleeing commuters appeared below. It was horrible to watch: a bottleneck at the base of the escalators caused an ugly stampede, during which the fittest and fastest thoughtlessly clambered over the slowest and weakest in their haste to reach safety. When the crowd had finally passed, they rushed forward to rescue an elderly man who lay sprawled at the top of the up escalator. He'd been trampled in the rush. Dragging him clear, they hoisted him over the barrier and unceremoniously shoved him towards the shelter of a solid wall.

A middle-aged black man, wearing a blue London Transport blazer, emerged from an office marked 'PRIVATE'. He surveyed the crouching detectives with disdain. Clifford Henry had worked at Liverpool Street station for twenty-three years, during which time he'd witnessed just about every type of tomfoolery imaginable; much of it committed by normally respectable city gents in expensively tailored suits. He was yet to meet an office worker who could drink two pints of lager without regressing to a state on the evolutionary scale that the average juvenile delinquent would be ashamed of.

Henry was more than a little deaf. He wore cumbersome hearing aids, which he thought were next to useless. The batteries never lasted very long, and he always forgot to carry spares. They had packed up earlier in the shift, which is why he hadn't heard the shots or the fleeing customer's screams. "Oi, you two. What d'ya think you're doing?" he demanded. "If you don't stop fooling around, I'll call the police."

Tyler flashed his warrant card angrily at the man, motioning him back. Henry ignored the dismissal. He strutted over to the two detectives and inspected Jack's warrant card carefully.

"What's this?"

"It's my warrant card," Jack hissed.

"I'm going to call the police..." Clifford began.

"We *are* the police," Jack snapped. "Now go back in your office. There's a man with a gun down there."

Henry frowned, wondering if he had heard correctly. "Don't be so ridiculous," he said, dismissively. The whole thing sounded utterly preposterous; this was London, not New York. But then, as he thought about it, doubt set in. The man who had just spoken didn't smell of booze, and he had an aura of authority, not to mention a badge.

Steering him by his arm, Tyler pointed Henry back in the direction he'd come from. "Get back in your office and get all the Central Line trains stopped at once. Whatever happens, make sure none of them stop at this station until I tell you otherwise," Jack instructed. "Do you understand?"

Henry nodded uncertainly. It was most irregular, but the policeman had said something about a gun. Henry decided to play it safe and do as he'd been told. Just in case. He hurried back to his office, fretting over the delays this would cause to his precious timetable. The station supervisor would blame him for this, no doubt. They always blamed someone. Why couldn't this have happened on someone else's shift?

———

Bull arrived just as Henry was leaving. "I heard the shots," he whispered. "Where is he?"

"Down there." Tyler pointed downwards.

Dillon half stood and risked a glimpse down the escalator.

"Can you see anything?" Jack asked.

A shake of the head answered his question.

"What do we do now, Jack?" Dillon asked, like they were spoilt for choice.

"We can either wait for the cavalry to arrive, and hope they turn up in time to make a difference, or we go in ourselves."

"We should definitely wait for backup," Steve Bull advised.

Dillon shook his head. "If a train comes in before the gun nuts get here, then we've lost him for good."

"Agreed," Tyler said.

"If we go down, how would you play it?"

"Take a platform each, and hope that one of us can sneak around and come up on him from behind while the other one distracts him."

"That's it?"

"Can you think of anything better?"

Dillon shook his head.

"I guess that's it then."

"I guess it is," Dillon said, unhappily.

"Don't do it," Steve Bull warned. "You'll get yourselves killed."

"If we're going to do this, it's got to be right now," Jack said, ignoring Bull.

Shaking his head as if to say, *I must be mad*, Dillon said, "Okay, let's get on with it."

As they moved forward, Dillon held out a hand, stopping Jack. "Look, I'll walk down the stairs like a normal passenger. You crouch down and ride the descending escalator. That way, if he's looking, he'll only see one person coming down. If he challenges me when I reach the bottom, there's still a chance you can take him out."

Jack stiffened. "If we're going to do that, I should be the one to draw his attention."

Dillon shrugged stoically. "I'm a newly promoted DI, I'm more expendable."

"That's bollocks, Dill."

"Take it or leave it, Jack."

Tyler could see there was no point in arguing. "All right, but be careful," he said as he made his way to the far escalator.

"You're not really going to do this, are you?" Bull asked, looking imploringly from one to the other.

"Yes, we are, so get back to the barriers and don't let anyone through. The last thing we need now is for some drunken twat to get themselves shot. And call for backup." Without waiting for a response, Tyler crouched down and stepped onto the descending escalator.

"Be careful," Bull said as he vanished from view.

Taking a long, deep breath, Dillon set off down the flight of steps between the two escalators.

Bull watched until Dillon's head disappeared, and then looked around wildly, seeking a phone. It was time to dial all the nines and get some help.

Dillon's descent into the bowels of Liverpool Street was buffeted by a surprisingly strong wind, which he guessed was being generated by trains pushing air through the tunnels ahead of them. The walls on either side of the escalators were peppered with posters in cheap tacky frames, most of which were advertising West End shows. Nestled between *The Lion King* and *Mamma Mia*, a shot of a woman's legs, long, slim and undeniably exquisite drew his attention. The legs were promoting a well-known brand of tights, and despite the urgency of the situation, Dillon found himself wondering if the model's face was half as pretty.

He strained his ears for signs of movement below, but the only noises that reached him came from the constant clanking of escalator machinery and the occasional roar of an approaching train. There was no sign of Jack as he glanced across to the down escalator, but he knew his friend was there, waiting for the signal to move.

Dillon stepped over a discarded copy of the Sun as he reached the bottom stair and padded towards the eastbound platform. He was almost certain the shots had come from that direction, although he knew sounds were easily distorted down here. He paused as he reached the platform entrance, signalling Tyler to go the other way, onto the westbound platform.

Dillon caught a momentary glimpse of Jack, a blur moving across the outer edge of his vision as he darted onto the westbound platform. Hopefully, he would be able to circle around behind Winston without being seen. That was the plan; all they had to do now was make it work.

Dillon cautiously poked his head around the corner, ready to whip it straight back at the slightest sign of trouble.

Nothing; the platform appeared empty. He took a deep breath, counted to five and stepped onto the platform, exposed and vulnerable. A wave of relief swept over him when he didn't immediately find himself staring down the barrel of a gun. He was just beginning to think that he might have picked the wrong platform when he heard the unmistakable sound of someone coughing just ahead.

He took a step forward and then stopped.

What was that?

Vibration travelled up through his feet, and a familiar noise, growing in volume like a banshee's wailing, emanated from the tunnel's mouth as a train approached. "Oh shit!" Dillon grimaced as the white, red and blue streak erupted out of the tunnel. He watched, aghast, as the long line of carriages sped by, knowing that Winston was as good as free if he managed to board a train. And then he realised that the train wasn't losing speed; it was going straight through without stopping.

As the train's noise and wind faded into insignificance, he heard the coughing again, but it was weaker this time. Whoever had made the noise had to be very close. It seemed to have come from a small recess just ahead. As Dillon moved slowly forward the limbic system in the lower half of his brain was already sending out signals to prepare his body for fight or flight. Taking a deep breath, Dillon geared himself up to pounce.

CHAPTER FOURTEEN

Jack had managed to sneak onto the westbound platform without being seen. *So far, so good*, he told himself as he massaged cramped sinews. The fact that Dillon had sent him this way indicated that the big man thought the killer was on the eastbound platform. As he stood there, waiting for his circulation to return to normal, Jack was suddenly engulfed by a sense of impending doom. He couldn't shake the strangely cloying feeling, which seemed to hover above him like a personalised storm cloud.

Well, it was too late to back out now.

———

Dillon recoiled as he came face to face with the occupant of the urine-scented recess. "Oh God!" he breathed, unaware that he had even spoken. Slumped on the floor in front of him lay a young British Transport policeman. A bright red circle was slowly spreading from the area immediately above his chest. The poor man was barely conscious and his pale face had contorted into a painful rictus. Dillon saw that he had somehow managed to prop himself up against the wall.

The officer, his breathing ragged, stared at Dillon through glazed eyes. "Get...back, not safe...get...help..." he rasped, the effort clearly sapping his remaining strength.

Dillon knelt down beside him and squeezed the younger man's hand reassuringly. "Help's on the way," he said, hoping it was. "Just hang in there a little longer."

There was an entry wound just below the shoulder, so hopefully the boy was going to be okay – unless, of course, the bullet had hit an artery and he was hemorrhaging internally, or it was a light caliber round that had hit a bone and bounced about inside his body. Dillon had attended post mortems on shooting victims where the entry wound was high up, as it was in this case, but the exit wound was down by the hip. The bullet had ricocheted downwards after striking bone, causing catastrophic damage as it did so. He prayed that wouldn't be the case here. He noticed there was a first aid kit attached to the BTP officer's utility belt. Hopefully, it contained bandages that Dillon could use to apply pressure to the wound in order to try and stop the bleeding.

Footsteps startled him.

"Don't move pig, or you'll get what he got," Winston announced as he emerged from the shadows, pointing the stubby revolver at Dillon's chest. Dillon stood up slowly, gazing into the man's eyes as he turned to face him. They were cold, cruel and full of hatred.

Winston motioned Dillon away from the injured man, gesturing with the gun, towards the track. "Move to the edge, pig. Nice an' slow, you know what I mean." He cocked the gun, to show that he meant business.

As he moved away from the wall, Dillon noticed a door ajar behind Winston. The gunman had obviously been watching him from inside there, waiting for Dillon to find the injured cop.

Dillon's appearance had complicated matters for Winston. He knew it wouldn't be long before the police arrived in strength, but if he could avoid capture until a train came in, he could still get away. He was sure the next one would stop.

He decided he'd pop this one too, just for the hell of it. After all, it wasn't as if he had anything to lose – the penalty for offing three pigs was no more severe than it was for offing one.

Dillon raised both hands in the air, being careful to move with exaggerated slowness. He didn't want his actions to provoke Winston unnecessarily, or to give him an excuse. He wondered where the hell Jack was. "Look, I'm unarmed and I won't do anything silly. I don't want to die. Just let me take this lad out of here and get him some help. It'll be better for you in the long run too, Claude." He spoke slowly, disarmingly, while walking slowly, ever so slowly, towards Winston. He needed to be a lot nearer if – no, when – the right moment presented itself.

"Don't use my fucking name, pig! I don't know you; you're not my friend," Winston spewed the words out in a fit of uncontrolled rage. He began waving the gun around dangerously, oblivious to the fact that it was cocked and would discharge under the slightest pressure.

Every fibre in Dillon's body cried out for him to dive down onto the floor, to take cover before it was too late, before this raving lunatic shot him dead, but he somehow forced himself to remain standing. He half expected a bullet to tear into him at any moment, and a part of him wondered if he would feel the impact before he heard the noise.

Suddenly there was movement behind Winston.

Jack!

Forcing himself to breathe deeply, Dillon took another step towards Winston. "You're brave enough with that gun, scumbag, but just how tough are you without it? Why don't we find out?" he taunted, staring the other man straight in the eye.

"Fuck you copper," Winston snarled. He had intended to usher the cop through the door before shooting him, but no one talked to him like that.

He pointed the gun at Dillon and fired.

———

After leaving work, The Disciple went straight to his lair. He had spent the day being nice to people he despised, and now he was feeling tired and crotchety. The drudgery of wearing his other persona for so many hours had drained him, and he desperately craved the solace of his own company.

He hadn't returned home since Sunday evening, and he grimaced at the thought of spending yet another uncomfortable night on the lumpy camp bed in the corner. Not that he would be getting any shut-eye for a while; there was still far too much to do before he could allow himself the luxury of sleep. For starters, he needed to case the house in Hanbury Street again, to confirm it was still accessible. There was no reason to think it wouldn't be; he had already checked it out several times, but one didn't achieve greatness by being sloppy.

He knew his plans for tomorrow night were incredibly ambitious, and the weaker part of him, the remnants of his old persona, was afraid he was biting off more than he could chew by going for the double whammy. Well, tough. He had made his mind up and he had no intention of changing it.

He had already disposed of the plastic sheeting that had been used to line the van when he took his first victim. It had been burned, along with all the clothing he had worn. The vehicle's insides had been scrubbed with bleach and vigorously swept. New plastic sheeting needed to be laid before tomorrow, and he would attend to that as soon as he changed into a paper suit.

At least he didn't have to keep looking over his shoulder, afraid the police were breathing down his neck; they were so far off the scent that he was almost tempted to start leaving them clues, just to make it more interesting.

Tomorrow night was going to be extremely challenging, but he had been thorough in his research and he knew his intended prey's routines inside out. He would require a little luck to pull this off, but he was confident he would have it; he could feel the power he'd attained from completing the first ritual cruising through his veins, and he knew it was already influencing destiny in his favour.

If there was a glitch – if, for some reason, he was unable to snatch the first one within the time frame he had allotted – he would just have to be pragmatic about it and move onto his second target. It wouldn't be the end of the world, although he had to admit that on a personal level it would really piss him off. The goading message he'd left at the first murder scene had been a clear statement of intent, letting the world know that greater things were to follow. Now he needed to back up his boast with a grand gesture. If he achieved success tomorrow, no one would ever be able to say that he had failed to live up to the promised hype.

Tyler made his way along the deserted westbound platform. About a third of the way down, he came to a door that said: *STAFF ONLY – STRICTLY NO ADMITTANCE.* He turned the handle carefully, praying it wasn't locked. The door swung inwards on well-oiled hinges revealing an unlit corridor that ran between the platforms.

Closing the door behind him, Jack crept along the dark passageway, which contained several storerooms and an assortment of industrial cleaning equipment, toward a distant shimmer of light, which he assumed was leaking in through the door to the eastbound platform. He moved as silently as he could, hugging the wall. After a while, he began to hear voices. Muffled at first, they gradually became clearer as he approached the eastbound platform. He noticed the platform door had been wedged open, which explained the sliver of light.

A sudden movement at ground level caught Jack's eye. Glancing down, he saw an enormous rat by the side of his foot. Jack drew in a sharp breath as the furry creature scuttled across his shoe and, seemingly unconcerned by Jack's presence, continued onwards without a backward glance.

As he stepped onto the eastbound platform Jack spotted Winston off to his right, no more than ten feet away. He had his back to Tyler and was pointing a gun at Dillon, who stood facing him, with both hands raised in the air. As Tyler assessed the situation Winston erupted into a screaming fit, recklessly waving the gun in the air.

And then the ranting was over and had Winston reached what hostage negotiators called the 'endgame moment'. Knowing that his partner had seconds to live, Tyler took a deep breath to oxygenate his blood, lowered his head, and charged.

Everything became a blur from that point onwards. In the instant that Tyler's body slammed into Winston, the gun went off, sounding incredibly loud. A grey cloud of smoke and cordite swirled around them as they clashed, its pungent odour stinging the back of Jack's throat. His ears were ringing painfully, distorting the sound of the struggle.

As his momentum carried them towards the tracks, Tyler wrapped his left arm around Winston's neck, clamping his forearm tight across the big man's windpipe and carotid artery. Jack's other hand grabbed Winston's gun hand, jarring it upward and outwards.

Powerful images flashed through Tyler's mind: Colin Franklin, last seen lying motionless in an east London street, a coffin, a Service funeral, Franklin's heavily pregnant wife being comforted by grieving family and friends, their unborn child growing up without a father. He saw Winston's smug face laughing at them from behind bars, mocking everything that young Franklin had stood for.

The images continued: Tracey Phillips lying on a cold mortuary slab, gutted like a fish; her family – he had found out earlier in the day that she had a young child of her own – struggling to cope. A pauper's grave with a little girl standing beside it, a handful of wild flowers, freshly picked, in her hand.

Lastly, he thought about Tony Dillon, realising that he didn't know if his friend had been hit or not. Tyler felt the images stoking his anger, and to his surprise, he realised that he really wanted to hurt Claude Winston.

Winston needed no such stimuli to summon aggression. He instinctively fought like a man berserk, thrashing and bucking with all his might as he tried to pull free and turn the gun on Tyler. Jack was lifted clear off his feet and swung around one hundred and eighty degrees, but he refused to let go. He knew that he was slowly strangling Winston, and he was determined not to stop until the mad bastard was down for good.

The struggle continued across the breadth of the platform. By now Winston was noticeably fighting for his every breath. He could feel his strength slipping away. As his vision became tunnelled he made a last-ditch effort and thrust himself backwards, smashing into the platform wall with all his considerable weight. He felt a satisfying thud as a surprised gasp came from behind, signalling that Tyler had been winded by the impact. Suddenly, the grip around his neck loosened and, sensing that the tables might just have been turned, he redoubled his efforts to dislodge his attacker.

Jack was dazed by the blow, but he was far from finished. If only he could knock the gun from Winston's hand, he would be free to move. Jack had been a good boxer in his younger days and he was confident that he could take Winston in a fair fight.

And then it didn't matter anymore. Dillon suddenly appeared in front of Winston, a fearsome battle rage contorting the normally calm features of his broad face. A shovel-like hand gripped Winston's wrist and squeezed until the man yelled in agony and released the gun. It fell to the floor and bounced down into the track below. Dillon's right hand exploded into Winston's fat stomach. The force of the blow was powerful enough to knock Jack – who was still holding on from behind – backwards. As Winston sank to his knees, his face ashen, Dillon delivered a forearm smash into the bridge of the drug dealer's nose. The snap of breaking bone was almost as loud as the gunshot had been on the empty platform. A sea of crimson erupted from the black man's battered face as he tumbled backward, unconscious.

Dillon studied Tyler, who was bending forward; hands on his knees, his breathing laboured.

"You took your bloody time. I thought you'd been shot," Tyler complained in between breaths.

"I thought you had him Jack, so I went to check on the lad."

"Lad? What lad?"

Dillon nodded towards the Transport cop on the floor.

"Oh God, not another one," Jack said, his face palling. "I didn't even see him." He rushed over to the injured officer, wondering if this was his fault too. "Hang on in there, mate. You're going to be okay," Tyler told him, not sure how true that was. *Christ*, Jack thought, *he doesn't look old enough to shave yet.*

The officer nodded weakly, in too much pain to talk.

Carefully removing the Constable's handcuffs, Jack ran back to join Dillon with their prisoner. "Help me turn this bastard over," he said.

Dillon looked around carefully. "Do you think there are cameras operating down here, Jack?" he asked.

Jack saw the malevolence in his friend's eyes. "Of course there are, so don't do anything silly. He's not worth it."

"So help me, I'm tempted to throw him onto the line and watch him fry," Dillon admitted, his voice thick with menace. He reached down with one hand and took hold of Winston's left arm. Then he grabbed the thick, beaded dreadlocks with the other hand, twisting them tightly to ensure a firm grip. Flexing his massive arms, Dillon unceremoniously hoisted the prisoner up in a deadlift. Using the motion to flip Winston over so that he faced the floor, Dillon let go of him. Winston fell forward like a stone, his chin striking the concrete with a heavy thud.

"That's for Colin Franklin, you bastard," he said through gritted teeth.

Dillon realised that several huge lumps of Winston's hair had come away in his hand. With a grimace, he cast them into the track and began to brush his hands.

"What did I just fucking say to you?" Jack snarled.

"It was an accident. He slipped."

"This isn't the bad old days, Dill. No one cares how good your motives are anymore. In the current climate if you put a foot out of line the brass won't think twice about putting you up before a discipline board."

"Does that include you?"

Tyler was shocked. "Of course not," he said defensively.

"It was an accident," Dillon repeated.

Tyler nodded; left it at that.

After searching Winston for additional weapons, they cuffed him and placed him in the recovery position, then returned to the injured Transport cop. They found a bandage in the first aid kit on his utility belt and tried to stem the bleeding with it. As Jack stood up to go and summon help, he heard the unmistakable sound of men in combat boots running. Moments later a host of heavily armed SO19 officers, toting an arsenal of MP5 machine guns and Glock pistols, burst onto the platform, fanning out as they went.

"Armed police! Nobody move!" Their leader shouted, as enough hardware to start a small war was levelled at Jack and Dillon.

As they left the platform, now clustered with emergency personnel, Steve Bull appeared at their side, his slender face fraught with worry. He handed them each a polystyrene cup containing coffee, which he'd purloined from a shop in the concourse.

"Any news on Colin, yet?" Jack asked.

"Nothing," Bull said, miserably.

There was a sudden flurry of activity behind them, on the platform where the BTP officer – they'd learned his name was Jenkins – lay. He had been there for over twenty minutes now, while the trauma team stabilised him. The area was off limits to non-essential personnel, which Tyler and Dillon were both now considered. Finally, something was happening.

They watched in strained silence as the ambulance crew carefully removed the injured transport cop from the platform. The Helicopter Emergency Medical Service doctor in attendance was a gunshot trauma specialist. He fastidiously supervised the paramedics as they held the various tubes and bottles in place during the difficult trip up the escalator.

Another ambulance crew had already removed Winston from the scene, with a strong police guard in attendance. He was still unconscious. The doctor had given him a brief examination, concluding that his nose, jaw and right cheekbones were all badly fractured. "He might not win any beauty contests for a while, but he should make a full recovery," he had informed them in a matter of fact tone.

"Pity," Dillon had responded, spitting the word out like venom.

A BTP Inspector, accompanying the injured officer, veered off from the stretcher party and approached them. "Chief Inspector Tyler?" he enquired in a strong Mancunian accent, his eyes flitting nervously from one to the other.

Jack acknowledged the man with a nod, his mind elsewhere. He desperately needed to get back above ground level, to find out how Franklin was doing. He had just finished handing the scene over to BTP CID; the necessary delay had been as agonising to him as any torture an inquisitor could have devised. Surely someone knew something by now, and if so, why hadn't they got word to Tyler?

"That's me. This is DI Dillon."

"I'm Inspector Dalton, BTP. I just wanted to thank you for looking after Constable Jenkins. He's been shot twice, but thankfully both bullets seem to have missed his vitals. The doctor thinks one's still lodged in the shoulder, though, because there's no exit wound for it." The BTP Inspector seemed at a loss as to what else to say and the silence quickly became strained. "Just thought you'd want to know," he finally said. Dalton was clearly shaken by the senseless wounding of one of his men.

Tyler knew exactly how he felt. *Welcome to the club, old son.* Jack kept the thought to himself.

The Inspector shook their hands formally, thanking them once again. With a final nod of the head, he rushed off to re-join the paramedics, who were now halfway up the escalator, intent on supervising Jenkins' removal to hospital.

Jack took a sip of his coffee and pulled a face. "I think I need something a little bit stronger," he remarked wearily.

"Yeah, me too," Dillon said, taking the unwanted cup from him.

"Come on. Let's get back to work," Tyler sighed.

According to the electronic clock mounted on the station wall, its red digits glowing brightly against a black background, the time was now 23:00hrs.

It had been one of the longest, most stressful days Jack could ever remember working, and it was far from over.

CHAPTER FIFTEEN

Emerging from the main entrance, Tyler spotted Steve Bull down by their car. He nudged Dillon's arm, pointed, and rushed down the steps, cutting through a string of uniforms surging the other way.

Winston's BMW had been cordoned off, and a City officer was standing guard. The road outside the station, already narrowed by roadworks, had been rendered completely impassable by abandoned police vehicles and ambulances. The glass-fronted buildings surrounding the station reflected the sea of pulsating blue light brilliantly.

Bull had his back towards them, and he was talking on the car radio.

"Is there any news on Colin Franklin yet?" Tyler asked as they reached the car.

"I've just spoken directly to the Yard." Bull's face was unreadable, but the strain in his voice was immediately evident.

"And?" Tony Dillon demanded, anxiously.

Steve Bull shook his head in misery. "Colin was still alive when the LAS took him off to the Royal London, but the CAD's not been updated on his condition since."

"Damn," Jack said. Not knowing Colin's fate was tearing him apart and, as cruel as it sounded, he would have almost preferred bad news to this.

"That might be a good sign," Bull said, hopefully.

Jack's face softened. "We can only hope," he said. "Are you okay? I know you and Colin were close."

"I'm fine," Bull lied.

Tyler nodded his understanding. "It's alright, Stevie," he said, placing a hand on the smaller man's shoulder. "C'mon, let's get over there on the hurry up. We can write this crap up later."

The Royal London Hospital is an austere building situated in the centre of Whitechapel High Street. Originally built in 1759, it was once the sanctuary of Joseph Carey Merrick, more commonly known by his cruel nom de guerre: the 'elephant man'.

While its grim Victorian facade hadn't changed much since Merrick's time, the hospital now boasted the Helicopter Emergency Medical Service and an impressive array of specialist consultants and advanced technical facilities; it had an Intensive Care Unit second to none.

As Tyler passed through the main entrance, he spotted Kelly Flowers and George Copeland standing beside a drinks dispenser opposite the reception desk. Copeland was jabbing the selector buttons aggressively.

For a second, Tyler faltered. This was the moment of truth. What on earth would he say to them if Colin had died? Dillon noted the slight hesitation in Jack's step but said nothing. He knew how badly his friend was taking this.

The detectives quickly crossed the hall to join their comrades, with Tyler taking the lead. Kelly Flowers was the first to notice their approach. A wave of relief swept over her pretty features as she nudged George and pointed in their direction. "Thank God you're safe," she said as Jack reached them. "We've all been so worried."

Kelly took a step towards Jack, instinctively reaching out to touch his arm, but then she stopped short, afraid he would think she was being too familiar. She needn't have worried. Jack wrapped his arm around the girl's shoulders and gave her a big hug. Kelly blushed, but Tyler was too preoccupied to notice. "How's Colin?" He asked, feeling his stomach constrict into a ball of ice. "Is he going to...I mean...How bad is it?"

"He's going to be fine," George said, not taking his eyes from the drink dispenser. "I'll take you to see him as soon as I get my money back from this thieving bastard machine." With that, he began rocking it.

"Why don't I take you through," Kelly offered quickly, conscious that the stern-faced lady sitting behind the reception counter was staring at Copeland disapprovingly. "George can join us after, assuming he doesn't get himself thrown out first." Without waiting for an answer, she set off along a white-walled corridor that led to the Accident and Emergency department. The triage area was packed with the walking wounded, some waiting patiently, others complaining about the long wait they had endured. The smell of Trigene was overwhelming, and it reminded Dillon of his recent trip to the mortuary.

When they reached a row of examination cubicles, all of which had their curtains drawn, Kelly stopped. "He's in the last but one cubicle," she explained.

Tyler nodded and set off towards it. As he reached for the curtain, it was drawn back from inside and Jack almost collided with a young nurse on her way out. She smiled and offered a polite apology.

Inside, Colin Franklin was propped up on a bed talking to Paul Evans. Apart from a large support bandage wrapped around his torso, and a whopper of a bump on his forehead, he appeared to be in remarkably good shape considering he had recently been shot.

On seeing Tyler, his face broke into an enormous grin. "Come in, guv. The boys told me that you and Mr Dillon went after the bastard that shot me. I only wish I'd able to go with you."

"I don't understand," Tyler said, dumbfounded. "You were hit! I saw you go down."

DC Evans leaned down and raised Franklin's bulletproof vest. "Colin's Met-vest saved his life." The remains of the bullet could still be seen, embedded in the Kevlar plate, just below chest level.

Tyler shook his head in disbelief. As always, the R for risk assessment contained within the standard IIMARCH briefing – a convoluted acronym which stood for Information, Intention, Method, Administration, Risk assessment, Communications, Human rights issues – had stipulated that all officers involved in the deployment were to be in possession of their Met-vest and Personal Protection Equipment, but he doubted anyone else on the team had actually bothered to wear any of it. He certainly hadn't. His equipment was sitting in the boot of the Omega, along with Dillon's and Steve's. "Get George," he told Kelly. "I want that thing bagged and exhibited, pronto."

Bull had been waiting patiently, but now he forced his way into the small treatment area, unceremoniously elbowing his way through his bigger team-mates until he reached Franklin's side. He clasped the younger man's hand affectionately. "I thought I was going to have to tell your wife you were dead," he said, blinking moisture from his eyes.

Franklin smiled up at Bull. "You're not gonna get rid of me that easy," he promised.

"Oh, please! All this sentimental crap is making me sick," Dillon told them.

Everyone in the cubicle laughed. They were all still alive, they had captured the bad guy, and even though there was still a lot of work to do, it looked as though the case was effectively solved. The mood quickly became jovial, and then boisterous as tension drained.

Tyler gave them a blow-by-blow account of what had happened after they left Commercial Street in pursuit of Winston's BMW. There were a few cheers when he recanted how Dillon had subdued Winston. Dillon acknowledged this with a modest bow.

The BTP officer's shooting was the low point of the story but, as his prognosis was good, the mood quickly livened up again. Eventually, a staff nurse came over and shooed them all out, complaining about the noise.

Franklin was to be kept in overnight for observation. Arrangements had already been made for his wife to be collected and brought to the hospital. They all promised to come back and visit again as soon as they could.

As they headed back to the car park, Steve Bull fell in beside Copeland. "What happened to Sandra Dawson? She was on the floor when we arrived. Was she hurt?" With all the excitement since then, Steve had almost forgotten about her.

"She's fine. Like the seasoned old pro that she is, she dived on the floor as soon as Winston pointed the gun at her."

"That's a relief," Bull said.

"She's been asking about you, you know."

"Really?"

"Yep. I reckon you're in there, sunshine."

"Fuck off."

"No, I'm serious. I don't even think she'd charge you."

Surprising a shudder, Bull quickly changed the subject. "What about the second shot?" he asked. "Was anyone else hurt?"

George shook his head. "Thankfully it went wild and just took a chunk out of a wall."

"Thank God."

George was suddenly sombre. "We've had a couple of close calls tonight."

"Tell me about it," Bull said with feeling.

"I'm glad you got the bastard though, Steve. What he did to that poor girl was downright evil."

"Right, pay attention," Tyler instructed. He was all business as the team gathered around him in the hospital car park. "Now he's in custody, I want Winston's flat under our control as soon as possible. There will be a briefing at Arbour Square in forty-five minutes. Do not be late." Without another word, Jack turned around and climbed into the back of the Omega.

Kelly Flowers lingered as she walked past the car, smiling down at Jack. He gave her a small wave in return. Dillon, who was just getting in, noticed the gooey-eyed look she gave Tyler. He rolled his eyes and grinned to himself. "I can't think why, but I reckon young Kelly has got the hots for you, Jack," he said, turning to face his friend.

"Don't be silly," Jack said.

"When we arrived, she made it very obvious that she'd been worried about you, but she didn't even ask me and Steve if we were okay. I don't think she even noticed we were there. I'm telling you, mate, the girl fancies you something rotten."

"You're imagining it," Tyler said, dismissively. Nonetheless, now that he thought about it, she had seemed rather pleased to see him.

Dillon raised a knowing eyebrow and smiled. "You know exactly what I'm talking about, don't pretend otherwise."

Jack was about to tell Dillon to mind his own business when Steve slipped into the driver's seat, stopping the conversation dead. He noticed the unusual silence at once. "I'm not interrupting anything am I?" he enquired casually.

"No," Tyler said firmly.

"Yes," Dillon said at the same time.

The two men looked at each other and began to laugh. Bull shrugged and started the car. He had long since quit trying to understand this pair.

CHAPTER SIXTEEN

Tuesday 2nd November 1999.

It was six-fifty-five a.m., and Jack had just finished updating his decision log. It had taken some pretty creative writing to justify the pursuit of Winston and all the carnage that had ensued. Still, they had got their man, and hopefully, that would be considered when the investigation was dissected and his operational decisions were reviewed.

The door to his Arbour Square office opened a fraction and Julia Prestwick, one of the HOLMES team, cautiously popped her head into the room.

Jack stared enquiringly at her through bleary eyes.

"Morning, sir," she said softly. "I hope I'm not bothering you. I know you've been up all night and I thought you might appreciate this." She produced a cup of steaming hot coffee. "It's only instant," she said, apologetically.

Jack rubbed at his neck, which was stiff from where he'd been slouching over his desk for so long. "Instant's fine, Julia," he croaked, feeling as though his tongue had morphed into sandpaper. He managed a feeble smile as she put the cup down in front of him. "Thank you, sweetheart," he said. "You're a lifesaver."

Julia's face lit up. She waited expectantly while he took his first sip, and then beamed when he nodded his approval.

Tyler studied the sway of her hips as she glided out of the office, moving with the grace of a model on the catwalk. No wonder every single bloke in the building – and a couple of the married ones, from what he had heard – was trying their damnedest to get into her knickers.

She stopped at the door, smiling again. "Call me if you need *anything* else." Julia was a terrible flirt, and she had an ability to make even a simple statement appear incredibly suggestive – another reason why she had so many admirers.

Dillon and Flowers passed Julia on her way out. Closing the door behind him, Dillon flopped down in one of the chairs opposite Jack's desk, closed his eyes and let out a long sigh. He looked all done in.

Kelly appeared equally exhausted as she sat down next to him. Stifling a yawn, she gave the coffee in Jack's hand a covetous glance.

After leaving the hospital, Jack's team had regrouped at Arbour Square to prepare for the next phase of the operation. Jack had liaised with Newham Borough, who had reluctantly provided two uniforms to guard Winston's flat until a warrant was obtained, a necessary precaution in case the local scumbags tried to sneak in and remove any incriminating evidence before the murder team got their act together.

Paul Evans had been tasked to wake up a friendly magistrate and get the warrant signed off. Charlie White was given the job of sorting out an armed guard for Winston and liaising with Witness Protection over Sandra Dawson.

Murray, who was also an Advance Exhibits Officer, had been dispatched to the hospital to seize all of Winston's clothing and belongings as evidence.

Copeland had arranged a full lift for Winston's BMW, which was being taken to the pound at Charlton pending a full forensic examination.

Once the warrant had been obtained, Dillon led a small group of officers, including Copeland and Flowers, over to Winston's flat to conduct a flash search. With their suspect in custody, they now had ready access to his keys, so getting in was no longer a problem.

A Police Search Advisor – or POLSA – accompanied by a specially trained search team would be tasked to pull the place apart once the flat had been forensicated by Sam Calvin and his cohorts.

As the driver of the pursuit car, Steve Bull had been written off to liaise with Traffic over the worryingly long list of vicinity only police accidents – or POLACCS, as they were known – that had occurred during the chase. Witness statements would eventually have to be taken from everyone affected by Winston's driving, but that could wait until after the Traffic bods had finished dealing with the Road Traffic Act side of the investigation.

The shootout had quickly become a major item across all the networks and, as the SIO, Tyler's first priority had been to ensure that the Yard's top brass were fully briefed and ready to deal with the impending shit storm. His first call had been to DCS Holland, who had gone nuclear when he discovered just how badly things had deteriorated after Tyler decided to follow Winston away from the flat, rather than just housing him for C_{II} to take on the following morning. Within seconds of saying goodbye to the DCS, the phone rang, and he was forced to go through the whole painful process again, this time with the area Commander, who had been even harder to placate. They say bad things happen in threes; sure enough, the phone had barely landed in its cradle when it started ringing again. It was the AC's Staff Officer, who had the raging hump because he hadn't been able to get through to Tyler earlier.

As if fielding the barrage of angry calls hadn't been hard enough in itself, the Yard's Central Press Office was being inundated with media enquiries, and an irate press officer, unable to reach him on the phone, had been paging him constantly. The first message had been firm but polite. The second had been more robust. By the time the fifth message arrived, a senior press officer had become involved, and he or she was demanding that Tyler drop whatever he was doing and call the press office at once. The messages had reached double figures now, and the latest one to come through, from a media and communications manager, who was presumably even more senior in rank, had warned him that if he wanted to keep his rank – and his testicles – he should make immediate contact. The pager's incessant vibrating was driving him mad. Wondering if this was what it felt to have a stalker, he had finally switched the annoying thing off.

"So, how did the flash search go?" Jack asked, hoping Dillon had some good news for him.

He didn't.

Under Copeland's guidance they had carried out as thorough a search as they could without jeopardising the scene from a forensic perspective, but they hadn't found anything to connect Winston to the murder. On a positive note, they had recovered a significant quantity of white powder, which they believed to be uncut cocaine. They had also seized ten rounds of .38 calibre ammunition, a bunch of stolen credit cards and driving licences, and several blank British passports. Under normal circumstances, a seizure like that would have been great news. Today, it felt like a very poor consolation prize.

"What's the score here?" Dillon asked.

Jack rolled his eyes, a look of exasperation crossing his face.

"I see. Like that, was it?" Dillon asked, sympathetically.

"Yep." Tyler took a deep breath before continuing. "I must've been given a dressing down by the entire chain of command for northeast London."

Dillon grimaced. "Really? That's quite impressive, even for you."

Tyler leaned an elbow on the edge of his desk and wearily buried his chin in the palm of his hand. "A new record, if I'm not mistaken." He looked hungover, which was pretty much on a par with how he felt. "Oh yeah, I almost forgot, the Chief Inspector at Information Room phoned me. He wanted to know what I was going to do about a certain DI who developed an acute case of selective deafness when ordered to disengage from a vehicle pursuit." His tone was one of mild rebuke, and he raised an eyebrow accusingly.

"What did you say?" Dillon asked, neutrally.

Jack allowed himself a mirthless smile. "I told him I was having trouble with my phone and couldn't hear him. He hung up on me after that."

Dillon grinned. "So, what now?" he asked, trying to stifle a yawn.

He felt fatigued to the point where he could no longer think straight, and he began rubbing his eyes, which were dry and sore. They immediately felt worse, as though he'd massaged grit into them.

"We've done all we can, for now," Jack told them. "As soon as you're finished downstairs, go home and get some sleep. I'll wait here to see Mr Holland, and then I'll do the same. The DNA results from the flesh under Tracey's nails won't be in till late today at the earliest. I'll ask Chris Deakin to call me at home if he hears anything."

"What time do you want everyone back in?" Dillon asked.

"Winston's going to be hospitalised for a good few days, which takes some of the pressure off us. The team has already been on the go for twenty-four hours solid, and if they don't get some sleep soon, they'll drop. Make sure they finish their statements, tidy up anything that's urgent and get away as quickly as they can. I don't want them back in today."

"What about the flat? Won't we need to supply an exhibits officer for that?"

Jack shook his head. "He didn't kill her there, Dill. I don't think we're going to get anything worthwhile out of that flat."

"But Sam Calvin's got people coming over to start work on it this morning," Dillon said. "George was sorting it out when Kelly and I came in to see you."

"I'll speak to Mr Holland. I'm sure he can blag us an exhibits officer from another team for a day."

"Okay, I'll spread the word. Steve'll be especially pleased, it means he can go around and visit Colin again later today."

"Tell him to pass on my regards if he does," Tyler said. "Now scat. Go get some rest. You've earned it."

As Dillon wearily descended the stairs towards the car park, he bumped into DCS Holland, who was on his way up.

"Ah, Dillon, I'm just on my way up to see Jack. Your team did damn good work catching Winston. Is everyone okay?"

"We're all fine, sir. Just a little tired."

"So, how long before we can bring Winston back for questioning?" Holland was eager to see him on the charge sheet as soon as possible.

"They reckon he'll be hospitalised for about a week."

Holland grimaced. A quick charge might have lessened the brass's interest in the carnage that preceded the arrest. It would have made the media easier to handle, too. "That's a pity, but it can't be helped, I suppose. What sort of security have we got on him?"

"An ARV crew was still there, the last I heard," Dillon said, "but I imagine the DPG will take over later this morning." It was policy that the crew of an SO19 Armed Response Vehicle should only be used to provide an armed hospital guard until a team from the Diplomatic Protection Group could take over.

"I see."

Holland cleared his throat, and then glanced around to make sure no one else was within earshot. Lowering his voice, he said, "I trust that the bastard was well and truly spoken to when he was arrested?" The inference being that the man had been given a good hiding for his troubles. Holland was old school. If a villain wanted to play rough, you made sure that you played rougher. That way, they thought twice about trying it on next time.

"He was most definitely spoken to, sir," Dillon confirmed. Holland didn't miss the fact that the large DI had deliberately avoided eye contact. It told him all he needed to know.

"Excellent," he said, passing Dillon on the stairs.

"Sir," Dillon replied dutifully, knowing that Holland had understood the unspoken answer to the unspoken question.

Did he get a good hiding?

Is the pope a Catholic? Does a bear shit in the woods? Would we let him get away with that, unscathed?

So, he got a good hiding, then?

He got spanked senseless.

Excellent!

By ten o'clock the last of Jack's team had gone off duty, leaving DS Deakin and a skeleton staff to hold the fort.

Holland, now fully appraised of the situation, would deal with the media circus. He had been ordered to attend the Yard for midday, and was to be present when the AC attended a media briefing to make a formal statement about the night's events. All in all, the hierarchy agreed, despite the mayhem that led up to the arrest, Tyler and his team had done well under the most difficult of circumstances. It was already being muted around the corridors of power at the Yard that Franklin should be nominated for a Commissioner's High Commendation.

―――――

When Johnson arrived at Arbour Square that morning he seemed preoccupied and irritable. He fussily inspected his desk, annoyed to find his 'in' tray full. Wendy Blake had only known him for a couple of days, but that was long enough. They exchanged strained pleasantries as he sat down, but after that, she only spoke to him about work-related matters, and then only when it was strictly necessary.

When he popped out to use the loo an hour or so later Dean Fletcher turned to her. "What's wrong, Wendy? You haven't said much today. It's not at all like you. Are you ill or something?"

She shook her head. "It's that new analyst, Dean. Something about that man makes my skin crawl."

Dean bristled. He was fond of Wendy, and if Johnson had been making her feel uncomfortable, he would have to have a quiet word.

"Don't say anything," Wendy said, seeing the expression on Dean's face.

"Wendy, we're one big happy family here, and I'm not having anyone come in and spoil things," Dean said firmly.

"It's fine, Dean," she said quickly. "He hasn't said or done anything, it's just the vibe that he gives off. Julia picked up on it, too. Apparently, a few of the girls have. They all reckon he's got a downer on women."

―――――

At four p.m. Chris Deakin came into the Intelligence Cell to give them an update. He had just received official confirmation from the FSS that the skin samples retrieved from Tracey's fingernails during the post-mortem examination were a DNA match for Claude Winston. Dean and Wendy were delighted. Even Johnson seemed pleased. "Have you told Mr Tyler yet?" he enquired.

"No," Deakin said. "He looked exhausted when he left, so I thought I'd let him sleep a little while longer. I'm just about to pop down and let the DCS know, but I wanted you guys to know first."

Johnson glanced at his watch. "I hadn't realised the time," he said, standing up. "I'm supposed to be attending a meeting at Whitechapel. Would there be any objection to my letting Mr Porter know about this development while I'm there?"

Deakin shrugged. "I suppose not," he said. "He is the Borough Commander. But you shouldn't let anyone else know until Mr Tyler has cleared it."

"Of course not," Johnson said, frostily. His tone implied that Deakin was an idiot for stating the obvious. He grabbed his jacket from the back of his chair and set off purposefully.

"Did he say anything to you about going over to Whitechapel today?" Dean asked Wendy as soon as Johnson had left the room.

"No," she said, "but he wouldn't, would he?"

"Seems a bit suspicious, if you ask me," Dean told her. "We get some important news and suddenly he remembers a meeting he's supposed to attend on his old ground. I reckon that bloke's a plant."

"Don't be silly, Dean. He couldn't possibly have known that the first murder he'd be assigned to when he joined us would happen on his old manor."

"I suppose not," Fletcher acknowledged, grudgingly. "But I bet he's reporting everything he finds out here straight back to his old paymaster."

"Why would he do that?" Wendy asked.

Fletcher shrugged. "Maybe he's keeping in with Porter so that he's got somewhere to run back to if things don't work out for him here."

"They can bloody well have him, as far as I'm concerned," she said with gusto.

The Disciple smiled as he walked into Whitechapel canteen. It was five p.m. and the canteen was starting to get busy. He could barely contain his excitement as he gazed around at the pathetic minions of law and order. What a joke they were. If only they knew the truth about him! But they didn't and never would.

He had prepared himself mentally and spiritually, and he felt replenished. He knew his superior intellect gave him a vast advantage over them; it enabled him to walk among them without drawing attention to himself. That was the supreme irony of it all. The wolf happily passed amongst the sheep, devouring them at will, and yet they welcomed him with open arms, trusting him explicitly.

It was simply delicious.

He acknowledged a detective standing in front of him in the line for the till. The man nodded politely. They would never catch him. Not in a million years! He would paint the streets with blood tonight, and there was nothing that anyone could do to stop him.

Nothing!

"DILLON!" Jack Tyler opened his eyes with a frightened start, aware that the terrifying screams that had woken him were his own. He claustrophobically pushed the quilt aside and sat up. "Dear God," he breathed, slowly rubbing his temples.

This was the third time it had happened, and the dream was becoming more intense with every rerun, flashing before his mind like a horror film on a loop.

As the mist cleared, he would find himself back on the railway platform with Dillon, fighting Winston. He watched helplessly as, in slow motion, the gun went off, again and again, the noise reverberating painfully within the confines of his tortured mind.

In his dream it was suddenly Dillon, not him, struggling with Winston as the gun discharged. As the two men moved apart Jack saw blood spraying everywhere as his friend fell to the floor, a massive hole in his chest, a look of disbelief on his dying face. Strangely, although the rest of his dream was played out in black and white, the blood was always a vivid red.

And then Steve Bull was running towards Dillon, shouting, "This is real life, not an episode of *The Sweeney*. People get killed in real life."

Jack was screaming his friend's name as Winston, laughing insanely, turned the gun on him. At this point, mercifully, he always managed to wake up.

He sat there, holding his head until the images faded and his heartbeat returned to something approaching normal. Running his fingers through his hair, Jack looked across at the alarm clock on his bedside table. It said six p.m. He had slept for a little over six hours. He groaned softly, knowing it was nowhere near enough.

Tyler took himself downstairs. Perhaps a cup of coffee and something to eat would help.

Chris Deakin had recently left a message on his answer phone, passing on the results of the DNA comparisons. It was the only message, which hopefully meant that nothing else of major importance had happened while he was sleeping.

With the DNA match and Dawson's evidence, he was confident they would be able to charge Winston, even if they failed to recover the murder weapon and Tracey's underwear. And yet there still remained a nagging doubt in the back of his mind that he found disturbing. It was probably nothing, but he would mention it to Dillon, get his view on it.

Shortly after 8 p.m., a lone figure hurried along Three Colts Lane, making for the railway arches. Pausing briefly to sniff the air like the predator he was, The Disciple made sure that no one was around to see him enter his lair. A light breeze was already blowing and it was beginning to drizzle. Heavy rain was forecast for later. He pulled up his collar to keep out the damp. Rain was good. It would serve him well tonight.

The Disciple no longer thought of himself by his given name. He saw that side of his personality as a grubby outer garment, waiting to be shed, as the butterfly within finally broke free of the chrysalis that encased it.

He had completed the preparatory stage and was now undergoing the transition, which would take him to a higher level of being. Smiling to himself he began to hum his tune. *What a ride. What a thrill. All I'm gonna do is Kill, Kill, Kill.*

It was time to strike again.

CHAPTER SEVENTEEN

The Disciple's battered van emerged from the lockup at precisely nine p.m. that evening.

Most of the surrounding arches were operated by an overhaul company that specialised in the maintenance and repair of London taxicabs, and while the area was always busy during the day, at night he could usually count on the cobbled streets being completely deserted.

Pausing at the main road, The Disciple glanced thoughtfully at the rucksack on the passenger seat beside him, running through his inventory in his head. Among other things, the bag contained his knives and scalpels, a Polaroid camera, a specially padded pair of rigid handcuffs, stolen from the police canteen three weeks ago, and a police issue radio he'd 'borrowed' for a few days. The rucksack also contained a scrunched up cool bag, smelling salts, and the artefacts and parchment he would need to perform the ceremony.

He gave his appearance a final check in the rear-view mirror. Tonight, he had opted for shoulder length brown hair, a drooping seventies moustache and tortoiseshell glasses with clear frames. He had left off the additional padding he'd worn for the first kill, making his midriff look a lot slimmer.

Satisfied with his disguise, he pulled into Cambridge Heath Road and set a course for Whitechapel. The noise level inside his head had gone right off the scale, the words of his twisted song forming a mantra of evil that he repeated over and over again.

He reminded himself not to exceed the speed limit, but his foot had other ideas; it wanted to press the gas pedal to the floor and keep it jammed there until he reached his destination and the bloodshed could begin all over again.

His mouth was parched. Without taking his eyes from the road, he leaned over and removed a bottle of sparkling mineral water from a side pocket in his rucksack. Wedging it between his thighs, he unscrewed it, one-handed, and drank greedily, savouring every drop of the precious liquid. Soon, he reminded himself, he would be able to savour another of life's precious liquids. He licked his lips as he contemplated the night's menu: sliced whore, chopped whore, and fillet of whore. "Patience, patience," he cautioned himself. There would be time aplenty to satisfy all his cravings tonight.

At that very moment, some twenty miles distant, Tyler was nearing the end of his workout. Breathing heavily, he looked down at the treadmill's control panel, spraying sweat everywhere. The digital readout told him he had completed two and a half miles.

Only another half-mile to go.

Jack glanced across at Dillon and was pleased to see that the big man looked every bit as fatigued as he felt, jogging on the treadmill immediately to his left. "I can't believe I let you talk me into doing this after all the hours we've put in over the last couple of days. I must be bloody mad!" The leisurely run he'd come for, which was just intended to shake the cobwebs off, was fast becoming an endurance test.

"Don't be such a wimp!" Dillon responded, increasing the speed of the machine despite the growing heaviness in his legs. "C'mon, I'll race you to the finish," he panted. "Loser buys the first round."

"You sadistic swine!" Tyler wheezed. It was all he could manage. Digging deep, he adjusted the speed control on his machine and forced himself to sprint the remaining distance. He wasn't going to be outperformed by Dillon, even if it killed him, which it probably would at this rate. He tried to shut out the pain in his legs by focusing on the music coming from the wall speakers behind him. Freddie Mercury was currently belting out *'Who wants to live forever'*, the song from the film, Highlander. As he listened to the lyrics, he thought about poor Tracey Phillips, who had barely lived at all.

Jack's lungs felt as though they were going to burst out of his chest when the alarm finally sounded. As the treadmill slowed to warm down speed, he glanced over at Dillon and was pleased to see that he'd finished just ahead of his partner. "I'm...never...going to...listen...to anything you say...ever again," Jack promised as he struggled to regain his breath.

Conceding defeat, Dillon slumped down on a mat next to the running machines and started massaging his calves.

Jack hobbled over to a large internal window that looked down onto the squash courts a floor below. Gasping in air, he spent a few moments watching two middle-aged men, with spreading waistlines and receding hairlines, stumble around the court, beetroot-faced.

"That could be us in a few years," he told his partner when he was finally able to speak again.

"What could?" Dillon asked from the mat, where he was impersonating a beached whale.

"Never mind," Jack said. When he'd phoned Dillon earlier, to discuss the case, they had both agreed that a trip to the gym, followed by a quick drink in the bar, might help them unwind. It had seemed like a really good idea at the time, but now they were both regretting their earlier enthusiasm.

"Let's get showered and have that drink," Tyler said, heading for the changing rooms on unsteady legs.

Dillon raised a hand, hoping that his partner would grab it and pull him up, but Jack had already gone. With a grimace, Tony Dillon slowly dragged himself to his feet and turned to follow Jack into the changing rooms – and immediately collided with a girl coming the other way. "I'm so sorry," he said, horrified at his clumsiness. "Are you okay?"

She smiled. "I'm fine, although I must admit it was like walking into a brick wall." She prodded his chest gently." You obviously work out a lot."

Dillon felt his face flush, but – as it was already beacon-red from where he'd been running flat out – he doubted any additional colour would make a discernible difference. He casually cast his eyes over her, ostensibly checking her out for any injuries. In reality, he was giving her figure the once over. The girl was blonde, in her mid-twenties, tanned, and wearing a baggy green tee shirt over a skin-tight purple leotard. Her face dimpled adorably as she smiled at him.

"Are you sure I didn't hurt you?" he asked, smiling back.

"I'm fine," she said, flexing her bicep. "See, I work out too."

"And how much longer do you plan to work out for tonight?" he asked, his earlier tiredness forgotten.

"I've just got ten-minutes to do on the cross trainer and then I'm all done," she said.

"Or you could just call it a night now join me for a drink in the bar," he suggested. "It's the least I can do after nearly knocking you over."

The girl appeared to consider the offer, and for a second Dillon thought she was going to accept. Then her pretty face creased into a frown. "I really need to finish my workout," she said, dashing his hopes.

"That's a pity, he said, trying to conceal his disappointment. "It would have been nice."

"It still might be," she said, grinning provocatively. "Keep me company while I jog, and perhaps we can have that drink afterwards."

Dillon puffed out his chest. "I just might do that," he said, treating her to his most debonair smile.

"Just to warn you, though, I'm with my friend, over there." She nodded towards a row of cross-trainers, where another girl, equally pretty, stood watching them. "I hope that doesn't put you off."

"Not at all," Dillon said, scarcely able to believe his luck. He gave the other girl a little wave and was rewarded with a smile.

———

The Disciple hated all women. The seed had been sown by an overbearing and controlling mother who had dominated and bullied him during his childhood years.

She had made his adolescence a living hell, never missing an opportunity to embarrass or demean him in front of others. He still flinched with shame when he recalled the day that she discovered a secret stash of porn magazines he'd kept under his bed. She had called him names like 'unclean' and 'perverted', as though sex was something sordid, and he was morally corrupt for wanting it. University had provided him with the perfect means to escape her clutches, and in all the years since he had graduated, he had never been back to visit the first woman that he had learned to hate.

He'd hated the boring string of girls he'd dated before getting married, and had relished finding different ways to make them feel as uncomfortable and miserable as his mother had made him over the years. He had quickly learned how to play cruel mind games; he would start off by being charismatic, charming and attentive, and then suddenly switch to being rude. Then he would turn on the charm again, just to confuse them. He would make promises and deliberately fail to keep them, and he would arrange to meet at really awkward times and then turn up very late and make them rush. During dates he would treat his companion in a way that made her uncomfortable; if she was the type of girl who was independent and liked to split the bill, he would make a point of choosing her food for her and paying for everything. If she was an old-fashioned girl, who wanted to be wined and dined like a princess, he would only order for him and he would find a way to make her pay for the entire meal. When it came to sex, he would insist on having it when she wasn't in the mood – or, even better, when she was on her period, if he thought that would make her particularly uncomfortable – but when she was in the mood, he would withhold it.

He also hated the worthless whores who gave him sexual gratification without saddling him with emotional baggage. He didn't have to make an effort to be nice to them; he didn't have to look them in the eye and feign affection; he didn't even have to waste his time with small talk or foreplay – it didn't matter if they enjoyed the experience as long as he did. The downside to having paid sex was that it was purely a business transaction for the girls, and he didn't have any of the emotional control over them that he had with his girlfriends.

When he was going through a particularly bad patch in his marriage, and the stress of this resulted in him struggling to get or maintain an erection, some of the girls started making adverse comments about his lack of size, or his inability to perform. This made him realise that his addiction to sex was allowing the whores – who, in his mind were the lowest of the low – to gain ascendancy over him, but for some inexplicable reason this only made him want them even more.

Yes, The Disciple hated all women, but there were three that he despised above all others: they were the Infector, the Blackmailer, and the Controller. These vile creatures, more than any other of their kind, had conspired to destroy his life – and they had very nearly succeeded.

Now it was his turn. What comes around goes around, as the saying went.

His first victim had, by necessity, been chosen at random; the next two, however, would be anything but. Their painful demise had been carefully planned, and he intended to enjoy every single delicious moment of it.

The Disciple had been on the streets for less than ten minutes when he spotted the Infector. The timing was so perfect that it had to be an omen. Leaning against a wall, he watched as she led a trick into a narrow cul-de-sac at the back of Brick Lane. It was a repulsive little place about twenty-five yards long by five yards wide, and it led to the rear of a large Indian restaurant. She had been using this spot for a few weeks now, and it was a definite come down from the underground car park where she had always taken him.

He hoped the hygiene levels inside the fancy fronted restaurant were better than those out back, where three huge bins overflowed with rotting food. The smell was putrid, even from a distance. Beneath the bins, rats fought amongst themselves for the most succulent morsels.

The Infector ignored the rodents as she walked past the bins and entered a tiny recess a few feet south of the kitchen. The Disciple watched in fascination as his intended victim, partially illuminated by light from the open kitchen door, bent forward, her legs crudely spread. The punter wriggled into position behind her and they began rocking backwards and forwards.

A few minutes later, they emerged from the alley and went their separate ways without as much as a goodbye. The Disciple waited until it was obvious that she was searching for new customers, and then he made his move.

Natasha, the name that she was using these days, was an anaemic looking woman in her mid-forties, with nicotine stained buck teeth. Her strong, Liverpudlian accent had an irritating nasal twang to it, and the revolting way in which she constantly poked a large ball of gum around her mouth with her tongue bore a striking resemblance to a cow chewing cud. Even if he hadn't already hated her for infecting him with the clap, this revolting trait would have been enough to make him want to kill her.

Natasha wore bright red PVC boots, a black leather skirt, and a red satin blouse. Her complexion was blotchy. To top it all, her hair was dyed bright pink.

She just had to die.

Even though he had once been a regular, she showed no signs of recognising him. Perhaps it was the disguise he was wearing; perhaps it was just that all her punters looked the same to her. He engaged her in small talk for a few seconds before steering the conversation around to business. Getting her to reveal her star sign was ridiculously easy – she was a Leo – but persuading her to accompany him to his van proved much less so. Natasha claimed she didn't want to vacate her spot in the alley in case someone else moved in while she was away. The reality was that she obviously felt safer there with a punter she didn't know. Maybe her pimp was nearby, ready to rush to her aid if she cried out.

The Disciple smiled disarmingly, confided in her that he was musophobic, and therefore terrified of rats, and offered to double her money if she humoured him. He could see the conflict in her eyes: natural caution versus greed.

In the end, greed won.

Once inside the van, The Disciple attacked her with awesome

savagery, beating her unconscious with a large crowbar, while cursing her for giving him the venereal disease that had ruined his life.

It was a simple matter for him to secure her after the beating. He cuffed her hands behind her back, being careful to wrap some thick material around her wrists first to avoid leaving any tell-tale marks. Then he ripped a length of material from her blood-soaked blouse and, after removing the unpleasant wad of chewing gum with two gloved fingers, stuffed it deep into her battered mouth, effectively gagging her. They didn't have far to go, and he wasn't overly concerned about the possibility of her asphyxiating.

The Disciple congratulated himself as he drove off. Once again, he had blended into his surroundings with consummate skill, like the true chameleon he was. He had snatched a jaded, streetwise prostitute from one of the busiest red-light districts in London without leaving any clues. He could go anywhere and do anything. There was no escaping his wrath.

His arrogance about such matters was understandable. When interviewed in the days that followed, neither the many restaurant workers nor the pimp, sitting in his car twenty yards from the alley, could shed any light on Natasha's sudden disappearance that night.

The only witnesses were the rats, but they weren't talking.

He took her to the derelict buildings at the far end of Hanbury Street, a site he had first identified weeks ago. He had visited it again last night, to make sure it was still fit for purpose.

He moved silently through a narrow passageway between the two derelict houses and slipped into the small yard at the rear of the one on the right. He hastily forced the door with a jemmy he'd brought from the van. The wood was old and it required little effort. He repeated the process on the front door, this time working from the inside out.

The killer quickly carried the unmoving form of his latest victim, now wrapped in a dustsheet, into the dark hall. In the gloom, he could only just about make out the layout. The stairs were on his left, two closed doors led to rooms on his right, and the hallway led straight back through to the kitchen, which in turn led out onto a small yard at the rear.

Dropping her unceremoniously, the killer made a final journey to the van to retrieve his bag. He would need to work quickly with this one, which was a great pity. He really wanted to take his time and savour his experience with Natasha to the same extent that he had with Tracey Phillips.

Breathing heavily, and covered in sweat, he checked his watch; the luminous dial showed him that it was now nine-thirty. Everything had gone perfectly, and he was slightly ahead of schedule, but he couldn't relax; it would only take one complication to completely derail his plans.

Moving quickly, the killer methodically laid the contents of his rucksack out before him to ensure easy access to his tools. With great reverence, he unwrapped the lambskin parchment, positioning it so that he could read its contents without losing control of the sacrificial whore.

When he was satisfied that everything was positioned exactly to his liking, he unscrewed a small jar of powerful smelling salts. He held them under the woman's nose, moving them slowly back and forth.

Initially, nothing happened, but after a few seconds, she began to respond. The first twitch of her head was almost imperceptible, but the movement gradually increased as she tried to resist inhaling the powerful fumes.

Natasha was suffering from a depressed skull fracture, but as the salts were thrust into her face again, she moaned softly, and half opened glazed eyes.

"Ah, that's better," he said. She turned her head towards the sound and tried to focus on the speaker. Despite her best efforts to stay awake, she began to slip into a coma.

"Wake up you filthy diseased whore, I want you with me for the ceremony," the killer said, impatiently. The voice confused Natasha as she drifted in and out of consciousness. She didn't remember going to a ceremony.

He shook her shoulders roughly. "Wake up, I said."

Her eyes blinked open and, this time, slowly focused. She experienced surprisingly little pain as she lay there trying to digest what was happening to her.

"Not long now," he whispered gently. He felt intensely aroused, and could hardly breathe as he reached behind him for the knife.

She began moaning softly in the darkness, a pitiful noise signifying her distress. It was important that she remain awake for this, to share the experience with him. He needed her to understand what was happening. Leaning close to her, his face only inches away from hers, The Disciple drove the Bowie knife deep into her genitalia. "This is for leaving me riddled with venereal disease," he snarled, closing his eyes in relish as she shuddered.

Placing a gloved hand over her gagged mouth to muffle the screams, he moved the blade deeper into her, probing and twisting, exploring with it. It was his penis and he was fucking her, thrusting deeper and harder until he reached the point of no return.

She was still alive, but only just. He wanted to postpone the final moment, prolong the experience for as long as possible.

This was all so intense. His nervous system felt electrified. Time itself seemed to slow down as every sense he possessed became unbelievably enhanced.

His hearing had somehow become painfully acute, to the extent that he could discern the distinctive rustle of all the different fabrics as their clothing touched. He could isolate the sound of her dying heart, still beating defiantly inside her chest but growing weaker as the life force ebbed out of her. He listened attentively to the glorious sound of her soft flesh tearing as he slowly moved the knife inside her. He paused momentarily, lifting his head to sniff the air like a wild animal. He could smell everything.

Everything!

He could differentiate between the thick layer of dust on the banister and an old newspaper across the hall. He could smell the fur of the rodents inhabiting the old house, and the pungent aroma of their droppings on nearby floorboards. He clearly recognised the rich coppery smell of fresh blood, a distinctive odour that triggered vivid recollections of his final moments with Tracey Phillips. The killer would not have been surprised to learn that scent tends to foster memory more readily than any other sense. Fragrances he had never noticed before were suddenly accessible to him. It was incredible, beyond his wildest dreams. It was as though he could now smell with his whole body and not just his nose, as though the various odours in the dank building were being suffused into his skin.

As the last embers of her life were extinguished, one question burned brightly in her mind. She struggled to ask it but her body wouldn't respond. Her tongue felt thick, as if it had swollen to fill her entire mouth. The Disciple saw the unasked question in her eyes as they tried to focus on him one final time. He smiled cruelly. "You want to know why I chose you, don't you? I can see it in your eyes." His voice was barely audible above her death rattle.

Another blade, a Finnish skinning knife, appeared in his left hand. Placing his right hand on the centre of her clammy forehead he rested the knife against the side of her neck.

"I'd gladly tell you," he said, conversationally, as the knife began to slice downwards with tremendous force.

"But then I'd have to kill you."

CHAPTER EIGHTEEN

Jack was sitting at the bar feeling mightily annoyed when Dillon finally showed his face.

He slid onto the next bar stool and signalled for the bartender. "Sorry, Jack," he said sheepishly.

"What took you so long? I thought you'd gone home until I remembered that it was me who'd driven us here." Jack looked at his watch. He had been sitting there, alone, for twenty-five minutes.

"Do you want another drink?" Dillon offered.

"I've already had two," Jack said, angrily. "What the hell happened to you?"

Dillon tried again to catch the bartender's eye. "I got talking, lost track of the time." He shrugged and spread his arms disarmingly. "You know how it is."

"No, not really," Jack said, huffily folding his arms across his chest and fixing Dillon with a cold stare. He was extremely unhappy that he'd been kept waiting, and he could just imagine the ear bashing he'd be getting right now if their positions had been reversed.

"Never mind, mate, I'm here now."

"You're unbelievable!" Tyler said, knocking back the last of his orange juice. He stood up to leave. "Come on, let's go."

"No, wait! Sit down, relax, and have another drink. It's my round." Dillon signalled the bartender again, successfully this time.

"Be with you in a minute, sir," the man called from the other end of the bar.

"What are you up to?" Jack asked suspiciously, but he sat back down nonetheless.

Dillon decided to be frank. "Look, I got talking to a girl called Karen. She's a real babe, and she's agreed to have a drink with me tonight."

"I see. Well, in that case, I don't want to play gooseberry so I'll leave you to it." Jack made to stand up again, but Dillon waved him back down.

"No, don't go. I need you to keep her mate occupied for me."

Jack's eyes narrowed. "Her mate?" That didn't sound good.

"Yeah, she's with her BFF, a girl called Fiona. I told Karen she could join us, so I need you to keep her company while I chat up Karen."

"I'm really not in the mood for this, Dill," Tyler said. And he wasn't; he was tired and grumpy, and his mind was preoccupied with the case.

"Don't be silly, it'll do you good to have a little female company."

"No offence, but any woman you try to set me up with must have something wrong with her, otherwise you'd be sniffing around her yourself."

"What do you mean?"

"I mean that this Fiona bird is probably a real pig or a certified bunny boiler or, knowing you, both."

"She's lovely, Jack, honest."

"She was probably dropped on her head as a baby."

Dillon shook his head vigorously. "No. She's a ..."

Tyler interrupted him, his tone cynical. "I can guess: A disfigured mutant with three eyes, grown in a test tube by a mad scientist doing experiments with radioactive plasma. I bet she glows in the dark!" He grimaced at the thought.

"No, no, no! Will you trust me? I wouldn't do that to you," Dillon protested.

"Oh, come on, Dill!" Jack exclaimed loudly. "Of course you would."

The bartender shot them a look of disapproval.

"Look behind you," Dillon whispered without moving his lips. He glanced over Jack's shoulder, pointing with his eyes. Following Dillon's gaze, Tyler glanced behind to see two girls, a blond and a brunette, approaching. He felt his jaw drop. If the theme from *Charlie's Angels* had suddenly started belting out of the bar's speakers, he would not have been surprised.

Dillon quickly moved forward to greet them. Smiling warmly, he ushered them onto seats at a nearby table with a flamboyant wave of his hand. "I'm so glad you could make it. Let me introduce you to my close friend and colleague, Jack Tyler. Jack, this is Karen and her friend, Fiona."

Jack was speechless as he shook their hands. To his amazement, both girls were tall, shapely and very easy on the eye! Nonetheless, he remained wary. There had to be a catch somewhere along the line if Dillon was involved. Fiona flashed him a dazzling smile, revealing perfectly aligned teeth. "It's nice to meet you, Jack," she said, with just a hint of shyness.

He surreptitiously ran his eyes over her as they sat down, guessing that she was in her late twenties or early thirties. The easy way that she moved, and her deportment in general, made him wonder if she might be a dancer of some sort. "My pleasure entirely," he responded. "Have you been coming here long?" Not a very original opening line, he realised, but he always felt awkward making small talk and it was literally all he could think of to say.

"A while, but I haven't seen you here before."

"There'd be no reason for you to remember me even if you had," Jack said, wishing he had been able to come up with something wittier instead.

"Oh, I'm fairly sure I'd have remembered you," she purred, green eyes glinting mischievously.

Jack swallowed, and felt his knees go weak. "I'd certainly have remembered you, too," he stammered, giving her a goofy smile. He signalled to Dillon. "I believe it's your round, Tony." Perhaps coming to the gym hadn't been such a bad idea after all he decided, returning his attention to Fiona.

Winston angrily pressed the off button on the remote and watched the TV screen flicker into blackness. He had propped himself up in his hospital bed to watch the late-night news, but the main story was the 'dramatic car chase and shootout in Central London', which had led to his earlier arrest. He was sick of hearing the actions of the police described as 'brave' and 'courageous'. The bastards had beaten the crap out of him.

His whole face was badly swollen and he could hardly see out of the left eye. The right eye was better, but not by much. His nose had been reset before he'd regained consciousness, and they had wired his broken jaw up tightly, making speech difficult. His cheekbone was badly bruised, but at least it wasn't broken, as they had first feared. On top of everything else, he had a concussion, and his motor reflexes were all over the place.

"Bullshit!" he shouted at the television set, and immediately winced at the pain the outburst caused him.

"Shut it, scumbag," the armed guard sitting in the corner warned. The officer had made his feelings for Winston clear from the start.

"Fuck you, too!" Winston muttered, turning over to face the window. At least he had been given a private room so he didn't have to suffer the noise and commotion of a general ward.

His solicitor had visited him earlier. The news he'd brought had been grim. He had actually laughed when Winston enquired about the likelihood of bail. It transpired that the entire incident on the platform, where Claude ruthlessly gunned down the young transport officer, had been caught on video. The uncut drugs had been discovered at his flat, along with a few other illicit items he had forgotten about. As if that wasn't bad enough, the bastards were trying to fit him up with the murder of Tracey Phillips.

And they called him dishonest!

He had told his brief that he hadn't even known she was dead, that he had been looking for her when they pounced on him. To his amazement, his lawyer hadn't even bothered to pretend that he believed him! Since when had solicitors started caring whether their clients were guilty or not? The soulless parasites were quick enough to take his money from him. He paid them for results, not excuses. He had told the skinny, turkey necked, four-eyed bookworm what he wanted in no uncertain terms. His demands got him precisely nowhere. Winston had finally kicked the man out in a fit of temper.

The doctors said that he wouldn't be fit enough to be discharged for a good few days, so at least he had some time to come up with a plan of escape. There was no way that he was going to go to prison. No way!

After Dillon excused himself and Karen, Jack Tyler had remained in the bar with Fiona until closing time. She turned out to be great company and, as he walked her to her car, he surprised himself by asking her to have dinner with him later in the week.

"I'd love to," she replied.

"That's great." He smiled, although he was already half regretting the impulse. This was a dreadfully inconvenient time to start seeing someone, not that there was ever a good time for him. They might have cracked the Phillips' case but there was still a hell of a lot of work to do before he could begin to relax.

They exchanged mobile phone numbers and he promised to call her in a day or so. Feeling pleased and nervous at the same time, he tucked the piece of paper she'd given him into his warrant card as she drove off. Fiona Barton was undeniably stunning, and he knew he should be feeling pleased with himself. Trouble was, he doubted they had any sort of a future together. She didn't seem the sort to sit around waiting for him to finish work, never knowing if he would get off on time or not.

His job wasn't exactly conducive to long-term relationships. Or was he using just work as an excuse to prevent himself from getting hurt all over again, the way he had with Jenny?

Perhaps he should consider hooking up with someone in the job, someone who understood how the system fucked up your social life. He bet Kelly Flowers would understand.

Jack scratched his head, wondering what had made him think about her in that way.

Now that he had, he had to admit that there was something about her that he found alluring.

In fact, since Dillon had pointed her out to him last night, as she walked past their car outside the hospital, he had started to become...

He wasn't really sure what he had started to become. Interested he supposed.

Interested?

Was that the right word to describe his feelings? Probably not, he thought cynically. Whatever, he had become aware of her, and he suddenly realised that he didn't want Kelly to find out about his date with Fiona, although God alone knew why she should care.

It was all Dillon's fault. If the big lug hadn't goaded him about Kelly last night, he wouldn't be thinking along these lines now.

Jack had been married once, but the relationship had lasted less than a year. He now accepted that the marriage had been completely wrong for them both. Of course, it was always easy to see such things clearly with hindsight. His wife detested his job; she liked the people he mixed with even less. She hated the frequency with which he phoned up to say that he'd be late home because he had 'prisoners in the bin'.

Most of all she hated the fact that he was independent.

The arguments had been explosive, especially when he missed one of the numerous social functions that she had committed them to. They say that 'make up' sex is great, and it can be, but it wears thin when it's the only kind of sex you ever have.

Jenny had been a glamorous, charismatic career girl who put her social standing before their relationship. They had grown apart quickly once the first cracks had appeared in their marriage. Jack hadn't been too surprised to discover that she had embarked on an affair with her boss. In one of their more heated arguments, he accused her of being willing to sleep with anyone who could advance her career prospects.

She had sneered at him, spitefully admitting it was something she would willingly consider. The divorce had been rushed through after that, the split uncontested by either party. Jenny had remained in the matrimonial home, and he had gone his own way, tail between his legs, to begin life anew. At least there were no children to be harmed by the separation.

Jack had remained on reasonably good terms with his ex-in-laws, Mr Justice Parker, QC and his wife, Elaine. They spoke infrequently but always sent each other birthday and Christmas cards. Jack occasionally drew Brendan Parker as the presiding Judge at one of his murder trials at the Bailey. It amused him that they acted like they didn't know each other in public but sometimes shared an afternoon sherry in Brendan's chambers after court.

For a long time after the divorce, the wounds had remained raw. As a coping mechanism, Jack ploughed himself into his work and avoided any form of serious commitment. There had been girlfriends along the way, of course, and that was fine until they started wanting to get serious.

He always made it clear that he wasn't ready for another commitment. Having been hurt once he was in no rush to repeat the experience. Once bitten, twice shy. At least, that's what they said.

And yet, Jack had always believed in his heart that the right woman for him was out there somewhere. He would know her when he found her, he felt certain of that. Perhaps it was time to start looking for her in earnest, while he was still young enough to enjoy a family and all that it entailed.

Jack was thirty-one years old and, while he wouldn't go so far as to say he was becoming broody, he had to admit that he was disappointed to have reached that age without having any children to share his life with.

Yes, he was close to his family, and he saw them regularly, but in general his life consisted of work, work-related piss ups with work-related friends and little else, unless you counted his thrice-weekly trips to the gym, which he often made with Tony Dillon, his work-related best mate. It was a sad and rather hollow existence if he was honest, and he would gladly have swapped the miserable freedom he had now for the joyful ball and chain of a loving wife and a couple of doting kids.

Increasingly, Jack found himself wondering what it would be like to have a son that he could teach to play football, a son he could take to Highbury to watch his beloved Arsenal.

He wanted a daughter, too. He wasn't sure what little girls liked, but he figured it would probably include wearing pretty dresses and playing with dolls.

Ideally, he would have one of each, which would be amazing. He could teach them both how to ride bicycles and fly kites, all kids loved that, and at weekends he could take them to the park, or the zoo. For family vacations, he could take them all to Disneyland in Florida, which was one of his favourite places in the whole world, and when they were old enough, he would teach them how to ski.

He imagined the joy of hearing his toddler's first words, especially if one of them were 'dad'; the pride of witnessing their first steps; the satisfaction of reading his children bedtime stories, and the protective love of nursing them while they were poorly.

Even the unpleasant aspects of parenthood, like changing dirty nappies and vomit stained clothing; or the lack of sleep most people he knew complained about while their kids were teething, didn't seem so bad anymore.

Yes, Jack had been – to coin a phrase – 'job-pissed' in his younger days, but now he realised that there were far more important things in life than work. He wanted these things, needed them. If only he could find someone to share them with.

Dillon, who had just finished saying farewell to Karen, ambled over, mistaking the longing expression on Jack's face for something else entirely.

He sniggered like a schoolboy and nudged Tyler's arm. "You sly old dog! I take it from the look on your face that things went well?"

"It was okay," Jack replied, giving nothing away. They crossed the nearly empty car park and stopped by Jack's car, a ten-year-old silver Mercedes E Class.

"Are you gonna see her again?" Dillon asked as he put his seatbelt on.

Jack gave a non-committal shrug and turned the ignition. "Maybe. What about you?"

"Of course!" Dillon seemed genuinely surprised that Jack should even ask him such a thing. "How could she resist me once I turned on the fabled Dillon charm?"

Jack laughed fondly. "Well, she is only human, I suppose."

At eleven-fifteen p.m. Geraldine Rye wearily locked the door to the Regency Enquiries Agency, a P.I. firm she had set up eighteen months ago following the unpleasantness that resulted in her being required to resign from the City of London Police.

Despite its posh sounding title, Regency was a shyster outfit based in a two-room let above a garment manufacturer in Mansell Street, and it had one employee: her.

Pushing her small brolly ahead of her like a shield, she gingerly stepped over the puddle that had formed a moat around the entrance step to her premises and emerged into the pelting rain.

Hands in pockets, and as motionless as a statue, The Disciple watched Rye from a darkened doorway that sheltered him from the downpour. The moment he spotted her, his stomach twisted with hatred, for this was the Blackmailer, the second of the three women who had ruined his life.

In her early thirties, Geraldine Rye was of average height and build, with a plain but not unattractive face. Unaware that she was being observed, Rye gave the door handle a quick twist to make sure the latch had caught and then set off towards the Aldgate one-way system at a brisk pace.

The Disciple remained stationary until she reached the subway. As soon as she committed, he pulled his collar up and sprinted back to his van, which was parked on a single yellow line nearby. The engine coughed once and then kicked into life. He slipped it into first and drove across the junction into Middlesex Street, coasting to a stop a few yards from the exit she should be appearing from at any moment. He switched on the hazard warning lights and waited impatiently.

He was angry with her for taking the subway; most sane people avoided the place after dark, and while he would have been quite happy for her to become a crime statistic on any other occasion, it would fuck his plans up completely if she had her bag snatched or her tits groped tonight.

The wipers jerked back and forth intermittently, struggling to clear a deluge that was leaving splash marks the size of fifty-pence pieces all over his windscreen. Normally, he found the pendulum-like movement quite soothing, but tonight it grated on him like nails down a blackboard.

Eventually, Rye emerged from the subway, shoulders slumped miserably and head buried beneath her little umbrella. Intent on dodging puddles, she passed by the battered van without giving it a second glance. The Disciple studied her receding figure in a rain-streaked wing-mirror, and smiled triumphantly when she entered Petticoat Lane. She was sticking to the same route she had taken every time he had followed her. He knew where she was heading next, and he had already identified the perfect spot to intercept her. All he had to do was get there ahead of her and let her walk into his arms.

Geraldine Rye was running late due to a telephone conference with a pathetically needy client who wouldn't get off the bloody phone, and now she was probably going to miss her train home. She cursed in a most unladylike fashion as her foot sank into a puddle she hadn't spotted and cold water flooded into her shoe. The bottom half of her coat, and her legs, were already soaked through, and she wondered why she had bothered putting up the useless compact umbrella; a Kleenex would have done a better job of keeping the rain at bay. She decided that she needed a stiff drink. If she was going to have to wait for the next train anyway, she might as well take advantage of the situation and stop off for a little tipple at the Wetherspoons next to the railway station. There might even be a nice warm fire on the go, and a seat in which she could sit down and dry off a little.

The door of a parked van slid open as she drew level with it, and the long-haired idiot who got out without looking nearly knocked her over. She stepped in yet another puddle as she sidestepped him. "Look out," she yelled angrily.

"Sorry," he said grudgingly, hurriedly closing the door behind him.

"Bloody idiot," she mumbled under her breath. Her right foot was squelching with every step now, and she stared ruefully at her suede shoes, wondering if they were ruined. Great, that would be another outlay she didn't need.

As she reached the rear of the van, the base of her skull suddenly exploded with indescribable pain. Night transformed into brightest day, and she seemed to be staring directly into the noonday sun, but then the world spiralled into blackness and the floor rushed up to meet her.

The music in The Disciple's head was becoming louder again as he drove into Mitre Street from Creechurch Lane. He already knew the Blackmailer was a Libra, which meant he would soon be devouring kidney. At least she wasn't another Leo; he didn't think his stomach could cope with eating heart twice in one night.

He slowed on the approach to Mitre Square and pulled over against the kerb as soon as he cleared the junction. There was nothing behind him. Grinding the gears, he eventually found reverse and carefully backed the van into the square. The side mirrors were next to useless in the rain, and with all the condensation it was causing on his windows he was virtually driving blind. Moving at a crawl, he concentrated on keeping the van parallel to the school playground, aware that there was a row of bollards somewhere behind him that prevented vehicular access to St. James Passage.

Thunk.

The van jolted to an abrupt halt. He had found the bollards. He jumped out and ran around to the rear to check for damage. Luckily, he had only been doing about 5 MPH. Apart from a minor kink on the bumper, there was no harm done.

Back in the van, he studied his environment carefully. The cobbled square was relatively small, approximately seventy feet by eighty. Mitre Street was directly in front of him, at the top of the square. The left side of the square was taken up by the gates to Sir John Cass's Foundation Primary School. There was a line of office blocks behind him and another along the right side of the square. A narrow pedestrian alleyway called Mitre Passage was located at the bottom right of the square, and St. James Passage, a wider pedestrian alley, was located at the bottom left of the square, immediately behind the Sherpa.

"This is where I drop you off," he told the unconscious woman lying bound and gagged in the back of his van. "But before I go, we're going to have a little fun." He thought for a moment and then grinned. "Well, when I say 'we', I actually mean 'me'."

He had decided long ago that the three women who had ruined his life would be left in historically relevant locations; it seemed a fitting homage to the man who had successfully completed the same series of rituals one hundred and eleven years earlier.

He had left the Infector in Hanbury Street because that was where Jack the Ripper had killed Anne Chapman, and he would leave the Blackmailer in Mitre Square because that was the deposition site for Catherine Eddows, another of the original Ripper's five canonical killings.

He stared with reverence at a spot on the floor just beyond the walled flowerbed in the southeast corner of the square, which had a solitary park bench in front of it.

Squinting through the rain covered windscreen, The Disciple carefully scanned the offices off to his right, allowing his eyes to linger on the building in the southwest corner of the square, at the junction with Mitre Street. To his relief and delight, there were no signs of movement anywhere.

Pulling his coat tight around him, he ventured out into the rain a second time to check out the buildings behind the van, and the two alleys; first Mitre Passage and then St. James Passage. The buildings were in total darkness and both alleys were deserted. He paused before getting back in the van, in order to study the night sky above. The downpour was torrential, and it showed no sign of letting up. The rain was his friend; it was another omen that this was all meant to be.

Satisfied it was safe to continue, he ducked into the rear compartment and pulled the dividing curtain closed. After removing his coat, The Disciple donned a pair of surgical gloves in readiness for the impending operation. When that was done, he surveyed the woman lying hogtied before him with clinical objectivity.

The Blackmailer would have to die in the van, which meant that slitting her throat was out of the question; an arterial bleed would be far too messy, even with all the plastic sheeting.

Strangulation seemed the logical alternative.

The Disciple sat astride Rye and wrapped his fingers around her neck, carefully probing until he found her windpipe. "You thought you could get away with blackmailing me, you filthy scheming harlot," he hissed, spraying her face with spittle. "You were wrong, and now you're going to pay the price. Like Shylock, I want my pound of flesh." Taking a deep breath, he flexed his fingers and then began to squeeze with all his might. Almost instantly, he felt her body start to shudder and wriggle beneath him as her air supply was cut off.

She seemed to take forever to die, but eventually, the convulsions diminished into minor twitches, and then Rye's body went totally limp. After checking for a pulse, The Disciple slumped down next to her, staring at his shaking hands and gasping for breath. He hadn't realised that strangulation was such hard work. In future, he decided, he would stick to using his trusty knife.

After a few seconds rest, he stood up on wobbly legs and switched on the van's internal light. The Blackmailer lay on the plastic-coated floor, staring up at him accusingly from sightless eyes. "Back in a moment," he told her, turning the light off again. The Disciple stuck his head through the cabin divider and spent a few seconds scanning the streets again. When he was satisfied that it was safe for him to continue, he ducked back inside and reached for his bag of goodies. "Now, where was I?" he asked Rye's corpse. Reaching for his bag, he quickly set about arranging his surgical instruments in readiness for the nephrectomy, and then slipped on a plastic surgical apron, which was already heavily bloodstained from the earlier procedures he'd carried out at Hanbury Street.

Strangely, now that she was dead, he felt no desire to insert his Bowie into her vagina, the way he had with his previous two victims. That would be perverse, like necrophilia, and he wasn't into that.

As he'd done for each of his previous victims, The Disciple carefully recited the satanic scripture before extracting the relevant organ. This was the third time in as many days, and he was reaching the point where he could remember the words without referring to the parchment.

He sensed the menacing presence of the deity he was summoning growing stronger with each word uttered, and his chest began to swell with joy as the spiritual empowerment guaranteed by the sacrifice began to take effect. He made the sign of the horned hand, which represents Baphomet: The Goat of Mendes, to pledge his allegiance to Lucifer, extending the two outer fingers of his left hand to represent the horns, and folding the inner two fingers over the thumb to represent the goat's head and beard.

When the chanting concluded, the Disciple began the medical procedure by making a wide incision below Rye's rib cage and cutting through several layers of fat and muscle in order to expose the kidney. There was no attempt at finesse; he needed to get in and get out, as fast as he could. Then he severed the connections to the blood vessels, adrenal gland, and ureter. Reaching inside, he removed the dripping organ in one piece. In a living patient, such a procedure could take up to three hours; he had done it in a matter of minutes. The second kidney took even less time to extract.

Once the organs were safely stored, he turned his attention to her breasts, carrying out a total mastectomy on both. After all, such needless mutilation was what distinguished the Ripper's work from that of any other killer; it would be expected, and he didn't want to disappoint. Acting on impulse, he decided to add a few flourishes to his work that were relevant to the reason she had been chosen. What did they say? *Hear no evil, see no evil, and speak no evil.* The Blackmailer would still be alive if she had abided by that simple mantra; instead, when he had approached her for some discreet assistance in tracing the Infector, who had seemingly dropped off of the face of the earth after giving him a dose of the clap, she had decided to try her hand at blackmailing him, threatening to reveal all to his wife unless he agreed to her extortionate demands.

Respecting client confidentiality obviously wasn't a priority for her, and it gave him immense satisfaction to know that she had paid the ultimate price for abusing the trust he had placed in her.

When he was finished, he carried her mutilated corpse through the rain and dropped it unceremoniously on the flowerbed. "At least, as compost, you might actually serve a purpose," he said spitefully. The Disciple lingered over the body, debating whether to slit her throat. There hardly seemed any point now that she was dead, but on the other hand, he liked to be consistent where he could. In the end, he knelt down beside her head, drew the Finnish skinning knife from its scabbard, and set to work. "Goodbye, and good riddance," he whispered, turning the nearly severed head to rest on her left shoulder.

Climbing back in the van, he quickly removed the blood-drenched nitrile gloves and apron, and checked his appearance. Satisfied, he started the engine and drove off calmly. As Mitre Square receded in his wing mirror, he wondered how long it would be before the Blackmailer was found.

The Disciple drove along Commercial Road for a while and then cut through the back doubles towards the Highway. Fighting to keep his eyes open, he steered the van into an unlit car park at the back of one of the predominantly Bangladeshi estates in Shadwell. It was one of several suitable locations he had identified during the preceding weeks. He pulled up opposite a couple of burnt out wrecks and killed the engine. The Disciple climbed into the rear and sat down in the darkness with his back against the cabin divider. He was physically and emotionally spent, and he was struggling to think clearly. Each trembling limb seemed to weigh a ton. He closed his eyes and sat still for a few moments, using the deep breathing techniques he'd learned to clear his mind.

Before commencing the second part of the ritual – the consummation of the organ – he splashed some water over his face and then drank the rest greedily; tossing the bottle aside after it had been drained. He was careful to take his time reading the parchment, ensuring that every word of the incantation was recited word perfect. Then, and only then, he ate from the still warm kidney. When the rite was finally over, he staggered back into the cab, wiped his bloodstained mouth on his sleeve and turned the key in the ignition. It was almost time to rest, but first, he had an important delivery to make.

CHAPTER NINETEEN

The young reporter was laughing merrily. The source of her amusement was a sleazy snippet of gossip her colleague, Julie Payne, had just shared with her during the ride from their Fleet Street office to her luxury apartment at Canary Wharf. It concerned a mutual acquaintance at a rival newspaper, a man who went to great pains to portray himself as a womanising playboy; a man who had recently been caught doing something promiscuous in one of the print room toilets.

With another man!

The raunchy tale appealed to her gutter level sense of humour.

The pair had left the *Daily Echo* offices forty-five minutes earlier, having spent a gruelling day putting the final touches to a political story they had been working on over the last three weeks. They had met the deadline for tomorrow's edition by the skin of their teeth.

The story had started with an anonymous tip-off that implied a high-profile politician had accepted a lucrative bung to award a government contract when there had been better value bids from elsewhere. Through an unofficial contact at BT, the reporter, Terri Miller, easily identified the caller, who had been silly enough to use a mobile phone registered in her own name. Miller started scrutinising every aspect of Elizabeth Wilson's life under a microscope, and quickly discovered that she was the former secretary to a recently appointed Junior Minister who was considered something of a flyer by the party hierarchy.

Miller lost no time in confronting Wilson, who tearfully confessed to calling the Echo in a moment of jealous rage, hoping to damage her ex-lover's reputation by breaking a story he had tried so hard to keep buried. It was yet to be determined just how much truth there was in Wilson's claims, but with the woman now willing to put her name to the accusation it was printable.

The article would deeply embarrass the government when it was published tomorrow. The Prime Minister would have no option but launch an immediate inquiry; guilty or not, the Party would drop the Junior Minister like the hot potato he had become.

They made a brief stop at an all-night bagel shop, and Miller braved a short dash through the heavy rain to buy freshly baked doughnuts.

A few minutes later, Julie drew up as close to the plate glass doors of the private apartment building as the topography would allow. The reporter waved goodbye to her friend, thanking her for the lift. Then, holding the collar of her Burberry up to protect her from the worst of the rain, she sprinted a few yards across the tarmac, splashing through puddles the size of small lakes and cursing as cold water flooded into shoes that were designed for summer use only.

"Damn this weather," the reporter grumbled to herself as she reached the shelter of the overhead canopy.

Julie watched from the warmth of her car as Teresa Miller, illuminated by a flash of lightning, fumbled with her keys at the entrance. Like the friend she was, Julie waited until Terri was safely inside the foyer before driving off.

The reporter lived on the top floor of the twenty-story building. Her two-bedroom, two-bathroom flat, which overlooked the river, was a present from her industrialist father.

Brushing water from her hair, Terri crossed the lavish marble floor to a bank of elevators. She removed her coat and shook it out while she waited for the next elevator to arrive. Her stockinged feet squelched inside her shoes every time she shifted her weight.

She studied herself in the mirrored interior during the short ride up. Terri was thirty years old, a pretty brunette with large brown eyes. She felt that the main flaw in her appearance was a stubby little nose, which she'd always disliked, but which the men in her life seemed to find cute. Not that there were many of them at the moment. She just didn't have the time or the energy!

Turning side on, she decided that her figure was acceptable. She wished that her bust was a bit bigger, but at least she had nice legs and a flat tummy, the result of swimming to county standard during her youth. She tensed her cheeks and prodded her rump, then gave a satisfied smile at the lack of wobble.

Terri moved closer to the mirror, examining her red-rimmed eyes critically. Her face was zombie pale, but given the ridiculous number of hours she was putting in at the moment that was hardly surprising. Seventy-hour weeks had become a regular occurrence for her, but that was the only way to get ahead in the dog eat dog business she had chosen as a profession.

Terri came from a privileged background, but she was determined to succeed on her own merit, and not just coast through life because of her parent's wealth. The flat was her one concession to that rule, and it was the only indulgence she permitted herself.

The elevator door opened with a melodic 'ping', and she stepped out, turning left towards her apartment. The hall lights flickered briefly as a loud clap of thunder signalled that the storm was intensifying.

Terri's concentration was focused on selecting the right key for her apartment, so she didn't see the man coming the other way, running for the lift. They collided forcefully, and the impact spun her sideways, knocking her keys from her hand. She was too startled to say anything as the man ducked into the closing lift without looking back. "I'm fine, thank you," she shouted angrily as the doors closed and the elevator began its descent.

She'd only caught a glimpse of him; he'd worn a long trench coat with the collar turned up, concealing the lower half of his face, and a fedora style hat that was pulled down to eye level, Humphrey Bogart style.

Who was that rude pig? His absolute lack of manners was astounding. He might have been in a rush but he could still have shouted an apology.

She picked up her keys and began rubbing her bruised shoulder. Perhaps he was staying with one of the neighbours. She would make a few discreet enquiries later, when people who lived regular lives were up and about.

As Terri walked along the hall, her body aching for rest, and her shoulder just aching, she noticed something on the floor outside her apartment. It was a large hat box tied with string. There was a letter pinned to the top. "Now what on earth can you be?" she asked the parcel as she bent to retrieve it. She held it up for examination, studying it under the hall light. There was no writing on it.

Strange.

She shook it carefully, to see if it rattled.

Nothing.

She read the name on the envelope: Teresa Miller. It was definitely meant for her, no mistake about that. Balancing her bag of doughnuts on top of the hat box, Terri opened the door awkwardly and stepped inside. She pushed the door closed with the back of her heel and kicked off her wet shoes.

She headed straight for the kitchen and prepared a strong cup of coffee to wash the jam doughnuts down with. While the percolator warmed up, she drew the kitchen and living room blinds. Sheet lightning illuminated the night sky above her apartment, followed almost instantly by an almighty crash of thunder that caused the double-glazed patio to rattle. She realised that the centre of the storm must be directly overhead and hoped it would pass quickly; she hated weather like this.

Once the coffee was made, she returned to the living room and sat down, putting the mysterious box on the coffee table next to her armchair.

Opening the envelope, she read the enclosed note:

My dearest Teresa,

I hope you find my little present interesting.
There are some pretty pictures too. I'll be in touch soon.
Enjoy.
P.S. I know you must be wondering who I am. Well, my true identity must remain a mystery, but for ease of reference I've chosen the name, Jack. That's how I want to be referred to from now on.

Frowning, she read the weird note again. What was this? Was someone with a perverse sense of humour trying to freak her out as a post-Halloween wind-up, or had a mentally defective oddball taken to stalking her? And how had he got into the building without a passkey?

She should probably call the cops. But first, she wanted to see what he'd sent her.

Was it chocolates?

Clothing?

What?

Suppressing a yawn, Terri put the letter down and started fiddling with the knot in the string that was wrapped around the mysterious item. She removed the lid and looked inside. It contained a blue cool bag, the sort of thing people used to keep their lunch fresh in hot weather. She unzipped it, peered inside cautiously, and immediately turned her nose up. "What the hell?"

Meat!

Someone had sent her a bag of fresh meat. Did the creep work in a butcher's shop?

Typical!

Why couldn't it be jewellery or flowers?

Putting the cool bag down next to her chair, she looked in the bottom of the box. The note had said something about photographs. There were three, and each one was wrapped in cling-film, presumably to make sure they didn't get any meat juice on them. Grimacing, Terri reached inside and gingerly picked them up. She might as well have a look at them before throwing the whole lot in the bin. She sipped her coffee appreciatively as she raised the first Polaroid.

Her eyes widened in horror. "Sweet Jesus!" she gasped, spilling her drink. Was this someone's idea of a sick joke? She examined the next shot. It was as revolting as the first, unbelievably vile in fact, and they both appeared genuine, not faked.

Surely not!

Even if they were real, why would anyone send something like that to her? She wasn't a crime reporter. She looked on the back of the photographs. Two of them had names written in red paint – at least she hoped it was paint.

One said: Geraldine. The other read: Natasha. The third was of a house, which was boarded up and looked derelict.

There was no way of telling if the grotesque figures featured in these pictures were authentic.

Terri Miller almost jumped out of her skin as the telephone rang, shattering the silence of her flat. "Shit!" She raised a hand to her chest, experiencing palpitations.

As she crossed the room, her mind full of morbid thoughts, she wondered who the hell could be calling her at this time of night. Perhaps it was Julie, just to say she had arrived home safely. Terri's hands were shaking as she fumbled for the receiver; she couldn't take her eyes off the grisly party bag just across the room.

"Hello?"

"*Did you get my present?*" The voice was a haunting whisper, devoid of feeling.

A chill ran down Teri's spine. "Who is this? I think you've got the wrong number."

"*It's the right number. We both know that, Teresa. As for who I am, I told you, you can call me Jack.*"

"I don't know anyone called Jack." As she spoke her eyes flew to the note she had just received.

"*You do now, Teresa.*" The disembodied voice was too close for comfort, like he was calling from a mobile outside her front door.

Oh my God! Terri couldn't recall bolting the front door. Security had never been an issue before. Wait! She had kicked it shut because her hands were full, but she hadn't checked to see that it had closed properly. What if she had left it ajar and he was already inside the apartment...?

She leaned across her desk and tried to peer into the hallway, but the phone cord wouldn't stretch that far. She craned her neck until the muscles ached, but she still couldn't see.

Outside, the storm was easing off a little. There were a full thirty seconds between lightning and thunder.

She knew the sensible thing to do was hang up and call the police, but professional curiosity got the better of her. "What do you want?" Terri demanded, trying a little too hard to sound calm.

"*What does anybody want?*" the sinister voice mocked. "*I want what is rightfully mine, and you are going to help me get it,*"

Terri scoffed, but it was pure bravado. "How could I possibly help you?"

"*By doing your job. I've decided that you should have the privilege of telling my story.*"

"What makes you think I want to tell your story?"

"*Most reporters would cut off their arm to get an interview with the man who is going to purge Whitechapel. You should be flattered that I've chosen to give you the exclusive.*"

Terri shook her head. "Maybe I'm not as ambitious as you think," she told him.

"Look," he snapped. "*You can either report on my work or become my work. It doesn't really matter to me. It's your choice, your life.*"

Terri felt the hairs on her nape stand on end. "Why me?" she asked, trying to suppress a shudder. "There are hundreds of reporters out there, and a lot of them are far more established than I am."

"*I like your work. You're just starting out and you have something to prove. I can relate to that.*"

"What exactly do you expect *me* to do?" She asked, unable to prevent an edge of fear creeping into her voice.

"*Have you got a pen ready?*"

She looked around frantically, scrabbling through the papers strewn across her desk until she found one. "Y-Yes, go on." Hands trembling, she wrote down the address he gave her, reading it back to confirm it. "What's so important about this place?" she asked.

"*Why don't you check it out yourself,*" he taunted. "*Remember this: you have nothing to fear from me if you do exactly as I say. I will be reading your column with interest, and we will speak again...soon.*"

The connection was severed.

Terri held the phone to her ear for what seemed an age, listening to the dialling tone in disbelief. And then she remembered the door. "Shit!" she exclaimed, dropping the phone and sprinting back to the hallway.

To her horror, the door was ajar.

Terri slammed it shut and rammed both deadbolts into place, and then she looked through the security peephole at the top of the door. The wide-angle glass revealed that the corridor was clear. With a sigh of relief, she sagged back against the door, her legs turning to jelly now that she was safe. And then it occurred to her that the killer could already be inside her apartment, hiding in one of the rooms, waiting for her.

She knew the living room and kitchen were clear, but what about the bedrooms, bathrooms and utility room? All the internal doors were closed, but she couldn't remember if they had been that way when she came in. Terri ran into the kitchen and grabbed the biggest knife she could find in the knife rack. Her heart was beating like a trip hammer as she frantically searched the other rooms, checking behind doors, pulling open cupboards, looking under beds. They were all clear. That only left the small utility room that housed her washing machine, spin dryer, and ironing equipment. Terri wiped her palm on her leg, then took hold of the brass door handle in her left hand and twisted it gently. Holding the knife out in front of her, she took a deep breath and pushed the door inwards as forcefully as she could.

There was a loud bang as it connected with something inside, and then a figure lunged forward out of the darkness, knocking the knife from her grasp. Terri screamed as they went down together, limbs entangled. Screaming, she thrashed out trying to twist free of her attacker's grasp and scrabble away. "No, please, don't hurt me," she sobbed, convinced she was going to end up like one of the unfortunates in the photographs. And then, as she broke free, she saw the knife on the floor in front of her, and hope mushroomed in her chest. If she could just reach that, then maybe she had a chance.

She scrabbled forward on all fours, wrapped her fingers tightly around the handle of the huge carving knife and spun back to face her attacker. The ironing board lay half inside the utility room, half out in the hallway. The three-quarter length leather jacket that she had hung over it several days ago lay in between the ironing board and her legs, where she had kicked it moments earlier.

Terri slowly stood up, exhausted by her exertions and breathing like she had just run a marathon. Returning to the spacious living room, Terri began pacing nervously up and down, hugging herself tightly as she tried to fight back the tears. She was shivering, despite the apartment's expensive climate control system, which was pre-programmed to operate at body temperature all year round. Without warning, a wave of nausea hit hard. "Oh God," she exclaimed. Cupping her hands to her mouth, she ran for the toilet. Surely this was some sort of twisted prank, she thought as she buried her head in the bowl; it was the sort of thing one of those male chauvinist bastards at the office would come up with.

But if it wasn't, then what a story!

After gargling liberal amounts of mouthwash to rid her mouth of the aftertaste of vomit, Terri rushed back to the lounge and retrieved her mobile phone from her handbag. Unlocking the phone, she hit the speed dial for Julie's flat.

A sleepy voice answered halfway through the eighth ring. "*...Hello?*"

"Julie. It's me, Terri. Get over here, right now, as fast as you can. It's an emergency..."

"*Are you alright...?*" Julie asked, her voice thick with concern.

In her mind's eye, the reporter pictured her friend sitting up in bed, her stomach turning over.

"I'm fine – at least I think I am," Teri said, running an unsteady hand through her hair. "Just get here quickly. You won't believe the friggin' story that's just landed in my lap."

Hanging up, Terri stumbled over to the built-in wall bar beside the large patio doors. Her entire body was shaking. She glanced back at the cool bag, remembering with a shudder what it contained. Suppressing the urge to gag again, she put some ice in a glass and unscrewed a bottle of brandy. She knew she ought to phone the police but, if she did, they would stop her from going to the address 'Jack' had given her, and she had no intention of letting them do that. No, she would just have to think of a bloody good reason to delay the call for a couple of hours, and hope she didn't get in trouble for doing so. She'd run it by her editor. He was pretty resourceful when it came to managing legality issues like that. She'd have to move like lightning before anyone else got a sniff of her story. But before she did anything else, she needed a drink. A bloody large one!

Replacing the telephone, The Disciple stepped out of the kiosk and into the rain, which had finally started to ease up. The thunder sounded distant now, somewhere off to the north. He studied the apartment block, deep in thought. For several seconds he remained that way, a statue carved from granite.

Bumping into the reporter had really shaken him. He had assumed that everyone in the building would be fast asleep, so when the elevator doors slid open and he came face to face with the one person he wanted to avoid, the blood in his veins had frozen. Instead of doing the sensible thing and just walking calmly by, he had drastically overreacted and barged her out of the way. He regretted his action, but it was done now. At least he didn't have to worry about being recognised. Not only were his features heavily disguised, he'd had his collar turned up and his hat pulled down.

He dreaded to think what his reaction would have been if she'd stumbled across him while he was making the delivery a few moments earlier. Would he have tried to bluff his way past her? Would he have fled down the fire escape at the end of the landing? He fondled the hilt of the Finnish skinning knife concealed in the small of his back, knowing that in his jittery state there could only have been one outcome.

He wondered what it would be like to kill someone as rich as

Teresa Miller, to have her blood on his hands, literally. Perhaps one day he would indulge himself and find out.

Now there was a thought...

Walking the four blocks to the little cobbled road in which the tatty Sherpa was parked proved surprisingly pleasant. The fresh air helped clear his aching head, dispelling some of the fatigue that was threatening to engulf him.

He completed the return journey from the quayside to his secret sanctuary at a leisurely pace, enjoying the peace and tranquility of an early morning drive through empty roads. Within a few short hours, he reflected, they would be jammed solid as the rush hour commuters caused their usual chaos, clogging up the arteries of the Capital as they did every day.

He was confident that the reporter would feel compelled to follow the bait he had so tantalisingly dangled before her pretty nose. She wouldn't be able to help herself; it was in the blood.

Blood!

He couldn't stop himself from thinking about how happy the spilling of her blood would make him feel. She might put on a sophisticated act, behaving like a cosmopolitan lady of charm, but he wasn't fooled.

She was a whore.

They were all whores at heart. Every last one of them! Just because she didn't stand on street corners advertising the fact didn't stop her from being a slut. They all sold themselves if the price was right. "Sluts," he muttered, feeling a spark of anger ignite inside his chest. He took a deep breath and released it slowly, trying to calm himself down. The desire to kill again was bubbling just beneath the surface, and he knew he needed to rein in the bloodlust before it spiralled out of control. If he started killing randomly, he would make mistakes and they would catch him.

He had killed three women in as many days, and the mental and physical strain of performing such an incredible feat had left him totally shattered. His mind was fuzzy, but it would be much clearer once he had rested properly, and it would need to be for what lay ahead.

His mind drifted back to Teresa Miller, and the shocked indignation on the pompous cow's face as they collided. The urge to punish her was strong in him. Perhaps, after the reporter had served her purpose....

But there was plenty of time to plan for that, if he decided it was what he really wanted.

CHAPTER TWENTY

Wednesday 3rd November 1999.

It was coming up to seven-thirty a.m. when The Disciple finally left his lock-up. The back of the van was still heavily bloodstained from the surgical intervention he'd carried out on Rye, and it would need to be thoroughly cleansed, but he could attend to that later. He needed to eat and recharge his internal batteries first, before he was totally burned out.

He had carefully stored his newest 'souvenirs' in safe places. The degradable items had gone in the long, chest shaped freezer that rested inconspicuously against the back wall of the lock-up. He had purchased it several weeks ago from a second-hand shop in Barking. Although it had seen much better days, it was more than adequate for his needs.

The Infector and Blackmailer's underwear were deposited inside a duffle bag that rested on the work surface between the large mirror and his disguise props. It already contained the knickers he had kept as a trophy after slaying Tracey Phillips.

He placed the blood-soaked clothing, the surgical apron, and the rubber gloves he had worn earlier in the evening in a black, plastic bin liner. This, in turn, was deposited in a large metal dustbin for future disposal by burning. Watching *CSI* programmes on TV had taught him a lot about forensics. The only safe way to dispose of any clothing that had come into contact with your victim was to burn it, and burn it well.

Without the makeup, his appearance was entirely different. There was no way that anyone who might've seen him a few hours earlier would recognise him now, not even the poor wretches whose battered corpses he'd hacked and torn at in such uncontrolled frenzy.

As he walked the short distance to Bethnal Green tube he noticed a lone black woman waiting at a bus shelter some fifty yards ahead. As the gap between them closed he saw that she was late middle-aged and plump, with a plain, homely face; he could easily picture her bouncing her many grandchildren up and down on her knee, laughing, telling jokes and reading them Roald Dahl stories. He wondered where she was going, but then he spotted the dark blue cloth of a nurse's uniform protruding from the bottom of her tan duffle coat, which was done up to combat the early morning chill. Black tights and rubber-soled shoes completed the outfit. Ah, so that was it, she was waiting for a bus to take her to the Royal London.

Their eyes met as he drew level and she nodded a polite good morning. The Disciple smiled a weary acknowledgment as he visualised himself slitting her throat. He knew how good it would make him feel to watch her blood spurt high in the air, gushing out of a neatly severed artery.

He quickly dispelled the dangerously compelling desires these thoughts conjured up.

Discipline had to be maintained at all times or his cover would be blown. It was just like being an undercover spy in communist Russia. He would have made a good spy, he thought, trying not to glance back at the woman.

A strong breeze was already clearing the grey clouds from the sky and the coming day promised to be a vast improvement on the preceding one.

He looked up as a police car whizzed past at high speed. The siren soon faded, but the killer continued to watch until the blue lights became a small glow in the distance. He wondered where they were going. Was their call connected to his work? They were certainly heading in the right direction.

He stopped to buy a morning paper from the stall outside the tube station. The wizened old proprietor was a real East End 'geezer', full of Cockney rhyming slang and dropped aitches.

Folding the Red Top under his arm, The Disciple walked the short distance to his favourite café. He ordered coffee and a fry up, and then took a seat by the window, where he could watch the world go by as he ate. Flicking through the newspaper while he waited for his food to arrive, the killer immediately spotted the name on the paper's lead story: Teresa Miller.

He smiled in satisfaction.

He had chosen well.

Standing alone, Tyler surveyed the body in silence. If Hell was the afterlife version of a jail sentence, he hoped the needless mutilation of this cadaver would guarantee that the perpetrator, a creature Jack envisaged as something less than human to start with, and all the more dangerous because of it, spent all of eternity in Prison Hades.

Like most detectives, or cops in general for that matter, he liked things to be clear-cut: cause and effect equals end result. Unfortunately, things rarely seemed to work out that way, at least not in real life.

In any homicide, it helped to know what motivated a person to commit such an extreme crime. Love, hate, greed, revenge, and jealousy; at least one of these factors usually appeared in the matrix.

It was equally true that, on the odd occasion, there was no discernible motive; the murder had occurred simply because the pressure of a particular situation, or of life in general, had proved too much, causing the killer to snap without warning.

He'd known from day one that this killer was different from any other he'd dealt with before; he'd said as much to Tony Dillon. No matter how hard he tried, he still found it impossible to fathom the evil behind these atrocities.

The woman lying before him had been senselessly murdered, her corpse unforgivably mutilated. A teenage boy had discovered her while cutting through St. James Passage on his morning paper round; it was an experience that would scar the poor sod for a long time to come.

As Tyler looked down at the lifeless husk on the flowerbed, he felt his anger rise like bile. There were those who argued that there were no evil people in the world, just individuals who were incredibly sick; Jack knew differently. This killer's actions went way beyond sick. They were acts of unspeakable evil, carried out by a dark force inhabiting a flesh-coated shell that was cleverly disguised to appear human.

The killing had occurred within City of London jurisdiction and, technically, this was their investigation. However, after lengthy discussions at the highest level, it had been agreed that it made sense for the Met to take primacy as this was part of an ongoing series they were already dealing with.

The forensic team was standing by to enter the crime scene, ready to begin the lengthy process of crime analysis. As usual, they had been instructed to wait until they were given a green light from the SIO. Sam Calvin, the Crime Scene Manager, had just arrived and was in the process of unloading his van.

Tyler asked for a few moments alone with the victim, so that he could study the scene without interruption. The deceased looked to be in her mid to late thirties at a guess. From the way she was dressed, Tyler doubted that she was a prostitute. Had the killer mistaken her for one? She was lying flat on her back, her right leg bent at a forty-five-degree angle, her left one straight. The full lips of her open mouth were already blue where cyanosis had set in.

"Poor cow," he said softly.

The woman's throat had been cut open in a similar fashion to Tracey Phillips, leaving a frightful wound that gaped open like a second hungry mouth. There was no evidence of an arterial bleed, so either she had been killed elsewhere and then dumped here or the incision had been inflicted post-mortem. Jack suspected the latter, and if that were the case it was a deviation from the previous attack. Both eyes had been removed, and her nose had been sliced off – her ears, too.

The second murder had been totally unexpected, and it had thrown a massive spanner in the works. Everyone had Winston pegged for the murder of Tracey Phillips, but he was in the hospital under armed guard and couldn't possibly have killed this woman. The implications were both obvious and catastrophic: Winston had an unbreakable alibi for the second murder, which effectively cleared him of the first. Not only were they back to square one, the fact that they had got it so wrong would leave the hindsight police, those pious bastards who earned a living out of criticising other people's honest mistakes, rubbing their hands with glee. The pressure to find the killer would now be magnified by a factor of ten, and if progress wasn't made pretty damn fast, heads would start to roll. Tyler pinched the bridge of his nose, reeling as his world threatened to spiral out of control.

When he felt able to focus again, Jack forced himself to concentrate on the victim's clothing, which had been soaked through by a combination of blood and rain. Her coat, a Burberry if he wasn't mistaken, was undone. Her dress had been sliced open from the neckline down to the hem, exposing her entire body, which had been hacked open in much the same fashion as the dress.

For some strange reason, the killer had modestly arranged the top sections of the dress to cover the woman's breasts. In contrast, the bottom had been deliberately peeled back to ensure her genitalia was fully exposed. As with Tracey, there was no sign of her underwear, and this woman definitely did not strike him as the type to go native.

In another deviation from the first killing, there was no obvious sign of genital mutilation.

Dillon appeared behind him, placing a large hand on his shoulder to get his attention.

"Sam Calvin's ready to start, Jack," he said quietly, gazing down at the lifeless form on the floor.

"Good. Bring him over please, Dill." Tyler spoke flatly, without taking his eyes from the body.

When Calvin arrived, he wasn't alone. "Jack, this is Dr Andrew Mackintosh. He's the same FME who attended the last one."

"Pleased to meet you," Mackintosh said formally. There was a hint of sadness in his eyes and Tyler was warmed by the man's obvious humanity.

"You're the unfortunate man in charge of this dreadful case, I take it?" the doctor asked softly.

Jack offered his rubber-gloved hand. "DCI Tyler, but please, call me Jack."

"Andrew Mackintosh. Most people call me Mack."

Tyler indicated the figure sprawled on the floor in front of them.

"I understand that you examined the girl in Quaker Street, Mack. I think this is the work of the same killer. Unfortunately, I can't get a pathologist down to examine her, so I could really do with a leg up. Anything you can give me would help."

The doctor nodded sombrely, understanding Tyler's needs all too well. "I'll do what I can, Jack, but don't expect too much at this stage," he warned.

The examination was thorough. Jack was impressed by Mackintosh's methodical approach. He stated his findings as he worked, seemingly unperturbed by their presence. "Tremendous force was used to cut the throat. The backbone is visible and the windpipe has been severed completely. I'm reluctant to commit myself without the benefit of an autopsy, as I'm sure you can appreciate...."

"But...?" Tyler encouraged.

"But I'm fairly confident this was done post-mortem. Even accounting for all the overnight rain, there is just too little blood."

"Any theory on why he would slit her throat after she was already dead?" Jack asked Calvin. He was desperate to understand what made this killer tick. Calvin shook his head in disgust. "There's no rational reason for it, not that I would expect this nutter to be well acquainted with rationality."

"You can see that the eyes are missing, gouged out as opposed to being surgically removed," Mackintosh, said continuing his examination, "whereas, her nose and ears have been cleanly sliced off." The FME paused as if struck by a sudden thought. "I wonder," he said, gently easing the victim's mouth open and peering inside. "Well, well, well," he declared.

"What?" Jack asked.

"The tongue has been cut out – or at least the front part of it."

"What made you think for to check that," Tyler asked, impressed.

Mackintosh gave a sad shrug. "I suddenly thought of the old adage: hear no evil; see no evil; speak no evil," he replied.

"And the nose?" Calvin asked.

"I don't know," Mackintosh said. "Smell no evil, maybe?"

Jack shook his head. "More like don't stick your nose where it's not wanted," he said, wondering if the facial carnage was the killer's way of sending them a cryptic message.

Mackintosh started probing the torso; his hands unnaturally pale in white rubber gloves.

"My God," Tyler gasped as the doctor peeled aside the top sections of the blood-drenched dress. Both breasts had been neatly sliced off. This was yet another disturbing deviation. Was the killer becoming more daring, the attacks more deranged as he grew in confidence? Was he experiencing a need to make each episode progressively more intense just to maintain the same thrill level?

Mackintosh said nothing as he stared up at the two policemen. The injuries spoke for themselves. There was no sign of the eyes, nose, tongue or the breasts in the immediate vicinity of the body. Dillon slipped away to organise an urgent search, making sure that it was done discreetly.

"The torso has been opened up from just below the ribs in a single, fairly neat cut, but until the pathologist has a poke around inside, we won't know how much internal damage has been caused."

"Do you think it was done here, Mack?" Jack asked.

The doctor gave the matter serious consideration. He looked around thoughtfully, taking his time before replying. "Very, very unlikely, I would say. He would have needed time to do all of this. A minimum of fifteen to twenty minutes, I reckon."

Jack let out a low whistle. The rain would have driven most people off the streets, but even so, Jack couldn't imagine the killer spending that much time in the open.

"But there are no lividity markings, Mack, so he must have moved her straight after she was killed."

"I agree, which probably means he killed her nearby and then brought her here in a vehicle," the doctor said.

The rain was a damned nuisance. They would be lucky to find any trace evidence from last night. It was another stroke of luck for the killer. So far, things were definitely going his way.

Hopefully, there would be CCTV covering the route into this place. If they could identify the killer's vehicle it would even the odds a little. Jack looked around the square. There were several wall-mounted cameras, but they all seemed to be pointing inwards, along the building line.

"One more thing that I feel I should mention," Mackintosh said reluctantly. He removed the gloves as he stood.

"Go on," Tyler said, eying him pensively.

"The cuts I've seen today strike me as anything but random, and I think your killer might have some sort of medical background. In fact, I wouldn't be surprised if the PM reveals he's been harvesting organs. Was anything missing from the last one?"

Jack shook his head. "No, not unless you count a section of her intestine, but we put that down to the fact that the killer had shredded her abdomen and rearranged her innards to taunt us. Tell me, Mack, did you suspect that the killer had medical knowledge when you examined the Phillips girl?" Jack asked.

The doctor hesitated a moment and then nodded. "I had my suspicions, but I wasn't sure, and as a professional, I only deal in solid facts."

"Well, between you and me, the pathologist shares your view that the killer has, at the very least, some rudimentary medical knowledge" Tyler confided. "But that's not public knowledge, and I would appreciate you keeping it to yourself for the time being."

"Don't worry; you can rely on my discretion, Jack. I won't mention this to anyone else," Mackintosh promised.

As the car pulled up in Hanbury Street, Julie turned to her friend with a look of trepidation.

"Look, Terri, I've been thinking. Maybe we shouldn't do this. Let's just call the police and let them handle it. It's what they get paid for. We'll still get the exclusive. What do you say, um?"

Teresa Miller rolled her eyes. If the truth were known, she wasn't too sure about this either. But they had talked it over in great detail before coming to their decision – a joint decision, democratically reached. If Julie was going to bottle out, then she should have done so back at the apartment, before Terri had called the city news desk to speak to their editor.

"Christ, Julie! It was hard enough persuading Deakin to let us run with this story in the first place," Terri said harshly. "Don't you dare let me down."

Julie's bottom lip began to quiver.

Terri closed her eyes and let out a long sigh. "I'm sorry, Jules," she, said, taking her friend's hand. Her voice was softer, kinder. "I know I act like I'm tough, but trust me, underneath I'm as scared as you. Look, we'll just make sure that we're not being taken for a ride by some joker who gets his kicks by scaring the shit out of dumb female reporters. If it's not a hoax we'll go straight to the cops. If the girls in those photos are already dead, then another few minutes won't hurt, will they?" she reasoned.

"I guess not," Julie agreed, although she sounded far from convinced. Her earlier resolve to go through with this was rapidly waning now that they were actually here. Still, she had to admit, Terri's suggestion made sense. And she had come to trust Terri implicitly.

As the two women got out of the car, Julie instinctively checked the settings on her digital camera. Like Terri, she was trying her hardest to establish herself in Fleet Street circles. Her aim was to obtain a permanent photographic post with one of the papers, but so far, the best she had managed was freelance status. There were plenty of freelancers on the circuit, and the competition was fierce, which meant she only worked on a part-time basis. She supplemented her spasmodic income by doing portrait photography at a local studio during the week, and by shooting occasional weddings.

Terri looked at the address she'd written in her notepad, and then started checking house numbers.

"What will we do if someone's still in there?" Julie fretted. "Or if it's all locked up?" The whole thing had seemed so incredibly adventurous back at the apartment, the intrepid reporter and her trusty photographer, fearlessly going into the unknown in search of a great story. Now that they had reached their destination, she was having second thoughts. Hell, she was having third, fourth and fifth thoughts as well. "I'm not trying to put obstacles in the way, Terri," Julie whined, "but what if the killer's luring us into a trap? We could end up like the poor bitches in those bloody Polaroids." She was unable to suppress a small but noticeable shudder.

"What was that for?" Terri demanded.

Julie sifted her feet uncomfortably. "I'm scared."

"Oh, don't be so silly," Terri said dismissively. "If he wanted me dead, he would've waited outside my apartment door and jumped me as soon as I got home. Why would he bother going to all this trouble?"

"Maybe he wanted to get us both together."

"Listen, Jules. On the phone, he gave me an address and said I should check it out. He told me it would be empty and the door would be open. If the house we want isn't both of those things we know that the caller is a crank and we can forget all about it. If he's right, then we call the police without being made to look like complete fools. Now, are you coming with me or do I go alone?" Terri stared hard at her friend, waiting impatiently for a reply.

"But we don't even know what we're looking for," Julie pointed out.

"He said there would be a message in clear view. He said we couldn't miss it."

"I must be mad!" Julie said unhappily. Nonetheless, she linked her arm through Terri's and started walking.

Typically, the house they were looking for turned out to be right down the other end of the street, nestled amongst half a dozen equally dilapidated buildings that were waiting to be demolished. Terri pulled out the Polaroid and compared the image to the derelict building standing in front of them. There could be no doubts, this was the place.

She raised an eyebrow at her photographer. "Why couldn't you have parked down this end of the street?"

"I was following your directions," Julie replied defensively.

"Excuses, excuses."

"But I –"

Terri held a hand out to silence her friend. "Julie, I'm just pulling your leg," she said, smiling kindly.

"Oh."

"Just trying to lighten the atmosphere," Terri explained, realising her attempt at humour had backfired.

"Ah."

The terraced house looked dark and foreboding, like something out of a sixties horror film. The street door and all the windows facing the street were boarded up. The wood appeared old, as if it had been there some time. The local yobs had decorated the lower panels with graffiti. Terri noticed there was a passageway between two of the houses, several doors along to their left. She nudged Julie's arm. "Look, there's a side entrance. Let's check around the back first," she whispered,

"Do we have to?" Julie asked, nervously.

"Yes, we bloody well do," Teri snapped. "C'mon, and make sure your camera's ready." She grabbed hold of the photographer's arm, dragging the reluctant woman after her.

They tiptoed through the dank passageway, ready to turn and run at the slightest sign of danger. Terri didn't really know what she was hoping to achieve by doing this. Perhaps, she admitted, she was just trying to prolong the inevitable moment when they tried the front door.

There was hardly any fencing left at the rear, so they had a clear view into the back yards of several houses on either side of them. They were all pretty much identical: small, overgrown with weeds, a coal bunker at the far end and several steps leading up to the house's rear door. A black cat sat on the bunker nearest them, eyeing them suspiciously. Julie pressed closer to Terri. "It's spooky back here," she whispered.

"Will you be quiet?" Terri scolded. She was trying to concentrate, and it was hard enough without having to endure stupid interruptions.

"Okay, you win," she eventually conceded, realising there was nothing to be gained by staying there. "Let's go back to the front."

Julie was more than happy to oblige, and a few seconds later they found themselves back outside the front door of the abandoned house.

"Oh well, I think we've put it off for as long as we can," Terri said, as much to herself as to Julie. Taking a deep breath, she approached the door, steeling herself for whatever might come. From a distance, the door had appeared quite secure, but as they reached it Terri realised that it was slightly ajar. There were fresh indentations in the frame. Had the mysterious Jack forced it open during the night? A padlock and clasp had been discarded in the nearby gutter, which tended to suggest that he had.

Terri's heart was pounding as she reached up to push the door. The hinges were stiff, and they creaked loudly, as though in pain.

"Hello...." Terri called meekly.

No response.

Clearing her throat, she tried again, louder this time. "Hello. Is anyone in here?" The words echoed back at her and then there was silence.

The two women exchanged worried looks. "Let's call the police," Julie suggested, and she tried to pull Terri away from the door.

Terri wrenched her arm free. "We're going in," she said firmly. Before Julie could argue the point further, she took a step into the darkened hall, dragging her friend with her. As soon as Terri let go of the door it swung shut, trapping them in stygian darkness.

The air inside was foul.

Julie whimpered.

Terri hushed her, feeling along the wall for a light switch. When she finally found one, it didn't work. She cursed in silence. "Can you hear that?" the reporter asked as something deep inside the house started clanking. "What is it?"

"I don't know," Julie said, her voice quivering. "But whatever it is, I wish it would stop."

"Wait there," Terri said as she edged forward nervously, following the line of the wall towards the rear of the house. There had to be a light somewhere. The floorboards groaned and creaked with every step she took.

Something scuttled across the floor in the dark, something fast.

"Terri, where are you?" Julie called from beside the door; she was becoming more stressed with every miserable second they spent in the house.

"I'm over here," Terri snapped, irritably.

"I can't see you."

"I'm looking for a light switch." Teri was beginning to think that Julie had been right: they should never have entered this dreadful place.

Just then, Julie had a moment of inspiration. "Wait a minute, I've got a pencil torch in my camera bag," she said, excitedly.

"Now she tells me," Terri mumbled, angrily. She could hear Julie fumbling in her bag, but she seemed to be having trouble. "What's happening?" she demanded.

"It's caught in my camera strap and I can't get it free," Julie explained in a fluster.

"Bring it over here," Terri snapped. Did she have to do everything herself?

"Okay," Julie said, clearly not enthralled by the prospect. "Hang on, I'm coming over." She moved into the interior, an arm outstretched to probe the blackness. "I think I've untangled it," the photographer said, fighting her way through the darkness. As she pulled the torch free, her right foot collided with something heavy that had been left on the floor. She tripped, and her forward momentum sent her tumbling to the ground, where she landed with a thud.

"Julie! Julie, are you okay? Speak to me!" Terri called out in alarm. She envisioned all sorts of terrible things happening in the dark.

"I'm alright, Terri. I just tripped over something in the dark." Julie sounded embarrassed but unharmed.

"Stay there and turn the torch on," Terri instructed.

Julie realised that she had landed in something wet. She rubbed her fingers together. Yuck! They were sticky. "What the hell...?" Sitting up, Julie turned the torch on, shining it over her palm.

It was red.

Julie directed the flashlight beam across the hall floor to find the object that had tripped her. What she saw would haunt her for the rest of her life. At first, she simply couldn't take it in.

Staring in wild-eyed shock from her blood-covered hand to the dead body beside her, Julie began to scream, and scream and scream.

CHAPTER TWENTY-ONE

Jack Tyler had just started briefing the photographer when his mobile rang.

"Excuse me," he said, undoing the paper suit and reaching into his jacket for the phone. The photographer nodded understandingly and began to snap away. Tyler glanced down at his unfinished case notes, grimacing. They would have to wait, too. He answered the phone with an impatient sigh. "Hello…"

"*Sir, DC Murray speaking –*"

Tyler blinked as the photographer's flash caught him off guard. "Who?"

"*DC Kevin Murray, sir, from Mr Quinlan's team.*"

"Oh, right. What is it, Kevin? I'm busy."

"*I'm in the incident room, boss. Thought you'd want to know straight away, there's been another one.*"

"Yes, I know. I'm already at the scene," Tyler said, impatiently.

"*No! I mean there's been another one on top of that!*"

"What?"

Tyler's features darkened as he listened to Murray's update; by the end of the call, he was in a dangerously foul mood.

Damn reporters!

He stormed out of the inner cordon and stripped off his protective oversuit. He looked around in anger, quickly locating the four people he needed. Firstly, he dragged Charlie White away from the conversation he was having with the HAT crew who had responded to the initial call-out, and handed control of the scene over to him, giving the surprised Scotsman the quickest briefing he had ever delivered. Then he set off to find the others.

Nick Bartholomew was leaning against the side of a squad car when he spotted Tyler striding towards him. The look on the boss's face was thunderous. "Sir?" he said pensively, hoping it wasn't his fault that Tyler was so pissed.

"How far is Hanbury Street from here, Nick?" Jack asked.

"Not far, sir. I know the way if –"

"Good. Come with me," Tyler said, and headed towards one of the Vauxhall Astra pool cars.

"Someone's in for it," Bartholomew observed as he moved into Tyler's slipstream.

Tyler made a small detour to where Dillon and Flowers were quizzing the uniforms who had been first to arrive on scene. "That'll have to wait," he said. "I need your help, so hop to it."

Kelly hastily took contact numbers from the bemused uniformed officers and told them she would be in touch before the end of their shift. "What's the matter with the boss?" she asked Dillon once they were alone.

"We'll find out soon enough," Dillon said, wondering the same thing.

As soon as they were all inside the car it sped off, the diesel engine clunking like the ditch pig it was. Bartholomew sat in front, navigating.

"Where's the fire, guys?" Dillon asked casually.

Bartholomew stayed silent.

"Another girl's been found dead in Hanbury Street," Jack explained, gripping the wheel harder as his anger fermented. "That's where we're going now. Kevin Murray just phoned me. Some prat of a reporter called Terry Miller found the body. He works for that new rag, *The London Echo*, and he's been withholding this information since 5 a.m."

"I don't follow, sir," Kelly said.

"At five a.m. this morning this twat, Miller, received a phone call from the killer, telling him where to find the body."

"Do what?" Dillon exclaimed, sitting forward.

"Oh yeah, and not only does the fuck-wit withhold the information, he swans off down to the scene to check it out for himself." Tyler shook his head incredulously. The more he thought about the dumb antics of the reporter, the more wound up he became.

Dillon said, "You're saying the killer phoned this reporter up and told him about the murder over two and a half hours ago?"

"That's the way Murray tells it, Dill."

"Surely, no reporter would be that stupid?" Bartholomew ventured.

"Don't you believe it," Kelly said with the cynicism of one who knows better.

"If this idiot reporter's had the scene to himself for a couple of hours, Nick, I dread to think what damage he's done," Tyler said.

"The whole thing could be contaminated beyond salvage," Dillon pointed out.

"I'll charge the bastard for obstruction if he's done that, Dill. I'll throw the bloody book at him," Tyler promised through gritted teeth.

Hanbury Street runs in an east to west zigzagging direction off Commercial Street. Nick directed Jack via Brick Lane, so when they reached the junction with Hanbury Street they encountered two huge 'no entry' signs. "I thought you knew this area?" Jack growled. He switched the headlights on and drove on, ignoring the signs.

"Sorry, boss, I forgot it was a one-way street," Nick said. He sounded crestfallen. Driving the RT car, with blue lights and siren on, he wouldn't have hesitated to take this route if it was necessary, but going through a no entry sign in an unmarked Astra, with no flashing lights or audible warning system, was extremely risky.

"Don't worry, mate," Dillon said, checking his seat belt worked. "We're only going one way."

Jack drove straight past Truman Brewery without giving it a second glance. Before the large building had been erected in 1970, a row of houses had occupied the site, including number twenty-nine Hanbury Street, where Annie Chapman's body had been left by Jack the Ripper in September 1888.

The Astra pulled up outside the derelict house a few moments later. An RT car, roof light still flashing, had already arrived. The driver was talking to two women, one of whom had a camera hanging from her neck. Both women looked badly shaken. The RT operator was standing grim-faced by the door, making sure that no one entered without permission.

"Like shutting the door after the horse has bolted," Dillon whispered to Kelly as they got out.

Jack showed his warrant card and introduced himself. He excused the uniform constable, making it clear he wanted to speak to the women alone. "I'm looking for a reporter named Terry Miller. Do you know where I can find him?" he said after dispensing with the formalities.

The women looked at each other uncomfortably. "I'm Terri Miller," The taller of the two said. She noted the look of surprise that flashed across Tyler's face and realised he had been expecting a man. "It's short for Teresa," she explained, getting the feeling that this stern-faced man wasn't impressed with what he saw.

Although he tried not to let it show, Jack found himself momentarily thrown off track. He had assumed he would be dealing with a cynical, hard-nosed, male reporter. The two women in front of him appeared anything but. He glanced at the one with the camera. She was dabbing her eyes with a handkerchief. Both looked as white as a sheet. "Where's the body?" he asked, fighting to keep the anger from his voice.

Terri indicated the house with a forlorn nod of her head. "In there. It's in the hall, by the stairs."

"Wait there," he said, pointedly. They regrouped at the rear of the Vauxhall. Jack broke open a new evidence bag and handed them each the customary paper suits, overshoes, latex gloves and white Victoria masks.

Once suited and booted, they entered the house in single file. Despite the trepidation he felt, Dillon took the lead, using a powerful Dragon Light Nick had purloined from the RT car to illuminate their path. Tyler and Bartholomew followed behind. Kelly remained at the door, keeping a watchful eye on the two women. One of the uniformed officers was writing up a scene log, the other began unrolling tape to instigate a cordon.

The rancid smell hit them as soon as they entered the hall; it was overpowering in the confined space. "Jesus!" Dillon exclaimed, his stomach turning. He had expected the cloying smell of death to be present, but it was the acrid stench of vomit that had stopped him in his tracks.

Jack pulled up the face mask, trying to filter out the worst of it. Bartholomew hurriedly produced a small jar of Tiger-Balm, which he frantically unscrewed while he held his breath. With a latex-coated index finger, he inserted a liberal amount into each nostril, and then passed it forward to the others.

The ground floor of the dilapidated old house was a mini disaster zone, with broken and missing floorboards everywhere. The body, which was hardly recognisable as human, was slumped in a heap at the side of a staircase that looked like it was about to disintegrate. Under the harsh light of the torch, it looked more like a tailor's dummy then a person.

Predictably, the unknown victim's throat had been cut. The nearly severed head sagged at an unnatural angle, resting in a large pool of semi-clotted blood. The woman's tongue protruded from her slack mouth.

"Shine the light directly on her head, Dill," Jack instructed.

Dillon nodded, and the beam settled on the dead woman's head. He forced himself to look, hoping it wouldn't make him feel giddy. The forehead had been partially caved in as a result of severe blunt force trauma.

"Jesus, talk about overkill," Bartholomew said from behind.

An eye was missing. Was that down to the killer, or had the resident rodents treated themselves to a midnight feast? And if it was the killer, why had he only taken the one eye? At Mitre Square, he had removed them both.

The woman had been laid open from sternum to pubic bone. The skin of her abdomen was folded back and she had been systematically disembowelled. The killer had tucked both of her hands up inside the empty stomach cavity. Was this a sinister ritual or merely a depraved private joke on the killer's part? A small bundle of intestines had been scooped out and placed on the left shoulder like a string of sausages. The detectives were mystified as to the significance of that. The pelvic region of her body had also been cut out. As with Tracey Phillips, it was obvious that something sharp had been violently inserted into her vagina.

As Dillon's shaking hand scythed the torch beam through the darkness, they saw there was blood everywhere. The body and the surrounding floorboards were covered in it. The arterial spray saturated the lower walls and the staircase. Two sets of red footprints could be seen, leaving a trail from the corpse to the door, and it looked as though someone had been rolling around in the blood.

There were several pools of vomit in the hallway, one of which covered the dead girl's feet. Jack wondered which of the two inept women waiting outside had thrown up.

"I bet it was the soppy tart with the camera," Dillon growled, as if reading his partner's mind. Jack didn't bother replying. He was too busy trying to work out if the body had been disturbed as a result of Miller's intrusion. He could just imagine them groping around in the dark, not giving a toss about the crime scene.

Moving cautiously, they entered the main living room. As Dillon shone the light across the walls, he saw the message. It was written in bold red letters and the blood had run in several places. It said:

The blood of whores will continue to flow freely in Whitechapel until I am appeased.
Jack the New Ripper.

"Another message," Jack said, stating the obvious. "This time he's signed off as 'Jack the New Ripper'. I wonder if he actually thinks he's a descendant of Jack the Ripper, or maybe even his reincarnation."

"He's taunting us, Jack. That's what he's doing," Dillon said quietly, his voice thick with frustration.

"I know. But our turn will come, despite the interference from those two prats outside. Let's not mention any of this to them, okay."

"You got it, guv," Bartholomew said quietly.

Dillon just grunted. He was beginning to feel very queasy, surrounded by so much blood and gore. It was almost enough to make him consider becoming a vegetarian.

"I don't know if it's relevant or not, guv, but the first message he left, the one in Quaker Street, was all written in capital letters. Well, look at this one. It's a mixture of caps and small letters," Bartholomew pointed out. Jack studied the message again, wondering why he hadn't spotted the difference.

"You're right, Nick. Well spotted! Mind you, until we get it photographed, and the two messages are compared by a handwriting specialist, we won't know whether or not the deviation in styles helps us any."

As they turned to leave the increasingly oppressive room, the torchlight flickered across a rickety table in the far corner, making its shadow dance up the side of the wall like a distorted phantom. Dillon noticed dark shapes on its surface, and he made a reluctant detour to check them out. "Oh my God, Jack. You'd better take a look at this." Neatly arranged on the dust-covered table were what remained of the girl's internal organs, which had been carefully removed from the now empty carcass.

As Jack edged forward for a closer inspection, a large brown, oily shape shot out from beneath the table, disappearing into the shadows by the hall door. All three men recoiled at the sudden movement and Tyler took an instinctive step backward, bumping into Dillon's arm. "Shit! I hate those damn things."

Dillon shone the dragon light back and forth, up and down, until he was satisfied that the room was clear of rodents. When he finally let it settle on the organs again, he saw that one – was that a heart? – had at least two big lumps missing from it.

"I think it's been partially eaten," Tyler said, struggling to keep his voice even. The culprit was presumably the rat that had just fled.

"We need to get the crime scene guys in here, pronto," Dillon said. "While there's still something left of the victim to preserve."

Bartholomew felt something drip on his face. He placed his hand on Dillon's arm, guiding the beam of light towards the ceiling. "Now what...?" Dillon demanded, and Jack could hear the unease in his voice. Bartholomew pointed upwards. He couldn't bring himself to speak.

Above their heads, the remainder of the dead girl's intestines had been wrapped around the empty light socket in the ceiling, draped across the room like make-do Christmas decorations, and then fastened to the boarded-up window.

"I've never seen anything like this," Bartholomew muttered, sickened by the rooms organised carnage. This was the work of a demon, not a man.

"None of us have," Tyler informed him, his voice brittle.

They returned to the street and the luxury of fresh air. Other members of the squad were already arriving, having been dispatched from the incident room by Murray.

Copeland headed straight over to Dillon, carrying a decision log. "I thought you might be in need of one of these," he said, waving the log in the air.

"What? Oh, thanks." Dillon said, relieving him of the decision log. He was tempted to tell George that what he was really in need of was a double brandy.

"You alright, boss? You look like you've seen a ghost," Copeland was surprised; he couldn't imagine too many things upsetting Dillon.

"Fine, George, fine. The smell in there is a little overpowering, that's all," Dillon explained, blowing the tiger-balm from his nose.

Copeland nodded his understanding. As an advanced exhibits officer, he knew all about bad smells. "The forensic team has been called out, and the FME will be here within the hour. What do you want me to do first?"

"Make sure that uniform lad's doing the scene log properly, please, George. Usual routine: record the details of everyone going in or out of the crime scene, along with times and reasons. Get him to show me, Nick and the DCI as going in fifteen minutes ago and coming out now." He checked his watch to confirm the exact times.

"Oh, and there are a couple of civvies who went in before our arrival. Make sure he's got their details. Also, we need to arrange enough lighting for several rooms as a matter of urgency and to make sure we have enough evidence bags and glass jars for a lot of exhibits. Oh yeah, we'll need a fucking great big net as well."

"Net?" Copeland sounded perplexed. "What do we need a big net for?"

"To catch the oversized rats that are dining on our victim, George," he said patting Copeland's arm.

"You're joking!" Copeland exclaimed, his jaw dropping.

"You'll see for yourself in a minute. Someone's going to have to stand guard in there, and who better than our best exhibits officer? Oh, and George, take my advice and tuck your trousers into your socks; it'll stop them running up your leg." He winked at Copeland who was looking rather pale.

Just then Dillon caught sight of Bartholomew. "Are you feeling okay, me old mate? You know, after going in there?" He studied Bartholomew's face carefully.

"Yeah, I'm okay," Bartholomew said in a shaky voice. "But if it's all the same to you, I don't want to go back in."

"Don't worry. You've done your bit. But I do need you to start the initial door-to-door enquiries. And tell the locals to set up a second cordon thirty yards back from the first one. That should be enough to protect the scene." As he spoke a couple of Panda cars pulled up, providing some much-needed additional resources.

"No problems, boss. Leave it to me. Just let me know what the DCI says to those poxy reporters, will you?" Nick said, breaking into a weak grin,

"Count on it." Dillon patted him on the arm and made his way back to Tyler.

"I've got the ball rolling here, Jack. And George has brought you a present." He handed the carbonated decision log to Tyler.

"Oh, great," Tyler said, "as if I haven't got enough paperwork already."

"Now, what are we going to do about these two, so called, journalists?" Dillon demanded.

Tyler smiled spitefully. "I think it's time we taught them both a lesson," he suggested, unzipping his white paper suit.

Kelly had moved the two 'newsies' out of the inner cordon. The three women were standing beside an old shape red Volkswagen Golf, which was parked a few doors down from the murder scene. Steve Bull was with them. "Morning," he said, nodding solemnly.

Tyler nodded back, curtly. "Stevie."

Dillon patted the smaller man's shoulder. "Nice to see that you're in a better mood today," he whispered.

"Did you find it?" Terri asked uneasily. She was careful to avert her gaze from Tyler's piercing stare.

"Yes, Miss Miller, we found 'it'."

"Please, call me Terri. This is Julie. I'm sorr –"

"Miss Miller," Jack cut in harshly, "which one of you threw up in there?" He scrutinised each one in turn, impatiently awaiting a reply.

"I – I'm afraid it was me," Julie began. "It's very embarrassing but I...."

"Have either of you moved the body at all?" Tyler continued.

"Not exactly," Terri said, evasively.

"What do you mean: 'not exactly'?" Dillon demanded.

"It's my fault. I'm sorry. I couldn't see in the dark and I...well, I kind of kicked the head when I tripped and..." Julie Payne bit her lip as tears welled up in her eyes.

"Bloody hell," Dillon muttered under his breath. The two women were like a female version of Abbott and Costello; they couldn't do anything right.

Terri put a protective arm around Julie as the photographer began to cry again.

Jack rolled his eyes and looked up to the heavens, wondering if, in some unknown way, he had offended God and was now being punished for it. He rubbed at the stubble on his chin, feeling the tiny bristles tickle the palm of his hand. "I need to know which one of you rolled around in the victim's blood." When neither one answered immediately, he continued: "Let me guess. That would also be you, Miss...?" he raised an accusing eyebrow at Julie.

"P – Payne. Julie Payne." Her voice, as she bowed her head in shame, was barely audible.

"Hah!" Dillon barked mirthlessly. "Payne by name: *pain* in the arse by nature!"

Tyler shot him a warning look.

"Really!" Terri protested. "I don't think that's very nice, Inspector." If no one else was going to stand up for Julie then she would. After all, it was because of her that Julie was there.

"Your trouble is that you just don't think," Dillon told her. Terri opened her mouth to argue but closed it again, realising that she was in a no-win situation. Instead, she crossed her arms in furious defiance.

"Miss Payne, can you remove your coat so that I can examine your clothing, please," Tyler asked. He spoke gently to avoid distressing her further. He was beginning to realise that Julie had been coerced into taking part in this foolish episode, probably against her better judgement. With Kelly's help, Julie struggled out of the three-quarter-length leather coat she had donned shortly after fleeing the house. Terri had insisted that she put it on to keep warm, knowing it would help battle the shock that was setting in.

The detectives immediately saw that her jeans and sweatshirt were saturated with blood. Dillon gave a derisive sigh and shook his head in exasperation. These two had pretty much destroyed his crime scene.

"We're going to have to ask you both to come back to the station. We'll need to take your clothing and then fingerprint and swab you. We'll also want detailed statements," Tyler stated as calmly as he could under the circumstances.

"What!" Terri exclaimed. "Can't we do that later? I've got a deadline to meet. Surely it can wait a little while?" She had an exclusive to file, and this was so...inconvenient.

"Miss Miller, you can either come back as a witness, under your own steam, or as a prisoner on charges of obstruction and perverting the course of justice. It's entirely your choice." Tyler's tone made it clear this wasn't a subject that was up for discussion.

"You wouldn't dare," Terri said defiantly.

Tyler's eyes hooded. "Try me."

"I'm coming," Julie said, emphasising her surrender by raising both bloodstained hands in a melodramatic fashion. Terri gave her a traitorous look, at the same time calculating whether Tyler really would detain her if she refused to go of her own accord.

"Miss Miller?" Jack enquired, testily.

Terri realised it was time to put up or shut up. "Aw, shit!" For a woman whose private education had cost her parents a considerable sum of money, she capitulated most ungraciously.

CHAPTER TWENTY-TWO

The two women were conveyed to Whitechapel police station in separate vehicles. Their escorts were under strict instructions not to speak to them, and the journey was completed in an uncomfortable silence, which did little to improve Terri Miller's mood.

When they arrived, they were photographed in their clothing, which was then seized, and they were fingerprinted and swabbed for DNA. Then they were placed in separate interview rooms and left to stew for another three-quarters of an hour. They were not offered refreshments. Nor were they given an indication as to how long they would be required. Whenever they asked what was going on, which in Miller's case was about every five minutes, they were given the same answer: "I'm sorry miss, but DCI Tyler is very busy right now. Someone will be along to see you in due course."

By the time Dillon and Evans arrived to take her statement, Terri was feeling utterly deflated. This, of course, was precisely what the detectives had intended. She told them about the mysterious man in her building, the meat-filled box he'd left outside her apartment, her shock at discovering the snapshots and how she had thought the whole thing was probably a hoax.

Terri played down her scheme to check out the house before

involving the police. She claimed she was motivated by a desire to prevent the emergency services from having their time wasted, not a selfish craving to get a story at any cost. Dillon noticed she couldn't meet their eye when she said that. Her narration ended with the arrival of the first patrol car and the murder squad officers themselves.

At one point, about halfway through recording her statement, Dillon abruptly stood up and walked out of the interview room, his square jaw set tightly. Miller, who was halfway through a sentence at the time, had no idea why he had left so suddenly. She assumed that he needed to communicate urgently with one of his colleagues. She thought that Dillon's conduct was extremely rude, but based on her limited experience of the man she concluded it was probably typical of him.

In truth, Dillon had left because he was on the verge of losing his temper with her, and that would have been highly unprofessional, especially as the interview was being taped.

He returned to the sparsely furnished room five minutes later, having regained his composure. He offered no explanation for his absence and continued the interrogation expertly.

In a nearby room, Bull and Flowers were conducting a similar interview with Julie Payne. She was faring much better than Terri, having been less antagonistic at the scene. During the interview she spoke candidly, holding nothing back. It soon became apparent that she had been an unwilling accomplice. At the end of the interview, Steve arranged for the locals to drop her off in Hanbury Street so that she could collect her car. She promised to contact them if anything new came to light.

By the time they pulled up outside the apartment block where Terri lived, the cool bag had been sitting in her living room for over six hours.

"Nice place, I suppose, but not my cup of tea," Flowers said, addressing Miller's reflection in the rearview mirror.

"Couldn't afford it anyway, kiddo, not on what they pay us," Paul Evans said as he opened his door.

In the back, Miller was smarting about her replacement clothing: an ill-fitting, all-in-one paper suit and cheap black plimsolls that were two sizes too big. She looked like an escaped convict. "I'll sue you if anyone sees me looking like this," she threatened the back of Flowers' head as the detective switched the engine off.

The rear child locks were on so Evans had to open the rear door to let Miller out. "There you go, Miss Miller," he said.

Terri slid out of the Astra in silence. She prayed the concierge would be busy in his little office and the foyer would be deserted. She would simply die of embarrassment if anyone she knew saw her looking like that. As she reached the halfway point between the car and the foyer, a black Porsche 911 convertible, its engine purring, glided to a halt next to the Astra. Cursing under her breath she raised her hand up to shield her face and increased the length of her step. "Hey Teresa, *nice threads!*" the driver shouted, studying her strange attire with amusement.

Tears of anger pricked Miller's eyes, and she thought she would simply die of shame. "I told you we should have used the back entrance," she complained, keeping her head bowed. "This is *so* embarrassing." Walking as briskly as she could without making her discomfort too obvious, Terri ignored the Porsche driver and focused on reaching the entrance.

Kelly glanced back inquisitively. The man sitting behind the wheel of the sports car was in his late twenties and deeply tanned. Not a single gelled hair was out of place. He wore an expensive blue silk shirt with matching red tie and braces. A thick gold bracelet dangled from his wrist as he waved at the reporter. "Cute," she said approvingly.

"What? Him?" Paul Evans asked, surprised.

"No, silly, the car," Kelly corrected him with an impish grin. Compared to the five-year-old Renault that she owned, the Porsche was positively sex on wheels. As for the driver, well she had her heart fixed on a real man; not some jumped up yuppie. She would leave that sort to the Terri Millers of this world.

"Do you know that bloke in the car then, Miss Miller?" Evans asked as he caught up with Terri. She ignored the question. "Look, he's waving at you. Don't you think you ought to wave back?" he persisted.

"Oh, shut up!" Terri snapped at him. She had never been so humiliated in all her life. As they reached the communal entrance Evans dropped back a tad, falling into step with his colleague.

"She doesn't seem particularly happy, does she?" he whispered to Kelly.

Kelly raised a finger to her lips and made a shushing sound. "We don't want to upset her ladyship, do we?"

"I heard that," Terri shouted without looking back. "And don't think I don't know that you're enjoying this."

"Hello, Mrs Phillips. This is Detective Chief Inspector Jack Tyler. I'm the officer in charge of the investigation into your daughter's murder." He wondered if he still would be, come the end of the day. The way things were going, it was far from being a certainty. "I'm sorry to trouble you, but there's been a development that I think you should know about."

This was the first time they had spoken, and Jack wasn't looking forward to the impending conversation. In fact, he was dreading it. After all, what could you possibly say to someone who had lost a loved one in the most brutal of circumstances? 'I'd like to offer my sincere condolences for your loss,' seemed woefully inadequate. For him, talking to the recently bereaved was one of the most difficult aspects of his job. Compared to that, a week in the witness box, being grilled by even the most ruthless and aggressive of defence barristers, seemed like a walk in the park.

Kelly had developed a good relationship with Rita, and had been keeping the elderly lady up to date on the investigation's progress, but it wouldn't be right for Rita Phillips to hear this particular piece of news from anyone else but the SIO.

Jack had just finished reading the background statement Kelly had taken from Mrs Phillips. Its content had saddened him. He noted, wryly, that everything about this case seemed to either sadden or enrage him. It probably wasn't the healthiest range of feelings to be flitting between.

He couldn't help thinking about the poor little girl who had been so cruelly orphaned. She was as much a victim as Tracey, if not more so, and now she would grow up deprived of a mother's love and guidance, never knowing that special bond that exists between parent and child. Jack, who had been blessed with two wonderful parents, grieved for her.

The inquest was due to open at the local Coroners Court the following morning, and Rita Phillips wanted to attend. Unfortunately, she was under the illusion that her daughter's murderer had been caught. That was his fault. When they'd nabbed Winston, Jack had authorised Kelly, in her role as Family Liaison Officer, to inform Mrs Phillips that they were confident they had the person responsible for her daughter's death in custody. He now realised that the disclosure had been a little premature, and he should have waited until charges were brought. He had meant well, of course, but he should have known better. In his haste to ease the old woman's pain, he had ignored the lingering doubts he had. Now he would have to pay the price for making such a stupid balls-up.

"Mrs Phillips, I wanted to tell you this before it hits the news," he began awkwardly. There was no easy way to say it. "The killer has struck again. There's been another murder. In fact, there have been two. It means the man we have in custody can't possibly be the person who murdered Tracey. I'm so sorry." Jack rubbed his eyes, trying to massage away the pain that was starting to develop behind them.

Silence.

He listened to her shallow breathing over the telephone, awaiting a response. His apology had sounded painfully inadequate, even to him.

"*I see,*" she eventually managed, her voice choked with despair. The swift capture of the man Rita believed responsible for Tracey's death had partially eased the searing pain she felt inside. While it wouldn't bring Tracey back, it would prevent anyone else from suffering like she had, and it would ensure that the killer was punished for his hideous crime. If the murderer escaped, it would make a mockery of British justice and everything that she and her late husband had believed in all their lives.

"Mrs Phillips, please don't give up hope," he implored her. "We are doing all we can, I promise you."

"*I know you are, Mr Tyler. It's just...it's just so hard.*" He could tell from the timbre of her voice that she was close to tears. The TV was loud in the background, a children's programme if he wasn't mistaken. He wondered if the little girl was sitting there with Rita, listening to her Granny, not really understanding what was going on but instinctively knowing that something was wrong. He imagined how agonisingly hard it must be for Rita Phillips, holding a difficult and painful conversation like this with him, and then having to pretend that everything was fine, for the little girl's sake. He prayed that neither he nor anyone he loved would ever have to go through anything remotely similar to what Rita and April were suffering right now.

"Look, Mrs Phillips, I'll arrange for DC Flowers to pick you up from home tomorrow at nine a.m. I'll be at Court myself. This is only a preliminary hearing, and it won't take long. We can sit down together and talk properly afterwards."

"*That's very kind of you, but it's no trouble to get the bus,*" she insisted. Rita was determined not to become a burden.

Tyler had dealt with so many spongers over the years, people who expected to be waited on, hand and foot. But Rita Phillips didn't fit into that category; she had pride. She was a fiercely independent woman, determined to stand on her own two feet. "Mrs Phillips – Rita – it's not a bother. Besides, you're an important witness to us and we don't want you being hounded by the press." He hoped that explanation would satisfy her. In truth, it was most unlikely that she would ever be called as a witness, or that the press would harass her.

"*Oh, I see,*" Rita said, and her voice softened. "*Well, in that case, I'd be most grateful for a lift.*"

"Good. I'll arrange it with Kelly Flowers and I'll see you in the morning."

After the call, Jack leaned back, hoisted his feet onto his desk and crossed his ankles. Folding his hands across his stomach, he let out a long sigh and swore profusely. The conversation had left him feeling extremely maudlin. It was a good thing that he ran a 'dry' office. If there had been a bottle of Jack Daniels sitting in his bottom drawer, he doubted he would have been able to resist a shot or two.

They needed a break, something to crack the case wide open, but lady luck just wasn't smiling down on them. It seemed as though they'd been working this case for months instead of days. With two live crime scenes on the go, every member of his team, plus all the other officers who had been drafted in to support them, was stretched to the limit. Even his OM and Receiver were out pounding the pavement today.

Jack glanced at his watch. It was four o'clock, already. The day was flying by. Tyler had personally spoken to the Coroner's Officer at the mortuary to clear the way for the two urgent special post mortems. The one on the girl from Mitre Square would be done first thing tomorrow, which meant he should get the preliminary report by early afternoon.

The SPM from the Hanbury Street murder would be carried out tomorrow afternoon, which meant he would have the prelim on her by mid-evening. Dillon had visibly paled when Jack delivered the bad news that he would have to attend two SPMs tomorrow.

Jack Tyler's style was to lead from the front, and he detested the tedious administrative responsibilities that came with the job. They were never ending, hung around his neck like a lead weight, and constantly restricted his freedom. After updating his decision log, Tyler wearily emerged from his office, walked along the corridor to the MIR, and placed copies of his latest log entries in the 'In' tray for Operation Crawley, the randomly generated name that Tracey's murder had been assigned. He smiled at Julia, the office temptress, on his way out.

"Would you like me to make you a cup of coffee?" Julia called after him.

"That's very kind, as long as it's no trouble."

"You can trouble me anytime," Julia purred.

―――

By the time the Scene Examiner arrived at Terri Miller's flat she had changed into some clothes of her own and was feeling slightly more human.

The Examiner was a quiet, introvert man in his middle thirties. He had an unkempt bush of curly brown hair that fell just below his collar and he wore metal-rimmed glasses, which contained enormous bottle-neck lenses that made his brown eyes seem much bigger than they really were. He introduced himself as Andy Baxter.

Baxter, who reminded Terri of your archetypal boffin, got straight down to business. He switched on the little iPod Nano that was clipped to his belt and started dusting the smooth surfaces of the apartment with fine white powder. He worked methodically, starting with the hallway and working back towards the living room. From his incessant humming, they quickly deduced that Baxter was an opera fan. When they asked what he was listening to, he shyly explained that he had a soft spot for the classic piano operas penned by the late German composer, Wagner.

"I hope he's more talented at scene examination then he is at humming opera," Kelly remarked, trying to lighten the atmosphere a little.

"Look, what exactly is the purpose of all this?" Terri demanded, wondering who was going to have to clear up the mess.

"You told us that, apart from you, Julie's the only person who's been in your flat recently. Is that right?" Evans enquired.

Terri nodded. "Yes. Sad but true. I've been so involved with my work that I've hardly been here at all, and I haven't had anyone over for dinner in −"

"The point is," Kelly interrupted, not the slightest bit interested in Miller's social life, "if we find prints belonging to anyone else, there's a good chance that they were left by the killer."

The colour drained from Terri's face, and she started looking around, trying to work out if anything had been disturbed. "You don't really think that...that *monster's* been in here, do you?" The idea that anyone − especially a bloodthirsty maniac − had been snooping around her apartment − going through her most intimate and private possessions − made her feel violated in some obscene way.

"Calm down, Miss Miller," Paul Evans soothed, "I've examined the locks and there are no signs of tampering, so I honestly don't think it's likely. But we have to check everything out, just to be sure."

Kelly moved over to the telephone, deep in thought. "Miss Miller, have you received any more phone calls, any at all since the killer spoke to you earlier?"

Terri checked the answer machine. There were no messages and no one had called before she and Julie left this morning. And she had used her mobile to speak to her editor. "No. And, please, call me Terri." The reporter smiled in a way that implied she wanted hostilities to cease.

Kelly nodded, smiling back. She had big reservations about Miller, but she had promised Paul she would try to keep an open mind. She picked up the telephone and dialled '1471'. "Right, let's see if our mystery man has left us a clue, shall we?"

"If he has, Kelly, it'll be because he doesn't mind us having it. This swine doesn't make many mistakes," Evans said quietly.

The electronic voice at the other end of the line repeated the eleven digits belonging to the last telephone number to call Terri, stating that the call had been made at five-fifteen that morning. "Thank goodness for British Telecom's call back service," Kelly said as she scribbled down the number on a pad by the phone. "We'll run a check on that when we get back," she told Terri, pocketing the piece of paper.

The cool bag and its wrappings were to be taken for immediate forensic and medical tests, but there was no doubt in anyone's mind that the flesh packed inside it was human. The Polaroids and their accompanying letter were placed straight into separate evidence bags; they, too, would be forensically examined back at the lab.

Baxter did a quick visual comparison between the prints he had found in the flat and the elimination prints Terri and Julie had provided before leaving the station. "Sorry, guys, we'll double check the results at the Yard, but I'm confident the only prints I've found match the two sets of elimination prints you've shown me." Baxter said this with utter conviction. He seemed disappointed that nothing more sinister had come to light during his examination.

"The place hasn't been wiped over, either. The dust patterns are equal and undisturbed, so I don't think anyone's been in and tried to hide the fact afterwards. No, I think you can safely say the place is clean." Baxter began to put his brushes and powder away, his job finished. After carefully collecting the cool bag he departed for the police forensic laboratory in Lambeth.

Evans opened the patio door and walked out onto the spacious balcony. He took a few moments to savour the splendid view it afforded of the river Thames, watching in fascination as a small tug made its way along the river, battling valiantly against the strong current. He could see the silhouette of the pilot in the tiny wheelhouse and a figure swaying on deck as the vessel pitched and rolled in the swell.

The temperature was starting to drop quite noticeably now that the sun was going down, but in contradiction to the abysmal conditions of yesterday it had been a pleasant autumnal day; cold, crisp and sunny. English weather was so temperamental, he reflected, just like his wife.

Terri Miller appeared beside him. "I've put some coffee on," she said.

"We don't want to cause you any bother."

"It's no bother."

"Well, in that case, I take mine white with two sugars," Evans said, gratefully.

On her way back in, Terri lingered at the doorway, giving him the impression that she had something on her mind. Evans raised an enquiring eyebrow, inviting her to speak if she wanted to.

"Look, I'm really sorry for all the trouble I've caused," Terri told him, and he thought he detected a trace of embarrassment, perhaps even a hint of remorse, in her voice. "For what it's worth, Julie was against it from the start. I guess I just got carried away with the idea of getting an exclusive story and acted irresponsibly." Terri was only just beginning to understand how rashly she had behaved; how selfish and insensitive she must appear.

Evans studied her intently. Was this genuine repentance? She certainly seemed sincere, but experience had taught him to be wary. Still, on the off chance that Terri's reparations were real, he would cut her some slack. "It's alright, love," he said, "we all mess up from time to time."

"Thank you, Paul. I don't think your Mr Tyler would be so forgiving, though. And as for that brutish Dillon character, I think he would have happily strung me up to be tarred and feathered!" She winced at the recollection of her interview with Dillon.

"They're good men, Terri. Admittedly, Mr Dillon is a little rough around the edges, but not everyone can be as silky smooth as me."

Miller grinned. "And you're so modest with it."

Evans chuckled, pleased that the ice between them had melted a little. The Welshman had a gift for making people around him relax. It was one of the first things Kelly had noticed when she joined the team.

Miller looked down at her feet. "So, what happens now? If Jack ... if the killer calls again?"

"We've got some technical people coming over soon," Evans explained. "They're going to rig up a recording device to your phone. Hopefully, we'll be able to trace any new calls that the killer makes. Kelly and I will wait here with you until the electrical wizards are finished."

"That's all very well in principle, but what if he calls from a phone box? Bugging my phone won't help you unless you can trace him to an address and arrest him." Terri didn't warm to the idea of having her calls monitored; it was a civil liberties infringement.

Evans smiled sympathetically. He understood her reluctance; he wouldn't want his private calls being recorded either. "Ah, Terri, love, we're not bugging the phone. We won't be able to listen in 'live time' to any calls. All we're doing is recording them for evidential purposes. It'll help us massively when the case comes to court."

"You've got to catch him first," she pointed out.

"We'll get him in the end, we always do, and the recordings will be played at trial. That sort of thing is dynamite in court."

Terri dry washed her face. "I'm not sure I can do it, Paul," she confided in a brittle voice that made her sound vulnerable. "I've seen what he can do, and I've never been so terrified in all my life. To think that he knows where I live, that he's been right outside my bloody door..." She shuddered and instinctively hugged herself. "The truth is I just want to run away and hide. The last thing I want to do is talk to him again."

"Terri, love, we need you to stay and help," Evans said. "You're the best chance that we've got to snare him."

"Would it be cowardly of me to say no?" Terri asked. All of a sudden, she seemed as naïve and defenceless as Paul's six-year-old daughter. "Jules has said I can move in with her for a while. You know, until this all blows over." Terri felt wretched for saying this, but her nerves were shot.

"No, not cowardly…"

"But not helpful either?" Terri was aware that she must seem very weak in Evans' eyes, and she hated herself for it.

"No," he admitted. "Not helpful."

Terri's ethos was that she had a solemn duty to discover the truth, no matter how deeply buried it was or how big a personal risk was involved, and to make sure that it was published for all to see. She dearly wanted to be the people's champion; noble, courageous and fearless in the face of adversity. She knew she had just been presented with a golden opportunity to prove she possessed the courage of her convictions – except that, when it came down to it, she wasn't really sure that she did. As much as it shamed her to admit it, she felt like a frightened little girl who was way out of her depth.

Under the circumstances, Terri just didn't know what to do for the best. If only she could seek her parent's counsel, but that was impossible. Her overly sensitive mother would be completely freaked out by something like this, and her father was a pretentious snob. The patronising multi-millionaire would just say something disparaging. He wouldn't understand that helping the police was the right thing – the decent thing – to do. Terri had long since rejected his exclusive circle of privilege and wealth, preferring to make her own path through life, even if it was an uphill struggle; and to make her own mistakes, even if the outcome was sometimes painful.

Evans sensed the inner turmoil the dilemma was causing, and he decided to give her some space. He leaned over the railings and checked on the progress of the little tug he had noticed earlier.

"I'm not sure about this, Paul. I really don't want to get involved," she said a few moments later.

With a sigh he walked over to Terri Miller, staring into her eyes with genuine concern. "I understand how you feel, and I won't pressure you into doing anything against your will. If you decide to stay and help us it has to be because you want to. If you want to move out, then that's fine, too. But you need to understand one thing: whether you like it or not, you already are involved, because the killer wants you involved, and that's got nothing to do with the police. If you chose to stay here you could be instrumental in helping us to catch a very dangerous man. As you said yourself, you've seen what he's capable of. We'll take every precaution that we can. A panic button will be rigged up from your bedroom to the local police station. If you press it at any time a message will cut into the local radio system and officers will attend at once, treating it as a high priority call. The door is solid, well hung and fitted with secure double locks and deadbolts. He's not going to get in there very easily, no matter what he tries." Evans paused, placing a tentative hand on each shoulder as he played his final card. "And it would make a hell of a story. I know you wouldn't be able to print everything you knew until it was over, but when the dust settles you would have a pretty awesome tale to tell. Hey, you could even write a book about it." That got her attention, he noticed. "Someone will, you know," he predicted, "even if you don't."

For several moments they stood there in silence, each one deep in thought. Terri anxiously chewed on her bottom lip as she contemplated her future, a nervous habit she'd had since childhood. She could feel Evans eyes on her as he waited patiently for her reply.

"Okay," she finally said. "I guess I could try and persuade Julie to move in with me for a week or so. We could look after each other while we give your plan a try." In her heart, she knew that she had to face her fear, no matter how daunting it might seem, or live in shame for the rest of her life. Her mind was made up, for better or for worse, and with the decision came a sense of relief. Terri tried to muster a smile for Evans, but she couldn't quite manage it.

"I'll get us that coffee," she said, trying to sound positive. As she went back inside, Kelly stepped onto the balcony, her shoulder length hair blowing gently in the morning breeze. "Nice view," she said, looking down.

"Uh-huh."

"So, will she do it?" Kelly enquired.

"Yes," Evans replied, softly.

"She's braver than I am," Kelly admitted, surprised that Terri had agreed to go along with the plan. She had anticipated that they would have to resort to strong-arm tactics to get her to play ball.

"I just hope we don't let her down if it all goes pear-shaped," Paul said.

The conversation was interrupted by the sound of the doorbell.

"That'll be the Technical Support Unit to plumb up the phone," Kelly said.

"I'll get it," Paul volunteered. "I think Terri's preoccupied."

"What a clusterfuck!" Holland raged. "When I went to bed last night, I was under the happy illusion that the murderer had been caught and the killing spree we were all so worried about had been prevented. It appears..." he paused and stared pointedly at Jack, who was standing uncomfortably before him. "...that I was somewhat misinformed." Holland was sitting behind his desk at Arbour Square, looking very agitated. His jacket was draped across the back of his chair, the top button of his shirt was undone and his tie was at half-mast. The clock on the wall told Tyler it was eight p.m.

"I'm sorry, sir," Jack said, not because he was but because he thought an apology was expected.

"Can you imagine my angst when I received a call this morning, informing me that another killing had occurred overnight, this time within City of London jurisdiction?"

Jack said nothing. What could he say?

"At first, I thought they were mistaken, especially when they said the victim didn't appear to be a prostitute, but as they talked me through the injuries my heart sank. The MO was identical; this had to be the work of the same fiend who murdered Tracey Phillips."

Tyler nodded, understandingly. He recalled feeling exactly the same way when he received an identical call at the crack of dawn.

"How could we have been so wrong?" Holland asked. He signalled that it was okay for Tyler to take a seat.

"Everything pointed to Winston," Jack said, sitting down wearily. "We were right to go with that."

"Maybe," Holland allowed, staring at Tyler with something akin to pity. "I'm sorry I gave this case to you, Jack," he said. "It was meant to challenge you, prepare you for bigger things further down the line, but I fear it has become something of a poisoned chalice. Now it's too late to remove you from harm's way, so you need to understand that neither of us will survive the fallout unless we get the right result."

Tyler shook his head defiantly. "I don't give a toss about my reputation, or my future promotion prospects. All I care about is catching the killer. And, if things go bad, I won't drag you down with me."

Holland smiled at Tyler's naïveté. "The game isn't played that way, Jack."

Jack's stomach tightened. "I know." Qualities such as honesty, integrity, and a hard work ethic were all well and good, but they wouldn't be enough to save either of them if media or political pressure forced the Yard to look for scapegoats further down the line. "Perhaps we should look at damage limitation," Tyler suggested.

Holland chuckled mirthlessly. "That boat sailed the moment the media cottoned on to the fact that there's a serial killer's running amok in Whitechapel."

"Hopefully, the press interest will blow over," Jack said, but his words sounded hollow, even to him. The New Ripper killings – the press was already calling them that – had received saturation TV coverage throughout the day, and he would be amazed if they didn't headline tomorrow's tabloids. The investigation been formally ramped up to Category A status.

Holland thumped his desk in anger. "No, it won't, Jack. We've had three murders in a week and, unless we catch the deranged psycho responsible, there are likely to be more in the near future."

"I appreciate that," Tyler said tetchily, "but we're doing our best."

"That's what every loser claims," Holland snapped. "We need to do more than just try our best. We need to get a result, and we need to get it bloody soon."

"Then I'd better get back to work and get you your bloody result," Tyler said, standing up.

"Not so fast, Jack. You and I have meetings to attend together tomorrow, and I need to go through a few things with you to make sure we're singing from the same song sheet." Holland pointed to the vacated seat, and Jack obediently returned, feeling very much like a schoolboy who had just been given detention.

"But I've got to attend the inquest for Tracey Phillips at Poplar tomorrow morning," Jack protested, hoping that would get him out of whatever Holland had planned.

"Send Dillon."

Jack shook his head. "I can't. He's already tied up with the post-mortems for today's victims."

Holland took a moment to digest this. "Okay, but the inquest will be a formality. The verdict will be unlawful killing by persons unknown. You could send Steve Bull."

Jack held firm. "I've promised to meet Rita Phillips, Tracey's mother. I can't let her down." Holland looked annoyed. "Very well, what time does the inquest start?"

"Ten o'clock."

"Not a problem, then. You'll be finished by midday, so that shouldn't interfere with our schedule," Holland said.

"Oh good," Tyler said, forcing a smile. "And what is our schedule, if you don't mind me asking?"

Holland explained that a Gold Group meeting had been arranged for one o'clock at Whitechapel. "That should last an hour or so," he said, "leaving us plenty of time to get up to the Yard for the 4 p.m. press briefing."

Jack left the room feeling angry and disheartened. As SIO, he had to have a finger in every pie, and at the moment it felt as though he was running out of fingers. He was constantly playing catch up, and every time he gained a little ground another obstacle would appear in his path, slowing him down again. He accepted that tomorrow morning had to be written off for the inquest, but at least that was a constructive use of his time, unlike the wasted afternoon he would now have to spend kowtowing to people he didn't give a hoot about. The burden of leading an investigation of this magnitude weighed heavily on him as he walked back to his office, leaving him feeling as though he was swimming against the tide; being pulled under relentlessly by an endless sea of bureaucracy, its treacherous currents running strong and deep.

CHAPTER TWENTY-THREE

Thursday 4TH November 1999

Although there was a distinct chill in the air, the sun shone brightly in a cloudless blue sky as Jack Tyler walked out of the District Line tube station in Bow Road.

The weather forecasters had predicted that today would be the finest day of the week, and it was looking as though they might be right for a change.

He made a quick stop in order to purchase a copy of the *Echo* from the small kiosk next to the station. Sure enough, Terri Miller's story was plastered all over the front page. He would read the article later. Tucking the newspaper under his arm, Jack dragged himself across the main road and trudged wearily up the steps into Bow police station. He showed his warrant card to the officer on the front desk and was shown through to the canteen where he had arranged to meet Tim Barton.

Barton was already there, finishing off a fried breakfast. "Morning, guv," he said, shovelling a fork full of bacon and egg into his mouth.

Jack ordered tea and toast and slumped down next to him. "Is everything ready?"

"All good to go," Barton said between chewing. "I've been on since six o'clock this morning, sorting out the paperwork for the inquest."

"Good."

After last night's tumultuous meeting with Holland, Tyler had stormed back to his office. Quietly seething, he slammed the door and immersed himself in a pile of statements and forensic reports that needed his attention, hoping to find something significant buried amongst the mundane. After three hours of fruitless digging, he finally gave up and called it a night. By then he was too tired to drive home, so he booked into a local budget hotel, took a long shower and then fell into bed. Sleep had been difficult, and when it finally came it was very fragmented. He awoke looking and feeling like one of the living dead.

They left Bow police station thirty minutes later. Tim's pool car was parked in the side road next to the station, MPS logbook prominently displayed on the dash to prevent the overly enthusiastic Traffic Wardens who patrolled the area issuing a ticket. Tim did a smart 'u' turn, drove up to the junction and pulled into Bow Road.

"This doesn't look good," Jack said. A line of cars stretched ahead of them as far as he could see. "Can we take a shortcut?"

"Afraid not, boss. It'll be just as bad whatever route we take."

"Terrific," Jack said.

"No, traffic," Tim responded wittily, only to be met with a caustic stare. "Sorry, no more jokes," he promised.

Conscious of the time, Tyler glanced down at his watch, wondering if he should phone the court and warn them that he might be a little late.

"Don't worry, boss. We'll get there in time," Barton assured him.

The traffic situation, already bad, was exacerbated by roadworks, which effectively narrowed the town-bound stretch down to one lane for a distance of about two hundred yards between the Shell garage and Mile End tube station.

Barton rolled his eyes. "Roadworks! I might've known."

Jack was horrified. "You mean you didn't?"

"They weren't here two days ago," Barton said, defensively.

Tyler didn't speak. He didn't have to. His face said it all.

"We'll be alright once we clear the next set of lights," Barton promised, hoping that he was right. Fed into a bottleneck, they crawled through the roadworks at a snail's pace. After what seemed like an age, they finally turned left into Burdett Road, where traffic was flowing normally. Tyler's watch said ten minutes before ten.

Five minutes later, they were in Poplar High Street, looking for the Coroners Court. They found it at the junction with Cottage Street, an old brick building that was much smaller than Tyler had expected. The double wooden doors at the front were closed. A square sign hung from the brickwork to the left of the entrance, and was painted a grubby yellow.

It read: *'Entrance to Public mortuary'*.

An arrow underneath pointed to a narrow, cobbled alley at the side of the building. They drew level, but it only appeared wide enough to take one car.

"Is that it?" Jack asked, jerking his thumb at the building, which reminding him of a miniature church, but without the charm.

"That's it," Barton confirmed.

"Park it around the back, if you can. I'll meet you inside," Tyler said, climbing out.

A large van with the legend *'BBC Outside Broadcasting Unit'* was parked in Simpson Road, almost opposite the court. An Independent Television News van sat right behind it.

The two crews had set their equipment up to cover the entrance in a pincer movement. He heard his name called out as he approached, but he didn't turn around. It would only anger Holland if he appeared on television again.

Tyler had never given evidence here before and, as he entered the shoddy building, he was surprised to see just how run down and cramped it was. Most people are surprised to discover that the Coroners Court is the most powerful court in the land. A summons to appear before it takes precedence over all others, even the powerful and prestigious Central Criminal Court at Old Bailey. Considering its status within the legal system, he found his current surroundings rather underwhelming. As his eyes acclimatised to the dark reception area, he spotted Kelly Flowers sitting, alone, on a wooden bench beside the courtroom entrance. Tyler walked over, wondering if Mrs Phillips had changed her mind about attending. He would understand if she had.

Sitting down beside Kelly, Jack leaned close enough to speak without fear of being overheard, aware that in these places even the slightest sound was amplified considerably. "Morning, Kelly. How long have you been here?"

"About fifteen minutes, sir. Traffic was much heavier than I'd expected."

"Where's Mrs Phillips?" he asked, scanning the foyer for someone who fitted the mental picture he had of her. Just then, Tim Barton came in. He spotted Tyler and made a beeline for him.

"She'll be back soon. She's just taken her granddaughter to the toilet." Kelly saw his eyes widen at that. Tyler obviously hadn't expected the little girl to be here. Well, she hadn't expected it herself, if the truth were known. "I'm sorry, sir, we had to bring little April with us. Rita hasn't got anyone she can leave her with."

"I appreciate that, Kelly," Jack said irritably, "but this is not the place for a kid."

"Don't worry. I'll stay out here with her while you and Tim take Rita inside." Kelly had taken quite a shine to the cute little girl dressed in her Sunday best.

"There's nothing else we can do, I suppose. I should have thought to ask her about the kid when we spoke on the phone."

Kelly nodded over Jack's shoulder. "Heads up, here they come," she warned. He stood up and turned to greet them. Rita Phillips was pretty much the way he'd imagined her to be. She was in her late sixties, and slightly underweight for her bone size, but that was probably a result of the stress Tracey had put her through these last few years. Her collar-length grey hair still had faint traces of blonde in it, and the pale blue eyes, which looked him up and down, were alert, worldly wise and full of character. Rita wore a three-quarter length camel hair coat over a conservatively cut blue dress with a crew neck. It was the kind of outfit that had probably looked old-fashioned even when it was brand new. Her brightly polished shoes appeared well worn and comfortable. Head up, back straight, chin jutted out defiantly; everything about her indicated that she was a woman who conducted herself with pride and dignity.

Jack had a feeling that he would like her immensely.

The little girl, trailing shyly behind her grandmother, seemed reluctant to approach them. She held the old woman's hand tightly and stood directly behind her, cautiously peering around the side of Rita's legs when she thought no one was looking.

He had a sneaking suspicion that she was probably far more uncomfortable with him and Barton than she was with the surroundings. Jack asked himself how many strange men, how many new 'uncles' or 'friends' she been forced to meet in her brief life? He wondered if they had been kind, cruel or simply indifferent towards her. He hoped that it was the former.

The unassuming innocence in those big blue eyes had a strange impact on him and he felt a lump forming in his throat as he looked down at her. Tyler didn't consider himself to be a sentimental man, but he was touched by the sweet gentleness that seemed to radiate from little April Phillips. Somehow, she seemed wise beyond her years. *You've been in the world before, little lady*, he thought, smiling tenderly. He remembered his own grandmother saying that to him once when he was small. It had sounded silly at the time but now it seemed to make perfect sense. "Hello, Mrs Phillips. I'm so very sorry that we have to meet like this," he said softly, taking her hand in both of his.

"Thank you, Mr Tyler. You've all been so kind to us. It's helped enormously to know that somebody cares," she said, her eyes never leaving his.

Jack bent down until his face was at the same level as April's. He slowly held out his right hand, smiling as he spoke. "You must be April. My name's Jack. I've heard a lot about you."

As he spoke the girl drew back, seeking refuge behind her grandmother's legs. Jack gazed up at Rita, seeking guidance.

"April's not too comfortable around men," Rita explained with great sadness. "I'm afraid she hasn't had much reason to trust them so far." She didn't add that Tracey had gone through a phase of bringing clients back to the flat whenever Rita was out; or that she used to lock April, often crying, always frightened, in her bedroom while she entertained them. Rita had found out about this practice by pure chance when her next-door neighbours called round one evening to complain. They had threatened to call in the police and social services unless it stopped.

Tracey had been out at the time, and Rita had waited up half the night for her to return, confronting her with the accusation the moment she stepped through the door. Tracey denied it, of course, but little April had, by that stage, told her nanny the shocking truth about the 'bad days', as the girl referred to them; days when she was repeatedly locked in the tiny room for hours at a time.

It was the very last straw for Rita. Tracey could ruin her own life if she wanted, Rita couldn't stop that, but she wasn't going to let her drag a poor defenceless child down into the gutter with her.

Rita had laid into her daughter over her cruel and reprehensible behaviour; she had threatened to throw her out, there and then. Shocked by the unexpected ferocity of her mother's wrath, the like of which she had never seen before, Tracey tearfully swore that she was sorry and that it would never happen again. Irrespective of how genuine her remorse seemed at the time, Rita had learned the hard way that she couldn't rely on the word of an addict, and so she had never left the child alone with her mother again.

Jack stood up slowly, still smiling tenderly down at the little girl who continued to cling to the one person she knew she could trust. "April, honey, not all men are bad. I hope that one day we can be friends." He wanted to reach out and touch her, to show her that he, at least, was sincere, but it didn't seem appropriate. The girl studied him closely for a moment, weighing him up, perhaps, before ducking back behind Mrs Phillips legs.

"And this is Tim Barton, one of my finest officers. He runs the office for me. If you ever need to speak to anyone urgently, and you can't get hold of Kelly or me, then you can trust Tim implicitly," Jack said.

"Hello, Mrs Phillips," Barton said, offering his hand. Barton excused himself as soon as the introductions were completed. He needed to get into the court to set up a table with his papers, in readiness for the hearing.

"Can we talk?" Jack asked as tactfully as he could. He glanced down at April as he spoke.

Rita Phillips nodded, understanding that he meant alone, without the child.

"Of course." Her voice sounded brittle, betraying the stress she was trying to conceal from her granddaughter.

He watched as she turned to the child. "April, darling, I'm just going to have a quiet chat with Mr Tyler. Will you be okay sitting here with Kelly? Will you look after her for me until I get back in a few minutes?"

April glanced up at Jack, a deep frown of uncertainty creasing her young brow. Then she looked across at Kelly, who immediately smiled at her. She finally returned her gaze to Rita, staring at the old woman with those big trusting eyes for a long moment before nodding. She sat down next to Kelly, releasing Rita's hand with great reluctance.

Jack guided Rita a few paces away before speaking. He continued to glance back at the child, noting that she seemed happy enough with Kelly Flowers. "Rita, I know that this is a very trying time for the two of you, and I want you to know that you can call us at any time if you need to. Do you understand what is going to happen today?"

"Yes, I think so. Kelly explained it to me on the way over; at least she tried to. It can be difficult to talk freely about such things with a child around."

"Well, there's not too much to it, really. The law requires that the inquest is opened as soon as possible, but this will be a straightforward decision for the Coroner, who will rule that Tracey was unlawfully killed by a person, or persons, unknown." Jack paused, considering his next words carefully. "Look, Rita, the medical details are not very nice. I need to warn you about that before we go inside. I –"

She raised a hand to cut him off. "I know, I know." She took a deep breath and let it out slowly. "Those dreadful murders in Whitechapel were plastered all over the TV yesterday. I'm not senile, so I can guess exactly what happened to my poor baby. And don't forget that I saw her in the morgue when I ... when I had to identify her." Her voice quivered and the colour completely drained from her face. A solitary tear ran down her cheek, and she turned away from him.

Tyler placed a gentle hand on her shoulder, waiting in silence while she gathered her emotions.

"I'm okay now," she said, turning back to face him again a few moments later.

Jack decided to change the subject. "Are you coping okay financially?" He suspected she would be too proud to ask for help, even if she needed it.

"Things are tight," she admitted, "but we get by."

"I'm not trying to pry; I'm just concerned for you and April. If you need help with the...well, with the funeral arrangements and the like, then the State is duty bound to provide it..." Her upraised hand silenced him for a second time.

"Mr Tyler, I know you mean well and I thank you, truly I do, but I'm not a pauper and I have a small amount of money put by. It's not much, and it was intended to pay for my own funeral in due course..." She smiled wanly at this point, pondering the bitter irony of what she was about to say. "...I thought that it would save my poor Tracey the worry of trying to find enough money to bury me when the time came." Inevitably, more tears were forming in Rita's eyes. Since the unexpected knock on her door early Monday morning, when the two baby-faced constables, their helmets tucked respectfully under their arms, had awkwardly delivered the death message, Rita had desperately tried to conceal her pain and grief from April. She had quickly mastered the art of crying silently, and each time the tears returned she would turn her head away, or use a newspaper to shield her face from April's view. And such simple things would set her off: this morning, when she heard a song that Tracey was fond of; last night, when she had cooked April one of Tracey's favourite meals; every single time Rita walked into Tracey's bedroom and saw her clothes hanging up, knowing that her fashion-conscious daughter would never wear the garments again.

"Look, Rita. You should really hang on to that money," Jack was saying. "You've got to think of April. She might need it one day. Why don't we sit down later, just you and me, and work out together exactly what needs to be done?"

She nodded, grudgingly. "I suppose it wouldn't hurt to talk about it, at least."

Tyler's heart went out to this poor woman and her grandchild. They were in a terrible predicament, through no fault of their own, and he would do everything in his power to help them. "We'll talk more, later – once the inquest is adjourned," he said, gently placing a reassuring hand on her shoulder as she sat down, next to Kelly.

"Thank you, Jack Tyler," she whispered, placing her hand over his for the briefest of moments.

April was visibly relieved to have her beloved grandmother back by her side, where the youngster firmly believed she belonged. She leaned over and subjected the old woman to a crushing embrace. Rita lovingly ran the arthritic fingers of her left hand through the child's shiny hair. At the same time, her other hand sought the familiar reassurance of the golden crucifix she wore around her neck. *Please, God, give me the strength to get through today,* she prayed.

Standing a few yards away, Jack watched the touching scene out of the corner of his eye. He felt woefully inadequate and desperately wished there was a way to comfort them in their time of need.

Kelly Flowers, as if somehow sensing the inner turmoil his thoughts were causing him, made her way over. For a few long moments, she stood there, trying to think of a tactful way to voice her concern without giving offence.

As he inhaled the subtle fragrance of her perfume, Tyler was acutely aware of her presence. He could actually feel the heat being radiated from her body. Kelly leaned closer to speak, her hand brushing against his as she moved. The sudden physical contact between them was electric, and it sent a small jolt right through him.

"You know, as much as you might want to, you can't heal all the wrongs in the world on your own," she pointed out. The words, quietly spoken, seemed very poignant to him as he turned to study her. Their faces were suddenly only inches apart, but she didn't back away, he noted with surprise and pleasure. He eyed her with mock suspicion. "Have you been talking to DI Dillon?" The words she'd just spoken could easily have come straight from the mouth of his overprotective partner.

Kelly smiled. "I don't need to talk to Tony Dillon to see that."

Before they could say anything more, the courtroom door opened and a slim, elderly man in the robes of an usher shuffled out and invited them into the courtroom.

Jack walked back over to Rita and placed a hand on her arm. "Are you going to be okay?"

"Yes, I think so," she replied in a weak voice that lacked conviction.

"Don't worry. I'll be right next to you all the time. If you need to go outside just tell me. Don't stay in there if it's too much for you to bear." He squeezed her arm gently. "Ready?"

She nodded uncertainly, allowing him to guide her through the wooden doors into the courtroom. As they sat down a small cluster of reporters, all keen to secure a seat in the limited space available, filed into the court. Tyler's face darkened as he caught sight of Terri Miller, dressed to kill in a stylish blue business suit, which had a lighter blue herringbone cheque running through it, and a garish red blouse. Holland had been right; the press coverage would continue to grow and grow until the killer was ultimately caught or another major news story eclipsed it.

Jack thought about the two TV crews opposite the building, waiting to film the grieving family when it emerged later in the day. He made a mental note to take Rita and the kid out of the courthouse via the back exit if there was one. With luck, they could get them away without being seen by the damned newsies.

The ancient usher walked across the room and stopped beneath a large portrait of Queen Elizabeth II. There was a much smaller version of the same image – at least Jack thought it was the same image – hanging on one of the walls in the main office, although some clever sod had added a curly moustache to the Queen's face in that one. "All rise," the usher instructed.

When everyone had stood up, the usher opened a wood panelled door theatrically and, with an air of dignified grace, the Coroner, Dr Montague DeVere, made his entrance. He paused to study the expectant crowd before walking the short distance to the raised platform on which his ornately carved chair awaited him. He bowed formally, an act reciprocated by court officials and those police officers present.

Dr DeVere sat down swiftly, motioning to the usher to continue with the opening procedure.

Jack reached over and took Rita's hand, holding it tightly. Without averting her eyes from the distinguished looking Coroner, she squeezed back.

"Here we go," he muttered under his breath.

CHAPTER TWENTY-FOUR

The building seemed strangely deserted now, Kelly reflected. She was reading a story from a book of assorted fairy tales. April Philips was a good listener. The child seemed more relaxed now that the tiny corridor had cleared of people, leaving them alone together.

Kelly had two nieces of her own, her elder sister's children. They were aged seven and four, and she had been reading stories like this to them since they were in nappies.

She wondered what would become of the child sitting so serenely on her lap. Would fate be kind to her in the coming years or would she end up going the same way as her mother?

As Kelly reached the end of the fable, the ageless tale of Snow White and the Seven Dwarfs, April looked up at her. "My nanny got me the video of Snow White from the market. Would you like to come home and watch it with me?" She spoke shyly, a look of eager anticipation accompanying the words.

"I would love to, April, but unfortunately I have lots of work to do. Maybe we could watch it another time?"

A frown appeared on the child's face as Kelly spoke, quickly followed by a look of disappointment. "That's okay," April responded sadly. "You don't have to come if you don't want to. My mummy didn't like doing things with me either." She looked down at her shoes as if she had been scolded.

Kelly mentally kicked herself. Thanks to the constant rejection she had suffered at the hands of her worthless mother, April had grown into a deeply insecure child with a very low opinion of herself. She thought Kelly was fobbing her off, making excuses just like her mother had.

Stupid! Stupid! Stupid! Kelly mentally kicked herself, and she was determined to rectify the mistake. "What other video's do you like, sweetheart?" she asked, trying to coax the child back into the conversation.

"Beauty and the Beast is my very best favourite," April told her, risking a coy glance up at Kelly as she spoke.

"Wow! That's my favourite, too!" Kelly exclaimed. The child looked at Kelly again, a smile beginning to form. She found herself intrigued by the grown up's sudden excitement. "Really?" she asked, eyes the size of dinner plates.

Kelly smiled. "Sure is!"

"My nanny said she would buy me a doll of 'Belle' for my birthday, but I don't think she will be able to, not now..." Her little voice, so full of energy and enthusiasm, faltered as she uttered the last few words, and her enchanting smile was replaced by an expression of infinite sadness.

"What's wrong, angel? You can tell me..." Kelly put her fingers under April's chin as she spoke, gently tilting the girl's head towards her. Kelly found herself close to tears as she stared into the endless sea of pain shimmering in the big blue eyes of the child on her lap. That was when it hit her, that April was just as much a victim of this obscene scumbag who proclaimed himself a modern-day Jack the Ripper as any of the three women he'd brutally hacked to death. "Why so sad, my little one?" she asked, instinctively drawing the child closer. April willingly snuggled into her, and Kelly began to rock her back and forth in a soothing rhythm that had always worked on her when she was April's age.

April's bottom lip began to quiver. "Now that mummy's gone to heaven to be with Jesus, my nanny will be too sad to play with me," she whispered.

"Oh April, I'm sure that's not true. Your nanny is under a lot of stress right now, but by the time your birthday comes around she'll be a whole lot better." Kelly tried to sound positive, kissing the girl's head gently. It occurred to Kelly that she wasn't doing a particularly good job of looking after April. She was supposed to keep the child happy and amused while the inquest went on, not reduce her to a sobbing wreck. She could feel her own eyes welling up now. What a fine chaperone she was turning out to be! She checked her watch. Oh God! They'd only been in the court for five minutes. If she carried on like this, the poor girl would be suicidal by the time they broke up!

———

Jack escorted Rita out of the courtroom after the inquest and led her to a secluded corner where they could talk freely. He could tell that she was still in a daze.

"Are you alright, Rita?" he asked, staring daggers at a reporter who had followed them out and was now lingering nearby. The man got the message and wandered off to re-join his colleagues who were milling by the exit, no doubt comparing notes and trying to come up with some eye-catching headers for their stories.

"No, I'm not." Her complexion turned a pale shade of green and she looked around with a sense of urgency. "Excuse me, Jack. I – I think I'm going to be sick." Clasping her hand to her mouth, Rita Phillips rushed off in the direction of the ladies toilet.

Damn! Jack thought. He looked across and signalled purposefully for Kelly to join him.

She came straight over, with April in tow.

"What's up, sir?" she asked anxiously.

"Rita's in the loo, throwing up. I think that you should go in after her."

Kelly looked down at April. "What about...?"

"Don't worry, we'll be fine." Tyler smiled, hoping that he wouldn't live to regret his words.

"Are you sure?"

"Just go," he said, firmly.

When they were alone together, Jack led April back to the bench. She sat down obediently, staring up at him with her big blue eyes.

"Listen," He began, searching for the right words. "I know that you've met a lot of bad men, but I'm not like them." He smiled again, conscious not to invade her personal space in case that intimidated her. She continued to view him sceptically, her expression one of distrust.

Probably heard it all before, huh, kid? Tyler thought, trying to see things from her perspective. He frowned, aware that he was totally out of his depth with children. Boy, this was going to be tough! None of the hardcore villains he'd dealt with over the years; none of the acid-tongued barristers who cross-examined him in the witness box, dissecting every word that he said in the hope of tripping him up, had managed to make him feel this uncomfortable in their presence.

"Okay, let's start again," he suggested, wishing that he had more experience with kids. April folded her arms across her chest, and the way she suddenly jutted her little chin out stubbornly reminded him of her grandmother, who had displayed the same mannerism earlier.

"Look, April, I didn't know your mummy, but I do know your granny. She's a very special lady and I want to help her. I want to help you too if you'll let me. I promise that I won't ever do anything to hurt either of you. I don't have any children of my own, but if I did, I would want to be as close to them as I could be, like your granny is to you." He paused, trying to marshal his thoughts. The harder he tried, the worse he seemed to be making it. With a dejected sigh, Jack Tyler sat down next to the little girl, pulling his tie loose. He scratched his head in frustration, wondering if he should just admit defeat and sit there quietly until Kelly came back with Rita.

"She's not my granny."

"What?" Jack asked, wondering what she meant by that.

"She's not my granny, *silly*. She's my nana." April explained this as if speaking to a retard.

Jack tried not to smile. "My mistake," he conceded, delighted that she had actually spoken to him.

April eyed him critically. "I thought policemen were s'posed to be clever."

Jack gave an apologetic shrug. "We're meant to be, little one, but I think I'm having a bit of an off week."

Tyler made it to the Gold Group meeting by the skin of his teeth. Having been caught in bad traffic earlier, he had decided to avoid the roads and catch a train, but there had been delays due to a signal failure. It was obviously going to be one of *those* days. Holland had given him a scathing look as he'd walked into the canteen, face flushed and breathing heavily.

The meeting was chaired by Chief Superintendent Porter, and held in the conference room at Whitechapel police station. Porter ushered the murder squad detectives into seats around the large table that dominated the bland room and introduced them to the other board members. Apart from Holland and Tyler, there was a stern-faced uniform Chief Inspector called George Chambers, who explained he was the Borough Operations officer, Inspector Ray Speed, who greeted them warmly, and several prominent members of the local community who formed the Borough's Lay Advisory Group. One of these was Dr Simon Pritchard from The Sutton Mission. Pritchard was delighted to inform the Gold Group that his wife had liaised with DS Bull earlier in the day and arrangements had been made for a small group of volunteers to be put at the detective's disposal over the weekend. The last person in attendance was Brian Johnson, the analyst. His presence had been specifically requested by Porter, and he had been tasked to prepare an intelligence overview for the meeting.

Lukewarm coffee and stale biscuits had been provided, but no one seemed interested in the refreshments.

Porter looked pale and tired, and he appeared to have lost a little weight; he was obviously feeling the strain.

After Holland's opening remarks, Tyler gave the Gold Group a general overview of the investigation to date. He wasn't prepared to disclose specific operational details in the presence of the civilian lay advisors, but he gave them enough of a flavour to make them feel involved. Porter made all the right noises, and showed concern and resolve in all the right places, but Tyler could tell he was far from happy.

They discussed resources; Holland pledged to increase the size of the investigation team and stated that all leave had been cancelled for the coming weekend and every available officer would be working. Chief Inspector Chambers informed them that he had liaised with the TSG, who would be supplying two whole units to the borough for a two-week period, starting the following Monday. In addition, also from Monday, all sector officers would have their shifts changed to provide extra cover during the evening hours. The streets would be flooded with officers, he said, which pleased the Lay Advisors, especially Dr Pritchard, but worried the detectives; their concern was that the drastically increased police presence would merely displace the killer.

Johnson then delivered a death by power-point presentation, showing graph after graph to demonstrate crime trends on the borough in the wards where the Ripper had struck. There were no surprises and nothing that took the enquiry further forward, but Porter and the LAG members seemed impressed.

Halfway through, Tyler leaned into Holland. "Like the old saying goes: 'bullshit baffles brains,'" he whispered.

Eventually, the meeting turned political, and Tyler was pretty much ignored while Porter and Holland discussed community impact issues with the LAG members.

After the meeting finished there was just about enough time to rush to the canteen and grab a takeaway coffee before setting off for the press conference at the Yard. A train was pulling in as they walked onto the platform. To Jack's relief, the Central Line was running without any delays, although the way the day was panning out, he wouldn't be surprised if something happened during the journey and they didn't make it to the Yard.

The press conference was to be held in the ground floor briefing room at NSY, which was already packed to capacity. As Tyler walked past the room, he spotted Miller standing in one corner talking to a colleague; she seemed to be following him around like a bad smell today.

The two detectives were led into an ante-room, away from the press, and told the assigned Press Liaison Officer would be with them shortly. Jack hoped it wouldn't be the same one whose pager messages he had repeatedly ignored after Winston's arrest. He was surprised to discover that Porter had also been invited and was due to address the camera when the individual interviews were given.

"What's he going to say?" Jack asked.

Holland shrugged. "Someone's got to do the community reassurance stuff, and that's never been your strong suit."

"I joined the job to catch villains, not be all pink and fluffy."

Holland sighed. "Jack, assuming we still have jobs by the time this investigation is over, you really will have to broaden your outlook and start thinking more globally if you want promotion."

"You say 'think globally', but I hear 'kiss arse'," Jack said, and immediately regretted it. Holland was right; the Job was changing, and if he wanted further advancement he would have to learn how to 'play the game'.

Holland shook his head in despair. "Think globally, Jack. We've got a serial killer roaming the streets of Whitechapel, killing and mutilating female victims. That's terrifying for the local community, and we need to reassure them before a general state of panic sets in."

"Good job Porter's here, then," Jack said dryly. "I'm sure he thinks globally all the time."

Before Holland could respond, a young Press Liaison Officer called Archie breezed into the room. He was pencil thin and exuded nervous energy from every pore; an unruly mop of brown hair bounced up and down as he walked. As soon as introductions were made, he began coaching them on what to say and how to respond to tricky questions. Jack noticed that the PLO's eyes glinted with enthusiasm, and guessed that he was fresh from university. *Give him a few more months and he'll be as jaded as everyone else*, Jack thought.

After running through the rules, Archie opened the door and peered into the corridor. "I just need to pop next door and get something," he told them. "I'll be back in two minutes. Don't leave the room until I return."

"Where do you reckon he's going?" Holland asked, thinking it was probably a quick trip to the loo.

"Probably gone to get us some more eggs to suck," Jack said.

When Archie reappeared five minutes later, he wasn't carrying any eggs, but he did have a shiny new clipboard. "Forgot my notes," he said by way of explanation, and promptly began flicking through them. This was to be a live broadcast, simultaneously filmed by all the major networks, Archie told them excitedly. The running order was: Holland, Tyler and then Porter. When the filming concluded, the detectives would be ushered away to sit down for a short question and answer session with the various tabloid reporters. Archie would invite anyone with a question to raise their hand, and he would nominate the lucky few who got to ask questions. That way, he could filter out potential troublemakers. Only when Archie was completely satisfied that they understood what was expected of them did he lead them into the crowded briefing room.

The press conference started promptly and, although it felt oppressive at times, both Holland and Tyler stuck to the party line, being helpful and informative without giving anything away. Like a proud parent, Archie gave little nods of approval to each of them as they came off camera. When it was Porter's turn, he cleared his throat and began to speak. "I want to say two things," he began, looking suitably solemn. "Firstly, I want to reassure the community of Whitechapel that we are doing everything humanly possible to catch the perpetrator. With immediate effect, there will be significantly increased patrols throughout the area, and these will remain in place until he is in custody." He paused for a moment, looking straight at the camera while considering his next words. "Secondly, I would like to speak directly to the killer, who I am convinced will be watching this broadcast."

Tyler and Holland were standing to Porter's side, just off camera. "What's he doing?" Jack whispered, alarmed.

"I don't know," Holland said quietly, "but this hasn't been sanctioned by me." Using a media broadcast to address a dangerous perpetrator directly was something that was generally best avoided. On the rare occasion that it was deemed necessary, the content had to be carefully scripted and properly approved.

Jack glanced around and spotted a very stressed looking Archie desperately trying to catch Porter's eye so that he could signal the Borough Commander to stop speaking. Porter either didn't see him or wilfully chose to ignore him. "You think you're cleverer than us," he continued, "but you are not. You're just deluded. You think you have power, but you don't. You are beyond pathetic. You think you can do anything you want. Well, take it from me, you can't. Start looking over your shoulder in fear, because we are closing in on you and we will not rest until you are safely behind bars, where you belong."

Jack grabbed Holland's forearm. "You need to stop him," he warned. "If the killer sees this, it will just antagonise him."

"You think I don't know that?" Holland hissed, pulling his arm free. "But I can't exactly drag him away while the camera's rolling, can I?"

Poor Archie had given up on subtlety and was now openly waving his clipboard at Porter to get his attention. Porter must have finally seen him because he gave a subtle nod and abruptly terminated his speech.

"Well," Jack said as Porter walked towards them, "If that's thinking globally, maybe I can manage it after all."

———

At exactly five to six, Terri Miller left the studios of Capital Radio in Leicester Square, having just recorded a short interview for the next drive time news bulletin. She went into the Radio Café at the base of the Capital building, and by the time the news started she was sitting comfortably at a little table, sipping an extra frothy cappuccino and watching the world through a tinted plate glass window. The Square itself was filled with the usual mishmash of tourists, shoppers, and office workers. Outside the café, two skateboarders were making a nuisance of themselves, and one of the waiters went outside to shoo them away. She watched them skate past a man doing a Little Tramp style shuffle for his girlfriend as she photographed him next to John

Doubleday's 1981 statue of Charlie Chaplin. The girl laughed at his antics as she put her camera away, and then looped her arm through his and dragged him off towards the Empire cinema on the north side of the Square.

Terri followed their progress until they disappeared inside the cinema, which had a massive billboard up for the latest Schwarzenegger blockbuster, *End of Days*. It had been ages since Terri had done something normal, like going to the cinema, and she found herself envying the couple.

When no one was looking, she slipped a pill into her mouth and washed it down with a mouthful of cappuccino. She disliked taking stimulants, but it was the only way to keep going at a time like this. As the only person yet to have spoken to the killer, she was being treated like a minor celebrity, much to the ire of some of her journo colleagues. She had already recorded brief slots for LBC and the BBC earlier in the day, and her next appointment was at the London offices of CNN, where she was due to film a live piece for them.

Since the police had taken her home, yesterday afternoon, her life had become unbelievably manic. She had remained at the apartment with Paul Evans, who was sweet, and Kelly Flowers, whom she wasn't sure she liked, until the telephone intercept and the panic button had both been installed.

The moment they left, she picked up the phone and, as Kelly had done earlier, dialled 1471 to obtain the number the killer had called her from. She knew it was local from the code, and instinct told her it would be close to the apartment block, so she went on a tour of the area, finding the kiosk on her third stop.

Smiling at her minor triumph, she'd immediately called Kelly on her mobile and asked her to return. The detectives arrived forty minutes later, this time with a different fingerprint man in tow. He examined the kiosk with his brushes and powders and managed to lift eight separate sets of prints, none of which were realistically likely to belong to the killer.

Terri had then made a mad dash to the Fleet Street office of London's newest daily for a crisis meeting with Giles Deakin, her esteemed editor. He had agreed that this situation, as deplorable as it was, presented the newspaper with a golden opportunity. Henceforth, Terri was to concentrate solely on this story; everything else was to be put on the back burner, at least for the time being. Deakin had even assigned her a researcher, who was to be at her beck and call for the duration. Julie Payne, who had reluctantly agreed to sleep over at her place for a few nights, was also posted to the small team. After enduring a painfully boring lecture on sub judice from a member of the legal team, to clarify what she could and couldn't print, Terri had finally started work on her first Ripper story. It had gone right down to the wire, but for the second time in a week, she had somehow managed to deliver her finished article minutes before the deadline.

This morning, Deakin had notified all the main TV and radio stations that Terri was the person the Whitechapel murderer had elected to speak through.

"Don't we want to keep any information he gives us to ourselves?" she'd asked, naively.

Deakin had responded with a sly grin. "We'll only tell them what we want them to know, darling. We won't be giving any exclusives away. All we're really doing is using them to get free publicity for your articles in the Echo."

"Oh!"

Deakin had tapped his skull knowingly. "You've got to use your noggin in this game, Terri," he said.

"Surely they'll realise that we're only using them?" Julie chipped in.

"Of course, but what choice do they have? Don't you think they would do the same to us, given the chance?"

Sure enough, within minutes of spreading the word, the first broadcasting company had called to arrange an interview. After that, the phone lines went into meltdown. And that was how Terri had ended up being interviewed at Capital FM today.

As soon as the news finished, she pulled out her phone and called her researcher. When he answered, she asked him to pull some stuff about the original Jack the Ripper from the archives. He'd already done that, he told her, clearly unimpressed that it had taken her so long to come up with such a basic request. She commended his initiative and asked him to run background checks on the three victims of the nineties version. That was next on his list, he said. Lastly, she instructed Clive Cullen to make a few discreet enquiries about Jack Tyler. She suggested that he should start with the Metropolitan Police Central Press Office, and ask for an official resume on Tyler's career. Cullen thanked her for the tip and sarcastically pointed out that he would never have thought of that on his own.

Smarmy git, she thought, as she finished the call.

The next thing on her list was to phone Deakin and ask him to start pumping his contacts for any gossip relating to Tyler. Deakin, she knew, had a half-dozen well-placed moles that the paper regularly quoted as 'a reliable source within the Metropolitan Police Service'.

She finished the call and looked at her watch again, conscious that she had a tight deadline to meet. Terri had been allocated the front page and a double page spread in the centre of tomorrow morning's paper. *That's not too shabby for a girl still fighting to become accepted*, she thought, allowing herself to feel a trifle smug.

The killer had been right when he said this was a big chance for her. With a little luck, and a lot of hard work, the story would establish her as a credible investigative journalist, and even the diehards would have to stop treating her like the new girl on the block. She had also decided to go with Paul's brilliant suggestion about keeping a diary and writing a book when it was all over. A quick glance at her watch revealed that the time for daydreaming was over; she had to crack on, while she still had some chemical induced energy left. Stifling a yawn, she left a decent tip on her table and set off towards Charing Cross Road, where she could hail a taxi. There was a lot of work to be done.

James Sadler was watching the evening news bulletin on a large, wall mounted TV in the practice's staff room. His receptionist, Doreen, was also there, preparing them both a cup of tea before the evening surgery got underway.

On screen, interspersed by snippets from the earlier press conference at NSY, Terri Miller was doing a sterling job of answering questions about the New Ripper killings.

"What do you think about these murders?" Doreen asked him as she waited for the kettle to boil.

"I don't think about them at all," he said.

"It's alright for you blokes," she continued, undeterred by his apparent lack of interest. "You're not the ones in danger, unlike us girls. Honestly, it's getting to the point where I'm terrified to go out alone."

As he often did when she rambled on, Sadler ignored her. He had been tied up dealing with patients for most of the day, and this was the first time that he'd seen the footage.

At that moment, Porter appeared on screen. *"Firstly, I want to reassure the community of Whitechapel that we are doing everything humanly possible to catch the perpetrator. With immediate effect, there will be significantly increased patrols throughout the area, and these will remain in place until he is in custody."*

Sadler yawned. That was the standard police response in a case like this.

"Secondly," Porter continued, *"I would like to speak directly to the killer, who I am convinced will be watching this broadcast."*

Sadler used the remote control to turn the sound up. "Be quiet, please, Doreen," he snapped at his receptionist, who seemed to have developed a bad case of verbal diarrhea and was completely oblivious to the fact that he was trying to follow what was being said in the broadcast.

"You think you're cleverer than us," Porter declared, staring straight into the camera lens for greater effect, *"but you are not. You're just deluded. You think you have power, but you don't. You are beyond pathetic. You think you can do anything you want. Well, take it from me, you can't. Start looking over your shoulder in fear, because we are closing in on you and we will not rest until you are safely behind bars, where you belong."*

"Bravo," Doreen said from behind. "It's about time one of them coppers had the balls to say something like that."

Sadler shook his head is despair. The woman really could be stupid at times. "Do you honestly think anything good can come possible out of an outburst like that?" he sneered, "because I would have thought it was blatantly obvious to anyone with half a brain that goading the killer can only make a bad situation worse."

Doreen crossed her arms defiantly. Unlike the other two doctors in the practice, who were both lovely, she found Sadler to be very opinionated at times. No wonder he was going through such an acrimonious divorce, if the rumours were to be believed.

"Well, I think it was very brave. It might not impress the likes of you, but it makes working class people like me feel much safer knowing that a man like him is looking out for us."

Sadler scoffed at that. "I think you'll find that he's only looking out for himself," he told her. He had never met Porter, but he knew the man was ambitious, and he was clearly trying to use all this free publicity to make a name for himself.

"In my humble opinion –"

"Sorry, Doreen," Sadler interrupted, standing up. "I've just remembered I've got to make a quick phone call before surgery starts."

"What about your tea?" she asked.

"Keep it warm for me," he shouted over his shoulder.

CHAPTER TWENTY-FIVE

Porter was getting ready to leave the office when there was a tentative knock on the door.

"Come in," he called, wondering who could be calling this late on a Thursday evening. After all, he wasn't the on-call senior; that was George Chambers. To his surprise, Brian Johnson poked his head around the door. "I was wondering if I might have a quick word," he said nervously.

Porter frowned, wondering what the buffoon could possibly want at this late hour. He didn't even work here anymore. "Yes, of course. Come in."

Johnson entered the room and shut the door after him. He approached the desk meekly and stood there saying nothing. Porter stared at him, waiting for the loathsome man to say something. He glanced at his watch impatiently to emphasise the point that he didn't have all night. "Well?"

"I saw you on TV earlier," Johnson said.

"Did you?" So, that was it. Johnson had come to do what he did best – kiss arse. Porter enjoyed having his ego stroked, and under normal circumstances he would have been quite content to sit there and soak up as many compliments as his admiring subordinate wanted to lavish upon him, but not tonight. Tonight, he was in a hurry and couldn't afford the time to indulge in small talk.

Johnson wrung his hands together in agitation. "Forgive me for saying this," he began, "but I really don't think it was a good idea to insult the Ripper the way you did. I've read quite a bit about serial killers, and what makes them tick, all the literature says it's not a good idea to provoke them."

Porter's face darkened. That was not the kind of feedback he had been expecting. Who did the presumptuous fool think he was speaking to? "Brian, we may have known each other for over a decade, but you need to remember your place. I'm a Chief Superintendent, you're an analyst. I don't think it's for you to question my judgement in these matters."

Johnson flinched at the rebuke. "No, of course not," he stammered. "I would never question your judgement, but I just don't think you realise how dangerous this Ripper chap is. I hope I'm not speaking out of place when I –"

"You are speaking out of place, Brian. I know exactly what I'm doing. Now, if there's nothing else, I have a busy evening planned and I'm in a rush. So, if you don't mind..." He pointed towards the door, making it clear the audience was over.

As Johnson, leaving the room with his tail firmly between his legs, closed the door behind him, the telephone on Porter's desk began to ring.

"Oh, for heaven's sake, now what?" he demanded, rolling his eyes in exasperation.

The general office was deserted when Tyler returned from the Yard so he switched the TV on and sat down in front of it, wearily plonking his feet up on the nearest desk. Unfortunately, when the screen came to life, the face staring back at him belonged to Terri Miller. His visage morphed into a mask of disdain as he quickly grabbed the remote and jabbed the mute button. If only it were that easy to silence the ambitious reporter in real life.

His MIR staff had printed out a ton of actions for allocation over the weekend; Holland had promised he would have so many people at his disposal that he wouldn't know what to do with them all. He seriously doubted that; there was so much CCTV still to gather and view, so many items of property to book in, and so many statements still to take that if a hundred officers paraded tomorrow, he would probably still be short.

The trilling sound of a telephone drifted out from his office. With a groan, Jack heaved himself to his feet and rushed across the incident room. Leaning across his desk, he snatched the handset from its cradle.

"DCI Tyler speaking."

"Tyler, this is Chief Superintendent Porter over at Whitechapel."

Tyler sat down, wondering why the Borough Commander was calling him at this late hour. *"I've just had a very nasty experience,"* Porter said, his voice trembling. *"The killer.... He – he just called me up and threatened me, said he was going to make me pay for disrespecting him on TV."*

Jack groaned inwardly. *This is what happens when you go off script at press conferences,* he thought, reaching for a notepad and pen. "Tell me exactly what he said."

"It was all very quick," Porter spluttered. *"He told me he'd watched my performance on TV, and he said that I was the pathetic and powerless one, not him. Then he said he couldn't allow my insolence to go unpunished, and that the next blood he spilled would be on my hands. Then, without another word, he hung up. The man is goading us, Tyler, and I want to know what you are going to do about it?"* Jack stared at the handset in disbelief. Porter had all but called the killer out on national TV, and now that his bravado had come back to bite him, he wanted to know what Jack was going to do about it. The fucking nerve of some people!

"What time did the call come in?" Jack asked, trying to keep the rising anger he felt out of his voice.

"A few minutes ago – I called you the moment he hung up."

"How did he come across?"

"Well, apart from sounding mentally unstable, there was a lot of anger in his voice."

"Can you describe his voice? For instance, was it deep or high pitched? Did he have a regional accent?"

"*I couldn't tell you, really. Everything he said was whispered, which made it sound very sinister, but there was no discernible accent.*"

"Were there any background noises that might identify where he was calling from?"

"*None that I could make out.*"

Jack closed his eyes. This was like trying to get blood out of a stone. Porter was a police officer, for Christ sake, he was supposed to be a professional witness, not a professional idiot. "I'll send someone straight over," he said. Maybe Dillon or Bull could get more out of Porter than he had been able to.

"But I'm about to leave," Porter protested. "*It's my wedding anniversary and I've got tickets to the theatre. My wife will give me hell if I'm late.*"

"That may be, but before you go anywhere, you'll need to provide a detailed statement about the call. I can have someone there in −"

"*No, that won't do at all,*" Porter snapped.

The pressure of the situation was obviously getting to the Divisional Commander; either that or he really was so under the thumb that he was genuinely terrified of upsetting his wife.

Tyler took a deep breath and spoke slowly. "Sir, this is very important. Apart from Miller, you are the only person, and more importantly, the only police officer, to have spoken to the killer. We need to debrief you properly."

After a moment's hesitation, Porter sighed melodramatically. "*I understand, really I do, but I can't let my wife down.*" There was a pause, and Tyler could picture Porter sitting there feeling conflicted, checking his watch anxiously. "*If I hurry, I can type a holding statement and e-mail it across. I'll put the signed original in a sealed envelope and leave it with the station officer for one of your lot to collect. I'm at the Yard all day tomorrow for a Borough Commander's meeting, but I'll write a more detailed account first thing on Monday morning. I'm sure that will be satisfactory.*"

It wasn't at all satisfactory, but there was no point in making a fuss; not when he was powerless to do anything about it. "Very well," Tyler conceded, "but I'll be sending someone over to debrief you properly first thing on Monday morning."

"*Of course,*" Porter said, sounding relieved. "*Look, I'm sorry if I seem a bit edgy, but that call was extremely disturbing.*"

"I understand that," Jack said, "but what's even more disturbing is that the killer has just announced his intention to strike again."

Porter immediately became ultra-defensive. "*I hope you're not suggesting it will be my fault if he kills again?*"

"No, I'm, not," Tyler said with forced calmness. He should have left it at that, he knew, but Porter needed to understand how difficult his attempt to impress the public with his hard man act had made Jack's job. "However, I do think your remarks today were ill-considered and inflammatory, and I do think you have antagonised him unnecessarily, which will undoubtedly put us under even more pressure."

There was a sharp intake of breath at the other end of the line. "*How dare you suggest that,*" Porter shouted, losing his cool.

Jerking the receiver away from his ear, Jack realised that he'd hit a nerve. *Good*, he thought.

"*My comments were considered and appropriate,*" Porter continued, angrily, "*and if you have any issue with anything I said, I suggest you go through proper channels and address your concerns to your superior.*"

"Don't worry," Tyler assured him. "I will. In the meantime, can you give me a contact number where I can reach you over the weekend if anything comes up?"

"*My contact details are in the Divisional Book One,*" Porter snapped, reminding Tyler of a petulant child. "*If you want them, you can get them from the Station Officer.*" Without a further word, he hung up.

For a moment, Tyler stared at the handset in disbelief. "What a cock," he said, dialling Holland's number. His boss needed to know about the call Porter had just received and the implications that came with it.

The Disciple had created something of a dilemma for himself by deviating from his original plan, which had been to make one sacrifice during the first week, and two in each of the second and third weeks. Unfortunately, his little spree of taking three in a week had put the

Yard under such intense pressure that it was now having to commit resources at an alarming rate. As of Monday, police patrols in Whitechapel would quadruple, making it far too risky to venture out next week. That left him with a simple choice: snatch his fourth victim before the patrols kicked in or go dormant for a couple of months and wait for life to return to normal. The problem with that latter option was that it required him to continue living a suffocating lie. He hated pretending to be someone he wasn't and showing subservience to the third bitch responsible for ruining his life, and he genuinely didn't think he could pull that act off for much longer. In the end, the decision proved simple. He already had commitments this evening, but he would go hunting again tomorrow night.

How did you get on?" Dillon asked, passing Jack a can of Seven-Up and a soggy paper bag containing fish and chips. He had just returned from a trip to the local chippie to get them some much-needed food. When he'd left, Jack had been about to start phoning around to try and muster some additional uniform patrols for the coming night.

Tyler grimaced. "I spoke to George Chambers, but he reckons the Late Turn relief at HT paraded under minimum strength today, and there's a stack of outstanding emergency calls that need to be answered. It's the same story at all the surrounding divisions. In short, the cupboard's empty."

"I'm not surprised," Dillon said, sagging into a chair opposite Tyler. "We can't realistically expect them to abandon their core business on the off chance that our killer might strike again." Yawning, he arched his back and stretched expansively, reminding Tyler of a cartoon bear awakening after its winter slumber. Yawn over, he began tearing open his food in a manner that would have done a grisly proud.

This was, Dillon realised, the first time he'd eaten since breakfast and he was suddenly famished. It had been a particularly gruelling day. He'd arrived at Poplar mortuary at eleven-thirty. After a cup of cheap instant coffee, provided by the ever bubbly and undeniably attractive Emma Drew, and the customary small talk about football, TV shows and who-was-shagging-who according to the gossip columns, he'd delivered a detailed briefing to the pathologist. That done, they all descended from the tiny first-floor office and crossed to the mortuary, where they donned their greens in Trigene scented silence. Dillon had then been forced to watch on as two human beings were systematically sliced and diced by Ben Claxton. Each procedure had taken approximately four hours, with a forty-five-minute break between the two autopsies. He had felt far too sick to eat during that time, unlike George Copeland, who found the whole experience deeply fascinating and had worked up quite an appetite by the time they broke for refreshments.

While Dillon had detested every second that he'd spent inside the mortuary, at least today's prolonged exposure to the gruesome sights and smells hadn't affected him to quite the same extent as they had during the post-mortem of Tracey Phillips a few days earlier. That said, he seriously doubted that he would ever be able to face eating spaghetti bolognese again, having seen and smelt it in Geraldine Rye's stomach contents.

At one point, towards the end of the day, he'd found himself mentally undressing Emma Drew as she stood next to him in her bloodstained greens. That had been a surreal experience!

Apart from the two of them, the office was empty – Jack had dismissed his flagging team at nine o'clock, which was by far the earliest they had finished all week. The poor sods had looked half-dead as they'd shuffled listlessly out of the office under strict instruction to return in ten short hours to start another gruelling shift. To their credit, not one of them had complained about the ridiculously long hours they were being asked to work. Tyler was proud of them, and he suspected their bank managers would be too when their wages were paid in!

Dillon had been tempted to stop off at the off-licence and grab a couple of cans to wash his dinner down with, but he had somehow resisted the urge. If the wheel came off – God forbid – it really wouldn't do to attend a crime scene smelling of booze.

"What about the TSG?" Dillon asked as he stuffed a huge hand full of chips into his mouth.

Jack shook his head. "I've spoken to the Chief Inspector at Information Room. The Commissioners Reserve are on a call-out in South London, dealing with a major public order situation, and are likely to be tied up for some time. As soon as they get released, he's going to send them to Whitechapel, but who knows when that will be, and they finish at two a.m. anyway."

Dillon took a long swig of his Tango and burped contentedly. "Well, we've done all we can. At least our arses are covered if anything does happen."

"True, but it doesn't sit well with me, knowing that sick bastard is out there just waiting to strike again, and there's fuck all we can do about it."

They ate in silence for a short while.

"Changing the subject slightly," Dillon said, wiping grease from his mouth with a paper napkin, "have you spoken to Fiona at all since the other night?"

Jack eyed him suspiciously. Dillon had a habit of trying to play cupid for him, and it always ended badly. "I haven't had a chance to even think about it," he said. "Why?"

Dillon shrugged. "It's just that I phoned Karen yesterday, and she suggested that the four of us do dinner sometime soon."

"Sure," Jack said, but he sounded very non-committal. "Next time you speak to her, explain how busy we've been and say we'll try and sort something out as soon as we wrap this case up."

"Leave it with me and I'll arrange something," Dillon said, knowing that was probably the only way he would ever get Jack to go. "Well, this isn't exactly what I had in mind for tonight, but cheers anyway," he said, raising his can to toast the occasion.

Tyler wearily raised his own can and clinked it against his partner's. "Here's to hoping the bastard decides to wait until next week before he makes another move. At least then the streets will be flooded with Old Bill and we might have half a chance of catching him."

"Amen," Dillon said, and burped again.

Just then, Chris Deakin popped his head around the door. "They smell amazing," he said, sniffing the air like a dog following a scent. "Mind if I nick a couple? I haven't eaten since lunchtime." Without waiting for a reply, he snatched up a fistful of chips and stuffed them into his mouth." For a moment he stood there, making appreciative noises as he chewed.

Dillon's jaw dropped. "So, do you actually want anything from us, Chris, or have you just come in here to steal all my food?" he demanded, testily.

Deakin smiled sheepishly, swallowed, and then licked his fingers. "I was going through Pilkington and Rye's nominal pages on HOLMES earlier, and I noticed they both used the same doctor's surgery in Whitechapel, so I've created an action for someone to pop along tomorrow morning and collect their medical records."

"Fair enough," Tyler said. "Was there anything else?"

"Well, it struck me as a strange coincidence that two of our victims should be registered at the same surgery, especially as one of them – Rye – lives in Chingford." Deakin said, eyeing Dillon's chips hungrily.

"Will you stop drooling over my food," Dillon complained, shooing him away.

"Sorry," Deakin said, "but they're very moreish."

"Maybe she just decided to register with a GP near her place of work because it's easier for her, especially if she often works long hours," Tyler suggested, dragging his OM back on topic.

Deakin nodded, and then quickly picked up some more chips, earning himself a fierce scowl from Dillon. "I think that's probably the case," he agreed, "but it was nagging at me so I did a bit of digging on the practice and saw that they have three doctors on the books: Dr Ahuja, Dr Agarwal, and Dr Sadler. Apparently, Dr Sadler is also an FME."

"Is this actually leading anywhere, or are you just stalling so that you can pilfer more of my chips?" Dillon asked. As he spoke, he pulled the remainder towards him and hovered over them protectively.

"A bit of both," Deakin admitted, grinning naughtily. "Anyway, I know it sounds a bit random, but earlier today I was on the phone to a mate of mine who works for CIB up at the Yard."

Dillon's eyes narrowed. "Why were you talking to the rubber heelers?" he asked, suspiciously. Like most rank and file officers, he instinctively distrusted anyone connected to the Complaints Investigation Bureau.

"We were just catching up," Deakin explained, "and when I asked him what case he was working on at the moment, he told me he'd just been assigned to look into an FME who works in East London. Apparently, the General Medical Council are conducting an investigation of their own following an anonymous tip off from a woman that a London based doctor is supplying drugs to local addicts in exchange for sexual favours. Obviously, as the man in question was one of our FMEs, they were obliged to notify the MPS."

"I don't suppose you managed to get this doctor's name?" Tyler asked.

"I did, actually," Deakin said, snatching a chip from under Dillon's nose and smiling triumphantly. "It was James Sadler."

CHAPTER TWENTY-SIX

Friday 5ᵀᴴ November 1999

Friday morning began as every other morning did during a live enquiry, with an office meeting. They were six days into the investigation, but they were no nearer to catching the elusive killer than they had been on day one. Still, that was the way it went sometimes, Tyler told his team. The trick was not to let it get you down, which was easier said than done when your suspect was still out there killing people.

Office meetings could sometimes run for an hour or more, but today there was nothing majorly new to discuss, and it only lasted twenty-minutes. After going through the latest developments, and receiving updates from his team on how their growing piles of actions were progressing, Tyler adjourned to his office to update his Decision Log, leaving Dillon to task the team with today's priorities.

He sat at his desk, pen poised. It was important that he marshal his thoughts properly before documenting an investigative strategy around Dr Sadler, and he took a few moments to do this.

Clearly, there was no evidence against the man, just an uncorroborated allegation from someone who wouldn't even provide their name, let alone make a statement, and therefore there was no justification for making him a suspect. However, given what Deakin had told them last night, Tyler thought that it was appropriate to declare him a Person of Interest.

He was mindful that he needed to tread carefully. According to GMC statistics, malicious allegations from disgruntled addicts were becoming more common, and he didn't want to set off a chain of events that could ultimately tarnish a good man's reputation without having something more substantial to go on than an anonymous tip off.

However, the tip off had been made just before the murder spree began, and it was too much of a coincidence for him to ignore, so although investigations by Complaints and the GMC were already underway, Tyler wanted his own people to check it out thoroughly.

With that in mind, he had instructed Chris Deakin to contact his friend at Complaints straight after the office meeting in order to set up an urgent conference. Ideally, he wanted all the information that CIB had on Dr Sadler to be made available to the enquiry team by close of play today.

Steve Bull had been tasked to touch base with the GMC and to grab everything that they had. Tyler was particularly keen to establish the date and time of the anonymous call. It was probably too much to hope that the GMC had logged the telephone number the informant had called in from. However, if they did have it on record, there were immediate lines of enquiry that Jack needed to set in motion.

First on the list was a subscriber's check. From this, they should be able to obtain the user's name and billing address. Even if the number belonged to an unregistered pre-pay mobile, the owner might have been dumb enough to have purchased the handset, or a subsequent text and minutes bundle with one of the major networks, with a credit card.

Secondly, there was a chance that if the anonymous call was made from a London phone booth the informant would be captured on CCTV. If they were able to get actual footage of the caller, and if it turned out to be either Geraldine Rye or Alice Pilkington, James Sadler would certainly have some very awkward questions to answer.

Charlie White stood outside the surgery entrance, waiting impatiently for it to open. He turned up his collar, tucked his hands into his pockets, and stamped his feet to ward of the cold. There was a biting wind sweeping down the High Street, and the recessed door of the surgery provided scant protection from it.

The sign on the door, which he could hardly read through the grime stained window, proclaimed that the surgery opened for business at eight-thirty, but that was still fifteen-minutes away.

He considered popping into a local café to grab a quick bacon sandwich and a cup of coffee, but he decided it would be more prudent to get the request in first. He knew from experience that attempts to obtain a victim's medical records tended to go one of two ways, depending on the attitude of the practice manager and the relevant GP. Sometimes, they were quite happy to hand the information straight over, but there were occasions when a practice manager could be awkward to the point of being obstructive, forcing the requesting officer to obtain a court order before they would release any personal information. Charlie was hoping everything would go smoothly this morning; otherwise he would be tied up all day sorting out the paperwork required to apply to a court for a production order.

It suddenly occurred to him that there was probably a staff entrance at the rear, and that he might be able to have a quick word with the practice manager before they opened for business if he could find it. If nothing else, it would get him out of this sodding wind tunnel.

It took him a few minutes, but Charlie eventually worked his way around to the rear of the building, where there was a small staff car park. A door to the practice was ajar, and he set off towards this, pleased that his initiative had paid dividends.

As he reached the door, a powerful motorbike pulled into the car park. The rider, clad in black leathers and a matching helmet, revved the machine loudly before switching it off and dismounting.

After setting the motorcycle on its stand, the leather clad figure walked towards the staff entrance and Charlie White. "This is a private car park," a muffled, male voice said from beneath the helmet. Its mirrored visor prevented White from seeing anything of the man's face. "The public entrance is around the front."

"Yes, I know," White said, producing his warrant card. "I wanted to have a quick word with the practice manager before the surgery opens."

James Sadler removed the helmet and starred at White in half recognition. "Don't I know you?" he asked.

White smiled. "Aye, you do. You gave me some painkillers at Whitechapel police station the other night when I had the headache from hell."

Sadler nodded. "Yes, I remember. You're the murder squad chap, aren't you?"

"That's me," White confirmed.

"You'd better come inside then," Sadler announced, walking straight past the Scotsman.

It was much warmer inside, and White undid his raincoat as he followed the doctor through to the reception area, where a slim, middle aged woman with fair hair stared at him in surprise.

"Doreen, would you be kind enough to find Patricia for me. This gentleman is from the police and he would like a quick word with her."

"Oh dear, I do hope she's not in any trouble," Doreen said, giving White a worried look.

"Don't worry," he reassured her. "I just need to speak to her about getting access to some medical records."

"Is this in relation to the prostitute murders?" Sadler asked after Doreen had gone off to find the practice manager.

"Aye, it is," White said. He produced two small photographs from inside his coat pocket and showed them to Sadler. "This one's called Alice Pilkington, although she used the name of Natasha when she was working, and this one's name is Geraldine Rye. She wasnae a sex worker, though. They're both registered as patients here. Do the names of faces ring any bells?"

Sadler studied the images carefully for a few seconds, and then shook his head. "No, I can't say I recall either of them, but to be fair, I see so many patients that they all blur into one after a while so I'm probably not the best person to ask."

Just then, Doreen returned with a prissy looking, plump woman in her early fifties, whose expression could not have been any sourer if she had been sucking lemons.

Oh dear, Charlie thought. *This wee wifey doesnae look the friendly type.*

"Hello, I'm Patricia Dolton, the practice manager," she announced, as though she were royalty. "How can I help you, Constable?"

White smiled inwardly. Dolton was a Scottish idiom for 'idiot'.

"Actually, I'm a detective sergeant. Charlie White's the name," he said, producing his warrant card for inspection. She donned the reading glasses that had been hanging from her neck and examined the identification carefully, as though she suspected that it might be a fake. When she had studied every word written on it – twice – she handed it back.

"So, how can I be of assistance?" she asked, taking a liberal squirt from a wall mounted sanitiser and rubbing her hands together vigorously to get rid of any unpleasant germs that might be ingrained in the police officer's warrant card.

Charlie took a deep breath and launched into an explanation that started with some detail about the three murders they were investigating, and concluded with a request for copies of the medical records of the two victims who were registered at the practice.

Although Doreen seemed riveted, Patricia was less impressed. "I see," she said when he had concluded. "Well, I will have to discuss it with the doctor they were registered with, and then we can make an informed decision. I'll get back to you sometime next week with an answer."

White shook his head. "Sorry, but that won't do. We have a killer on the loose and we really need to make this happen today, even if it means getting a production order from court." He looked across at Dr Sadler, who had watched the exchange with detached interest. "I'm sure Dr Sadler will be sympathetic to our request, what with him being an FME and all. And I'm sure he'll vouch for me when I say that patient confidentiality goes out the window when said patient has been murdered. What do you say, doc?"

Being awarded an FME contract was a very good earner, White knew, and he very much doubted that Sadler would want to be seen as obstructive when the police were conducting such a high-profile murder investigation. After all, you don't bite the hand that feeds you, as the saying goes.

Sadler appeared to consider his stance on the matter, but White could already see in the other man's eyes that he was going to give in.

"I'm sure we can accommodate your request today," Sadler declared a moment later. "Doreen, can you check the system and confirm which GP these ladies were registered with, please," he asked the receptionist without taking his eyes off the detective.

White affected a look of boredom, but inwardly he was feeling mightily pleased as he listened to the receptionist tapping away at her computer keyboard behind him.

"They're both shown as your patients, Dr Sadler," she stated as soon as the typing stopped.

"I see," Sadler said. "In that case, Patricia, I have no objections to their release. I'll leave you to prepare a copy of the two women's records for the officer as I have to prepare for my first appointment." With that, he was gone.

"If you'd like to take a seat in the waiting area," Patricia told him, frostily. "I'll print out the information you require. We will, of course, require a receipt."

Of course," White said, wondering if she planned to suck any more lemons while she was out of the room.

When he was alone with the receptionist, the atmosphere immediately became friendlier. "You know, it's strange that Dr Sadler didn't recognise those women's names," she said, lowering her voice conspiratorially.

"Is it?" Charlie asked. "Why's that?"

"Well, Ms Pilkington, was always coming in here and making a right nuisance of herself. Between you and me," she said, looking around to make sure they couldn't be overheard, "she was a vile woman. She was always drunk, and she had such a foul mouth on her."

White raised an eyebrow. "Interesting," he said. "And what did Dr Sadler think of her?"

"Oh, he couldn't stand her," Doreen said. "He was always complaining that once she was in his office, he couldn't get her out, and sometimes she was up there with him for absolute ages."

Is that a fact?

"Oh yes," Doreen confirmed. "God knows why he didn't strike her off the surgery register. She did more than enough to justify his refusing to treat her anymore."

Perhaps it was because the randy old sod was sticking more than his thermometer in her mouth when he was examining her? White kept the thought to himself.

The day passed by uneventfully, and with Daylight Savings Time having ended on 31st October, the clocks had gone back an hour, so it was almost dark by five-o'clock.

There had been intermittent showers during the early afternoon, but they had finally cleared up and it looked like it was going to stay dry for Bonfire Night.

Although a lot of the organised displays weren't taking place until tomorrow evening, it wasn't long before the fireworks started. They were sporadic at first; just a few Bangers and Rockets, but by eight-o'clock the racket was almost incessant as the night sky was repeatedly lit up by explosions of bright colour.

Tyler and Dillon were oblivious to what was going on outside as they sat in the office, going through the information that had come in during the day. Unfortunately, there was nothing to get them even remotely excited.

Deakin's buddy from Complaints had given them everything he had on Sadler, which was basically a copy of what the GMC had given him. It took them precisely nowhere.

The GMC had confirmed that an anonymous female had rung

them at 13:00 hours on Wednesday 27th October. Refusing to provide any personal details, she had made a rushed allegation and then hung up. The voice had sounded muffled, as though the caller had wrapped a handkerchief or something around the mouthpiece to disguise her voice. The only good news was that the GMC did, in fact, have a note of the incoming number. The call had been made from a 020 number, which meant it had originated from within the Greater London area.

Reggie, the team's resident phone expert, had already submitted a subscriber check, but that wouldn't come back in until Monday at the earliest. This was because the SPOC – Single Point of Contact – at the Telephone Investigation Unit was unwilling to treat it as a priority submission. Apparently, he had explained, it didn't meet the criteria laid out in their Standard Operating Procedures.

The GMC had made some enquiries into Sadler's prescribing history following the accusation, but nothing untoward had been revealed.

According to the investigator at the GMC, Sadler had been qualified for nearly twenty-years, and had been on the FME approved list for five. He had an impeccable record, and in the absence of any additional material to corroborate it, this allegation was likely to be resulted as malicious and unfounded.

Despite what Charlie had told them upon his return from the doctor's surgery this morning, Jack knew they didn't have enough grounds to interview Sadler.

What they had against him was so flimsy that it would be stretching the imagination to even consider using the term 'circumstantial evidence' to describe it: An anonymous woman had complained that he was receiving sexual favours in exchange for prescribing controlled drugs to prostitutes and drug addicts a few days before the first murder occurred – not that his prescribing history in any way supported that claim; he just happened to be the GP for two of the New Ripper's victims; he had claimed not to recognise Alice Pilkington's name or her photograph, although his receptionist was adamant that the sex worker often came in to see Dr Sadler and spent ages his office each time she visited.

Sadler and his legal representative would simply laugh at them if they interviewed him on the basis of that. No, unless supporting evidence came to light over the coming days, they wouldn't be going anywhere near Dr Sadler.

All they could do now was hope the subs check would identify a telephone kiosk that was covered by local authority CCTV, and that this would provide them with footage of whoever made the call. Even then, unless it transpired that the caller was Pilkington or Rye their enquiries would hit a brick wall.

"This is so frustrating," Jack complained. "I feel like we're just wasting valuable time and resources following this Sadler allegation up."

"We don't have a choice, mate," Dillon told him.

"I know," Jack snapped, "but it seems to me that all we do at the moment is chase shadows and grasp at straws."

"Jack," Dillon soothed, "we're working in strict compliance with the Murder Manual framework, and we're doing everything that's humanly possible to find the bastard who's murdering these women. Over the past few days we've taken a stack of statements, and we've seized a tonne of CCTV. God alone knows how long it's going to take Paul Evans to view all that footage. We're pursuing multiple lines of enquiries relating to telephone numbers, financial histories, and various vehicles that have been seen in the vicinity of the crime scenes during the relevant times. We've also carried out the requisite anniversary visits and leaflet drops. All the forensic material gathered from the three crime scenes is being processed, and we've had more publicity on this case than any other job I can ever remember working on. Something will eventually give, and when it does, we will catch him."

"I know, Dill," Jack said, miserably, "but when?"

"You're still worried that he'll strike again at any moment?" Dillon asked, studying his friend carefully.

"I'm absolutely convinced he will," Jack confessed.

Dillon sighed. "All we can do is spread the word for everyone to be extra vigilant and try and get the uniform patrols in Whitechapel increased over the weekend," he said.

Jack gave a mirthless laugh. "I've already tried doing that. Apparently, Bonfire Night weekend is one of the busiest times of the year for the emergency services and they expect to be run ragged dealing with all the calls that come in."

"You know, having all those extra people out and about, enjoying themselves at firework displays and bonfire parties, means the streets are going to be buzzing tonight. That might just work to our advantage," Dillon said, trying to sound positive.

"It might," Jack agreed, sounding incredibly morose. "Or it might work to his."

It was nearly midnight, everywhere was shrouded in dense mist from where all the fireworks had been set off earlier, and it was raining again. Not that The Disciple was complaining. The rain was his friend. Statistically speaking, it was a known fact that far less crime was committed during periods of inclement weather than at any other time. It was also a known fact that even the most conscientious police officers were reluctant to get out of their nice cosy patrol cars without an extremely good reason when it was pissing down.

Spookily, despite the weather forecast predicting a cool, dry evening, the downpour had begun within minutes of him starting tonight's hunt. It was, he knew, yet another sign of his growing power.

Now that all the fireworks had finally stopped, the streets seemed eerily quiet, especially for for a Friday night. That wasn't going to be a problem; there was always action to be found somewhere in Whitechapel if you knew where to look, and The Disciple knew exactly where to look.

He picked up his fourth victim in Middlesex Street. Her name turned out to be Sonia, and she was an anorexic mixed-race girl in her late teens with a face full of angry pimples. She seemed awkward and embarrassed when he broached the subject of sex, giving him the impression that she hadn't been on the game for very long. As soon as a price was agreed he patted the passenger seat impatiently, indicating that she should join him inside the van. She climbed in, brushing water from the shoulders of her plastic jacket.

Tonight's disguise consisted of a black-haired wig, worn under a flat cap, a stick-on goatee and a pair of circular glasses.

Given that he was the most wanted man in London, he wanted to get off the streets as soon as possible. With that in mind, he pulled away from the kerb the instant she closed her door.

"Where are we going?" Sonia demanded, pulling her seatbelt on. There was a note of apprehension in her voice, but he knew her anxiety stemmed from the fact that no money had changed hands yet as opposed to any fears she might have over her safety.

The rain was getting worse by the minute, and he increased the speed of the wipers to compensate, not that it made much difference.

"I know a quiet place not too far from here, where we won't be disturbed by the police." He did, too. Tracey Phillips had very considerately shown it to him on the night he had killed her.

"That's all well and good, but you haven't paid for my services yet."

"Oh, don't worry," he promised, "I'll make sure you get your just reward." He tried to smile but it came out as a grimace. The music in his head was becoming louder again, and he made a conscious attempt to dull it down so that he would be able to hear her reply.

"You'd better," she warned him, "because I ain't performing till I've been paid."

"I'm a Capricorn," The Disciple lied. "What's your star sign?"

She glanced sideways at him, the hint of a frown creasing her brow. Her face said: *Are you for real?*

The Disciple took a deep breath and repeated the question, making a huge effort to sound friendly.

There was an awkward silence, and he could tell from the vexed expression on her face that she was on the verge of having a strop. "I'm an Aires," she eventually told him. "What's it to you?"

The Disciple shrugged. "Just making conversation," he said, trying to keep the mood jovial. He wasn't sure that she had answered truthfully, and as the ritual would be rendered useless unless he consumed the organ that corresponded to her Zodiacal sign, he decided to ask her again as soon as they reached their destination. Only the next time he asked, there would be a knife at her throat, and she would be made painfully aware of the consequences of lying to him.

Sonia clearly wasn't impressed with this feeble attempt at small talk. "Tell you what; you can talk to me all you want after you pay me. Till then..." She raised her right hand to her mouth, mimed zipping up her lips, and then crossed her arms defiantly.

My, you're a feisty one, he thought. She had seemed so demure when he'd first spoken to her. *Well*, he mused, *it just goes to show how deceiving looks can be, and I should know.*

"Don't worry," he told her, using his most reassuring tone, "We're nearly there, and I promise I'll give you exactly what you deserve the moment we arrive."

CHAPTER TWENTY-SEVEN

Monday 8th November 1999

"Heads up, everyone. Here they come," Evans warned as he entered the conference room. He had just hot-footed it from Tyler's office, where the DCI, Dillon, and Holland had been squirreled away since seven o'clock that morning, discussing the case. He had interrupted their meeting just as it was finishing, excitedly informing them about an explosive piece of CCTV evidence he had literally just found. He knew they would want to be forewarned before the main meeting started; bosses always liked to be told about new developments in advance of the plebs.

Evans took a seat near the rear of the room, next to Kelly Flowers, so he could access the video when the time came. The chairs had been neatly arranged in rows of ten to form three semicircles facing the whiteboard.

It was eight o'clock on the dot when Tyler, Dillon, and Holland entered the conference room. The extended team of thirty officers stood up respectfully and all conversation died.

"Thank you. Please be seated. You might as well make yourself comfortable because we're going to be here a while," Holland informed them grimly. "Right, we're entering the second week of Operation Crawley. I want to start by thanking you all for your hard work and your dedication to duty. I'm aware that some of you have already worked seven long days on the trot, and you will probably have to work another seven before you get a day off. The only consolation I can offer is that your bank balances will all be considerably healthier by the time this investigation concludes." That was certainly true; most of the command had just worked two twelve-hour shifts at double time after he'd cancelled their weekend leave. In addition, he dreaded to think how many hours of time-and-a-third overtime Tyler's team had clocked up during the first week, not to mention all the double time they had earned on the day that the case had broken, when they had been called in on their day off. At this rate, the command would be facing bankruptcy before the killer was put behind bars.

"So far, all we've had to show for our valiant efforts are three victims and a shit load of bad press." Holland allowed himself a brief smile. "But we're still very much in the race. The forensic and CCTV work you've all been breaking your backs to get through is finally beginning to pay dividends, and a much clearer picture is emerging. We're breathing down the bastard's neck, and it's only a matter of time before we take him down. DCI Tyler will update you on some interesting developments in a moment. First, the Commissioner has asked me to pass on his best wishes and inform you that he has complete trust in you, even if you are bleeding his budget dry!"

"Phew! That's a relief," Bull said, theatrically wiping his brow. Everyone laughed, including Holland, and the atmosphere lightened a little.

"When poor Tracey Phillips died last Monday," Holland continued, "we all hoped that she was a one-off. None of us expected another murder, let alone two, to happen so quickly afterwards. Since then we've all been on tenterhooks because we half expect another one to occur at any bloody second."

"Thanks to Chief Superintendent Porter goading the killer on TV,"

Murray said, and his words generated several nods of agreement and a few derisive groans.

"Indeed," Holland allowed. "Now, it has to be said that AMIP has been put in an unenviable position. The eyes of the nation are focused on us, with everyone and their dog demanding a quick result. Well, it might not happen quite as quickly as everyone wants, but I have no doubts whatsoever that we'll get them their bloody result in the end. So, that's it from me. DCI Tyler and his core role officers are now going to talk us through what we've achieved so far." With that, he sat down next to Tyler.

"Thank you," Tyler said. "I want to start by reiterating what the boss has already said and add my own thanks for all your hard work to date. We're dealing with a serial killer who appears to be driven by a pathological hatred of women. We don't know what has made him like this, or why he has chosen now to start his killing spree. He strikes randomly, but at least his attacks are confined to one division. This is great news if you live in Walthamstow or East Ham but pretty shitty if you happen to live or work in Whitechapel. Results are finally starting to come in. We're going to talk through what we know about each victim and look at the forensic, CCTV and witness evidence relating to each one. I would normally ask Chris to take the lead on this as OM, but he's been rushed off his feet for the past few days carrying out some High Priority actions for me, so his deputy, Tim, is going to walk us through the investigation and I'll do my usual and interrupt as we go along. Over to you, Tim."

Tim Barton stood up and took centre stage. He flipped through his briefing notes, aware that everyone was waiting for him to start. Clearing his throat, he began.

"Okay. Victim number one: Tracey Phillips, a twenty-two-year-old white female, unmarried, with no permanent love interest unless you count her pimp, Claude Winston..."

"Evil slag," Dillon growled under his breath.

"...who is currently recovering in hospital from injuries he received after his face accidentally collided with a platform floor...several times...while he was resisting arrest."

This revelation brought laughter, a few cheers, and smiles all around. Dillon sat there quietly, the picture of innocence. Holland raised a finger to his lips and the room quickly quietened down.

"Unfortunately, while he's looking at some very serious jail time, we now know he's not responsible for Tracey's death." Barton turned the page before continuing.

"She leaves behind a five-year-old child and an elderly mother. Tracey was a South London girl, a prostitute, who worked around Commercial Street and lived in a nearby squat. The last confirmed sighting we have of her is at about 01:25 hours in Quaker Street on Sunday 31st October, and that was by her best friend, Sandra Dawson, a fellow prostitute. Dawson popped off to use the loo shortly after, and when she came back approximately fifteen minutes later, Tracey had gone. Her mutilated body was found the following morning at a nearby building site by the watchman. As there are no witnesses, we don't know if she went there of her own volition or was abducted. In the past week, we've conducted door to door enquiries with every shop, pub, business and residential premises in the vicinity of her last sighting and the body deposition site. We've done this for all three victims, and nothing useful has come out of any of it. Over the weekend, with the help of the charity workers Steve Bull rustled up from the Sutton Mission, we've interviewed every sex worker we could find – forty-two in total. If they can be believed, none of them has a Scooby about what happened to any of our victims. We've had PCSOs handing out witness appeal leaflets to the public all week." He held one up for them to see. "They contain the usual message. You know, requesting information or sightings from anyone who was in the area on the night in question, and naturally, they promise complete confidentiality for anyone coming forward." He contemptuously screwed the A5 sized leaflet up into a ball and threw it into a wastebasket. "So far, we've drawn a complete blank," he told them with a bittersweet smile. His tone implied the exercise had been a complete waste of time and money.

"But it's still early days yet. Someone could be wrestling with their conscience, trying to pluck up the nerve to contact us with information that could lead to a vital breakthrough," DC Richard Jarvis piped up from the back of the room. Jarvis, fresh-faced and fair-haired, was the youngest member of Jack's team. He was also the newest. A Cambridge University graduate who only joined the Job four years ago, he spoke with a frightfully posh accent, which sometimes made him the butt of jokes for some of the old sweats. Jarvis took the jibes in his stride, retorting that if he had a pound for every time one of the old farts told him they might not have attended Cambridge but they were graduates of the 'University of Life', he would be a rich man.

"That university education your parents paid for was wasted on you, wasn't it?" Murray said, eyeing Jarvis with scorn.

Copeland snorted. "Sounds like something straight out of the detective training manual."

"Okay, so we have no witnesses," Jack said, killing the banter before it could start. "We've discussed applying for a reward to be sanctioned, and if we are no further forward by the end of the week DCS Holland will speak to the AC about making it happen. Kelly, what about CCTV?" Kelly had spent the entire weekend assisting Paul Evans, the enquiry's dedicated CCTV officer, to view the footage. She had sat staring at a screen for so many hours that she was surprised her eyes hadn't turned square.

Kelly stood up hesitantly and walked over to the TV-video combination. "Could somebody flick the light switch for me, please," she asked, switching the TV combo on.

"I'd like to do more than flick the lights for you, sweetheart," Murray leered, Les Dawson style, and was rewarded with a slap across the back of the head from Steve Bull.

Kelly smiled at his chivalry. "Thank you, Steve."

"Thank you, Steve," Murray mimicked, and he had to duck quickly to avoid a second blow. Once the lights were out, she played the tape. It was in black and white and the quality was dubious. The picture flickered briefly and then settled. Flowers gave a commentary to augment the picture.

"Right, I've reviewed the bulk of the footage relating to Tracey and Alice. Paul has been looking at everything relating to Geraldine. Unfortunately, the spot in Quaker Street where Tracey and her mates were plying for trade isn't covered by CCTV, but there's a local authority camera further along Commercial Road that provides coverage of the junction, so we can see vehicles turning into or pulling out of Quaker Street. There is also a private wall-mounted CCTV system further along Quaker Street, about a hundred yards past the used car lot, so we've effectively got footage of the only two routes she could have taken to get in and out of Quaker Street. We have identified Winston's BMW turning into Quaker Street at 01:23 hours, and we now know that was how Tracey arrived. Furthermore, we can safely say that Tracey didn't leave the area on foot, which means she must have gotten into a vehicle, either of her own accord or under duress. The viewing parameters the DI set for the first murder required us to search for any vehicles that appeared to be engaging in kerb-crawling. These were allocated High Priority Trace-Identify-Eliminate actions, and I know that quite a few of you were kept very busy visiting the registered keepers of all these cars over the weekend."

"I had a very awkward conversation with one man who vehemently denied being anywhere near the area," Jarvis said. "At least he did until his wife popped out to make us tea. Then he was practically down on his knees begging me not to say anything in front of her. It was a bit sad really."

Murray looked at him as though he were retarded. "You really are in the wrong job, you know that, right?"

"I know all these seemingly pointless TIE actions have been a royal pain in the arse for some of you," Dillon said, "but they were important, and they have helped us to eliminate about ninety percent of people who appeared on the CCTV. Kelly, tell these good people – and DC Murray – what we are left with."

"As Mr Dillon says, after sorting the wheat from the chaff, we now have a shortlist of five vehicles of interest. They all turn up at Quaker Street several times during the relevant period. Four of these vehicles are cars." She played a brief section of footage showing four different cars. The date and time stamp on the screen changed along with each of the vehicles. Kelly pressed the pause button as a battered Leyland Sherpa van appeared centre screen. The frozen picture wasn't good enough to make out the driver's face and the registration plate was covered with dirt. The only noticeable feature was that one of the headlights was badly out of alignment. "I want to draw your attention to this van. It's the fifth vehicle on our shortlist and I think it's the most likely vehicle for our killer to be using. Why? Because a van like that can be parked inconspicuously almost anywhere, with someone in the back watching his targets through blacked out windows. We do it all the time. It's quick, simple and can be moved around to suit your needs. It's also the perfect way to transport a messy victim from 'A' to 'B' without drawing attention. That's all the CCTV relating to Tracey, but I'll talk more about this van a bit later."

"Right," Jack said as Kelly sat down, "talk us through the forensics next, if you would, Tim. George, feel free to join in."

Tim Barton had sat down to watch the CCTV, but now he stood up again. "I've got Sam Calvin's crime scene report here. It won't come as a surprise to any of you to hear that the killer didn't leave us any fingerprints, shoeprints or DNA at the scene. That would have made our lives far too easy. We didn't recover any foreign trace fibres from her clothing either." He allowed himself an ironic smile. "And, as you all know, the DNA hit we got from the flesh beneath her nails turned out to be a red herring."

Tim picked up a document with the FSS logo on and started flicking through it. "Blood pattern analysis is interesting. The experts have given us their interpretation of her final moments based on the shape, pattern, and radius of her blood fall. Due to the high arterial spatter pattern they found, they reckon that our man slit her throat from behind, while she was still standing up and had blood pressure, and stood back as she thrashed around like a fish out of water. The blood pattern peaks and dips in line with the heartbeat and spirals down dramatically as she collapses to the floor. They think she was bound when the cut was inflicted, which would account for her severely restricted range of movement." Barton grimaced as he imagined the killer standing back, just out of range of the blood spray, watching dispassionately as she bled to death. "The autopsy supports our theory that her arms were tied behind her," he added.

"Handcuffed, you mean," George Copeland corrected.

"Yes, that's right. Thank you, George," Barton said, flicking through his papers to find the pathologist's report. "George, you were at the SPM. It's probably best if you talk us through that."

"Two different types of knife were used," Copeland said, quoting from memory, "one being a twelve or thirteen-inch serrated hunting knife, which was rammed up her muff – we worked out the blade length from the extent of the damage inflicted. The throat was cut from behind, right to left, indicating that the killer is left-handed. The pathologist reckons the abdominal cuts were surgical in nature, and a scalpel was probably used. Parts of her intestines are missing – they were never recovered at the scene. The obvious conclusion, as distasteful as it is, is that chummy removed them and took them with him."

"Perhaps the sick fucker is a cannibal," Charlie White suggested. Why else would anyone take human flesh with them after a kill?

"That's an astute observation, Charlie. We'll come back to that point a little later," Tyler said, not wanting to be pulled off topic or jump ahead of the script. "Any sign of infectious disease or STDs?" he asked.

Tim shook his head. "Nope, according to the pathologist's report and the preliminary toxicology results, there were no signs of HIV, Hepatitis, or any historical or current Sexually Transmitted Disease."

"Can you confirm there was no trace of recent sex?" Jack asked.

"I can. Firstly, we know she was banged up in a south London nick for eighteen-hours over the weekend for kiting stolen checks. When she was released, she went straight home and called her pimp, who collected her and drove her to Quaker Street. Sandra Dawson confirms she didn't go off with anyone before she disappeared. Secondly, there was definitely no seamen or traces of spermicide inside her."

Traces of semen had been found in the vaginal wall of rape victims up to fourteen days after intercourse, despite the fact that the traumatised women had rinsed themselves raw. It could still be found in the mouth up to thirty-six hours after ejaculation, and no amount of teeth cleaning or gargling could completely obliterate it. A complete absence of any foreign DNA in a career prostitute like Tracey indicated that she practiced safe sex – unusual for a declining junkie. But there were still ways to get a perpetrator's DNA off of a victim, even after protected sex.

"Was she combed, swabbed and taped?" Holland asked.

"She was," George confirmed. "Tracey's pubic hair was combed for foreign hair; there were none. Her skin, vagina, and anus were swabbed for alien DNA transmitted via the sweat of a client; nothing was found. As you know, we all constantly shed minuscule flakes of skin. She was tested for any microscopic deposits belonging to the killer, or anyone else. Guess what? Zilch. The pathologist is confident that something would have turned up if she had been out shagging before the killer struck. For it not to have done so, the bloke would have had to have been kitted out in a condom that covered his entire body, not just his dick. Even then, there would probably be traces of the spermicide condoms are coated in, which I believe is most commonly nonoxynol-9. Conclusion: she was done in before she could open shop."

"Open her legs, he means," Murray sniggered in Grier's ear, earning himself a disapproving glare from Dillon.

"Interestingly," Barton said, "there were marks on the body that suggested she had been wearing underwear, but this was never recovered."

"So, he's a trophy taker as well as a cannibal," White said.

"We'll come back to that possibility in a little while," Tyler said. "At this point, I want to ask Chris Deakin to talk us through the financial enquiries he's been making for me."

Chris Deakin leaned forward in his chair. "For those of you who don't know, I worked on the fraud squad in a past life so the boss asked me to conduct some enquiries into the money that was found in the deceased's possession."

"Hopefully," Jack interjected, "you have all had time to read the briefing document that DI Dillon prepared, and are all aware that Tracey Phillips had three brand new ten-pound notes in her purse when her body was found," This was said for the benefit of the officers who had been seconded to the enquiry over the weekend.

"When we examined the notes, we immediately saw that they were numbered consecutively," Deakin continued. "This suggested they were newly printed notes that had been issued together by a bank or building society, most probably through a hole in the wall. To cut a long story short, I made some enquiries with my old banking contacts and confirmed this was the case. Two Production Orders later, I can tell you that the notes were issued from a Nat West ATM in Whitechapel Road. The notes were part of a batch placed in the ATM on the morning of Saturday 30th October. It has taken some doing, but I've finally obtained a list of every person who made a withdrawal of thirty-pounds or more between then and 06:00 hours on Monday 1st November. Not only that, but there is a CCTV camera covering the cash point – there have been robberies in the area – and we have now received the digital download of the footage for the relevant period."

"We know from Sandra Dawson that Tracey didn't have a penny on her when she arrived in Quaker Street," Jack said. "Sandra even purchased two rocks of crack for Tracey because she didn't have any money to buy them herself, yet when her body was found she suddenly had thirty-pounds in her purse. I think our killer gave Tracey that cash. I think if we identify who made the withdrawal, we identify our killer."

"How would we ever be able to prove that?" Murray asked.

Jack smiled. "George, how do we prove it?"

"I had the notes treated with ninhydrin at the lab. We recovered two clear sets of fingerprints. One belonged to our victim; the other is not on the system, meaning it belongs to someone who has never been arrested."

"We have three brand new notes, fresh from the cash machine," Jack said, "with two sets of fingerprints on them. One set belongs to the deceased. If the unidentified prints on the notes match the person who made the withdrawal, I think a jury will be persuaded that he is our killer." He could almost hear the cogs turning as the detectives mulled this over, and he held up a hand to stem the questions that were clearly forming in their minds. "As the meeting goes on, we're going to be introducing some supporting evidence, so save your questions until the end, when you have the full picture."

"I have names and addresses for all the people making withdrawals," Deakin said. "I'll pin it up in the MIR straight after the meeting. I would like you all to read through it to see if any names jump out at you. Brian, Dean, Wendy, I'll issue HP actions for PNC checks and very basic research to be carried out on each one. HP actions will also be issued this morning for every name on the list to be visited. We'll require statements from all of them to see what they did with the money. We'll also need elim prints and voluntary DNA samples from everyone on the list to eliminate them from our enquiries."

"I understand why we need prints, but why do we need DNA samples as well?" Charlie White asked.

"All will be revealed," Tyler said cryptically. "Just bear with us for a few minutes longer and I promise it will all make sense."

"Right, I think that just about covers victim number one," Holland said. "Let's move on to victim number two."

"One last thing before we move on," Jack said. "I take it you are all aware of the 'Jack's back' message he painted in the victim's blood at the body deposition site? We'll talk about all the messages the killer's left us in due course. For the moment, all you need to know is he left a message telling us to be afraid because –" he made air quotes with his fingers "– Jack's back." He nodded for Barton to continue.

CHAPTER TWENTY-EIGHT

At the same time as the detectives were starting their meeting in the conference room at Arbour Square, Sarah Pritchard and her husband Simon were sitting down over a cup of coffee for their regular Monday morning tête-à-tête to discuss the Mission's plans and priorities for the coming week.

Sarah had spent the night in the small flat above the Mission, which is where she had been staying for the last three weeks, since she had moved out of the matrimonial home to give them both some breathing space. Although their marriage was on the rocks, neither of them had allowed the cracks – some would say chasms – that had developed in their personal life to interfere with their professional relationship.

"So, how did you get on over the weekend?" Simon Pritchard asked his wife, more out of politeness than interest. Much to Sarah's ire, he had flatly refused to join the group of volunteers she'd assembled to assist the local constabulary in canvassing the area's sex workers, stating that he preferred managing the business side of the operation to being 'hands on' with the clients in the way she so dearly loved to be. Besides, he told her, there was a black-tie event at his Masonic Lodge on Saturday night, and she knew he hated to miss those.

"It went well, all things considering," she replied.

"Did any of the girls you spoke to see anything?" he asked.

No, they didn't; at least none of them admitted to seeing anything."

Pritchard huffed. "A complete waste of your time, then," he said, dismissively. "You should have come with me. I had a whale of a time."

Sarah bristled. He could be such a smarmy bastard at times. "Actually, it wasn't a complete waste of time. I doubt the girls would have spoken to the police at all if we hadn't been there, and we managed to interest a few of them in our intervention project. If even one of them takes up our offer, that'll be another girl off the streets and out of danger."

Simon Pritchard snorted derisively. "Trouble is, for every one you save two more take their place. Besides, most of the girls that we supposedly 'save' end up back on the streets within a few months of leaving the Mission. Makes you wonder why we bother."

Sarah thumped her desk so hard it made her hand sting. "It doesn't make me wonder," she snapped. Tears prickled at her eyes. "I don't know why you bother if you think what we're trying to achieve here is such a waste of time."

No one could ever accuse Sarah of being a quitter and in spite of everything that had gone wrong between them she remained fully committed to working through the problems in their marriage, which ironically were all of his making. He claimed he was equally committed to sorting things out, but when he spoke so dismissively about the Mission and its legacy, it made her wonder if her husband was less worried about losing her than he was about losing the money and lifestyle her inheritance had given him.

As was his way, Simon Pritchard immediately backed down and showed contrition. "I'm so sorry, dear," he said, pinching the bridge of his nose. "I've got a bit of a migraine this morning, and you know how cranky that can make me. I didn't mean it the way it came across. I'm sure the police were very grateful for all the help they received, and I agree wholeheartedly that any situation that gives us a chance to promote the good work we do should be embraced."

Sarah nodded, seemingly appeased. "They were very grateful," she said, recalling how pleased Steve Bull and his colleagues had been about the support the volunteers had given them at such short notice.

"There is one thing that has come to light, though," Sarah admitted uneasily, "and I don't know if I should mention it to Steve or not."

"Do tell," he said, intrigued.

"Last night one of the sex workers pulled me aside and confided that she was having real problems with one of her clients. Apparently, he's a bit of a deviant."

"Aren't they all in your book?" he said sarcastically.

"I make no secret of the fact that I am repulsed by any man who feels the need to pay for sex," she said, her eyes boring into his like twin laser beams, "but this man doesn't only want sex, he gets off on hurting the girls, and he often says very disturbing things when he's – you know – approaching climax."

"Like what?" Pritchard asked, sitting forward expectantly.

Sarah shook her head in disgust. "He describes the ways he'd like to hurt them in graphic detail. It seems to really turn him on."

"Why haven't you told the police?" he asked.

She gave a lame shrug. "The girl asked me not to. Apparently, this client claims to be a local police officer. She caught a glimpse of his rank, or rather his lack of it, on Saturday night, as he'd forgotten to remove his lanyard from around his neck when he visited her. It transpires that he's actually a member of the civil staff."

"What about his name," Pritchard asked. "Did she see that?"

Sarah nodded. "Yes, he told her his name was Brian, but the name on the badge said Henry Boyden."

"Bloody hell," Pritchard said, looking shocked. "Surely it's not the same Henry Boyden who volunteers here?"

"I think it is," Sarah said, "and I think I'm going to have to break her confidence and tell Steve Bull."

"Victim number two is Alice Patricia Pilkington, currently using the street name of 'Natasha,' Tim Barton said. "She was a forty-five-year-old prostitute, originally from Liverpool but more recently residing on the Isle of Dogs. No known dependents or relatives, at least not in the big smoke. We identified her through her fingerprints. Unsurprisingly, she has some petty form for soliciting, theft-shoplifting and being drunk and disorderly. She wasn't a drug addict, although she apparently liked a good drink."

"Don't we all," Charlie White said, longingly.

"True," Barton said, "but it looks like she was shit faced more often than not. According to the pathologist she had chronic progressive deterioration of the liver."

"What does that mean?" Grier asked Murray, who was sitting beside him.

"It means she was a pisshead," Murray replied sarcastically, and a little too loudly.

"Quiet." Holland barked. Murray shifted uneasily in his seat. Grier folded his arms and sat up straight, like a schoolboy at assembly time.

"She was also syphilitic, and it looks like she had Chlamydia, too," Barton said, reading from his notes.

After making sure that Holland was looking elsewhere, Murray leaned into Grier and shielded his mouth with his hand. "Oi," he whispered, "do you know what the doctor said when one of his patients died from an STD?"

Eyes rigidly glued to the front, Grier gave a subtle shake of his head. The last thing he needed, as a probationer plod, was get another bollocking from a Detective Chief Superintendent.

"We've got a gonorrhoea!" Murray said, sniggering like a naughty five-year-old. Luckily, no one seemed to hear him.

"Her pimp was the last person to see her alive," Barton was saying. "According to him, at approximately 21:10 hours on Tuesday 2nd November she was being rogered by a trick in an alley at the back of a restaurant in Brick Lane. He knows this because he was listening to the Champions League match on the radio in his car, which was parked nearby. Traces of seamen were found in Alice's vagina, or what was left of it, and we think this is most likely from the client her pimp mentioned in his statement. We've sent a sample off for DNA profiling, and if we get a result, we will obviously issue an action to statement him."

"Wonder if the stupid sod has started itching yet?" Copeland said, shaking his head in disbelief. "She had syphilis and Chlamydia. What sort of idiot would have unprotected sex with a prostitute?"

"Alice normally handed her takings over to her pimp for safekeeping after each trick," Barton said. "When she hadn't reappeared by half-past-nine he thought he'd better go and check on her, but she had vanished from the face of the earth."

"Did he call the cops?" Copeland asked.

"Don't be daft! He just assumed the lazy cow – his words, not mine – had skived off to the pub for a drink."

"Sounds like a nice, caring sort of bloke," Charlie White remarked.

"He was a real charmer," Barton told him. "When we told him she was dead, his first worry was that he would be out of pocket till he replaced her."

"You think the mutilation of Tracey's body was bad, but what he did to Alice was ten times worse," Jack said, taking up the narrative where Barton had left off. "We found her in a derelict house in Hanbury Street." His voice became embittered as he described what happened next. "You all know the story: two selfish reporters get a call from the killer, and instead of calling the police, they popped over to the crime scene and did their best to destroy it, all in the name of journalism. What did the post-mortem reveal, George?"

"The victim was beaten about the head and face with an iron bar, four heavy blows in all. She had a depressed skull fracture and compression of the brain. In an identical manner to Tracey Phillips, the serrated hunting knife was repeatedly rammed into her vagina while she was still alive in what I can only describe as some form of perverted intercourse. Her womb and uterus were literally shredded like mincemeat. Her throat was cut with such force that the head was almost severed clean off. The blood spatter indicates that she was lying down for all of this."

Jack raised a hand, indicating that George should stop. "The pathologist and crime scene reports are in the MIR, along with all the record photography. You should take the time to familiarise yourself with them over the next couple of days if you haven't done so already." He could tell from the mixed facial expressions in his audience that some of the detectives, mainly the advanced exhibits officers, would be very keen to read the reports and view the photographs, while others would rather chew their own arm off.

"Carry on, George."

"The killer opened her torso using surgical cuts and removed every internal organ from her body. The way he did this implies at least rudimentary medical knowledge. One eye was missing; we initially wondered if the killer had removed it, but upon closer examination, it quickly became apparent that one of the resident rodents was responsible. For some unfathomable reason, the killer folded her hands into her stomach cavity." He used his own hands to demonstrate the position they had been placed in. "He then carefully arranged her innards in the front room for us to find. Although most of her intestines were hung up like Christmas decorations, he left a small section over one shoulder. God alone knows why."

"Because he's fucking evil personified," Charlie White said, putting into words what every other person in the room was thinking.

Watching Nick Bartholomew's face completely drain of colour while George described the macabre scene, Dillon felt a twinge of sympathy. He guessed that the poor lad was having a flashback to the traumatic experience, and he recalled the sheer horror that had registered on Nick's face when he'd realised that the victim's blood was dripping down on him from one of the freshly harvested organs the killer had suspended from the ceiling.

"There was another message in blood, written on a wall in the living room," Jack said. "There are photographs in the MIR for those of you that didn't attend the scene. As with Tracey, we have reason to believe Alice was wearing underwear, but this has never been recovered. So, I think Charlie is spot on when he says our man is a trophy taker. I also think Charlie hit the nail on the head when he talked about our boy being a cannibal. George, would you tell our colleagues what we found when we examined the victim's heart, please."

Charlie White was looking mightily pleased with himself over his two astute deductions, Jack noted, suppressing a grin.

"The heart had a great big chunk missing from it," George informed them. "Two bites worth, to be precise. Because the place was infested with giant rats –" He suppressed a shudder as he recalled the constant scuttling noises they had made during the long hours he'd spent inside that hell house, first processing the scene with Sam Calvin and then supervising the removal of evidence. "– we naturally assumed that the victim's eye had just been an aperitif and the discerning rat that ate it had returned to have heart for his main course. It turns out we were wrong. We know this for two reasons: Firstly, a forensic odontologist has examined the photographs and plaster cast we took from the heart, concluding that the bite marks were definitely made by a human. Secondly, we swabbed the heart and, to our shock and delight, we obtained a human male DNA profile. Unfortunately, like the fingerprints on the bank notes, the owner isn't in the system."

"Whose brilliant idea was it to swab the heart, may I ask?" Dillon enquired.

George rolled his eyes. "It was your idea, boss."

"Oh yes, so it was," Dillon said, smiling contentedly. "I have so many brilliant ideas that it's hard to keep track."

"So, I'm not a betting man," Tyler said, "but even I wouldn't mind a little wager that the fingerprints on the notes we found in Tracey's purse and the DNA we found on Alice's part eaten heart came from the same person. Kelly, I'll pass the mantle to you so you can delight us with the next exciting instalment of your CCTV adventures."

Kelly resumed her station by the TV-video combo. When the lights were dimmed, she began playing the next segment in her CCTV compilation.

"Remember the van I showed you earlier?" she asked. "Well, although, typically, there is no CCTV coverage of the spot where Alice Pilkington was working or the house in Hanbury Street where she was found, we do have footage from cameras covering other parts of Brick Lane and other sections of Hanbury Street. Guess what? We found footage of a white Sherpa van with an out of alignment headlight driving along Brick Lane at 21:05 hours, just a few minutes before Alice was last seen by her pimp. We also have footage of an identical van driving into Hanbury Street at 21:27 hours. Lastly, we have footage of what we say is the same van leaving Hanbury Street at 22:45 hours."

Bull's face contorted as he did the mental arithmetic. "So, he was alone in that house with her for an hour and a quarter?" he said, shuddering.

"Looks like it, "Dillon said.

"That's sterling work, Kelly," Jack said. "Well done."

Kelly beamed. "Thank you. Paul and I locked ourselves away in a quiet room on Saturday morning, and we've been going at it pretty much non-stop ever since." It was only when the giggling started that Kelly realised what she had said, and she immediately blushed beetroot. Thankfully, as the lights were still down, nobody realised the true extent of her embarrassment.

"When this meeting is over, run off a couple of working copies of your compilation for us to use to brief the TSG and divisional lads later, then hot foot the original footage of this and Paul's latest find straight up to the technical lab at Newlands Park to see if the picture can be computer enhanced. Make sure they know it's a priority job. I want a result on this yesterday, if not sooner."

"Yes, sir," she said, resuming her seat next to Paul Evans, who nudged her arm and winked at her. "Don't say a word," she warned.

"Wouldn't dream of it," he said, grinning at her obvious discomfort.

"Right," Holland said, checking his watch, "let's move on to victim number three."

Tim Barton stood up again. "Right, this is where things start to get even more interesting. Victim number three is Geraldine Elizabeth Rye, a thirty-three-year-old white female; she was required to resign from City of London Old Bill eighteen-months ago over some vague corruption allegations that were never proven."

Dillon stared at Murray. He was about to ask if they knew each other as they had both been investigated for corruption at about the same time, but then he felt Jack place a restraining hand on his arm. *Am I really that predictable?* he wondered.

"At the time of her demise," Barton said, "she was a self-employed private eye – having set up a tinpot firm called Regency Enquiries Agency in Mansell Street. Rye was single, lived in Chingford, and caught the train into Liverpool Street each day to work. Her elderly parents moved to Murcia in Spain a few years ago, and she has no other family in the UK. She had a season ticket in her pocket, and we believe she had just finished work and was heading for the station when she was taken. That's supported by her phone records, which shows she had a fifteen-minute call that ended at 21:10 hours on Tuesday 2nd November. We traced the number and spoke to the caller, a client who had rung her for an update on a sensitive matrimonial enquiry she was conducting for him. He was miffed that she had terminated his very important call halfway through the conversation just so that she wouldn't miss her train. Unprofessional, he called it."

Murray sneered knowingly. "It sounds to me like his wife was over the side."

"He wouldn't elaborate on the nature of the work Rye was doing for him," Barton said, "but reading between the lines I would say that seems likely. If the poor cow had stayed on the line to discuss his wife's affair a few minutes longer she would probably still be alive."

"Yeah, but then someone else would be dead in her place," Steve Bull pointed out.

"Probably," Tim agreed. "Anyway, Paul Evans has been plotting the route Rye took from the office to the station, and he will take you through the CCTV we've found of her shortly. Unlike Phillips and Pilkington, Rye was not, and never had been, a sex worker. She was wearing designer clothing and there is no way that anyone would ever mistake her for one. She had no STDs or other infectious conditions, and there was no sign of recent sexual activity."

Murray laughed wickedly. "I had a quick look through her diary when we searched her home address over the weekend," he said. "From what I could tell, she hadn't had it off for so long that her gash had practically healed up."

Holland's eyes drilled into Murray's. He wasn't averse to a bit of smutty humour, but not when ladies were present. "Kevin, if you can't say anything constructive don't say anything at all," he warned.

"Sorry, sir," Murray said, avoiding eye contact. "No offence meant; I was just trying to provide a bit of background detail for the team."

"Her body was found in Mitre Square by some poor sod taking a shortcut on his paper round at 07:15 hours on Wednesday 3rd November," Barton said, resuming where he had left off. "The cause of death was strangulation. After he killed her, he slit her throat from ear to ear, again almost severing the head."

Bartholomew grimaced. "He must be using one hell of a sharp knife," he said.

"Sharp or not, it takes an incredible amount of force to nearly sever a head with one cut," Steve Bull added.

"He didn't stop there," Tim told them. "Both eyes were gouged out, and her nose, ears, and tongue were also removed. As if that's not enough, he sliced off both breasts, and surgically removed her kidneys."

Richard Jarvis raised a hand. "How long would it have taken him to do that?" he asked. "I mean, I can understand him taking his time inside the house in Hanbury Street, but with Geraldine, he was working out in the open and must have been very exposed. Anyone could have stumbled across him while he was dissecting her. It seems way too reckless to me."

"It's a good point, Dick," Tyler said. "But we think he killed her in the back of the van and operated on her post-mortem. We think that's why he strangled her, because he couldn't afford her to bleed out inside his van."

"Yeah, but chopping a body up inside a van is still pretty ballsy," Jarvis said.

"Not when you take into account that it was one of the wettest nights of the year," Dillon said. "The risks of him being interrupted would have been minimal."

"Was a message left at the scene, like with the others?" Susan Sergeant asked. DS Sergeant, or Sergeant Sergeant as her colleagues liked to call her, was one of the newcomers who had only joined the team on Saturday. She was a tall, slim girl in her late twenties with strawberry blond hair – woe betide anyone who dared to call it ginger in her presence – and a soft Irish lilt.

"No message at the scene," Barton said.

"And I take it she was subjected to vaginal mutilation like the others?" Susie asked.

"Actually, no," Barton said. "We're not sure why, but the hunting knife wasn't used to shred her reproductive organs like it was with the other two."

"The killer deviated from his established pattern in three ways with his third victim," Jack said. "Firstly, she isn't a prostitute; secondly, there is no genital mutilation; thirdly, there was no message left at the scene. We've been trying to figure out why for days. The lack of a message doesn't overly concern us. We think the letter and photographs he sent Terri Miller were his message to us. It's the lack of genital mutilation that confuses us. Were her reproductive organs left intact because the killer only feels the need to mutilate prostitutes in this way, possibly because one of them infected him at some point? That's DI Sigmund Dillon's theory, by the way."

Dillon arched an eyebrow and affected a look of superiority.

"I'm not just a pretty face, you know. There's a mine of useful information stored in this computer-like cranium," he said, tapping the side of his head. "Unlike you lot, I've read Freud's theory that repressing your unconscious mind governs your everyday behaviour."

"Really, boss," Steve Bull said, grinning mischievously. "I didn't think they covered subjects like that in The Beano!"

"Or," Jack said, keen to keep the meeting on track, "is the lack of injury to her nether regions simply because the sadistic bastard had no interest in committing genital mutilation on someone who was already dead?"

"He'll plead insanity when we catch him," Holland predicted with the cynicism of one who had seen too many sane killers play that card before. "Full psychiatric evaluations will be carried out prior to trial, so we might get a better idea of what makes him tick then, but I seriously doubt it."

"Right, Paul, your turn to talk us through the CCTV," Jack said.

"As you know," Evans said, grinning broadly, "me and little Kelly have been going at it non-stop all weekend." This generated a welcome outbreak of laughter, which he acknowledged with a bow. Kelly laughed and blushed in equal measures. "But in between that we did manage to view some CCTV." This resulted in more laughter from the team and more blushing from Kelly.

Evans inserted a cassette into the video player, and Kelly obligingly turned out the light for him. Evans then pressed the play button and began his commentary. "This is footage of Rye crossing under the one-way system at Aldgate at 23:20 hours on Tuesday 2nd November. It's absolutely pissing down, which affects picture quality somewhat, but you can just about make her out here." He tapped the screen with his pen. "As you can see, she's wearing a three-quarter length Burberry overcoat and carrying a dinky little umbrella." The picture changed to show the view from another camera. "Now we have her walking along Petticoat Lane on her way to Liverpool Street." The picture flickered and changed again, providing a view from a third camera. "Now, this clip is hot off the press. Although Rye is only a dot in the distance –" he tapped the screen again with his pen to pinpoint her for the audience "– I want you to concentrate on what happens next."

Sensing something interesting was about to happen, everyone leaned forward to get a better view of the footage. The camera was obviously mounted high on a lamppost. It provided a poor-quality long-distance shot of a solitary figure holding an umbrella above its head. The figure, Rye, was walking along the nearside pavement and moving away from the camera. As she approached a stationary van, which was parked with its bonnet facing the camera, the offside door suddenly slid open and a silhouetted figure emerged from the driver's seat. The movements were masculine, indicating it was a man. Evans paused the frame. "Anyone notice anything significant about this van?"

In the darkness, both Grier and Jarvis raised their hands.

"It's got a headlight badly out of alignment," Susan Sergeant said.

"That's right, it has," Evans said, pressing play again. It was impossible to tell what colour the male from the van was, but he did seem to have quite long hair. Rye swerved around the driver and continued walking towards the rear of the vehicle without a backward glance. After a moment, the driver followed her and they both suddenly disappeared behind the vehicle. About forty seconds later, the driver came back into view, alone. He got into the van and within seconds it pulled away. There was no trace of Rye.

"I'm convinced," Evans said dramatically, "that what you just saw there was the killer abducting Geraldine Rye," He rewound the tape as he spoke. "I'll play that clip again for you." This was the big find he had interrupted the bosses meeting for earlier.

CHAPTER TWENTY-NINE

Henry Boyden was filling in the last few details on a lost property report when Simon Pritchard entered the station office at Whitechapel police station. He was a few minutes early for his nine o'clock appointment with Charles Porter so he waited patiently for Boyden to finish. As soon as Boyden buzzed him through, Pritchard looked around carefully and, seeing they were all alone, whispered conspiratorially in the station officer's ear.

"You may have a bit of a problem," he said. "One of the whores you've been shagging has made a complaint to my wife about your behaviour."

Boyden felt his sphincter loosen. "Who was it?" he demanded, face ashen with worry. "What did she say?"

"Sarah wouldn't tell me, but I think she plans to report you to the murder squad."

Boyden's eyes widened. "Why would she report me to the murder squad?" he asked in a shaky voice.

Pritchard laughed mirthlessly. "Because, you blithering idiot, she thinks you might be the Ripper,"

"That's ridiculous," Boyden said, but he looked very worried.

"I've turned a blind eye to your inappropriate shagging because we're in the same lodge, but I can't protect you if you step over the line and start hurting the tarts."

"I haven't hurt anyone, I swear," Boyden said, wide-eyed. "I might be a little rough at times, but I've never marked one of them."

Pritchard nodded. "I believe you, but others may not. I'll try and convince Sarah to drop it but you should stay away from the Mission until this has all blown over."

"I will," Boyden promised. But Pritchard was already heading for the elevator.

―――

The meeting had been going strong for the best part of two hours and Tyler could see that people were starting to flag. He considered giving them a ten-minute break to grab a cup of coffee and take a leak, but on reflection, he decided against it. They were nearly finished now and it would be better to press on and just get it over with.

"Okay," Tyler said, "the killer left a cool bag containing human flesh outside Terri Miller's plush Canary Wharf apartment. We still haven't worked out how he got into the building unseen as there is a concierge on duty twenty-four hours a day. I'm guessing that the night duty bloke had slipped into the back office for a kip, but he swears he was wide awake and at his post all night. Unfortunately, there's no internal CCTV, so we'll probably never know for sure. The bag and the flesh have been sent to the lab for fingerprint and DNA testing. George, how is that progressing?"

"The flesh has been visually examined. Basically, he sent Miller one of the breasts he removed from Rye. It doesn't appear to have any bite marks on it, but it's been swabbed for DNA anyway, and I hope to have the results back by the end of play today. The bag has already been tested and is negative for prints and DNA."

"What about the handwriting comparisons, and the forensic testing of the letter and three Polaroid photographs he sent Miller?" Jack asked.

"We've sent photographs of the two painted messages, the names written on the back of two of the Polaroids, and the letter up to Scotland," George said. "There's a woman in Edinburgh who's probably the best handwriting expert in the business. I spoke to her on the phone last week and her initial findings are quite encouraging. We're pretty confident we can prove the same hand wrote all three texts. The letter itself has been sent to the lab for ESDA testing and will then be chemically treated for fingerprints. Likewise, the three Polaroid photos that Miller received will also be tested for DNA and fingerprints."

"When will we get the results back?" Tyler asked.

"Not sure, boss," Copeland confessed. "I'll chase it up after the meeting." He made a quick note in his daybook to ensure he remembered.'

Grier raised a tentative hand. "Excuse me," he said, and then blushed when every head in the room turned to look at him. "Sorry to be so dim, but what's ESDA?"

"It's an Electrostatic Detection Apparatus," George explained. Grier stared at him blankly. George smiled indulgently and explained in layman's terms. "Imagine a suspect wrote something down in a notebook, and because they didn't want anyone else to know what they had written they tore out the page. How would we find out what they wrote?"

"I guess you would either have to find the page they tore out or ask them," Grier said.

George nodded. "Or – if you had access to the notebook – you could have the page underneath the one that was torn out ESDA tested. The chances are that an invisible indentation of what was written on the missing page will be on it, showing you exactly what the suspect wrote."

"Cool," Grier said, impressed.

"Paul, has Miller received any more telephone calls?" Tyler asked.

"No, sir," Evans said. "But the recording equipment is all in place so, if he does call, we should get a good quality recording of his voice. Also, we've received permission from her editor to install a similar recording device at her office, and that goes in later today."

"Right, so we've now gone through all the evidence relating to the three victims," Jack said. "As you can see, we are slowly putting together a very solid case against the killer, and I'm confident that when we do finally catch him the evidence will be overwhelming. The problem is catching him in the first place. At the moment, we have no suspects, although we do have one Person of Interest, Dr James Sadler."

"For those of you who don't yet know," Dillon said, taking over the narrative, "on 27th October, a few days before Tracey Phillips was murdered, the GMC received an anonymous tip off from a female who claimed Sadler was giving out controlled drugs in exchange for sexual favours. I should point out that his prescribing history has been checked and does not support this allegation. Sadler, it turns out, is the GP for two of our victims, Pilkington and Rye. Whitey obtained their medical records last Friday, and I feel obliged to say that Sadler made no effort to block the request. The only thing that bothers me a little bit is that when Charlie told him their names and showed him their photographs, he claimed not to recognise either one."

"In his defence, boss," Charlie cut in, "he did say he sees so many people that they all blur into one."

"Also," Deakin said, "the name James Sadler isn't on my list of people who withdrew money from the ATM. The nearest match to it is someone called Nadia Sadler, and she made a withdrawal of one-hundred-pounds."

"Have you compared their addresses?" Jack asked. "Just to make sure she's not his wife."

Deakin looked up from his list, and Jack could see that he was a little embarrassed. "Er, no, sorry, I didn't, but I'll do it as soon as the meeting is over."

"Reggie's put in a subs request on the number the GMC were called from," Dillon said, continuing from where he had left off. "That should be back in today or tomorrow. If it relates to a pay phone that's covered by CCTV, we might get some footage of the caller. If not –" he shrugged – "there's probably not a lot more we can do in relation to Sadler at this moment in time."

"So," Tyler said. "If anyone has any bright ideas about what else we could be doing to catch the swine responsible for killing these women we'd very much like to hear them."

Silence.

A few coughs and someone's shoe tapping against the leg of a chair.

"No suggestions?" Tyler said.

"I suggest we break for coffee," Dillon said, stifling a yawn.

There were universal nods of agreement.

Tyler gave him a 'well, that wasn't particularly helpful', look. "Before we stop, I want to briefly discuss what makes our killer tick. Yesterday, I spent an hour on the phone with a forensic psychologist the National Crime Faculty recommended, and I have commissioned him to prepare a profile for us. In the meantime, I'm gonna run you through the psychobabble he shared with me. It might help us to develop a better understanding of our quarry."

Steve Bull didn't have much faith in psychologists. "You'd have got more insight from reading one of Mr Dillon's Beano comics, boss," he told Tyler.

"Let's get on with it, shall we, Jack," Holland instructed, giving Tyler the feeling that the boss was starting to get a little tetchy. Maybe it was just the fact that the cost of using the NCF recommended expert to prepare a profile was probably going to be in the region of several thousand pounds, and he didn't take kindly to one of his staff effectively saying the whole thing was a complete waste of time and money.

"Quite often, or so I'm told, serial killers don't have a discernible motive, although they do tend to follow a predictable pattern. On reflection, I think that describes our suspect rather well. They usually operate in defined geographical areas –"

"Like Whitechapel?" Jarvis asked.

"Yes, Dick, like Whitechapel. Often, but not always, the killings are sexually motivated. They certainly seem to be in this case. Unlike in the films, where the killer is always a dysfunctional loner, the majority of serial killers don't live alone; they hide in plain sight by having families and being gainfully employed. And it's a misnomer that once they start killing, they can't stop. My greatest fear with this bastard," Jack confided, "is that he will stop killing as suddenly as he started and disappear back into the woodwork without a trace."

"Don't worry, Jack, we'll get him, even if he goes to ground," Dillon said, and the sentiment was immediately echoed around the room with such passion that it made Tyler feel humbled.

"Serial killers tend to have a type," he said when they had quietened down. "For instance, Ted Bundy's victims were all pretty young girls, college students if I remember correctly. They were all similar in appearance to a woman who had jilted him because she thought he was all mouth and trousers and was never going to amount to anything."

"Who's Ted Bundy?" Grier asked.

"He was a famous American serial killer who kidnapped, raped and murdered numerous women in the seventies, long before you were born," Holland said.

"As for having a type, I thought our killer had a vendetta against prostitutes, at first," Tyler said, "but I've had to recalibrate that theory in light of Geraldine Rye's murder. Now I'm wondering if he just hates all women. Either way, something must have set him off. I mean there must be a catalyst that triggered his spree."

"Realistically, I don't think we're going to find any answers until he's in custody," Dillon said. "And while all this mumbo-jumbo is enlightening, none of it is going to help us catch him. For instance, knowing his crimes are sexually motivated, and that he only operates in Whitechapel, didn't help us anticipate that he would kill two women in one night."

"Come on then, Sigmund bloody Freud," Tyler challenged, "tell us why do you think he did that?"

Dillon shrugged. "Personally, I don't think he had a reason. I wouldn't be surprised if he only set out to kill one, the prostitute, and something happened afterwards to make him kill again."

"Like what?" Charlie White asked.

Dillon shrugged. "No idea. Perhaps it was road rage or something. Perhaps she looked like the woman who jilted him years ago for being all mouth and no trousers, à la Ted Bundy."

DC Wendy Blake raised a hand. "I might have an idea about why he did that," she said timidly. Wendy didn't like being in the spotlight. She was quite content to work in the shadows and let others take centre stage.

Tyler smiled encouragingly. "We're open to suggestions, Wendy. The floor is all yours."

"Well," she began nervously, "I started reading a book about Jack the Ripper when we took on this case," she told the assembled detectives, "and a couple of the things that have come out during the meeting have struck a chord with me. The original Ripper had a double event too. I wonder if our man is just copying him. Also, the original Ripper left bodies in the back yard of a house in Hanbury Street and at Mitre Square. Again, maybe the new Ripper –"

"Please don't call him that," Holland said forcefully. "Perhaps he genuinely thinks he's a reincarnation of that fiend, or his descendant, or maybe he just hallucinates that the Ripper's ghost is telling him to kill in his name. Personally, I doubt all of that. Call me cynical, but I think he just wants the notoriety that comes with the Ripper tag. After all, it worked wonders for Peter Sutcliffe. The media are lapping it up. They use the Ripper moniker to sell newspapers, but a by-product of doing that is that they're giving fame and notoriety to a deranged monster who will probably get a book deal out of it, and then make a mint selling the films rights after he's banged up." Holland was becoming more worked up as he went on. "I will not have my staff accord him that accolade. He is vermin. He is filth. He is just another unknown killer to us and I would be extremely grateful if everyone here refrains from calling him 'The New Ripper'." The room had gone completely silent, as tends to happen when a Detective Chief Superintendent loses his rag.

"I'm sorry, sir," Wendy said, crestfallen.

"Not at all, my dear," Holland said. Having vented his fury he was feeling a little mean for snapping at her like that. "Please carry on."

Wendy fidgeted nervously in her chair. "I was just trying to make the point that the killer is duplicating some of the things the original Ripper did as some sort of tribute to him. That's why he deposited two of his victims at locations the original Ripper used, and that's why he had a double event of his own."

"Where did the original Ripper leave the other bodies?" Dillon asked. "Do you know?"

"There were five canonical killings in 1888," Wendy said. She held up an A3 sheet of paper. "I took the liberty of printing this street map off and cross-referencing it with the deposition sites for both the 1888 killings and the 1999 murders. The historical sites are all marked by red circles and the 1999 sites are marked with blue circles. There are red circles in Durward Street, which in 1888 was known as Bucks Row, Hanbury Street, Berner Street, Mitre Square and Whites Row, which is where Miller's Court was. The blue circles are in Quaker Street, Mitre Square, and Hanbury Street."

"So, our boy isn't following the exact pattern of his hero?" Jack said. "He isn't leaving every victim at locations his namesake used in 1888, only some of them."

"Well," Wendy said, "even if he's clinically insane, and I'm not saying he is, it would be stupid to do that. After all, he's got to realise that we will make the connection at some point. If he was mirroring the original Ripper that closely, all we'd have to do to catch him would be stake out the next deposition site."

"That makes a lot of sense, Wendy," Steve Bull said, admiringly.

"What about the dates of the murders?" Jack asked. "Do they match?" If they did, they might at least get an insight into the killer's intended timetable.

Wendy shook her head emphatically. "No, they don't. The killings we're investigating bear no resemblance to those of the 1888 killings." She opened her day book and read from her notes. "Mary Ann Nichols was discovered on Friday 31st August; Annie Chapman was discovered in Hanbury Street on Saturday 8th September; Elizabeth Stride and Catherine Eddows were the Ripper's double event, both were killed on 30th September – Eddows was dumped in Mitre Square; and finally, Mary Jane Kelly was found at her home address, thirteen Miller's Court, off Dorset Street on 9th November."

"Well done, Wendy," Jack said. "What you've just said makes a lot of sense and actually makes things much clearer in my mind. If I had a gold star, I would give you one."

"And a gold star," Murray sniggered under his breath. Grier made a mental note not to sit anywhere near him again in future meetings.

"Right," Tyler said, "I think everyone has had enough. Grab a coffee and then back in here in ten minutes for tasking."

"I'm bloody gasping," Dillon said. "And as it's your turn to pay, I think I'll have a Belgium Bun as well."

As the detectives stood up and began to file out, Derek Peterson appeared in the doorway, looking harried. When he spotted Holland, Tyler, and Dillon he waved a piece of paper at them and began fighting his way through the oncoming crowd.

"Are you alright, Derek?" Tyler asked when he reached them. The older man was a bit flushed and breathing hard, as though he had just come from the gym, and judging from the girth of his waistline the gym wasn't somewhere he went very often.

"I've been looking all over the building for you, sir," he said, panting and fanning his face with the sheet of paper. "I'm sorry to be the bearer of bad news but another mutilated body has been found just off Commercial Street. The HAT car is on its way there now."

Jack felt his stomach tighten. Every time the phone had rung over the weekend, he had feared it would be a call to notify him about another murder. When he'd woken up this morning, he had experienced a tremendous sense of relief; somehow, despite Porter doing his level best to push the killer over the edge, they had dodged a bullet – or rather a knife.

Dillon's shoulders slumped and he let out a pitiful moan. "Oh well," he said, stoically, "I didn't really want that coffee and bun you were going to buy me anyway."

CHAPTER THIRTY

The crime scene was a covered loading bay inside the grounds of a large distribution warehouse located within spitting distance of Commercial Street. The property was surrounded by a nine-foot perimeter wall. Entry was gained via a pair of wrought iron gates that opened inwards. Although the building was alarmed there were no other security features in place.

The body, which had been left between two HGVs, had been discovered at nine o'clock that morning when one of the drivers inspected his rig in accordance with company policy to make sure it had no damage or defects that would stop him from taking it out.

Inspector Speed was the duty officer, and his grim countenance told Jack that this wasn't going to be pretty.

"We've got to stop meeting like this," Jack said, shaking the duty officer's hand. Dillon and Bull followed suit.

"This is even worse than the last one I attended," Speed warned. "The FME has been and gone, reckons the body has been there for a couple of days. That fits in with what the manager told me about their opening hours. Apparently, they shut up shop at six o'clock on Friday evening and, as no one works over the weekend, the place was deserted until this morning. The warehouse staff clock on at seven and the first trucks are normally loaded up by eight, but they had a big union meeting this morning to discuss some changes to working conditions that are about to come into force, so they didn't start loading until nearly nine."

Jack grunted. That meant the killer would have either taken her late on Friday night or during the early hours of Saturday morning. Biting back his anger, he wondered how Porter would react when he discovered the killer had struck again so soon after his provocative comments were aired on TV. Would he be overcome with guilt? Or would he defend his outburst by claiming the killer would have done this anyway, regardless of what he said? And, to be fair, Jack admitted, maybe the killer would have.

"I don't suppose there's any CCTV inside the yard?" Jack asked.

Speed barked out a short, humourless laugh. "Apparently, they've been thinking about installing CCTV and motion activated lights because they're sick of coming into work and finding used condoms strewn all over the loading bay floors, but they haven't gotten around to it yet."

Jack raised an eyebrow. "I take it that means this place sees a lot of action from the local sex workers?" he asked.

"Seems that way," Speed said, "but to the best of my knowledge it's not a location that's ever been flagged up on our radar."

"Who found the body?" Dillon asked.

"One of the lorry drivers found her. Poor sod fainted and cracked his head against the side of the truck on his way to the floor. The paramedics have already checked him out and he's in the main office talking to one of my lads."

"I'll get one of our lot to take a statement," Steve Bull said, and slipped away to organise it.

"How was she killed?" Jack asked.

Speed blew out his breath and shrugged. "I really wouldn't know where to start with this one," he said. "Perhaps it's best I just show you the body so you can see for yourselves."

That sounded ominous. "Well," Dillon said unhappily, "I suppose we'd better get on with it, then."

Speed led them to the edge of the inner cordon, where they

donned paper suits, rubber gloves, and overshoes. They were logged in by a bored looking constable, and then Speed walked them over to the two HGVs parked by the furthest loading bay.

"She's in there," Speed said, stopping at the front of the first vehicle.

"Aren't you coming with us?" Dillon asked.

Speed shook his head, emphatically. "Once was enough."

The two detectives swapped surprised glances. Was it really that bad?

Jack cleared his throat. "Right," he said. "We'll catch up with you afterwards. Lead the way, Dill."

"After you," Dillon insisted, waving Tyler forward theatrically.

As they entered the narrow passage formed by the two high bodied HGVs, they saw Sam Calvin standing with his back to them, clad as he always was in his Tyvek protective coveralls. A similarly clad photographer stood slightly in front of the Crime Scene Manager, legs akimbo as he bent over a figure lying motionless on the cold concrete floor. The photographer's flash went off several times in rapid succession as they approached.

"What've we got, Sam?" Jack asked, tapping Calvin on the shoulder.

Calvin turned around. "Hello, Jack. You're not going to believe what the sick bastard has done this time," he said, moving to one side so that Tyler and Dillon could get a clear view of the corpse of the floor.

"Sweet Jesus!" Dillon gasped.

The sight that met their eyes was difficult to describe: grotesque; bizarre; warped; disgusting; reprehensible. All of these adjectives fit, but none of them came close to doing the macabre diorama justice. The victim had been arranged so that she was flat on her back with her limbs extended to form the shape of a star. Her clothing had been cut off and discarded all around her. Her legs had been pulled wide apart, and her decapitated head had been placed between them, its mouth forced open and pressed against what was left of her vagina to create a sickening parody of oral sex. There were multiple incised wounds, some shallow but most penetrating, visible on the front of her torso. In contrast, there were no signs of defensive wounds to the fingers, hands or arms, which indicated that she hadn't been able to put up any resistance to the barrage of blows. The girl's skin had turned a mottled grey from the loss of blood, making it impossible to determine what colour it had been in life. For his piece de resistance, the killer had skillfully flayed the skin that had once covered her face. Despite the rainfall that had beleaguered the city over the weekend, blood staining was clearly visible on the floor and across the sides of both lorries.

The photographer ambled over to them, pulling his face mask down. He acknowledged Tyler with a nod. "Hello again," he said to Dillon. "Guess we'll both be going back to Poplar tomorrow for the PM. Mind you," he said, grinning wickedly, "it looks like the Ripper has already done most of the work for the pathologist." He chortled at his little joke and seemed disappointed when neither of the detectives joined in.

Dillon mentally scratched his head, trying to remember the nerdy looking twat's name. They had met last week, during the post-mortem on Tracey Phillips. And then it came to him. "Hello, Ned," he said, forcing a smile.

"Isn't George here today?" Ned asked.

Dillon recalled that the two sick fuckers had a bit of a bromance going on, which no doubt stemmed from their shared interest in all things gruesome. "He'll be here shortly," Dillon told him.

"Good, good," Ned said, swapping the lens on his camera for a bigger one he'd just removed from his bag. "Well, I'd better get back to work. The body isn't going to photograph itself."

"If it did," Dillon told him, "you'd be out of a job."

―――――

Sarah Pritchard stood at the edge of the outer cordon, looking in anxiously. She had pleaded with the constable on guard to be allowed inside so that she could speak with the murder squad detectives, but he'd told her she would have to wait until someone came out as he was under strict orders not to let any unauthorised personnel in. At least, when she'd told him that it was really important and that it related to the Ripper murders, he'd allowed her to leave the Mission's mini-bus parked on a double yellow opposite the warehouse, under the proviso that she would move it straight away if the road got busy.

When Charise had called through to her office forty minutes earlier, to inform her that another Ripper murder had just been reported on the radio, Sarah had immediately feared the worst. What if the victim was Cassandra Newly, the prostitute who had confided in her that Henry Boyden had been roughing her and a couple of the other girls up? What if Boyden was the Ripper and he had murdered her? If that turned out to be so, the knowledge that she might have saved the poor girl's life by passing the information onto Steve Bull earlier would torture her for the rest of her days. Guilt twisted her insides as she dialled Steve's office number, praying he would pick up and dispel her fears by confirming that the body wasn't Cassandra's. There was no reply, which probably meant he was down at the scene. She wasn't comfortable speaking to anyone else about this, so she decided the only thing to do was attend the scene in person and find Steve. But how could she when she didn't even know where it was?

Sarah was an extremely resourceful woman, so it didn't take her long to come up with a solution. She telephoned her husband, who was having one of his LAG meetings with Charles Porter at Whitechapel this morning. Whatever failings Simon had, and there were many, he was one of the most persuasive people she had ever met; if anyone could find out where the scene was, it was him. Sure enough, Simon had called her back within minutes with the information she sought. The moment she hung up, Sarah grabbed the keys from reception, told Charise to hold the fort, and jumped in the Mission's green mini-bus. She had driven straight there, determined to find Bull and get some answers, but, so far, she hadn't had much luck in that department. Sarah had already been standing in the freezing cold, surrounded by a dozen disgruntled workers who had been evicted from the warehouse, for a little over twenty minutes. She had managed to eavesdrop snippets of their conversations, hoping to learn something about the latest murder, but all they seemed interested in was the gossip about Dave from finance shagging a girl from the typing pool, Ada dumping her shit of a boyfriend who, having got her pregnant, was demanding she have an abortion because he wasn't ready to be a dad, and what the union were going to do about the unpopular changes to working practices that the company had proposed this morning.

Two outside broadcasting units, one from the BBC and one from Sky, had turned up a short time ago, parking on either side of her minibus and boxing it in. Before long, the journalists had started circulating amongst the crowd, interrogating them for information, and she wondered if they would have more luck that she had. Just when she was on the point of giving up and going back to the Mission, tail between her legs, she spotted Steve Bull walking across the yard.

"Steve! DS Bull," she called out, waving frantically to get his attention.

Having just tasked Richard Jarvis to take a statement from Billy Briggs, the driver who had discovered the body, Bull was on his way back to the deposition site when he heard his name being called. Looking around, he spotted Sarah and made his way over.

"Hello Sarah," he said, surprised to see her at the scene. "What brings you here?"

Sarah bit her bottom lip. "Steve, I heard about the murder. I need you to tell me the victim's name." She was trying to remain calm, but it wasn't easy.

Bull studied her carefully, confused by her distress. "We don't know her name yet," he said guardedly. "But even if we did, I couldn't disclose it to you without the DCI's authority. Why do you ask? And why are you so upset? Is something wrong?"

She nodded and a single tear ran down the side of her left cheek.

This was perplexing. Bull ducked under the cordon tape, wrapped an arm around her shoulder and led her to one side, well away from any onlookers. "Okay," he said when they were alone. "What is it?"

The words spilled out of her. "I should have told you this on Saturday when I found out, but Cassandra made me promise I wouldn't say anything."

"Slow down," Steve told her, placing a hand on each shoulder to steady her. "Who's Cassandra? And what should you have told me?"

"Cassandra Newly is a sex worker. She's one of the girls we canvassed on Saturday evening. When I told her about the rehabilitation work we do at the Mission she asked if there was anything we could do to help her get off the game and turn her life around. We never turn anyone who asks for our help away so I invited her along to one of our meetings, with a view to entering her into a programme. When I asked her, what had happened to make her feel this way, she confided that she and a couple of other girls were having real problems with a particularly nasty client, and this had made her realise she couldn't continue living like that."

Steve's eyes narrowed. "What sort of problems?"

"Well, he was becoming increasingly rough with them, and saying deeply disturbing things about what he wanted to do with them. He was talking about cutting them up and slicing them open, and they were scared he might actually do this. It all sounded really perverse when she told me."

Steve felt his pulse quicken. Could this be the break they needed to catch the bastard? "Why didn't you tell me about this at the time?" he asked, wondering if it was because she didn't trust him.

Sarah took a deep breath. "I'm sorry," she said, bowing her head in shame. "I know how lame this sounds now, but I was just trying to do the right thing by Cassandra."

Bull was annoyed, but he knew there was no point in berating her. "Did she give you a name for this client?"

Sarah nodded. "Yes, he told all the girls that his name was Brian and that he was a cop. That's why they were all afraid to say anything."

"So, what changed?"

"He came to see her late on Saturday evening. He was a little drunk, and he was still wearing his ID on a lanyard around his neck. He'd obviously forgotten to remove it after work. She caught a glimpse of his personal details. Turns out he's not a cop after all; he's a civilian called Henry Boyden."

The name meant nothing to Steve Bull, but it would be easy enough to check out. "And you're worried that this Boyden bloke is the killer and that his latest victim might be Cassandra?"

"At first I was dubious," she admitted. "I know Henry Boyden – not well I grant you – but he seems like a nice person. He works at Whitechapel police station, and he's been doing some voluntary work at the charity for the last couple of months."

"How did that come about?" Bull asked, astonished that anyone working the kind of shifts police employees were required to perform could possibly find the time to do charity work. It all sounded a bit suspect to him.

"He's in my husband's lodge."

"Lodge?"

"They're both Masons," she explained. "Simon got talking to him at one of their meetings and Henry seemed genuinely interested in what we did. One thing led to another, and before long he had started volunteering."

"Tell me you didn't withhold this information just because he seems like a nice person?" Steve pleaded. The trouble with people like Sarah, he knew from past experience, was that they always wanted to see the best in people, and it made them fucking gullible.

"No," Sarah said, exasperated that he should think her so naive. The tears, triggered by guilt and remorse, were flowing freely now. "Oh, Steve, I'm so sorry I didn't tell you all of this straight away, but I was trying to protect her. I swear that I had already made up my mind to pass on the information before I heard about the murder; I was just trying to work out how best to do it without revealing Cassandra's identity. And now it might all be too late."

It might be, Steve thought. *And if it is, you'll have to live with that.* "There's nothing you can do here, so why don't you go back to the Mission," he told her. "I'll make some urgent enquiries and talk to you later. Do you know the names of the other two girls?"

Sarah dabbed at her eyes. "I only know their first names. One was a redhead called Trudy and the other was a mixed-race girl called Sonia. They all do their soliciting around Middlesex Street, I think."

"Okay, leave it to me," Steve said, heading back towards the cordon. "I'll speak to you later."

Ned was pestering Dillon again. He had finished the record photography of the body and was waiting for Calvin and Tyler to finish their big forensics Pow-Wow and say what they wanted him to do next.

"Actually, it's a bit of a result, going back to Poplar tomorrow," Ned was saying.

The photographer's sanity, along with his choice of hair stylist, was definitely questionable, Dillon decided. "Is it? Why?"

"I think that the mortuary technician fancies me," Ned confided.

Dillon disguised his laughter with a cough. "What, Fred Dawkins?" he said, trying to keep a straight face.

Ned looked totally confused. "Who's Fred Dawkins?"

There was no one called Fred Dawkins, as far as Dillon knew. "Big ugly brute of a man, bald head, squashed nose; he's got 'love' and 'hate' tattooed across his knuckles. Oh, and he has a bit of a problem with body odour. Come to think of it, you two would make a nice couple: Fred and Ned."

"No, not Fred," Ned said, turning his nose up indignantly. "I'm talking about the delectable Emma Drew."

"How could you possibly think Emma fancies you?" Dillon scoffed. He gave Ned a look that implied the photographer was deluded.

Ned's face did mock offended. Then it lit up in a mischievous grin. "Oh, do I detect the presence of the green-eyed monster?" he teased. "Come on, admit it, you're just jealous because girls like her always pick suave, sophisticated, intellectual types like me over knuckle-dragging apes like you."

Dillon folded both arms across his barrel of a chest. "And you're so modest with it," he said sarcastically.

"Very," Ned agreed. "Don't tell me you didn't see her giving me the eye last week, flirting with me and rubbing up against me while I was photographing that girl's body on the slab."

Dillon shuddered. That was just plain creepy.

"Anyway," Ned continued, "I'm not seeing anyone at the moment so I've decided to ask her out next time we speak."

Dillon didn't like the sound of that. Nerdy Ned was actually quite a nice guy, but Emma could do so much better. He decided to change tack.

"I think you're misreading the signals, old son," Dillon said kindly. "I wasn't trying to say that she would prefer me to you. I was trying to say that she would prefer someone like Kelly Flowers to either of us, if you get my drift." He winked, conspiratorially.

Ned looked confused for a moment, and then the penny dropped. "You mean she's gay?" he asked, horrified.

"I'm afraid so, mate. Better men than either of us have been blown out by that girl. But, hey, if you want to ask her out, be my guest. I just don't want to see a sensitive guy like you get humiliated."

Ned looked crestfallen. "I can't believe she's gay," he said.

"Who's gay?"

Both men spun around to see George Copeland standing behind them.

"Don't creep up on people like that," Dillon scolded, wondering how much the tubby exhibits officer had heard.

"Who's gay?" George repeated. He loved a bit of gossip, and this sounded juicy.

"Emma Drew from Poplar mortuary," Ned said.

George seemed sceptical. "Emma? Are you sure?"

"Mr Dillon was just telling me," Ned said.

George stared at Dillon with undisguised suspicion. What was the big lug up to now? "I didn't know Emma batted for the other side, and I've known her for years." He didn't mention that he also knew her ex-boyfriend.

Dillon was starting to feel rather uncomfortable. "It's probably best that we keep it to ourselves," he said quickly. "I mean, I'm sure she'll come out when she's good and ready, but we don't want to cause her any grief by broadcasting her sexuality before she's ready to tell the world."

"No, of course not," Ned agreed. He had a cousin who was gay, and he knew how hard it had been for her to come out to her parents.

Thankfully, Dillon was spared further discomfort because, at that point, Tyler and Calvin's conversation broke up and the CSM wasted no time in whisking Ned and George away.

"So, what forensic priorities did you agree with Sam?" Dillon asked, grateful for the reprieve.

Before Tyler could answer, Steve Bull appeared, looking excited. "Sorry to interrupt," he said," but I've just been talking to Sarah

Pritchard outside the cordon, and I think you two are going to want to hear this."

———

Henry Boyden felt like shit. He had hardly slept a wink last night, and he hadn't been able to face eating anything all morning. One of the whores had complained about the way he had treated her, but what exactly had she said? Hopefully, Simon could make it all go away, but what if he couldn't and Sarah Pritchard went to the police about him? What would he say if they questioned him? This could ruin everything. He was due to work a late shift today, his third in a row, but maybe it would be better to phone in sick. He needed time to think; to get his story together in case he was interrogated.

His wife had noticed that he wasn't himself as soon as he'd joined her and the kids for breakfast this morning, but he had managed to put her off the scent by saying he had a touch of the shits, probably the result of eating an iffy sandwich he'd purchased from the canteen the day before. Mornings in their house tended to be chaotic, but somehow Sandra always managed to get the kids dressed, fed and out of the house on time with military precision. Unable to relax, Henry Boyden had spent the majority of the morning sitting on the sofa fretting about his future.

He switched on the radio just in time to catch the eleven o'clock news, and what he heard chilled him to the bone: There had been another Ripper murder in Whitechapel. This really wasn't a good time for someone to allege that he'd been roughing up prostitutes.

———

"Listen up," Dillon said, kicking the briefing off. It was three o'clock already, and the day had passed in a blur. The six detectives he'd assembled to carry out the arrest were crammed in Tyler's office, clustered around the desk he had commandeered. "The information we have is that a forty-year-old white male called Henry Clive Boyden frequently uses the services of prostitutes in the

Whitechapel area. He has become increasingly violent towards several of the girls in recent weeks, assaulting them during sex and threatening to come back and cut them up in a manner that is consistent with the injuries inflicted by our killer. We know from a source that one of the girls he's been threatening is a mixed-race girl called Sonia. Our latest victim is mixed race. She wasn't carrying any ID, so we had a dead set of fingerprints taken at the scene and rushed up to the Yard. The results were phoned through about fifteen minutes ago, and guess what: her name is Sonia Wilcox. Is that a coincidence? I don't think so." From the expression on the arrest team's faces, neither did they.

"Boyden's been telling the girls a few porky pies about who he is," Dillon continued. "He's been claiming to be a police officer named Brian. In fact, he's a civilian station officer at Whitechapel. It seems that Boyden's done some voluntary work for the Sutton Mission over the last couple of months, and we believe he may have been using that as a screen to legitimise his contact with the working girls. Anyway, Dean's done some flash research for us. What have you found out, Deano?"

"Well," Dean began, "he's no trace on the PNC, or on the CRIS, CRIMINT or CAD databases. I checked with Human Resources to see if there was anything interesting or relevant in his personnel file about his previous work experience. Get this – he served in the army medical corps."

Paul Evans let out a low whistle. "So, he definitely has some rudimentary medical knowledge." Boyden was starting to look like a good suspect.

"That's right," Dean confirmed. "Then I checked with the duties office to see what he was working on the nights our killer struck. Turns out he was off duty on both the night Tracey was murdered and the night of the double event. We know the fourth victim was killed over the weekend, probably on Friday evening. Boyden did an early shift on Friday, so he could easily have snatched her that evening. He worked late shifts over the weekend, but they finish at ten o'clock."

"So even if she wasn't killed until Saturday night, he could still have done it," Dillon said.

"What's he working today?" Jarvis asked, wondering if they were going to have to arrest him at work.

"He was supposed to be doing another late shift, but he phoned in sick this morning," Dean said."

"Where does he live, Deano?" Charlie White enquired.

"Boyden actually lives in the borough. He's got a place in Vallance Road – not far from where the Kray twins grew up – lives there with his wife and two nippers, both of whom are primary school age. There are no dogs as far as I can tell."

"What about vehicles?" Dillon asked.

"I did a VODS check on the home address and found one vehicle, a Ford Mondeo." Dean read out the registration number.

"No Sherpa vans?" White asked hopefully.

"Afraid not," Dean said. "But, if he is the killer, he'd hardly be stupid enough to register his death wagon with the DVLA, would he?"

"I suppose not," White allowed. "It would have been nice though".

"The only other thing you need to know about Boyden," Dean said, "is that he's on Chris Deakin's list of people making withdrawals from the Nat West ATM. He withdrew fifty-pounds on Saturday 30th October." When Jack had phoned in earlier, asking for fast time research to be carried out, the first thing Dean Fletcher had done was walk through to the MIR and run his eyes down the list that had been pinned up. "Fuck me," he'd said to himself when he came across Boyden's name. "We could be onto something with this Herbert."

"Boyden is now a named suspect," Dillon told them. "The intention today is to arrest him at his home address in Vallance Road, and to secure the premises as a crime scene. I want us in before his wife and kids get home; it'll be less grief that way. The method will be for an arrest team led by Charlie White to attend the address straight after this briefing. I've arranged for some uniform to meet you there to assist with entry and to secure it when we're finished. Once he's arrested, I want him taken to a police station off the division – can't exactly bang him up in the nick where he works, can we. We don't think our killer's working with anyone else so there's no need to apply to keep him incommunicado. Let's move onto roles: DCs Evans and Jarvis will arrest; as George Copeland is still tied up at the scene of the latest killing, DC Murray will be the exhibits officer; you two," he nodded at Dean Fletcher and Colin Green, a stony-faced detective in his mid-thirties who had been seconded in from another team over the weekend, "will act as searching officers."

Both men nodded their understanding.

Dillon then went through the more mundane aspects of the IIMARCH briefing – covering the risk assessment, methods of communication to be used, admin protocols and any Human Rights Act issues that might have a bearing on their actions.

"Anyone have any questions?" Dillon asked when he'd concluded the briefing, looking at each man in turn. There were none. "Good. In that case, go and arrest yourselves a serial killer."

The arrest team filed out of the office, clearly excited by the prospect of catching the killer. They quickly organised themselves for the impending operation, grabbing log books for cars, checking their officer safety equipment and making sure their radios had fully charged batteries. Murray put together an exhibits bag, making sure they had everything they needed for a search. Colin Green asked if anyone knew the way to the target address as he didn't have a clue. Luckily, several of the others knew the area well.

Brian Johnson observed them preparing to go out and arrest his friend with a heavy heart. There was no way that Henry could be the Ripper. He might like a bit of kinky sex, and he might even be a little rough with the prostitutes he used, but a killer? Never! Besides, hadn't Boyden recently told him that he was happily married these days and had no interest in using prostitutes anymore?

Johnson knew that he wasn't exactly an easy man to get along with, which was probably why Henry was the only real friend that he had left. He desperately wanted to help the poor fool, but what could he possibly do? What would Boyden do in his place if their positions were reversed?

The answer came to him surprisingly easily.

Taking a deep breath to steady his nerves, Brian Johnson slipped out of the office and made his way along the corridor until he came to DCI Quinlan's office. The lights were off and no one was inside. He glanced up and down the corridor to satisfy himself that no one else was around, and then he opened the door and stepped inside. Closing the door quietly behind him, Johnson moved swiftly to the desk and snatched the phone from its cradle with a trembling hand. Keeping his eyes fixed on the door and praying that no one would walk in on him, he dialled a number from memory and waited impatiently for it to be picked up at the other end.

"Listen to me," he whispered the moment it was, "I haven't got time to explain, but the police have got it into their heads that you're the Ripper. They're on their way around to your house right now."

CHAPTER THIRTY-ONE

"This is all a terrible mistake," Boyden sobbed. "I'm not the Ripper. I didn't kill those girls." He was finding the tiny interview room hot and oppressive, and the walls felt as though they were slowly closing in on him. Susan Sergeant and Steve Bull stared at him in detached silence from the opposite side of the table.

They had found Boyden hiding in the tiny loft of his house, crouching between the rafters; a half-packed bag had been discovered lying open on his bed, along with a train timetable and some cash. It looked like he had been preparing to do a hasty runner.

As per the instructions Dillon issued when they'd phoned in to confirm they had their man, Paul Evans and Richard Jarvis had driven him straight to Walthamstow police station in Forest Road, where a cell had been reserved. After relating the facts of the arrest to the custody sergeant and going through the booking-in procedure, they had escorted a dazed-looking Boyden off to a detention room to strip search him and bag all his clothing. A variety of samples had been authorised. Jarvis had taken the non-intimate samples himself: hand swabs, nail cuttings and scrapings, hair follicles and mouth swabs for DNA. Surprisingly, Boyden had readily consented to provide intimate samples as well, and the FME had been summoned to take blood, urine and lastly, penile swabs – no matter how tough a criminal was, or how much of a fight he put up upon arrest, Evans was yet to encounter a man whose eyes didn't show fear as he was led away for penile swabs.

A wet set of Boyden's fingerprints were taken, and these were rushed straight up to the Yard by young Terry Grier for urgent comparison against the prints found on the three ten-pound notes that had been in the first victim's purse.

Nothing ever happens quickly when someone is taken into custody. When they arrived at Walthamstow police station at four-thirty p.m. there had only been one other person in front of them, a crappy shoplifter from one of the shops in Walthamstow market, but it had still taken over an hour and a half to book their prisoner in and bag all his belongings. Then they had waited a further two hours for the FME to arrive and take the intimate samples.

Although the interview team, DS Bull and DS Sergeant, had arrived at six p.m., it was getting on for half-past eight by the time they finally sat Boyden down for interview. The good news was that Boyden had consented to be interviewed without a solicitor present. Generally speaking, people tended to do this for one of two reasons: firstly, because they were innocent and wanted to clear their name; secondly, because they thought there was no evidence against them and the police were just grasping at straws. They wondered which scenario applied to Henry Boyden.

"Mr Boyden," Susie began. "Can you confirm for the benefit of the tape that you understand the caution that I have just given you?"

Wiping a long trail of snot along the back of his hand, Boyden nodded. The accompanying whimper could hardly be called a word.

"It's an audiotape, not a video. I need you to speak," Susan said with studied patience.

Boyden sniffed again. "Yes, I understand," he confirmed.

"And can you tell us why you have chosen to be interviewed without legal representation?" she asked.

Boyden shrugged. His bottom lip was trembling and he was looking so sorry for himself – or perhaps he was just sorry for being caught – that it was verging on the pathetic. "I don't need a solicitor," he said, wiping his eyes. "I'm not the Ripper."

Dillon had chosen Bull and Sergeant to carry out the interviews because of their vast combined experience in this field. It had also occurred to him that, if Boyden was the killer, he probably wouldn't react well to having a strong, confident woman like Susie interrogate him. With luck, it would provoke a reaction. So far, all it had provoked was tears.

The first interview was all about getting an account from him. They began by asking him to tell them about his job, the voluntary work that he did, and his family; as soon as he started talking about his family the waterworks started all over again. Understandably, Boyden was desperate to know what his wife had been told and how she had reacted. When Susie explained that they hadn't told her anything yet, he latched onto this, pleading with them not to reveal the nature of his arrest to her.

"It's going to come out, Henry," Steve said, "whether we say anything or not."

Henry Boyden buried his head in his hands and let out a howl of pain. His world was falling apart around him and he was powerless to do anything about it. "Can't you at least refrain from mentioning the girls I've been seeing?" he wept. "It would break her heart. Please, please, please don't do that to her." There was desperation in his voice.

Sergeant eyed him with disdain. As Steve Bull had already said, Boyden's wife was going to find out; there was no way of avoiding it, and he needed to face up to the fact that the devastation, shock and betrayal she would feel would be his fault, and his alone.

When the self-pitying wailing finally stopped, they asked him about his service in the army medical corps and discussed the extent of his training and the depth of his knowledge. Once that topic was exhausted, they moved onto each of the four victims: did he know them? Had he ever met them, either socially or through work? Had he, perhaps, dealt with them while volunteering for the Sutton Mission? What about Cassandra Newly, did he know her? What about a red-haired prostitute called Trudy, who hung around Middlesex Street with Cassandra and Sonia Wilcox? Had he ever assaulted any of them or made threats to harm them? Had he ever given them any money or other gifts? The questions went on and on. Eventually, they asked him to account for his movements on the nights of the four murders, encouraging him to provide alibi evidence that would help clear his name, if it existed.

Bull had asked Reg Parker to make an urgent application for Boyden's phone records from the TIU as soon as he'd been declared a suspect, but like the DNA, these results wouldn't be back until the following day. Annoyingly, the fingerprint results hadn't come back yet, either, so that would have to wait, too.

At nine-forty-five they reached a point in the proceedings where it seemed appropriate to break for the night and, after updating the custody officer, an exhausted Boyden was returned to his cell to be bedded down for the night.

"Tell my wife I love her," he called out as they slammed the cell door shut and closed the wicket.

"What do you think?" Steve asked Susie as soon as they were out of the custody suite. "Is he our man?"

Susie scrunched her face up in thought. "I don't know, but I'm not getting the sort of vibe I'd expect from a man who's just killed four women. And he doesn't seem to have any trouble talking to me." There had been no displays of hostility, resentment or anger towards her from Boyden.

Steve Bull shrugged. "I can't call it either way," he admitted, which was unusual for him. He could normally tell if a suspect was guilty within minutes of commencing an interview. "Tell you what, let's give the boss an update and then we can grab some food and Foxtrot Oscar back to base."

"What did Steve say?" Dillon demanded the moment that Tyler put the phone down. They were sitting in Jack's office discussing the day's progress over a cup of coffee. The door was closed to reduce the noise from the outer office, which was still a hive of activity.

"Hold on a sec," Tyler said as he finished off the last of the notes that he'd made during his fifteen-minute conversation with Bull. There were reams of them. He took a quick sip of coffee when he finished and then sat back in his chair, flexing the cramped fingers of his right hand. "Well, at least Boyden's talking," he said, which was better than being met with a string of 'no comment' replies.

"Has he made a full and frank confession?" Dillon asked, mockingly.

Jack chortled. "His stance is that he hasn't killed anyone and this is all a big mistake."

Dillon snorted. "Well, that's hardly surprising, is it? If he is our man, he's not going to roll over just because we've got him in the bin. He's far too arrogant for that."

Tyler grunted his agreement and drank some more coffee. "He denied knowing Tracey Phillips, Alice Pilkington or Geraldine Rye and showed no signs of recognition when their photographs were produced. He initially denied knowing any working girls called Sonia, Trudy or Cassandra, but when they showed him an old custody image of Sonia what's-her-name his face went as white as a sheet."

Dillon scoffed. "I bet it did."

"Anyway, in a nutshell, his story is that he met Sonia through the voluntary work he does for the Sutton Mission but he never learned her name."

"Did he admit to banging her?"

"He was a bit coy at first, but he eventually confessed to having sex with her several times over a period of weeks."

"Is he claiming she's the only one he's been seeing to?"

"No, he admitted to having sex with a couple of other girls he picked up in the vicinity of Middlesex Street, but of course he doesn't know their names.

"And what about the allegation this Cassandra bird's made about him knocking them about and threatening to cut them up?"

"He was unhappy about that, indignant even. While he accepts that he might have been a little rough at times, he's adamant that it was always with their prior consent. He claims it was all just a harmless sex game. All the girls were well compensated for indulging him in his fantasy. He swears it was all consensual role-play and that he would never have harmed any of them."

"Yeah, right," Dillon sneered, contemptuously. "So, why does he think she would go crying to Sarah Pritchard about him and make something like that up?"

"Steve told me he sees himself as the victim of a malicious allegation, which has been made out of spite because he refused to start paying them double when they decided to up their prices."

"What a fucking sleazebag," Dillon said, shaking his head in disgust. "Why is he saying they put their prices up?"

"He reckons that when the Ripper murders started, the girls got together and told him he would have to double their money if he wanted to keep playing his sordid little games with them. They called it danger money."

"What, so they suddenly felt threatened by him? Why, did he start upping his levels of aggression towards them?"

Jack shook his head. "Not according to Boyden. He claims they just sensed a business opportunity, and when he wouldn't go along with it, they decided to ruin his life. He blames them; he blames us. The one person he won't attribute any blame to is himself."

"What did this reptile say about his movements during the nights of the murders?"

Jack checked his notes. "He said he was home asleep with his wife."

"That should be easy enough to check," Dillon said. "Who's taking a statement from her?"

Jack's face clouded. "I lumbered poor little Kelly with that," he said, guiltily.

Dillon grimaced. He didn't envy her that task one little bit. "I bet she's gonna really thank you for that."

There was a knock on the door and Chris Deakin popped his head in. "Sorry to disturb you, boss, but Terry Grier is on the line asking for you."

They followed Deakin through to the MIR and Jack picked up the phone lying on Deakin's desk. "Hello, Terry. Have you got a result for me yet?" He listened carefully for a few seconds, digesting what he'd been told, and then he thanked Grier for letting him know and told the youngster to get back as quickly as he could. Hanging up, Tyler turned to find everyone in the MIR staring at him expectantly.

"Well?" Dillon demanded, impatiently.

"The fingerprints aren't his," Jack told them, feeling numb.

After receiving the bad news from Terry Grier, Jack sent everyone home. "Get some sleep," he told them wearily. "We've still got a lot of work to do before this case is over, and unless we get some rest, we won't be able to function properly."

Disheartened, he'd hardly said a word to Dillon during the drive home. He was beginning to wonder if they would ever catch the fiend. They had never caught the original Ripper, after all, and Peter Sutcliffe's reign as the Yorkshire Ripper had lasted for five whole years. His capture, when it eventually came, had been something of a fluke. A routine patrol had stopped to check out two people sitting in a parked car; the driver was Sutcliffe and his passenger was a twenty-four-year-old prostitute called Olivia. One of the officers, a probationer, had carried out a PNC check on the vehicle, which revealed that it was on false plates. Sutcliffe was duly arrested for this and taken to Dewsbury police station, where he was questioned in relation to the Yorkshire Ripper murders because it was felt that he matched many of the killer's known physical characteristics. On the afternoon of 4th January 1981, following two days of intensive questioning, Sutcliffe had declared that he was the Yorkshire Ripper and had gone on to provide detailed accounts of all the attacks he'd carried out between 1969 and 1981. Tyler wondered how long the monster they were hunting would remain at large, and if he'd be caught out so innocuously.

When he got home, Tyler threw his clothes on the floor and staggered into bed, where he immediately fell into a deep sleep.

CHAPTER THIRTY-TWO

Tuesday 9th November 1999

When the alarm went off, seemingly only seconds after he had fallen asleep, Tyler stared at his clock in bleary-eyed confusion. Surely it couldn't be six-thirty a.m. already?

Unfortunately, it was.

Jack felt physically sick as he stood up. His head was throbbing like he had a hangover and his body ached like he'd had a kicking. He wondered if he was coming down with something or just dehydrated. He greedily gulped down the pint of water that he'd taken up to bed but had been too tired to drink, and then dragged himself through to the en-suite bathroom, where he showered and shaved. He dressed in a trance-like state and then trudged downstairs to make coffee. He wasn't remotely hungry, but he forced down a bowl of Sugar Puffs and two slices of peanut buttered toast.

Thankfully, for once, Dillon had the good grace not to be his usual annoying self during the long drive into work, and they had made the journey in companionable silence.

"Why can't every morning be like that?" Jack made the mistake of asking as they ascended the stairs into Arbour Square.

Dillon stopped in his tracks. "Charming!" he said. "I make the effort to get up extra early so I can drive all the way to yours and chauffer you into work because I know how delicate you are in the morning, and what do I get as thanks? Insults, that's what. I can't help it if I like mornings and you don't. It's the best time of the –"

Tyler turned on him and made a stop sign with his hand. "Don't say it!" he warned. "Just don't say it."

"– day," Dillon said, defiantly.

"I told you not to say it," Tyler growled, and the bickering started.

The mood in the office was flat, and everyone seemed subdued as they waited for the eight o'clock meeting to commence. Almost everyone looked tired enough to drop, and one or two of the detectives were starting to look ill. When Boyden had been propped up as a suspect the day before, a wave of euphoria had swept through the team, giving everyone a much-needed boost of morale. They had finally caught a break.

That all changed when the fingerprint results came in, dashing their hopes that charges were imminent, and life could finally start getting back to normal.

Jack opened the meeting by repeating the depressing results of the fingerprint comparisons, and then promptly handed over to Steve and Susie to run the team through what Boyden had said during interview.

Once that was done, Jack nodded to Kelly Flowers, who he noted was looking very pale. "Kelly, can you tell us what Mrs Boyden said in her statement, please."

"Well," Flowers said, letting out a very long sigh, "for starters, she was severely pissed off that I wouldn't tell her exactly why her husband had been arrested. I eventually calmed her down by explaining that I wasn't being obstructive; I simply couldn't divulge the details without her husband's explicit consent. Anyway, when I asked her if she could account for his movements on the nights of the four murders, she immediately sussed why I was asking and went ballistic. When she did finally calm down, she confirmed that hubby had been at home in bed with her every night last week. If she's telling the truth, and I think she is, then he's definitely not our man."

"So, what now?" Charlie White asked. "Surely, if the fingerprints don't match and his wifey is giving him an alibi, then he's not our man. We might as well let him go now, and save ourselves some time."

"We wait until the DNA results come in," Jack said, firmly. "Detention wasn't authorised until four-thirty yesterday afternoon, so we've got plenty of time left on the custody clock. I'm not convinced he's our boy either, Whitey, but we can't take any chances."

"The boss is right," Dillon said. "There's no way on earth that the foreign DNA we found on our victim's heart could have landed there by accident. If Boyden's DNA is a match for that, we know he's guilty, it's that simple. It just means the wife is lying to protect him and the unidentified fingerprints on the notes got there innocently. If that's the case, we'll have to work out how later on."

"George, I know it normally takes thirty-six hours but can you get straight onto the FSS and see if you can pull any strings," Jack said. He didn't like the idea of keeping Boyden in custody for a moment longer than absolutely necessary, but there was no way he could risk releasing him until he was eliminated as a suspect.

"I'll do it straight after the meeting," George assured him.

"Do it now," Jack said. "You can phone from my office if you want some privacy." Copeland nodded obediently, gathered his notes and disappeared into the DCI's office.

"Are we going to charge him in relation to any of the prostitutes he's been roughing up?" Nick Bartholomew asked, wondering why he seemed to be the only person thinking along these lines.

Jack shook his head. "What are we going to charge him with, Nick?" he asked. "Sonia's dead so we can't get a statement from her. Cassandra what's-her-face has refused to make a statement, and we haven't even been able to identify the redhead called Trudy."

Bartholomew thought about this. What Tyler had said seemed to fly in the face of justice. "So, he just walks free?" Surely, that couldn't be right?

"We don't like it any more than you do, mate," Dillon said, "but without some actual evidence there's nothing we can do about it."

"At the very least what he's been doing must be a discipline offence," Bartholomew protested. The idea that he might end up having to work alongside a man who treated women that way was repugnant.

"Don't worry, Nick," Tyler assured him. "Everything we've got, including his admissions to using local prostitutes to indulge his sexual fantasies, will be passed to the rubber heelers. He will be suspended pending a full disciplinary investigation."

"I reckon he'll end up getting the tin-tack," Dillon said, "but, ultimately, that's for Complaints to worry about. We have much bigger fish to fry, remember?"

"Yes, sir," Bartholomew said, hoping Dillon was right about Boyden being fired. It would be a travesty if he walked away from this without at least losing his job.

Jack checked his watch and stood up. "Right, I've got to shoot off as I'm due at Poplar Coroner's Court this morning for the inquests on victims two and three. Poor old Mr Dillon needs to get a wiggle on, too, as he's attending victim four's post-mortem. Chris Deakin's in charge until we return. Chris, I'll leave you to finish the briefing and allocate the day's taskings and actions." Tyler headed for the door with Dillon in tow. "Good luck," he shouted over his shoulder, "and let's all try and keep upbeat. We will get him in the end."

Jack walked out of the Coroner's Court shortly before midday. The sky was clear and the sun was shining. The two inquests had been a formality, as he'd known they would be. At least this time there had been no grieving relatives or film crews to contend with. He wondered how Dillon was getting on, and for a heartbeat he considered popping into the mortuary to find out, but there was really no point in both of them going back to the office smelling of death so he decided against it, opting instead to hunt for a Costa or a Starbucks and grab a large coffee.

Once he was sitting comfortably with his steaming hot latte and a slice of millionaire's shortbread, he turned on his mobile phone and called the office, wondering if there had been any interesting developments.

As it turned out, there had.

———

Dillon removed his coveralls as soon as they reached the mortuary's ante-chamber. Although he hadn't been standing near enough to get any of the victim's blood or other bodily fluids over him, the smell of death had still seeped into their very fabric, and so he held the greens at arm's length and wrinkled his nose as he dropped them into the basket for used garments. Then he tossed the plastic overshoes into the bin and washed his hands twice, just to be on the safe side. After a quick chat with Ben Claxton, to make sure he hadn't omitted anything of relevance from his notes, he accompanied George Copeland and Emma Drew into the latter's office for a quick cup of coffee. Nerdy Ned the photographer declined Emma's offer to join them, explaining that he had another assignment to go to. Privately, and with some relish, Dillon suspected that poor old Ned had lost interest in socialising with her now that he thought Emma batted for the other side.

George drank his coffee quickly and went off to start loading the exhibits van, leaving Dillon alone with Emma. "So," he said, feeling the need to fill the silence, "what time have they got you working till today?"

"Why?" Emma asked, eyeing him mischievously. "Surely you weren't thinking of asking me out, what with me being gay?"

Dillon blushed, gulped down a mouthful of coffee in order to buy himself a few seconds grace, and then stammered something in gibberish.

Emma laughed at his discomfort. "You do think I'm gay, don't you?" she asked, moving closer. "Only, a little birdie whispered in my ear that you told Ned I wasn't interested in men. Is that true?"

Bloody hell! Dillon thought, angrily. *George big-mouth Copeland has grassed me up!* No wonder the tubby git had shot off sharpish, he must have known Emma was going to bring this up.

Dillon cleared his throat and ran a finger around his collar, which suddenly felt very tight. He couldn't deny it, not when her source was Copeland. "It's not like it sounds," he said, hastily raising his hands to placate her.

Emma folded her arms across her chest. "Oh? And how exactly does it sound?" she asked, sweetly.

Dillon's mouth opened and then closed, and he felt himself wilting under her gaze. His mind went into overdrive as he tried to concoct an answer that wouldn't drop him further in the shit. And then, out of nowhere, inspiration struck. "I was only repeating what Kevin Murray told me," he said.

The look of amusement was gone in an instant, and Emma's face clouded with anger. "That nasty little turd," she fumed. "I should have known."

Dillon breathed a sigh of relief. It had been a bit of gamble, blaming Murray, but the man had a reputation for letting his hands wander when he was around the girls, and he wasn't averse to calling any woman who complained about him a lesbian. As an advance exhibits officer, he was someone that Emma would already know; and in Dillon's experience, to know Murray was to dislike him.

"Why do you say that?" Dillon asked, and then answered his own question. "Don't tell me, he tried it on with you and you said no?"

Emma nodded, shuddering at the recollection of creep features brushing against her on the dance floor at a recent leaving do; gyrating his skinny hips as he pointed at his crotch and invited her to play with his extendable baton. "I most certainly did. I wouldn't go out with that slimy little toad if he was the last man alive. Plus, I don't generally date coppers – no offence, but I know what most of you lot are like."

"None taken," Dillon said. He knew what most coppers were like, too.

"I made the mistake of going out with one once," Emma said. "Bloody heathen had the cheek to sniff me when he thought I wasn't looking, to see if I still smelled of death."

"That's terrible," Dillon said, shaking his head like it was the worst thing he had ever heard. "I would never do a thing like that."

"Anyway, I knew Kevin's nose was out of joint when I turned him down, but I didn't think he'd stoop to spreading rumours about me."

"I'm not surprised," Dillon confided. "I've never trusted him."

"To be honest," Emma said coyly, "I thought you'd told Ned that I was gay because he was going to ask me out and you were jealous. I thought it was rather sweet, and I was going to tease you about it. I didn't bloody well realise that you really thought I was gay."

Shit, Dillon thought. *She thought it was sweet that I was lying to put Ned off asking her out. I could have got away with it, but now I've made the situation worse by blaming twat features!*

"Just you wait until I see that little cretin," Emma said, vindictively. "I'm going to cut his tiny shrivelled bollocks off with a rusty knife."

Dillon held up his hands to calm her. "Perhaps the best thing is to say nothing," he advised. "You don't want to give that petty little knobhead the pleasure of seeing he's rattled you."

Emma's eyes narrowed. "You don't strike me as the kind of man to forgive and forget. I would have thought you'd be all for me cutting his gonads off."

"Oh, I would be, normally," Dillon admitted, but even he drew the line at turning a man into a eunuch for something he hadn't done – even a man like Murray. "I suspect he was only saying it out of insecurity, to stop people taking the piss out of him over you giving him the cold shoulder."

Emma wasn't buying that. "Yeah, right! That man's got the skin of a rhino; he wouldn't care what anyone else thought about him."

"Tell you what," Dillon said, "why don't you let me have a quiet word with him on your behalf. There's no love lost between us, and I'll put the fear of God into him."

Emma thought about this for a few moments. "I had heard you two didn't get on," she said. "Very well, I'll let you sort him out," she agreed, "but only on one condition."

"Name it," Dillon said, feeling inwardly relieved.

"You buy me dinner."

Dillon smiled. "Deal," he said offering her his paw-like hand to shake. Maybe dating a mortuary technician wouldn't be so bad after all. And, knowing that she didn't normally date coppers, made him feel privileged.

"I can't think of any better way to piss that weasel off than by dating his least favourite boss," she said. "Can you?"

That wiped the smile from Dillon's face. "No, I suppose not," he agreed.

Jack was feeling quite chuffed as he hung up fifteen minutes later. Having been briefed by Deakin, he'd given detailed instructions on how he wanted this latest development progressed. He made a quick call to update Holland, and then he took a leisurely stroll back to the mortuary, arriving just in time to see Tony Dillon emerge from the building with a strikingly pretty girl at his side. The two of them seemed very cosy together, and Tyler couldn't help but marvel at his randy partner's ability to pull just about anything that moved.

When Dillon caught sight of him, he whispered something in the girl's ear and squeezed her arm affectionately, and then he ambled over to meet Jack.

"I see you smell of death again," Tyler said, fanning his nose with his hand.

Dillon sniffed the air around him several times, and then he sniffed his sleeve. "You know what, Jack, I hate to say this but I think I'm getting used to it."

"She seems nice," Tyler said, nodding towards the girl, who was now chatting to Copeland as he finished loading his van. "Although, I doubt Karen would be overly keen on her."

"Don't even go there," Dillon warned.

"Is that the mortuary attendant everyone raves about?"

Dillon nodded. "It is."

"Does she smell as manky as you?" Tyler asked, grinning.

"Probably," Dillon admitted, "but I bet she scrubs up very nicely when she's in her own time."

"You know it'll all end in tears, don't you?" Tyler told his friend.

"What will?" Dillon asked, guardedly.

"When Karen and mortuary girl both find out that you've been dating the other one," Jack explained. "Ouch! It doesn't even bear thinking about."

"I haven't been out with either of them yet, and you've already got me pegged as a two-timer! Thanks, mate."

"Oh, I'm sorry," Jack said, although his sarcastic tone made it clear he wasn't. "I've obviously misjudged your intentions."

"I'm telling you, you've got me all wrong," Dillon insisted, piously.

Tyler rolled his eyes. "When you come out with crap like that, I half expect your nose to grow a couple of foot longer," Jack told him.

Dillon grinned, mischievously. "Okay, you got me," he confessed. "So, how long do you reckon I would be able to get away with it before they found out?"

"Not long enough," Jack said. "But enough about your love life, what did the pathologist say?"

"Only what we expected," Dillon told him. "Claxton thinks the killer slit her throat first, and then mutilated her genitalia with his hunting knife. He isn't sure which followed next, the flaying of her face or the frenzied stabbing that turned her torso into a pincushion. The pathologist stopped counting the incisions when he reached eighty-eight. Lastly, the killer decapitated her; Claxton is satisfied that this was done after she expired."

"Any sign of recent sexual activity?"

Dillon grimaced and shook his head. "Jack, how could anyone possibly tell? Honestly, if you went into Tesco and bought a pound of mince it would probably be less shredded than that poor girl's womb was. We'll just have to wait and see what turns up when the forensics come back. Anyway, how did you get on?"

Tyler gave a bored shrug. "The inquests went exactly as expected. However, I do have an interesting, hot off the press, update for you," he told his partner. "I'll fill you in on the way back to the factory."

Steve Bull led a dishevelled looking Henry Boyden out of his cell and through to the custody office. Boyden's hair was sticking up and he smelled slightly of body odour; a night in the cells will do that.

Today's custody sergeant was a stern-faced female in her mid-thirties. She wore a pair of horn-rimmed glasses that made her look like a librarian, and her brown hair was swept back in a ponytail. "What's happening with this man?" she asked, eyeing Boyden with disapproval. "I was told you were awaiting forensic results before further interviews could be conducted."

"That's right," Bull told her. "We were waiting for DNA and fingerprint comparisons to come back, but they're all in now, and I can tell you that Mr Boyden's fingerprints and DNA don't match that of the Whitechapel killer. Therefore, we will be taking no further action against him in relation to the matters for which he was arrested."

A wave of intense relief flooded through Boyden as this was said, and he had to hold onto the custody officer's desk to stop his legs from giving way. "I told you I didn't kill those girls," he said angrily, "but you wouldn't listen, and now you've ruined my marriage and my life. I'm going to sue the lot of you for wrongful arrest, false imprisonment and defamation of character."

Ignoring the outburst, the custody sergeant turned to her gaoler. "Harry, be a love and dig out this man's belongings, please. As soon as they're restored to him, I can show him the door." Boyden had been a complete pain in the arse all morning, with his non-stop whingeing, and the custody officer couldn't wait to get rid of him; if he hadn't been complaining about being locked up for something he hadn't done, he had been demanding to be allowed to ring his wife. Unfortunately, Mrs Boyden had made it abundantly clear that she didn't want her husband to contact her, and he had gone into a right strop when he'd been informed of this, blaming the murder squad for poisoning her mind and turning her against him.

"Actually," Steve Bull said. "You might want to hold off on doing that." He turned to Nick Bartholomew, who was standing behind him. "Nick, do you want to do the honours?"

Bartholomew stepped forwards. He knew Boyden by sight, enough to say hello in passing, but nothing more.

"Henry Boyden," he said showing the detained man his warrant card. "I'm Constable Nick Bartholomew, and I am arresting you on suspicion of the murder of a sex worker called Connie Williams, which occurred in Shacklewell Lane, Stoke Newington during the early hours of 20th December 1995." He went on to give the caution, but Boyden wasn't listening.

He looked as though he had just been slapped. "No, this can't be happening," he cried, staring at them in a combination of disbelief and horror. "You can't do this to me. I know what you're trying to do. You couldn't get me for the Ripper murders so now you're trying to fit me up with something else." He turned to the custody officer, a look of desperation on his face. "Surely you're not going to let them get away with this?" he pleaded.

"Is there any evidence?" The custody officer asked Bull.

Bull nodded, solemnly. "He's bang to rights on this one, but I'm not in a position to disclose the nature of the evidence at this stage."

The custody officer nodded her understanding; the murder team obviously had forensic evidence, but before they disclosed it, they wanted to give Boyden a chance to hang himself out to dry. "Mr Boyden," she said, leaning forward with a bored look on her face. "If I were you, I'd think about getting a solicitor. I have a feeling you're going to be with us for a long time to come."

CHAPTER THIRTY-THREE

Friday 12th November 1999

The second week of Operation Crawley was drawing to a close, and while they were no nearer to solving the four Whitechapel murders, Tyler's team had at least managed to close a cold case that had been sitting on the books for the past four years.

The post-mortem of Connie Williams, which had been carried out on 23rd December 1995, had yielded a significant amount of forensic evidence. There had been semen in her vagina, and traces of skin had been found under the fingernails of her right hand. Some of this had been hers, but some of it had been foreign. Unfortunately, the profile obtained from the foreign DNA hadn't matched anyone who was in the system at that time. However, the profile obtained from these samples had proved to be a one-hundred-per-cent match for Boyden's DNA when it was run through the system while he was in custody for the Whitechapel killings.

During the first interview, they revealed that his semen had been found in the victim's vagina. Boyden had simply given them a *'so what'* shrug and blithely told the interviewing officers that he had no recollection of the event, although he accepted that he had used the dead girl's services at some point. "That doesn't make me a killer," he'd announced defiantly. By the time they rose for a quick break, Boyden had been full of smiles, confident that they had nothing of any real substance against him and he would soon walk free.

The second interview commenced with the revelation that traces of blood and some skin fragments had been found under her fingernails, from where she had tried to fight her assailant off, and this was also a perfect match for his DNA profile. That wiped the smug smile from his face. There was no easy way to explain this away, and from the moment its existence had been disclosed he had known he was in serious trouble. His solicitor hastily requested that they take another break in order for him to consult with his client, and when they resumed – on the advice of his solicitor – Boyden had immediately gone into 'no comment' mode.

Boyden's face was ashen when he was charged with Connie Williams' murder late that evening, and he looked close to tears as the custody sergeant denied him bail on the basis that he posed a flight risk.

Following a second sleepless night in the cells, Group Four had whisked him off to Waltham Forest Magistrates Court, along with all the other non-bailable prisoners.

Boyden's first court appearance lasted a matter of minutes, and he had only spoken once, briefly, to confirm his personal details. Dillon had taken the stand to outline the case against him and to make objections to bail, and then the defence solicitor had made an impassioned bail application on behalf of his client. The three worldly wise Magistrates who made up the presiding panel had listened attentively, and then promptly dismissed the application, remanding a broken looking Boyden to HMP Pentonville to await trial.

Claude Winston had also been released from hospital earlier in the week, and to Jack's utter dismay, Holland had given the case to Andrew Quinlan's team to deal with.

Holland defended the decision by explaining that Tyler's team was drowning under the combined weight of work being generated by the

Whitechapel murders and the cold case that Henry Boyden had been sheeted for. It would have been unfair – not to mention irresponsible – to load them up with a third case. Tyler knew the boss was right, but losing the investigation to another team still rankled.

After a series of interviews that had lasted two days, Winston had been charged with numerous offences, the most serious being two counts of attempted murder, possession of a loaded firearm with intent to endanger life, and possession of a couple of kilos of class A drugs with intent to supply. Like Boyden, bail had been refused, both at the police station and at Magistrates Court, and he had been remanded into custody to await trial.

While the Whitechapel killings hadn't been solved yet, the detectives were making steady progress, and the case against the killer was growing stronger with every passing day.

Paul Evans had done some great work with the CCTV. He had found some interesting new footage, which had been seized from a private system in Mitre Street. The camera had been wall mounted on a building that sat almost directly opposite the junction with Mitre Square. The footage, timed at 23:26 hours on Tuesday 2nd November 1999, showed a white Sherpa van pulling over against the opposite kerb, just beyond the junction with Mitre Square, and then reversing back into the square. The same van could be seen pulling out of Mitre Square thirty-eight minutes later. Unfortunately, the camera hadn't captured anything that occurred inside Mitre Square, but its footage did afford them their first real look at the van driver's face. While the heavy rain blurred the image a little, it was still good enough for the detectives to make out that the Whitechapel killer was a white male of indeterminate age with long hair and a slightly droopy moustache, and he was clearly wearing glasses.

Evans printed off some stills for distribution. When Charlie White was shown these, and asked if he recognised the man, he proclaimed that, unless the suspect was wearing a wig and fake moustache, which seemed highly unlikely to him, it definitely couldn't be James Sadler.

Dillon, who had been sitting with Charlie in the canteen when Evans brought the stills down for viewing, remarked that the man's glasses and moustache were reminiscent of the look George Harrison had sported in the 1970s. "We should issue an order, with immediate effect, for anyone resembling one of the Beatles to be stopped," he had suggested helpfully. The three of them had then spent the rest of the day seeing who could work the most titles of Beatles songs into their conversations, much to everyone else's annoyance.

The result of the subscriber check on the number that called the GMC on 27th October hadn't come back in until Wednesday morning. Unfortunately, the telephone box it belonged to was located in a quiet East End street, nowhere near any CCTV cameras. At Dillon's behest, Reggie had since requested billing and cell site location mapping for the entire previous week on Sadler's mobile telephone, having obtained his number from the GMC. This would tell them who he had been in contact with during that time and give them a good idea of his movements, but it would take the TIU a few days to prepare. They all accepted that this tactic probably represented their final shot at finding anything tangible to link Sadler to the four killings. Unless something came out of theses checks, the doctor would cease to be a POI.

One of the highlights of the week had been yesterday afternoon's unexpected visit from Colin Franklin, who was still convalescing from the rib injuries he had sustained while trying to arrest Claude Winston. Colin was in good spirits and wanted to hear all the latest news and gossip. He was gutted to have missed out on all the overtime his colleagues had earned, and he hoped there would still be some money in the pot when he returned to active duty. His wife was due to drop any day now, he informed them excitedly, and he was both looking forward to and dreading the sprog's arrival at the same time.

It was mid-afternoon when Tyler fielded an unexpected call from Charles Porter over at Whitechapel. Dillon had gone to the lab for a forensic meeting with Sam Calvin earlier in the day and, when the phone rang, he half expected it to be the big man calling to blag a lift from the tube station.

"How can I help you?" he'd asked warily, hoping the conversation wouldn't deteriorate into another argument.

"*I think you had better send someone over,*" Porter had told him. "*The Ripper has just sent me a rather gruesome present.*"

Thirty minutes after receiving the call, Tyler entered Porter's office, accompanied by Steve Bull and George Copeland. Porter was sitting behind his desk, and from the look of it, he was halfway through writing a statement. To his surprise, he saw that Simon Pritchard was also present.

For once, Porter looked relieved to see the Murder Squad officers. He rose to greet them and then indicated a small white shoe box that was sitting on a table to the side of his desk. The box had been opened, and the lid was sitting next to it. "This is the offending article," Porter explained. "It was addressed to me, but when I opened it there was a second note inside, telling me to pass it onto you. I'm afraid we had no idea what it contained and so we've both touched it with our bare hands."

Tyler walked over to the table and peeked inside the open box. As Porter had told him on the phone, there was a lump of cellophane-wrapped meat sitting on a bed of what looked like greaseproof paper. Tyler grimaced. "George, can you take care of this thing," he asked, pointing to the flesh filled shoe box.

"Leave it to me," George said, opening his exhibit bag to get the appropriate packaging out.

Tyler turned to the Divisional Commander. "Where's the note?"

Porter returned to his desk and retrieved an A4 sheet of paper, which he held at arm's length. At least he'd had the good sense to place it inside a clear evidence bag, Tyler observed. In keeping with the killer's previous messages, this one also appeared to have been written in the victim's blood, and it had run in a number of places. Taking the bag, Tyler read the enclosed note carefully.

My dear Inspector Tyler,

I hope you enjoy this kidney as much as I enjoyed the first. This woman's death may have occurred by my hand, but it was your moronic colleague's words that brought it about. I trust he will all be more respectful when talking to the media about me in future.
Your obedient servant,
Jack the New Ripper.

Jack read the disgusting note in silence and then handed it to Bull.

Porter immediately produced a second clear evidence bag, which contained a smaller sheet of paper. "This is the note he sent to me," he said with some distaste.

Jack took it and studied the text, which had also been inked in blood.

Chief Superintendent Moron,
I've sent you a little souvenir to remind you that this woman's blood is as much on your hands as it is on mine. When you're done with it, give it to Jack Tyler. He, at least, is a worthy adversary, and I think of him as my very own Inspector Abberline.
Jack the New Ripper.

"How and when was the box delivered?" Tyler asked Chief Superintendent Moron.

"Well," Porter said, looking across to Pritchard, "I think Simon is probably better placed to explain that."

"Yes," Pritchard said. "I suppose I am."

"I'm listening," Tyler said, wondering why Porter had deferred to the civilian.

"I popped into the station this afternoon to speak to Charles about Henry Boyden, who I understand was charged with murder earlier in the week. Because of the voluntary work he's been doing for the charity over the last couple of months, Sarah and I wanted to make sure that his terrible conduct won't reflect badly on us. I mean, can you imagine the headlines: Sutton Mission charity worker murders prostitute! Anyway, as I was about to walk up the station steps, a motorcycle courier pulled up and called me over. I assumed he was going to ask me for directions, but I was wrong. What he actually wanted was for me to drop that –" he indicated the shoe box "– into the station office on his behalf as he was running late and still had loads of deliveries to make. He assured me it was nothing valuable and didn't need to be signed for, so I thought I'd do the chap a favour. When I noticed it was addressed to Charles, here, I bypassed the station office and brought it straight up to him. It was only when he opened it that we realised what it was."

"Can you describe this man for me?" Tyler asked.

"Well, not really," Pritchard said. "He was wearing a helmet with the visor down, and he had on black leathers, gloves, and motorcycle boots."

"What about his eye or skin colour?" Tyler asked.

Pritchard shook his head apologetically. "I couldn't see either. The visor was mirrored, you see, so all I could see in it was my own reflection, and every inch of his body was covered by his biking outfit."

Oh great! Tyler thought, struck by the similarities between this conversation and the one he'd had with Porter the other night. "What about his accent?" he asked, without any real hope.

"Well, it was sort of normal; not posh, not cockney, not any accent that I could recognise to be honest," Pritchard said. "It was a little muffled by the helmet, which didn't help."

Tyler let out an impatient sigh. "What can you tell me about the motorbike," he asked. Surely Pritchard would be able to recall its colour or the brand or a part of the index.

"Well, it had an engine and two wheels," Pritchard said, and immediately regretted doing so when he saw that Tyler's face had clouded with anger. "Forgive me," he said quickly. "I didn't mean to sound flippant. It's just that I really don't know anything about motorcycles. Not my thing, I'm afraid. The only thing I noticed was that the engine sounded powerful."

Tyler ignored the apology, which he suspected was as false as the man's smile. "Have either of you actually handled the notes or touched the cellophane wrapping on the meat that's inside the shoe box?"

Porter and Pritchard exchanged guilty looks, like a couple of choirboys who had just been caught looking at a dirty magazine by the vicar.

"Well," Porter said, and then cleared his throat. "We both handled the notes, but we didn't touch the meat inside the box, did we, Simon?"

Pritchard squirmed uncomfortably. "Actually, Charles, I did prod it a couple of times," he admitted sheepishly "out of professional curiosity."

Tyler gave him a piercing stare. He could completely understand them handling the box, and even the notes to a certain extent, but what sort of fuckwit would start prodding a package of human flesh? The cellophane would now potentially be contaminated by his DNA and his sodding fingerprints.

Pritchard must have read his mind, or more likely the scathing expression on his face, because he stared back indignantly. "I am a doctor, you know," he proclaimed, as if that justified his actions.

"I think the meat in that box is beyond needing a doctor," Jack pointed out acerbically, "don't you?"

It was almost six o'clock by the time Tyler arrived back at Arbour Square, and after making himself a strong cup of coffee, he rang Holland to give him an update. "At a guess, I'd say the meat will turn out to be Geraldine Rye's missing breast and one of her kidneys," Jack said. He shuddered as he recalled the rancid smell wafting out of the shoe box; no matter how many times he was exposed to it, he would never get used to the sickly sweet odour of rotting flesh.

Holland wasn't pleased by the revelation. *"Let's hope the press doesn't get hold of that, Jack. I'm sick of seeing this case plastered over every newspaper I read."*

After ending the call, Jack went straight to the CCTV viewing room and found Paul Evans. "Paul, drop what you're doing and come with me." When they were in his office, Tyler explained all about the latest development. "It stands to reason that the motorcyclist Pritchard spoke to was the killer, so I want you to hot foot it over to the Borough CCTV control room and see if you can pick him up on camera."

Evans face dropped. "What, now?" He had been hoping the team would be dismissed at a reasonable hour today. After all, this was their thirteenth day at work without a break. Dillon had recently broken the news that the entire team was having its leave cancelled again, and would have to work a second weekend on the trot. Some of the money grabbing bastards had been chuffed to hear the news, but not Paul Evans – he had a life.

"Sorry, Paul," Tyler said, "but needs must, and all that. The front of the station isn't covered by camera, but surely the surrounding area will be." He repeated the generic – and totally useless – description Pritchard had provided of the courier and his motorcycle, and then, as an afterthought, described the good doctor. "Pritchard doesn't recall the exact time he arrived at the nick, so you might have to do a bit of work to pick him up before he gets there." He gave Evans the most likely route that Pritchard would have taken if he had come straight from the Sutton Mission. "I don't need to tell you how important this could be for us," Tyler said. "Even if you can't follow the bike back to an address, at least try and get me a registration number."

"I'll do my best," Evans promised, hurriedly donning his jacket. Tyler clearly had a bee in his bonnet over this; he wanted answers, and he wanted them quickly. Paul Evans realised that he was in for a very late finish.

"Good evening, London Echo offices, how can I help you?" The singsong voice of the telephonist grated on The Disciple. He tried to put a face to the voice and imagined how nice it would be to silence it once and for all.

"Put me through to Terri Miller," he demanded, tapping the glass pane of the telephone kiosk in agitation.

"Who shall I say is calling, sir?" The receptionist's manner became frosty; no doubt she was annoyed by the tone of his voice.

"Tell her that it's Jack. And if you value your scrawny little life, be quick about it," he hissed menacingly.

"*Jack? You mean...? Hold on, please.*" He sensed her fear and realised she had been primed to expect his call.

He smiled in satisfaction.

"*The line's ringing for you, sir.*" She told him, unable to mask her discomfort. The phone was picked up after the fourth ring.

"*Terri Miller speaking.*" The tautness in her voice told him that she already knew exactly who was calling. It was possible that the receptionist had forewarned her, although he didn't think there had been enough time for her to do that. Perhaps they had set an extension aside purely for incoming calls from him. That would make more sense. "Cut the crap. You know who this is. I've got a newsflash for you: Jack Tyler received a little present from me this afternoon at Whitechapel police station. You know the sort of gifts I send, don't you?" Her sudden intake of breath answered that question nicely.

"*I know you've done some terrible things,*" she began, reciting the speech that she and Giles Deakin had prepared in anticipation of him calling her again, "*but we can get you the very best psychiatric help if you'll just turn yourself in. You don't have to be afraid of the police. You could come here and we would ensure you had legal representation...*"

Miller rattled him with her meaningless talk. What was she playing at? It didn't make sense to provoke him like this. Unless, of course, the call was being taped and she was planning to use it as propaganda to promote her newspaper. Well, wasn't that what he had effectively told her to do? To get him the publicity he craved. He allowed himself a small, malicious smile. She was playing a dangerous game, one that could not end well for her...but, if that was what she wanted, then so be it.

"Let me tell you what I need. I need to feel the warm blood of the damned flow through my fingers. Don't play games with me or you could find yourself becoming a donor! If you want to live, call Tyler and ask him about my gift."

"*I'll call him,*" Miller promised, "*but first I want you to tell me why you're doing this. If you really want me to do your story justice, the least you can do is give me something to work with.*"

The Disciple thought about this for a moment. Perhaps she was right. Perhaps there was a way of giving her an insight that she could draw inspiration from. "Very well," he said, as an idea struck him. "You want something to work with? I've got just the thing in mind. Wait by the phone; I'll call you back later tonight." With that, he slammed down the receiver and stormed out of the phone box.

"Dear God, did he threaten to kill me halfway through that conversation?" Terri asked her editor the moment the Ripper hung up. She felt her knees starting to buckle, and quickly sank into the easy chair beside Deakin's desk before they gave way altogether.

"Yes, he did, and on audio tape too!" Giles Deakin beamed. Looking very much like the cat that had swallowed the canary, he raised his glass of wine to salute the three other people who had gathered in his office when the Ripper's call had come in.

"By Jove, old girl, you just got another exclusive for the paper. I wasn't sure about letting you run with this at first, but I'm glad I did now. When this is all over, we've got to seriously consider doing a serialisation of the case, or perhaps a pull out for the Sunday issue." He stroked the side of her face and handed her a glass of white wine.

Still in a daze, Terri automatically took the glass. "I'm going to write a book," she informed him, downing its contents in one.

"A book," Deakin said, grinning enthusiastically. "What a super idea."

"Are you okay, Terri?" Julie asked, taking her friend's hand. Like everyone else in the room, she had listened to the conversation via a desk-mounted speaker. But, unlike Giles and his pompous solicitor – whose only concern was whether what they were doing was technically legal – she had accompanied Terri to the house of horror in Hanbury Street, and she had seen the gruesome gift the Ripper had left outside Terri's apartment.

"I'm fine, just fine," Terri said, sounding anything but.

"Major Incident Room, DCI Tyler speaking," he said into the receiver.

"*Hello Chief Inspector, it's Terri Miller here, from the Echo...*"

Tyler grimaced. "What can I do for you?" he asked coldly.

"*I've just had a call from the Ripper. We recorded it on the equipment Paul Evans had installed.*"

Tyler sat up at that. "What did he say?" he asked, a little surprised that she had actually called this in so quickly.

"*He told me he had made a delivery to you at Whitechapel police station and he ordered me to ask you about it. He threatened that something unpleasant would happen if I didn't.*"

Jack found himself wondering whether she'd added the last bit for effect, or as an excuse to phone him and sniff around, but he dismissed the idea almost at once. She wasn't stupid. She wouldn't say anything that could be easily disproved by listening to the tape.

But what should he tell her? Whatever he said, she would almost certainly publish it. He thought carefully before answering. "Miss Miller, I did receive a delivery this afternoon from someone claiming to be the Ripper. I'm not in a position to disclose what it contained. Suffice to say we are treating the matter as serious, and we're exploring all avenues to prove or disprove its authenticity." He made as bland a statement as he could, speaking without actually saying anything.

"*I see,*" she said, clearly disappointed.

"I'm sorry, Miss Miller. I appreciate your call and I'll send someone straight over to collect the tape, but I can't disclose any more details at the moment," he explained, knowing he couldn't ostracise her completely; they needed her continued co-operation too much.

"*Will you be able to tell me more about this later?*" she asked, hopefully. He rolled his eyes. Reporters! Didn't they ever let things drop?

"We'll have to see," he informed her, noncommittally. "Now, if that's all, I'll say goodbye."

"There's one more thing," Miller said, uneasily. "*He told me he was going to call back later tonight, and that I should wait by the phone. I have a horrible feeling that he intends to do something terrible.*"

Jack felt his pulse quicken. "What makes you think that?" he asked.

"*Just the tone of his voice,*" she said, knowing how corny that must sound. "*There was something deeply unsettling about the way he told me to wait by the phone. It was as if he didn't want me to miss out on whatever nastiness he had planned."*

"Thank you for letting me know," Jack said. "I really hope you're wrong about this feeling of yours, but in the meantime, I'll make sure all our patrols are fully aware of the need to be extra vigilant. If I give you my job mobile, will you call me straight back if you hear anything more?"

"*Of course*," she promised, and noted the number. "*Good night, Chief Inspector*," she said, "*and don't take this the wrong way, but I really hope we don't have to speak again tonight.*"

"Me too," Tyler said. Shaking his head, he put the phone down.

"Dean!" he shouted, as Fletcher walked past his office. "I've got a job for you."

CHAPTER THIRTY-FOUR

The Disciple lingered on the corner opposite the lockup until he was completely sure that no one had followed him. When he was satisfied that it was safe to move, he crossed the road quickly, keeping his head tucked down and his face hidden by his collar.

With nimble fingers he unlocked the heavy wooden door and slipped inside, cursing his neighbour's security lighting as he always did.

Re-locking the door from inside – you could never be too careful – he reached out into the cloying darkness, his fingers probing the cold wall for the lights, which were located just below an ancient fuse box that any self-respecting electrician would have condemned as lethal.

Once found, he flicked the small row of switches down, illuminating the centre of the cavernous arch in a weak beam of yellowish light. For a moment he stood perfectly still, soaking up the atmosphere of his lair.

The Disciple felt more at home here than he did anywhere else, including the house that he called home. Perhaps it was because everything in this crumbling place reflected the decay that festered in his soul. Perhaps it was just that here, unlike anywhere else, he didn't need to wear theatrical props and cheap make-up to shield his identity from the rest of society.

And while most people would have found the interior sinister and oppressive, to him it was a warm and comfortable place, one in which he felt secure and protected from the outside world. He enjoyed spending as much time here as he could.

He crossed to the far side of the archway and sat down at the worktop he'd installed especially for his makeup and props. Switching on the small light mounted above his mirror, he studied his reflection thoughtfully. "Good evening, Jack," he said to the image in the glass. "It's time to go out hunting again."

He had decided against wearing a disguise tonight. There was no need as his intended victim already knew his name. In fact, she knew everything about him – well, he smiled, almost everything.

He was about to head over to the van when he caught sight of the duffle bag resting against the old chest freezer. As eager as he was to get going, he couldn't deny himself the few moments it would take to inspect its precious contents. Opening the drawstring, he reached inside, removing the panties he'd procured from his first four victims. For a moment he stared at them in reverence. Then, raising them to his face, one at a time, he closed his eyes and inhaled deeply. A fantastic explosion of light and colour filled his mind as the sight, smell and touch of the material recreated the intense feelings he associated with each of the original events.

"How am I ever going to give this up?" he asked the underwear. But give it up he must once tonight's final ritual was completed.

The Disciple reluctantly returned his trophies to the duffle bag and then went over to inspect his van. With a final glance around his lair to make sure that nothing had been forgotten, he turned off all the internal lights and pulled opened the doors to the street.

He had to assume that, by now, the detectives knew the type and colour of van he was using; they might even have the index number. Thankfully, it no longer mattered, not since he had stumbled across a burnt-out Sherpa in Shadwell during the night of the double event. Its discovery in such fortuitous circumstances had obviously been another omen – and in a moment of pure inspiration, he had swapped the number plates on the charred wreck with his own. The following day, he had spent several tedious hours spraying his van dark green. The paint job was blotchy in places but that was irrelevant. Unless anyone compared the VIN on the engine and chassis to the registration number, it would pass for the vehicle whose identity it had taken on.

These simple precautions should ensure that the police didn't give him a second glance tonight, and after that it wouldn't matter.

He had been sorely tempted to sacrifice the third bitch responsible for ruining his life at her place of work and then leave her mutilated body to be discovered on Monday morning. It would be easy, and it would negate the need for him to take the van out, but it didn't fit in with his plan to send her off in style.

In 1888, the Ripper's final victim, Mary Kelly, had been slaughtered in her grubby little Miller's Court bedsit – it was the only one of the five canonical murders to have been committed inside a building. He intended to emulate that feat, only he wanted the building in question to be his lair. After all these years of marriage, it seemed only right and proper that she should be allowed to see this hallowed place before she died.

A dull ache had formed behind his eyes, as it did every time he started thinking about the final ritual. Perversely, now that he was so close to achieving his goal, he couldn't shake the feeling that something was going to go wrong at the last moment. As he massaged his eyeballs with his left thumb and forefinger, he could feel the little tendrils of pain spreading right back into his brain.

Sitting in the driver's seat of his van, engine running, The Disciple closed his eyes and focussed on his breathing, counting up to ten with each inhalation and down from ten to zero with each exhalation. After a couple of minutes, the stress related pain began to subside and his head began to feel a little clearer.

Once the van had cleared the archway, he stopped and ran back to close and lock the double doors. Climbing back into the van, he checked his watch.

It read: 20:45 hours.

It was finally time to go and get the third bitch responsible for ruining his life, but first, he had to find a phone box and make a very important call.

As if on cue, the rain started.

Several minutes later, The Disciple pulled up sharply outside a bright red telephone kiosk. It was the third one he'd tried; the other two had been vandalised and were no longer usable. He had stopped on a double yellow line, but it was nearly nine o'clock and he didn't anticipate being there very long. Thankfully, this one was still in working order and he quickly dialled the number from memory.

"*Good evening, New Scotland Yard. Can I help you?*"

"Yes, you can put me through to the Incident Room dealing with the Ripper murders, please."

"*One moment, please, while I try to connect you...*" The line went dead on him and he wondered if the idiot had cut him off. He was considering hanging up and redialing when a new voice suddenly came on the line.

"*Incident room, DC Jarvis speaking, can I help you?*"

The Disciple quickly wrapped a handkerchief around the mouthpiece, to disguise his voice in case the call was being recorded. He spoke very slowly, trying to make his voice sound deeper. "I want to speak to Jack Tyler," he said.

"*I'm sorry but I can hardly hear you,*" Jarvis told him. "*You'll have to speak up.*"

"I want to speak to Jack Tyler," the killer repeated irritably, keeping his voice to a whisper.

"*I'm sorry but Mr Tyler's office is in another part of the building. Can I take a message and get him to call you back? Hello...? Hello...? Are you still there, caller?*" but the killer had already hung up.

In the Incident Room, Jarvis stared uncomprehendingly at the handset for several seconds before replacing it in its cradle.

"What was that all about?" Kevin Murray asked from across the room, where he was sitting with his feet up on a desk.

"I don't know. We got cut off. Still, I guess they'll call back if it's important."

"I guess they will." Murray agreed, turning his attention to more pressing matters, namely the centrefold pinup in the latest issue of Playboy Magazine.

The Disciple phoned New Scotland Yard again, this time requesting to be transferred straight through to DCI Tyler at Arbour Square. The line briefly went dead, and then it was ringing again. He licked his lips nervously. In his mind, he went over the monologue he'd rehearsed earlier.

The phone continued to ring.

Where the hell was Tyler?

"Come on, you clever bastard," he hissed. "Where are you?" Suddenly, from out of nowhere, a fit of rage engulfed him and he found himself banging the phone against the side of the kiosk as hard as he could, cracking the plastic around the earpiece. The pain behind his eyes had returned with a vengeance. Struggling to regain control, he looked around, fearful that someone passing by might have seen his outburst. Luckily, there was no one nearby.

The ringing continued, and he began to wonder if Tyler had already left.

"*Hello, Jack Tyler speaking,*" a voice suddenly announced, and The Disciple was so surprised that he almost dropped the phone.

"*Hello?*" the voice continued. "*Is anybody there...?*"

Inside his office, Tyler shrugged his shoulders at Dillon, who impatiently mimed hanging up.

They had been on their way out of the office when the phone had started ringing, and although Dillon had done his level best to dissuade him, Tyler had dutifully returned to answer it. He had been feeling a little skittish since his earlier conversation with Terri Miller, and every time the office phone or his mobile had rung, he had instantly been filled with dread.

"Aw, come on, Jack. Put the bloody thing down and let's go grab a beer," Dillon complained, moodily. The intensity of the investigation had been relentless, and he had persuaded Jack to stop off for a quick one on the way home, just to unwind.

"Hold on, Dill, just in case there's been a development," Jack insisted.

Dillon rolled his eyes. The Yard's Press Bureau had run a massive publicity campaign to ensure that everyone and their dog was aware of the significantly increased patrols, and he found it hard to believe that the killer would be stupid enough to try and snatch another victim tonight.

"I'm sure that what the killer said to Miller was just an empty threat to impress her," Dillon said. "And, anyway, there's probably more coppers roaming the streets of Whitechapel at the moment than there are civilians."

Tyler motioned for him to be quiet. Unless he was mistaken, he could hear breathing at the other end of the line. "Is anyone there?" he asked again, and this time he tried to sound less aggressive.

"*Jack Tyler?*" The words were little more than a whisper.

Tyler sat down, holding a hand up to silence his friend, who had annoyingly started to whistle the tune for the football chant '*why are we waiting*'.

"Speaking," Tyler said, and Dillon immediately noticed the edge that had crept into his voice.

"*Do you know who this is?*" the voice asked.

"I'm sure you'll tell me in your own time," Tyler said, trying to sound bored. With his free hand, he urgently motioned for Dillon to pass him a pen.

"*It's me: your nemesis. I thought it was about time for us to talk, one Jack to another, so to speak.*"

Tyler felt his stomach constrict into a tight ball. He scribbled frantically on a sheet of memo pad: *I think this is the Ripper calling,* and held it up for his partner to read.

Dillon's jaw dropped. Springing out of the chair he'd just flopped into, he mouthed the words: '*Keep him talking*', and shot out of the room.

"How do I know that this isn't a hoax call?" Tyler demanded, stalling for time. He knew – he just knew – that this was for real.

He could almost feel the darkness within the killer's soul pulsating down the phone line. Without realising he was doing so, he moved the receiver slightly away from his face, as though the man's madness might infect him if he held it too close.

"I think you're bright enough to recognise the real deal when you encounter it, Jack. You don't mind if I call you Jack, do you?"

Jack realised that the killer was enjoying this moment.

"But just in case you're not, I'll establish my credibility by asking you how you liked the kidney and shrivelled breast that I sent you via Chief Superintendent Moron this afternoon."

Tyler's heart missed a beat. It *was* the killer beyond a shadow of a doubt; no one else could've known what the gruesome delivery contained, or the precise wording he had used to describe Porter. "How did you know how to find me here?" Tyler asked, suspiciously.

"Rest assured, I always know where to find you, Jack. I know everything there is to know about you. I could even tell you what you're wearing today if you wanted me to," the killer boasted.

"That won't be necessary," Jack said, doing his best to sound unimpressed. The killer was letting him know that he was close, that he could see without being seen. It was an unnerving thought. Had the killer been watching him? Had he been following him? Did he know where Jack and his team lived? It was highly unlikely, but even the possibility that he might was enough to send a shiver down Tyler's spine.

"Why are you doing this? Why are you killing these women?" Jack asked. Perhaps, if the killer really wanted to talk, he might actually be prepared to answer a few questions.

"Why? Because they are whores, that's why. I thought that would be obvious, even to a wooden-top like you."

"Geraldine Rye wasn't a whore, but that didn't stop you from killing her," Tyler said, angered by the killer's callous disregard for human life.

"*Which one was she?*" The killer asked, sounding confused. "*I don't have any idea who you are talking about. Surely you don't expect me to know any of the strumpet's names?*"

"The last woman you murdered," Tyler told him through gritted teeth. "You snatched her from Brick Lane and dumped her body in Mitre Square."

"*Ah, her,*" the killer said. "*Well, she looked like a whore to me, walking the streets alone at that time of night. What else would she be doing?*"

Tyler was appalled. *My God*, he thought. *This fiend sees all women as whores, whether they are on the game or not.* "Listen," he began, forcing himself to speak calmly, "There's no need for any further killing. Why don't you give yourself up and let us get you the help you need?"

At that point, Dillon reappeared, breathing heavily and holding a small portable tape recorder in his hand. He held it up in front of Jack and pointed at the phone. Tyler nodded and Dillon clipped the microphone to the receiver.

"*You think I need help?*" The Ripper snarled, his voice climbing several decibels. "*I'm not the one who needs help. If anyone needs help, then it's you, because you really haven't got a clue as to what I am, where I am, or what I'll do next. You're not in my league, Jack Tyler, not even bloody close to it.*"

Shit! He's going to hang up, Jack thought, racking his mind for a way to keep the killer talking.

"You're right," he said, quickly. "You're absolutely right. I don't have a clue about you, so why don't you even the odds by giving me a hint – or are you scared that I might find you if you level the playing field?"

Inside the telephone box, the killer's face grew taut. Tyler was mocking him. How dare the fool presume that he was afraid of a mere policeman! The murder squad detectives were intellectual insects, incapable of comprehending the magnitude of his genius. That they could threaten the outcome of his plan was inconceivable; that they had the sheer audacity to believe that they could catch him was an insult too great to ignore. It didn't matter how many 'clues' they managed to scrape together, the end result would still be the same – and he would prove it to them, once and for all.

"Me! Scared of you?" The Disciple ridiculed. "Don't make me laugh. Was my namesake scared of Inspector Abberline? I don't think so." He paused for a moment to gather his thoughts. "You can't begin to understand the power that I now wield, Chief Inspector. I can't be stopped, and I won't be found. Mark my words, I will disappear after the fifth, when the final ritual is complete, and you will be left chasing shadows, absolutely no wiser than you are now."

The music was playing inside his head again, and the volume control had been cranked up to the max. He had to shout to be heard above the ear-shattering din it was making.

"I will kill again, Jack Tyler, within the next twenty-four hours, and I'll do it right under your very noses. Heed my warning, I'll shred the next one like so much mincemeat, and there's nothing that you or your pathetic minions can do about it. You'll be eating humble pie the next time we speak; just you wait and see. You dared to challenge the New Ripper. Well, stop me if you can..."

The line went dead abruptly.

Tyler stared at the handset in horror. "Oh, shit!" was all he could manage to say.

"What's wrong? What did he say?" Dillon demanded, hitting the rewind button.

"I think I might have upset him," Jack admitted, replacing the handset in its cradle.

"What did he say?" Dillon repeated.

"He said he'd kill again within the next twenty-four hours, Dill. He also said the fifth would be his last – and he said something about disappearing after completing the final ritual, whatever that means. I think I pissed him off by baiting him, but I didn't know what else to do." Tyler ran his hands through his short hair. "Did you manage to record anything he said?"

"Let's find out," Dillon said, pressing the play button.

"*...Me! Scared of you? Don't make me laugh. Was my namesake scared of Inspector Abberline?*" The quality wasn't the best, but it was plenty good enough for the lab to get a voice comparison from.

"If you want a drink that badly, Dill, then I suggest you put the kettle on. I hate to say this, but we're not going anywhere for a while."

With a heavy heart, Tyler reached for the phone. Holland was going to love this – not.

CHAPTER THIRTY-FIVE

At ten past nine, Sarah Pritchard was still sitting at her desk in the Sutton Mission, catching up with a few last-minute admin issues. Charise had gone home hours ago to get ready for a Friday night out with some old university friends, and all the evening volunteers had long since gone forth to help the less fortunate.

The Mission had a completely different, more serene, vibe during the evening, and it was one that she rather liked. Once the hustle and bustle of the working day had petered out, and she no longer had to deal with a constant stream of interruptions from her staff and some of their more needy clients, she found that she could get so much more done, which was one of the reasons why she often worked late.

Simon had called a few minutes ago to apologise for running late, and to reassure her that he hadn't forgotten their date and would be there to collect her shortly.

It seemed weird – but in a nice way – that they were actually going out for dinner together again. They hadn't done anything like that since he had committed the indiscretion that had torn their marriage apart.

She wondered if he was taking her somewhere intimate. Perhaps he wanted to say something to her – something important? But surely, if he was going to all the trouble of taking her to a restaurant, it was unlikely to be anything bad. Perhaps, she allowed herself to hope, they were going to turn a corner in their troubled relationship and he was finally going to try and put things right between them.

Was that too much to hope for?

As if on cue, Simon Pritchard poked his head around her office door. "Are you ready?" he asked.

Sarah nodded. "Just give me two seconds to send this email and I'll be with you," she said, smiling up at him.

When the call-out arrived, the Commissioners Reserve were playing cards in the canteen at Limehouse police station, having just started their refreshment break.

"Call-out!" PC Jay Smith shouted as he walked in from the Control Room, where he'd just been to collect a printout containing details of the call-out.

Inspector Perry Twist, the unit commander, signalled for Smith to join him at the far end of the canteen, where he was enjoying a cup of tea with the four carrier supervisors.

He read the printout and gave an unimpressed grunt. Then he passed it to Sergeant Bob Beach, who sat to his immediate left.

"Load of bollocks if you ask me," Twist said, dismissing Smith. "They already have two whole units of TSG posted to the borough every evening this week. That's eight carriers. And that's without all the local aid that's been drummed up. Talk about overkill! What possible difference do they expect us to make? We won't rush out from grub for that. What do you think Bob?"

"You're probably right, guv," Bob Beach said tactfully, although the way he saw it, the Metropolitan Police was a disciplined service, and they had just been instructed to proceed immediately to Whitechapel division and commence high visibility patrols. It was wrong of Twist to ignore the order, although he was undoubtedly right about them not making a difference once they got there. "But my crew has finished eating. We could head over to HT and fly the flag for a while, just to be on the safe side. The rest of the unit can join us after grub."

After considering this for a moment, Twist grunted a grudging approval. "Off you go, then," he said.

As he led them out into the rear yard, Beach could hear his crew moaning like a bunch of sulking children about having had their break shortened. He glanced at his watch as they climbed aboard the carrier. It was twenty past nine.

"So much for a proper grub break," he said, wistfully.

The Disciple angrily swerved the van over in Vallance Road, stopping opposite Vallance Gardens. He was only a few minutes away from his lair, but the bitch was stirring already. He had obviously miscalculated the amount of chloroform he'd given her because, somehow, against all the odds, she had pulled down her blindfold and staggered to her feet, and she was now trying to wriggle out of the rigid handcuffs. Having somehow removed the gag he'd rammed halfway down her throat, she was making a hell of a racket, and he couldn't risk driving her into his lair while she was carrying on like that in case someone heard and called the police.

He left the engine running, and hurriedly climbed through the dividing curtain. He knew that, in the half-light, his advancing form would appear as a menacing silhouette to her. As she tried to back away from him, eyes wide with terror, and screaming like a demented banshee, he punched her on the point of the chin. To his immense satisfaction, she dropped like a stone and the awful noise immediately stopped.

He loomed over her, ready to lash out again if she so much as moved, but to his relief she remained still and silent.

His fist ached from the jarring impact of the punch, and he flexed it gently to make sure that nothing was damaged. Then he knelt down and checked her pulse and pupil dilation. She wouldn't be out for long but, hopefully, he would have enough time to get her into his lair, where he could sedate her properly. He put the blindfold back on, and stuck an even bigger wad of clothing into her mouth – now, when she came around, she would be far too busy trying to breath to even think about screaming – and then tied her feet together, wishing he'd done that in the first place.

To his great surprise, the third bitch responsible for ruining his life was already beginning to stir as he stood up, and he watched without pity as she drunkenly struggled into a sitting position, resting her back against one of the plastic-coated sides of the van. He briefly considered striking her again, but it quickly became apparent that she was far too dazed to cause him any further problems.

Tyler was writing furiously when the telephone rang. "Oh, for goodness sake," he snapped, staring daggers at it. The bloody thing hadn't stopped since he'd upgraded the threat assessment for the killer striking again to imminent; at this rate he would never get his decision log up to speed. "DCI Tyler," he said.

"*Sir, Paul Evans here. Sorry to disturb you, but I'm a little confused.*"

The Welshman sounded tired, Tyler thought. "I know how you feel," he said. "That's my default setting these days. How can I help you to become less confused, Paul?"

"*Can I confirm that you wanted me to see if I could pick up Dr Pritchard on his way to the nick, and then follow him there?*"

"That's right," Tyler confirmed.

"*And then, once he arrived, I was going to wait until this motorcycle courier turned up and see if I can follow him off?*"

"Yep, you're on the money so far."

"*So, here's the thing: I finally managed to acquire Dr Pritchard on CCTV walking along Cambridge Heath Road towards Bethnal Green tube station. Then I followed him along Roman Road on a different camera and actually watched him turn left into Victoria Park Square, which is where the nick is. It's a bit of a long-eye view, so not ideal, but I can see him clearly enough for my purposes.*"

"That's excellent work, Paul," Tyler said, impressed.

"*I figure it would take him a minute at most to reach the front office after he turns the corner and I lose sight of him."*

"Sounds reasonable," Tyler agreed.

"So why is it that I've watched the CCTV for half an hour either side of his arrival at Whitechapel nick and not one motorcycle turned into or out of Victoria Park Square during that time?"

"Are you sure?" Tyler said, replaying Pritchard's account in his head. "It must have done."

"I'm absolutely positive it didn't, boss. And there's one other thing – I only got a brief glance of it, but I'd swear that Pritchard has got a white shoe box tucked under his arm in the footage from the Cambridge Heath Road camera. Who took Pritchard's statement, if you don't mind me asking?"

"Mr Porter took his statement, as a matter of fact," Tyler said. "He was halfway through writing it when we arrived so I let him finish it."

"That probably explains it then," Evans said. *"It must be a mistake. Old man Porter probably wrote the events down out of sequence."*

Tyler couldn't help but smile. "Actually, Pritchard gave me a verbal account of what happened, which correlates to what's in the statement, so unless you think I made a mistake too..."

"I would never even dare think such a thing, boss," Evans promised hastily.

Tyler's mind had gone into hyper-drive. "I have a nasty suspicion Simon Pritchard deliberately lied to us, Paul. And I can only think of one reason for doing that."

"Fuck me! Does that mean what I think it does?" Evans asked.

"I think it does, Paul," Tyler said, suddenly very excited. "You've done great work, and you might have just given us the break we so desperately need."

The Disciple's latest victim was very groggy, and very confused. She tried to focus her eyes as she sat up, but the world around her was in darkness. Head throbbing unmercifully, she sagged back against something cold and hard. She couldn't close her mouth; it was as though her jaw had been wedged open. There was vibration all around her. Try as she might, she couldn't remember what had happened.

Was she ill?

Had she collapsed?

Where was her husband?

A bittersweet odour permeated the air; a strange cocktail of different smells, the like of which she had never before encountered. It seemed to consist of a mixture of gasoline, disinfectant and, what else...?

Plastic...?

Yes, that was it, plastic. There was something else, too – something chemically. It reminded her of hospitals.

And she could hear the gentle pitter-patter of rain on metal. Was she in a shed with a corrugated roof? She tried to move her arms, and then her legs, but neither responded and she began to panic. Had her neck been broken? Was she now a paraplegic? She tried to cry out, but only a muffled squeal escaped. That was when the realisation that she was bound and gagged hit home.

Oh my God I've been kidnapped! She thought, beginning to hyperventilate.

Where was she?

How long had she been there?

What was going to happen to her?

Somebody help me! She screamed, but her gag muffled the words and she almost choked from the effort. Hot tears began to prickle her eyes.

A rustling in front of her broke the silence; the noise told her that she was not alone. Someone was there with her, watching her.

Oh, my good God!

And then, in a moment of spine-tingling clarity, it all came flooding back to her. Her husband had done this to her – her own husband!

But why?

It made absolutely no sense whatsoever. He was an intelligent man – a man of science, and he had never demonstrated the slightest capacity for violence in all the years she had known him – which begged the disturbing question: had she ever truly known him at all?

They had been chatting quite amiably, and he had gallantly held her coat open for her as she slipped it on. Standing behind her, he had tenderly placed his hands on her shoulders and whispered that he was really looking forward to spending some quality time with her tonight. There had been affection in his voice, or so she had thought. And then, in the blink of an eye, his arm had wrapped itself tightly around her neck like a python crushing its prey. Pulling her body against his, her husband had used his free hand to clamp a foul-smelling cloth over her face. The powerful chemical it contained had immediately made the world around her spin.

She had a blurry recollection of him lowering her down to the floor, but after that, there were only uncoordinated snippets of consciousness. She vaguely recalled him ranting about not being the pathetic 'yes man' she thought he was while he was securing her hands and applying the gag. There had been something else, too – something about how she was a controlling bitch who had ruined his life – but she had passed out before his diatribe had finished.

What could possibly have made him say those terrible things? All she had ever done was to try and help him become a better person. She had given him love, money, a purpose in life; she had even forgiven him for shagging one of the street workers he was supposed to be helping. Of course, she had given him hell over it, but what had he expected her to do, turn a blind eye and carry on like nothing had happened? Ironically, in spite of his abhorrent transgressions, she had never given up on him, and she had fought so hard to salvage their marriage. How many other women would have done that?

And then she recalled the weird singing – well, it more like chanting really – she'd heard as she'd drifted back into consciousness a few moments ago, only to find herself laying on her back and being bumped around in the darkness. "What a ride! What a thrill! I'm Jack the New Ripper, and I love to kill, kill kill..." She had recognised the toneless voice immediately – her husband couldn't sing in tune to save his life.

Hot bile rose to the back of her throat as she truly began to comprehend the futility of her situation.

She was going to die.

The man she had so naively – so bloody foolishly – believed still loved her was, in fact, a demented serial killer. He had already slaughtered four defenceless women and she was going to be the fifth.

She was going to be made to suffer miserably, and then she was going to die a dreadful, unholy death at her the hands of her own husband, the man the media had reveled in labeling 'Jack the New Ripper'.

Like countless others, Sarah had read Terri Miller's gripping articles in the Echo, and she had followed the TV coverage avidly, so she knew exactly what to expect from this demon.

She knew she should try and escape, but there was absolutely no fight left in her, and all she could do was lean back against the cold wall of the van and await her fate. And then she heard a new sound, a sound that froze the blood in her veins. It was the sound of laughter, soft and sibilant. The twisted bastard was enjoying this.

———

As soon as he'd put the phone down on Paul Evans, Jack Tyler scrabbled together every available body he could find. A team of detectives, led by Steve Bull, were dispatched to the Sutton Mission. Another team, this one commanded by Charlie White, was sent to Pritchard's home address in Loughton. Wendy was tasked with circulating him as wanted-missing on the Police National Computer. After that, she was to ensure that his status and description was circulated on all local and Met wide radio channels. Locating and arresting Simon Pritchard was now their overriding priority, and pretty much everything else had been put on hold until this was achieved.

The Chief Inspector at IR had been rather annoyed when Tyler had called a few minutes ago to request that a carrier be sent to each of the addresses to support his officers. "I don't have a limitless supply of policemen," he'd told Tyler, testily. "You've already used up every floating resource I have. The only way I can give you two carriers is if I redeploy some of the aid that's already patrolling Whitechapel, which might actually be a good thing. We've got so many police vehicles driving around that bloody division that the roads are more clogged up now than they normally get at the height of the rush hour!"

The moment the two arrest teams left the building, Tyler settled himself in his office and started reviewing his notes. Pritchard's story about helping out a courier who was running late was pure fiction – they could prove that, and the only conceivable reason for lying about how and when he received the box was that he was the killer. The more Jack thought about it, the more sense it made: Pritchard hadn't been in practice for many years, but he had the requisite medical knowledge; he had easy access to the area's street workers – they all knew him from his charity work so he would be able to move amongst them without drawing attention or suspicion.

What didn't make sense – at least not yet – was why he was doing this. What possible motive could he have?

Tyler dug out the notes he'd made while speaking to the forensic psychologist. The quack had explained that, although there might not be a discernible relationship between the serial killer and his victims, that didn't mean there was no motive. The trick was to think less like a detective and more like a psychotic. Often, for people suffering from psychosis or other forms of mental illness, the anger, rage, and hostility they felt towards a particular subgroup of the population – in this case, women, particularly sex workers – provided all the motivation they would ever need. Sometimes, it was the power and thrill of what they did, or the need to act out repressed sexual desires that motivated them. The psychologist had suggested it was probably a combination all of these factors that drove the New Ripper to commit his atrocities.

Talk about hedging your bets!

Tyler was cautiously optimistic that Pritchard was indeed their man, but he wasn't going to allow himself to get carried away until they had irrefutable evidence – he had made that mistake twice already, with Winston and Boyden. Both had looked like extremely good suspects on paper, but neither had turned out to be the man they were after.

Dillon appeared, carrying two steaming hot mugs of coffee. "There you go, mate," he said, handing one over. "You'll feel better with some caffeine inside you."

"Cheers, Dill," Tyler said, taking a sip and burning his lip.

"Oh yeah," Dillon said, seeing his friend wince. "Julia said be careful, it's hot."

CHAPTER THIRTY-SIX

Simon Pritchard viciously pulled the blindfold off. Even in the darkness, he could see the fear in her eyes. For once he was the one in control, not her. It generated a feeling of warmth in the pit of his stomach. He knelt down and leaned over her, studying her face intently, wondering what the third bitch responsible for ruining his life was thinking now that the tables were turned. He caressed her cheek, relishing the way she flinched at the contact. When she tried to edge back, he grabbed hold of her hair and yanked her head around until he was staring straight into her terror-stricken eyes. When he was satisfied that she wouldn't scream, he removed the gag from her mouth.

Sarah Pritchard gasped, and then gratefully filled her lungs with air. "Please, don't kill me," she pleaded. "I don't want to die."

The Disciple shrugged. "No one ever does."

"I told Charise we were having dinner together tonight," she sobbed. "When my body turns up it will be obvious that you did it. You would never get away with it." Surely, he could see that murdering her would cost him his freedom?

There was a maniacal intensity to his laugh. "Simon Pritchard won't be killing you," he purred. "Jack the New Ripper will have that honour. Trust me, Sarah. No one will ever consider me a potential suspect when your corpse shows up." He said this with absolute confidence. "Don't worry, though, I promise to play my part as the grieving husband perfectly. I've already chosen you a lovely tombstone."

"But it makes no sense. Why would the Ripper kill me? He only kills prostitutes." Sarah knew that wasn't strictly true. She had read about the woman who had been abducted on her way to the train station after finishing work, but surely that had been a case of mistaken identity.

"Ah, but the Ripper has a very good reason to kill you," he explained, knowingly. "Tell me, what's even worse than all those vile parasitic whores swarming through our streets like cockroaches?" He studied her face to see if she could guess, but she just stared at him blankly, her mind frozen by fear. "No idea? Well, the answer is a woman who empowers them; a woman who gives them money and shelter and arranges free accommodation and health checks so that they can continue to seduce, infect and exploit the unsuspecting, fundamentally good men who fall prey to their charms – a woman like you, Sarah. You are nothing but a Jezebel – a false prophet. Your so-called charity provides a safe haven from which the dregs of society are free to spread their filth and corruption, with you presiding over it like the Queen of Whores you are. Like it or not, Sweet Sister Sarah, you are every bit as culpable for the actions of the harlots you protect as they are themselves, perhaps even more so in some cases."

"No," she said, sobbing quietly. "You're distorting the truth. That charity is my life, and I thought it was yours, too."

He shook his head and made a horrible screeching noise that was meant to imitate the electronic buzzer that TV game show contestants hear when they get the answer wrong. "Uhhh-uhhh."

"Simon, I'm begging you, before it's too late, please let me go. You won't get away with this. How are you going to keep my disappearance a secret?"

He cocked his head to one side and stared at her in exasperation. "Why on earth would you think I want to keep it a secret?"

"Because the moment someone finds out, you'll be done for," she said, desperately trying to make him understand.

Pritchard bristled. He was so incredibly fed up with this interfering cow always thinking that she knew better, of her constant criticism of every idea and plan that he had ever come up with. Even now, as she cowered down before him, begging for her worthless life, she was still managing to find fault. Unbelievable! He knew he should wait until they were safely ensconced in his lair, but he couldn't allow her to speak to him like that anymore – she needed a reality check, and he was going to give her one, right here and now.

"In a minute I'm going to make a phone call. If you scream, I will kill you on the spot. Do you believe me? It's important that you do," he said, and nodded towards a huge serrated hunting knife that had magically appeared in his left hand.

Sarah nodded, hesitantly at first and then more forcefully when she saw how angry her feeble response was making him. Releasing her hair, he reached into his jacket and removed a mobile phone. She watched in fearful fascination as he keyed the buttons.

"Now remember, no screaming," he warned.

While watching his every move fearfully, Sarah rubbed the side of her face. Her jaw still ached terribly, but she no longer thought it was broken. By now, her eyes had adjusted to the darkness, and she was confident that they were in the back of a van. She considered screaming for help but dismissed the idea almost at once. She had no way of knowing where they were. For all she knew they could be out in the middle of nowhere, a field or an abandoned building in which she could scream until she was blue in the face and still not be heard. Besides, there was no doubt in her mind that she would be dead before the first cry ended. The deranged man in front of her was a complete stranger, not the husband she had loved for so many years.

"Please," she said, desperately trying not to let her fear show, "I've only ever loved you. Why are you doing this to me? Surely we can sort this out without you hurting me?" She tried to keep her voice calm and reasonable, appealing to his better nature. He was a doctor, for Christ's sake. Weren't they sworn to protect life?

The Disciple smiled indulgently and held a finger to his lips while making a shushing noise.

"We'll talk after," he promised.

A flicker of hope danced across her heart. Maybe there was a slim chance of surviving this after all.

And then he was through to the newspaper again.

"Get me Teresa Miller at once..."

Miller was still at her desk in the main office, putting the finishing touches on her latest article covering the Ripper case. It was infuriating that Tyler had declined to confirm that the flesh delivered by the Ripper was human, as the killer had inferred, and not a pound of stewing steak from the local butcher's shop, but she had managed to find a way around that.

As luck would have it, after being blanked by Tyler, she had spoken to a rather naive trainee lab technician who had been present when the ghoulish shoe box full of human flesh had been delivered for forensic examination. Claiming to be a police officer calling for an update on behalf of DCI Tyler, she had been told that the box contained a human kidney and a neatly severed mammary gland.

The article made splendid reading if she said so herself – and she did – and, as Tyler hadn't asked her to withhold any of the details, she would print the story in all its glory.

Deakin suddenly ran out of his office and began jumping up and down like a Jack in the box. When she frowned at him quizzically, he began waving his arms frantically. "Terri, it's him again. Get your arse over here now," he bellowed across the room, causing heads to turn.

"Shit!" she exclaimed, as a jolt of adrenaline flooded through her.

"Miller speaking," she said, a few seconds later, having sashayed her way through an obstacle course made of desks.

"*Who was that?*" the now familiar voice hissed suspiciously. "*Who answered the phone?*"

"It was my editor, Giles. He was manning the phone for me. It's cool. You can trust him," she soothed, mentally kicking herself for not staying by the special phone line they'd set up.

"*I'll decide who I can and can't trust, Terri, and it's not fucking him,*" the sinister voice reprimanded her fiercely.

"I – I'm sorry," she told him, recoiling at the ferocity of his anger.

"*I have someone here I want you to listen to. Don't ask her any questions. Don't say a word. If you speak, I will kill her and it will be your fault. Do you understand these instructions, Terri?*" He said the words so casually that she thought she'd misheard for a moment.

"*I asked you a question.*" The anger was back in his voice.

"You want me to listen to someone speak, is that right?" she clarified.

"*Just listen. Do not talk. Understand?*"

"Okay. Whatever you say, but who am I going to be talking to?" Miller asked, not really understanding what the killer wanted from her. A new voice came on the phone. It was a woman's voice, utterly terrified, and it was possibly the saddest thing Terri Miller had ever heard.

"*Help me, please. Tell him he doesn't have to do this. I don't want to die...*" The sheer desperation in Sarah Pritchard's words broke Terri Miller's heart. The phone was taken away, and the woman's pleas for help faded until all Miller could hear was the killer's breathing.

Terri clasped her hand over the mouthpiece to prevent the killer hearing. "Jesus Christ, he's taken another one. Oh God! Giles, I think he's going to kill her over the phone. Quick, call the police," she urged her editor.

She could hardly breathe; it felt as though the killer's hand had reached into her chest cavity and was now squeezing her heart.

"Are you sure?" Deakin asked, paling.

"Just do it, will you," Terri pleaded. In the background, on the other end of the line, she could hear the Ripper speaking to his captive.

"Please, don't hurt her..." Terri begged. She cast a sideways glance at Giles. He was on the other phone, gesturing animatedly.

The sound of the slap was distinctive, even over the phone. It was accompanied by a scream, then silence. Terri flinched. She nearly called out to the woman, to make sure she was okay, but she stopped herself just in time. The killer's words echoed in her mind: *Don't say a word. If you speak, I will kill her and it will be your fault.*

She rammed the receiver tightly against her ear, hardly daring to breathe in case the noise it made blocked out something important at the other end. And then, after what seemed an eternity, the killer spoke again.

"*My guest and I are going to bid you farewell shortly, but don't worry, we'll call you back again before too long.*"

"Wait! Is she okay? Have you hurt her? Can I talk to her again?" Terri had to know the answer to these questions.

"*Don't fret about the Queen of Whores. She's still alive – for now. I want you to pass a message onto Jack Tyler from me. Tell him that he should've taken me more seriously.*"

In the back of the van, Sarah Pritchard cowered in the far corner, between the rear wheel arch and the back doors. A trickle of blood ran down the side of her face where he'd hit her. She watched as her husband casually turned his back on her and reached for something in the darkness. Dazed from the blow, she was only half-aware of the words he spoke into the mobile phone.

"...tell him that he should have taken me more seriously."

When he turned to face her again, there was an insane glint in his eyes. She could have sworn that they were glowing red in the dark, like those of a demon. He advanced on her slowly, his movements purposeful and sinister.

"No, keep back, please. Don't hurt me again..." she pleaded, trying in vain to wriggle backwards. The Disciple sat astride her stomach, pinning her to the floor with his knees.

"Listen to this, Terri. It's the sound of my redemption," he whispered into the phone. Then, holding the mobile towards her face with his right hand, the killer raised his left hand high above him. Following the movement with her eyes, Sarah instantly recognised the fearful shape of the claw hammer. Wide-eyed, she opened her mouth to scream, but it was too late. With a sickening thud, the hammer crashed into her shoulder, shattering the clavicle.

He hit her a second time for good measure. Sarah Pritchard's screams stopped after the second blow, as she slipped into unconsciousness. "There," The Disciple said in satisfaction. "Did you hear that, Terri? Are you enjoying the show?"

"*NO! Stop it, please. This is insane,*" Miller's voice screamed at him. He wondered why, if it was so bad, she hadn't hung up on him. He knew she wouldn't, of course. It was too good a story to pass up: holding a telephone conversation with Jack the New Ripper while he toyed with his latest victim. "I'm going to cut her throat, Terri," he teased her. He wasn't, of course. That would come much later, when they were back at the lair.

"*NOOOOOOO!*" The anguish in Miller's voice was simply delicious.

He very much doubted that this is what Miller had in mind when she'd asked him to open up to her so that she could do his story justice, but her request had proved quite inspirational. To be able to share this moment with someone who would be alive to talk about it afterwards was just incredible. The third bitch responsible for ruining his life stirred. He had to admire her durability. The Queen of Whores was virtually indestructible.

"Oh my Lord, he's going to kill her, Giles. I can hear him moving about, getting ready." Miller was close to tears. She wanted a story of course, what reporter didn't, but this went beyond the pale. If she thought it would have stopped him, she would have hung up, but she knew it wouldn't. The only thing she could think to do was find a way to keep him talking until the police arrived. Maybe they could trace the call.

"Please, talk to me," she shouted into the phone. "Talk to me damn you or I'll hang up," she cried, hoping to call his bluff.

The sound of movement stopped abruptly. There followed an uncomfortable silence and she began to wonder if the signal had been lost. She could tell he was using a mobile because of the intermittent echo. And then she heard his breathing again and a wave of relief flooded over her.

"*What's the matter, Terri? I thought you wanted my story. Think of how many newspapers this will sell.*" His voice, cruel and mocking, made her feel hollow and unclean. As if sensing her thoughts, The Disciple went on the attack. "*You prove my point for me, Terri. All women are whores. You might not sell your body for sex, but you are willing to abandon your principles and sleep with the devil just to get your name in print and sell a few measly newspapers. What's the difference? Tell me that, if you can.*"

"I –" Terri opened her mouth to refute the hurtful allegation, but somehow nothing would come out. There was a cruel perception in his words that had stung her. Surely, he was wrong? Surely, she was better than that?

"*Exactly,*" he smirked. "*Well, Terri, it's been fun, but I've got a throat to slit so I'm going to say goodbye for now. We'll talk again later.*"

"Wait, don't go," she pleaded, but the line had already gone dead. "He rang off." Terri Miller said, appalled. She was close to hysteria and she felt thoroughly sick. Holding her head in her hands, Terri slumped forward on the desk. "Dear God, what have I done?" she asked, ashen-faced.

"It's not your fault, sweetheart," Deakin told her.

"It *is* my fault, Giles. He's only doing this to impress me. If I had refused to play his stupid games none of this would be happening. It's no wonder that that cop, Dillon, looked at me with such contempt." She angrily wiped a tear away from the corner of her eye.

"Listen to me, old girl," Deakin said firmly. "It is not your fault. This monster doesn't do things to please you or anyone else. He's mad, and he's evil. It's as simple as that. If the truth be known, you're as much a victim as that poor cow he's got trapped." Deakin spoke with growing anger. Miller was a good reporter; she didn't deserve to be reduced to this.

"Oh Giles," She said, looking across at him. "That poor, poor woman…" Unable to contain her anguish a moment longer, Terri Miller finally broke down and cried.

Deakin placed a gentle hand on her shoulder. He knew there was nothing he could say to ease her pain, so he didn't speak at all. He just knelt down beside her and wrapped his arms around her protectively. If need be, he would hold her like that all night. When the tears finally stopped, he would fix her a strong drink and try and get her to talk about it.

At that moment the door opened and a stern-faced detective strode in.

CHAPTER THIRTY-SEVEN

PC Patrick Reeve pointed at a battered green van parked with its rear end askew from the kerb, as though it had pulled over in a hurry. He couldn't see anyone sitting in the cab, but the lights were on, and a plume of exhaust fumes could be seen coming from the rear of the vehicle, so the engine was obviously running.

"What about that one?" he suggested.

"There's no one in it," PC Ron Stedman said, dismissively. "It's probably a delivery driver who's stopped for a quick piss in the park."

"Or," Reeve countered, "the driver could have seen us coming towards him and legged it because there's a dead body in the back."

"Imbecilic comments like that are the main reason some of our colleagues call us the Thick and Stupid Group," Stedman pointed out, his voice oozing sarcasm.

Reeve wasn't going to be put off that easily. "But they want us to stop Sherpa vans," he protested. "We should stop and find the driver. He can't be far."

The two men were polar opposites; Patrick Reeve – or Seventies Cop as he was referred to on the unit because his views and mannerisms could have been straight lifts from some of the classic policing shows from that era – was tall and skinny, although he did have a little beer belly that hung over the front of his belt. His uniform trousers were a couple of inches too short for him, and they looked as though he regularly slept in them. Although bald, he proudly sported a Pancho Villa style moustache that drooped miserably over the sides of his lips. Ronald Stedman, on the other hand, was tall, broad, with a military buzz cut; his uniform was always immaculate and the only thing sharper than his trouser creases was his tongue.

"No, they want us to stop white Sherpa vans," Stedman corrected his operator in a condescending tone. "White Sherpa vans with a headlight out of alignment, to be precise, not green ones. Honestly, you're such a pillock!"

Reeves face reddened and his moustache twitched angrily. "Well it might not be white, but it is a Sherpa, and it does have a headlight out of alignment, so I vote we should still check it out."

Stedman rolled his eyes. They were meant to be looking for a murderer, not giving someone a traffic ticket for leaving a vehicle unattended with its engine running. "Hello, is anyone in there?" He leaned over and rapped his knuckles against Reeve's bald head several times. "Just as I thought, the lights are on but no one's home."

"Get off," Reeve said, sweeping Stedman's hand away. He tapped his nose. "This is telling me something's not right with that van and I vote we check it out."

Stead glanced over his shoulder at PS Beach. "Sorry about Reevo, Sarge. He recently went into hospital for a vasectomy but they gave him a lobotomy by mistake."

Beach smiled indulgently. Carrier humour was all right in small doses, but it could quickly become tiresome. Besides, Reeve did have a point, and more importantly, he had good coppering instincts. "Do a slow drive by," he instructed. "Let's see if the back doors are open."

Stedman reluctantly altered his course, and several seconds later they drew level with the old van. Reeve's shoulders sagged in disappointment when he saw the rear doors were firmly closed.

"See, no one's in it." Stedman gloated. "Like I said, the driver's obviously been caught short and has nipped into the park to relieve himself."

"Yeah, right," Reeve's voice dripped with skepticism. "If he's in the park, he's more likely to be getting some ganja from a local dealer or to having it off with a prossie," he argued.

"Do we really care?" Stedman asked. He was bored with the conversation. Obviously, he would have had a very different view if the van had been white, but it wasn't. It was green. He pressed the accelerator pedal and the carrier surged forward.

"Hang on a second, Ron." PC Sid Wallis called from the rear seat. "Back her up, will you."

"What's up, Sid? What have you seen?" Ron Stedman asked, putting the carrier's selector into reverse.

"I just saw the van start rocking from side to side. Why is it doing that if no one's in it?"

Reeve smiled triumphantly at his driver. "What did I tell you?"

"Oh shut up and wipe that silly grin off your face, you silly old git," Stedman snapped. "If I wanted to listen to an arsehole, I'd fart."

Reeve grinned. "No one likes a sore loser," he said, nudging Stedman with his elbow.

The Disciple heard voices, and then came the unmistakable crackle of a radio.

He froze.

The police were outside his van.

They couldn't possibly be looking for him, could they?

He looked down at his wife; afraid she would call out and spoil everything. To his relief, she was still unconscious. He covered her mouth, anyway, digging his nails hard into the flesh in case she woke up and started crying out. He tried to control his breathing. If he just stayed still, without making any noise, the Old Bill might go –

BANG, BANG, BANG. He flinched as they hammered on the side of his van.

An authoritative voice shouted, "Police. Come out of the van, now."

What should he do?

If he went out, they would arrest him.

If he didn't go out, they might open the driver's door, which he had stupidly left unlocked, and find him here in the back with the third bitch responsible for ruining his life.

Was there any way out of this?

There had to be. It was his destiny to complete the rituals and ascend to a higher level of being.

Moving quickly, he slipped the knife into the rear of his waistband. He grabbed the gag and stuck it back in her mouth, cringing when she made a low moaning noise in protest.

BANG, BANG, BANG. His heart missed a beat as they hammered again, more forcefully than the first time.

"Hurry up. We can hear you moving about. Come out now." The voice sounded impatient, angry even.

"I'm coming," he called back, frantically wiping his sweaty hands on his wife's clothing and then climbing back through the divider into the cab.

"Can I help you, officers?" The Disciple asked, having wound down the driver's window.

"Is this your van?" PC Wallis asked.

"Yes, it is." He smiled, trying to act naturally.

"Step out of the vehicle, please," Wallis said.

"But it's raining," The Disciple protested.

"Step out of the vehicle," Wallis repeated, and it was clear from his tone that there was no room for discussion. The Disciple grudgingly obliged, standing with his back to the open driver's door.

"What are you doing here, then?" PC Jay Smith asked, openly suspicious.

"I just stopped for a moment to secure something that had worked its way loose in the back. I'm finished now though, so I'll be off if that's okay." The Disciple made to climb back behind the wheel.

"Hang on, mate. We're not finished with you yet," Stedman told him, firmly. Maybe Reevo was right about this van. Maybe something hooky was going on here.

"But I really ought to be going," The Disciple protested.

"You're not going anywhere, sunshine. I reckon you've got a prostitute in the back of your van," Smith said. He couldn't understand why anyone would want to pay for sex, especially with some of the gremlins that worked around here. If his entire body were covered in a condom, from head to toe, and they were paying him instead of the other way around, he still wouldn't let one of the local working girls anywhere near him.

"No. I told you, I stopped to adjust something in the back," The Disciple said lamely. His eyes darted about nervously as he weighed up his chances of escape.

Wallis saw this, and he and Smith exchanged a knowing look. Something smelled wrong to them.

"Can you switch the engine off and step away from the van," Wallis said, moving in closer to cover him.

"I can't. There's – there's a problem with the battery. If I turn it off then I won't be able to start it again," The Disciple lied. His only realistic hope of escape lay in keeping the engine running. If he could just find an excuse to get back in the driving seat, he might just have half a chance.

"Just step away from the vehicle, please," Wallis repeated, dashing his hopes. After a moment's hesitation, the killer reluctantly obeyed.

Smith opened his notebook "What's your name?" His tone was openly hostile.

"Mr Bradley," he said, picking the name out of thin air.

"What's your full name?"

The Disciple looked down at his shoes, thinking: *fuck you, you Nazi*.

Smith nudged his arm and said, "I asked you your name."

The Disciple shifted his feet uneasily. "David Bradley," he said. David had been his father's name.

Their pompous attitude was turning his fear into anger. He was determined to escape, if only to humiliate these fools. They clearly didn't have a clue that the arrest of their collective careers was almost within their grasp.

"Have you got any driving documents on you, Mr Bradley?" Smith asked. He wished that he'd thought to bring a flashlight off of the carrier with him. There was something odd about the guy's face, but it was too dark to see exactly what it was.

"No, I'm sorry, I haven't," The Disciple shrugged apologetically.

The trick now would be in getting them to drop their guard. If he could just convince them that he was a nerd and not a threat.

"Is the van registered to you, Mr Bradley?" Sergeant Beach asked, speaking for the first time since he'd got off the bus.

"Er, no, it's not. I've not had it long, you see."

"That's what they all say, pal." Wallis sneered. "Open the back, please. Let's see who's in there, shall we?"

"I've told you, there's no one in there." The Disciple said this a little too quickly and immediately regretted it. A trickle of sweat ran down the centre of his back, and he licked his lips, suddenly aware that his mouth was dry.

"Then you won't mind opening the back to show us, will you?" Smith said, forcefully. He grabbed hold of the rear door handle and twisted.

Nothing happened.

It was locked.

Smith frowned. The van had just rocked slightly. Had someone just moved inside or was it merely where he'd pulled the handle?

And then he heard a muffled voice. It sounded like someone stifling a sob. Without a doubt, it came from inside the vehicle.

"What was that?" Beach asked, having heard it too.

"Okay, wise guy, I've had enough of your lies. There's someone inside this van. Open the bloody thing, right now," Smith said, moving towards the killer aggressively.

"Okay, okay. Look, it's true. I've got a girl in the back of my van, but we haven't done anything, I swear. You stopped us before we could." The Disciple wrung his hands together as if begging for mercy.

Smith rolled his eyes. These kerb crawlers were so pathetic. He'd be begging them not to tell his wife and kids next. "Open the van up, Mr Bradley," he said flatly. The killer nodded, eager to please, or at least eager not to upset them more than he already had.

"Okay, but the back door's jammed. I'll have to climb through the back and open it from inside. Unless one of you wants to do it?" he knew that none of the officers would want to get in the back, not with the whore there.

"Just get on with it," Wallis said. He was pissed off with this insignificant little twerp. The quicker they dealt with him, the quicker they could get on with searching for the murderer.

The Disciple started walking towards the driver's door. He made himself walk very slowly. It was important not to appear too eager. He paused with one foot inside the cabin, looking back at the group of officers gathered by the rear doors. "Are you sure one of you chaps doesn't want to do this?" he asked.

"Just get on with it, will you," Smith snapped impatiently.

"Well, if you're sure," The Disciple said to himself.

He slid onto the driver's seat and carefully put the van into gear, praying that the gearbox wouldn't crunch, as it was sometimes prone to do in first.

It went in perfectly.

He shook his head in disbelief. This was almost too easy, not that he could afford to relax just yet. He took a deep breath, released the handbrake, and then ground the accelerator into to the floor. The van rocketed off towards the main road. The last thing the killer saw in his rearview mirror was the small cluster of policemen standing in a cloud of black fumes, a look of total shock on their faces.

The TSG officers all scrambled for the carrier, furious with themselves for having been hoodwinked. The Sherpa had a good head start on them, and their vehicle was facing in completely the wrong direction.

"Shall I put it up on the Main-Set, Sarge?" Reeve asked breathlessly.

"Are you kidding? It's bad enough that we let the fucker give us the slip, without telling the whole world about it," Beach snarled. "Ron, you had better catch him up or I'll be using your gonads to play conkers with."

Stedman grimaced at the thought. The power steering and superb turning circle of the Mercedes Sprint made manoeuvering relatively easy, but they would have to drive like the very wind if they were to have any chance of catching the Sherpa, which was no more than a speck in the distance.

"Did anyone get the registration number?" Beach shouted above the wail of the siren. "Please tell me one of you got the registration number." He looked around expectantly.

"Don't worry, skipper. I've got it." Smith said, tapping his notebook.

"I wonder why he's doing a runner?" Wallis asked. "Surely it's not over a poxy hooker?"

"Stranger things have happened," PC David Dixon put in. He had remained on the wagon when the others had alighted to check out the van, figuring it didn't require six officers to handle one suspect

"Yeah, well, when we catch him, and after I kick his nuts into his neck, you can ask him," Smith told them viciously. In ten bloody years of frontline policing, he'd never let a suspect escape; he didn't intend to start now.

"Can't you drive this bloody thing any faster, Ron?" he yelled.

The Disciple picked up speed once he entered Commercial Street. He watched as the needle crept up to fifty, then on towards sixty. His wife rolled around in the back, tossed from side to side as the van swayed like a small boat in high seas. He ignored her screams as he headed for the Aldgate one-way system, cursing the slower moving traffic that impeded his progress.

"Come on, arsehole, get out of my way." He flashed his lights and sounded his horn at the car in front until it moved over and let him by. He figured that, with luck, he had a thirty-to-forty-second start on his pursuers. If fate was smiling on him that might be just enough time to lose them, especially in this rain – was it his imagination or had the downpour gotten worse since he had driven off? Pritchard knew he needed to make some more headway. If he could make the one-way system before they caught up with him, his chances of escape would be doubled.

With that objective in mind, he pulled onto the wrong side of the road, zigzagging around a half dozen cars, trucks and buses before returning to the correct lane. Luckily, there wasn't much traffic coming the other way. But that would change soon enough. There was a main arterial road up ahead. He looked in the mirror and saw tiny blue lights appear in the distance. For a second, he thought that they had turned right instead of left, that they had gone the wrong way.

But he was mistaken.

They were coming after him, speeding along the road outside the line of vehicles in which he was now stuck.

Damn!

The Disciple floored the accelerator again and the engine roared. There was no point in subtlety now; they would catch him up in seconds unless he acted quickly and decisively. He pulled onto the wrong side of the road again, forcing an oncoming motorcyclist up onto the pavement. Red traffic lights loomed ahead but he didn't ease off the gas pedal. The carrier was still a fair way behind him, but it was much nearer than it had been the last time he looked.

"There he is!" Reeve pointed as the Sherpa suddenly pulled out of the line of traffic way up ahead.

"I told you he'd gone left, didn't I?" Stedman roared triumphantly. In all the confusion of turning their bus around, they had suffered a temporary loss of vision just as the van had reached the junction with Commercial Street. Vital seconds were lost while they argued amongst themselves whether to turn left or right. In the end, Stedman had ignored them all and gone with his gut instinct. As they sailed past the sluggish line of vehicles heading for Aldgate, he allowed himself a grim smile. His decision had been vindicated and they were back in the game. "Come on, baby, don't let me down now," he coaxed, stamping his foot to the floor. The carrier was diesel powered, and although it wasn't too bad once you got the speed up, it was hard work trying to get it there in the first place.

"You can get on the Main-Set now, PC Reeve," Beach shouted from behind.

CHAPTER THIRTY-EIGHT

Kelly Flowers was heading back towards the office after a gruelling two-hour long Family Liaison meeting with Geraldine Rye's elderly parents, who had flown in from Murcia a few days ago to identify the body and make funeral arrangements. She sometimes wondered why she had ever volunteered to become a FLO because each deployment seemed to drain so much out of her. Maybe she should...

The sudden transmission on the Main-Set startled her.

"*MP, MP, active message, Uniform 366. We're chasing a dark green Sherpa van, Commercial Street towards the Aldgate one-way system...vehicle possibly concerned in the abduction of a prostitute...*"

"Shit!" She said, pulling over. That wasn't far away, and they were heading straight towards her current location. The pursuing vehicle's operator had clearly said that the bandit vehicle was a Sherpa van, like the one their suspect was using. But the Ripper's van was white, not green. Could he have started using a different vehicle?

"I wonder...?" she said, reaching for her mobile phone.

―――

The Sherpa, skidding along the wet tarmac, was locked on a collision course with an island that separated the two busy streams of traffic where the main road narrowed before joining the Aldgate one-way system. A deadly looking lamppost protruded from the island's centre, where it waited patiently to cleave the van in two. The impact would prove fatal; of that he was sure, but a wonderful calmness had descended over Pritchard and, somehow, he knew it would all be okay.

All four tyres screeched, and the rear of the van fishtailed crazily, as he stood on the brakes. At the very last moment, he came off them and gunned the accelerator, spinning the steering wheel hard to the right at the same time, just like he'd seen Stig Blomqvist do in one of those rally driving videos that he so enjoyed watching. The van might not be on a par with Stig's rally spec Audi Quatro, but all four wheels remained grounded as he dragged it clear of the island and into the one-way system, and that was good enough for him.

Entering the one-way system against the flow of traffic, there was no time for conscious thought. The Disciple simply buried the accelerator into the floor and drove straight at oncoming vehicles, trusting that the dark deity he worshiped would part them so that he could escape his pursuers, just as the Hebrew God had parted the waters of the Red Sea for Moses as he fled the Egyptian army.

Horns were sounding all around him; loud, angry, sustained blasts that he regarded with complete impunity. Fear was imprinted on the faces of the oncoming drivers who swerved to avoid him, but he remained calm, secure in the knowledge that celestial forces were watching over him.

The police carrier was still following, but more cautiously now. It was beginning to drop back again.

YES!

He could do this. He could lose them and still kill the third bitch responsible for ruining his life exactly as scheduled. He would have to get rid of the van, of course, but he had a contingency plan for that. After months of preparation, he prided himself on having a strategy to deal with every possible eventuality. "Don't you worry, my Queen of Whores," he shouted into the back. "We'll play our little game, yet."

"The TSG are doing what?" Dillon said into the phone, which was clamped against his right ear. He could hardly hear Kelly's response, so he rammed a sausage-shaped forefinger into his left ear to block out the background noise. "Say that again" he instructed. Flowers repeated her news about the chase on the Main-Set and asked him what she should do.

"We'll be right over, Kelly, love. Just you wait there," he told her excitedly. Hanging up, he began to pull his jacket on.

Tyler studied his partner from across the room. "What's happening, Dill?" he asked, anxiously.

"We need to move fast, Jack," Dillon told him. "I'll explain on the way."

The Disciple had cleared the one-way system in one piece, as he'd known he would, but he had left a trail of carnage in his wake. Still, what did it matter if a few sheep got hurt along the way, as long as the ritual sacrifices were completed according to satanic scripture and he attained a higher level of consciousness?

He took a series of left and right turns through the quieter side streets, until he reached cobbled roads lined with large warehouses. They were near the river Thames now, and well away from the main drag.

The police were no longer in pursuit. His flight had caused a major pile up, grinding the road behind him to a messy halt, and the cops would have to stop and deal with that.

He knew the chasing officers would have circulated his details over the radio, and that their colleagues would be out in strength, scouring the streets for him. They would expect him to remain in Whitechapel, which was why he was now heading towards Limehouse. He would scan the local channels on his 'borrowed' radio as soon as he got the chance.

A single set of headlights appeared in his mirror, causing him to miss a heartbeat. He studied them intently, half expecting flashing blue lights to come on. He made a left turn. The car followed at a distance but made no effort to gain on him. As he turned another corner, he saw that it was a dark blue Ford Escort with a single female occupant.

He breathed a sigh of relief. It was just some silly cow going about her business, leading her humdrum life, oblivious to the fact that she was following the most dangerous man in London.

An idea came to him. He knew of an abandoned warehouse further along the river, near a pub he used to frequent in his misbegotten youth. He would take the Queen of Whores there.

He continued into Wapping High Street, towards West Pier, leaving the affluence of the Docks far behind. The third bitch responsible for ruining his life continued to moan in the back, presumably calling for help.

He yelled at her to be quiet.

Her constant whining was making it hard for him to think clearly.

He continued for some distance, finally pulling into a dead end turning that led down to an old quay. The Escort drove straight by, its driver not even looking in his direction.

He got out, locked the van and walked along the path that meandered down to the tall decaying warehouse. The smell of the river was very strong, here.

He looked at his watch: Ten o'clock.

If he killed her here, down by the river, he would be able to make his way back to the Sutton Mission later and come back in the minibus to collect her corpse, which he could drop off at his chosen deposition site sometime over the weekend.

The Disciple paused in the shadows, studying the warehouse carefully. He wondered if it really was as abandoned as it looked. He'd have to check; it wouldn't do to gatecrash a vagrant's home or stumble across a pair of young lovers who had nowhere better to go.

The rain was easing off, and it looked as if it would soon stop altogether. That was good – he was convinced that the rain only came when he needed its protection.

Treading carefully, he made his way forward along the quayside. He wasn't worried about the third bitch responsible for ruining his life. Before leaving the van, he'd given her another, stronger dose of chloroform, and he had rebound her far more securely. He had also swapped the rigid handcuffs from a front stack position to a rear back-to-back position. Even if she woke up, she wouldn't be able to move, and she could literally scream her lungs out around here and no one would hear her. Anyway, he wouldn't be gone long, and then she wouldn't have any lungs left to scream with.

He smiled at that.

Sergeant Robert Beach surveyed the wreckage in front of him. The carrier's path was completely blocked by a twisted pile of metal that had once been four cars and a French registered articulated tractor-trailer unit that had slewed sideways.

It sickened him to watch as the Sherpa van faded from view, having cleared the one-way system fifty short yards ahead.

"Fuck, fuck, fuck." Ron Stedman yelled, kicking the iron grill of his vehicle.

"It's alright, Ron. It's not your fault. You did well not to end up embedded in that lot," he gestured at the damaged vehicles littering the road.

"I've circulated its last known location and direction, but no one's managed to pick it up yet," Reeve told them.

"Right then," Beach said, tilting his cap back on his head, cowboy style. "We'd better start dealing with this mess."

Kelly sat in her car nervously covering the junction that the Sherpa had turned in to. She had almost followed it in, but had spotted the dead-end sign at the last moment.

Driving straight by, she had turned around at the next junction and driven back with her lights out. She now faced a dilemma: did she wait where she was in the hope of picking him up again when he left – assuming he did – or did she venture in after him?

Kelly had picked the van up purely by accident. It had simply pulled out in front of her as she sat in her car waiting for Tyler and

Dillon to arrive. She had immediately tried to warn the MP radio operator and summon assistance, but to her horror the microphone on her Main-Set was defective and she couldn't transmit. Instead, she'd had to listen with mounting frustration as units converged on all the wrong places.

She had set off after the van without thinking it through, and by the time it occurred to her to use her phone, it had unhelpfully slid off the seat during a turn and was sliding around in the passenger footwell.

With her only means of communication out of reach until she could stop and retrieve it, she had trailed the van through unfamiliar streets, becoming increasingly lost.

Now that the van had stopped, she needed to phone in and summon the cavalry – but first, she needed to find a street name and get her bearings.

She switched off the car's internal light and then opened the door, slipping out of the Escort as quietly as she could. Kelly padded past the turning the killer had driven into, looking for road signs.

There were none.

SHIT!

The van was parked about one hundred and fifty yards in, against a narrow path that led down to an abandoned looking warehouse on the quay. The layout made the footpath difficult to spot from the road.

She scanned the road, hoping to see a pedestrian; anyone would do as long as they could tell her where she was, but it was like being stranded in a ghost town. A thin mist was creeping in from the river, making the air damp.

Kelly jogged further along the street until she reached the main road. There, at last, was a sign: WAPPING HIGH STREET, E1.

Relief flooded over her as she reached into her pocket, fumbling for her mobile phone, which she had recovered from underneath the front passenger seat before leaving the car. Now that she had a road name, she could get some much-needed help. Kelly unlocked the keypad and dialled Tyler's mobile from memory.

Nothing happened. "What the...?" She looked down in horror, to see that the signal strength read zero bars. "You have got to be joking," she said to the phone, moving it around to get a signal.

Still nothing.

She began to jog back towards her car, hoping to pick up a signal along the way. Once inside, she checked it again. One bar was showing; a weak signal, but hopefully it would be enough. Kelly pressed redial. "Please work," she begged it. She immediately heard a ringtone, thank God, but why wasn't Tyler answering his bloody phone?

Tyler felt strangely redundant as he stood beside the police carrier, watching in silence as the TSG lads dealt with the accident with practised ease. Two traffic cars had also arrived, one containing a scowling Traffic Sergeant. Hopefully, no blame would be attached to the carrier's driver when the mean faced Traffic Sergeant had finished his investigation.

They had stumbled across the vicinity only POLACC purely by chance, on their way to RVP with Kelly. Upon arrival, both detectives had expected to find the Sherpa at the epicentre of the crash, its driver safely detained. Unfortunately, that hadn't been the case.

Jack showed his warrant card to one of the TSG lads, a bald-headed man with a droopy ginger moustache, and asked what was going on, only to be informed that the van had been lost and that numerous units were scouring the area for it.

Jack described Kelly Flowers to him, asking if he could shed any light on her whereabouts. PC Reeve scratched his bald head thoughtfully and then said that he hadn't seen anyone matching that description.

Grim-faced, Jack hurriedly returned to the pool car, where his partner waited impatiently.

"Give her another ring, will you, Dill," Tyler instructed as he climbed in. He was seriously worried about Kelly. They had been trying to call her back for ages, but all they could get was her damned voice mail service, and until the road was cleared, they couldn't get to the agreed RVP to meet her.

The only pool car that had been available was a diesel Astra that was ready for the scrap yard. It didn't have a Main-Set, and neither of them had thought to bring along a portable.

As they were walking back to their ride, Tyler's Nokia suddenly rang, making him jump. "Hopefully, this is Kelly," he said.

"It could be." Dillon agreed, holding up his own phone. "I'm still getting her bloody answer machine."

When he finally managed to pull his cell phone out of his pocket, Jack keyed the green button with gusto. "Tyler speaking..."

"Guv, it's me, Kelly. Just listen, I haven't got a very good signal. I'm in Wapping High Street, E1. I've followed the van here. It's parked up but I need some —" The line went dead.

"Damn!" Tyler cursed, trying to get his bearings. Where was Wapping High Street in relation to their present location? And what did she think she was doing following the van on her own? "Get in the car," he ordered, unlocking the doors as he spoke. "I think Kelly needs our help on the hurry up." He turned the ignition, and the car started clunking like the unrefined beast it was. Fighting the lumpy gear stick, he eventually managed to find first and gunned the accelerator. "Plot me the fastest route to Wapping High Street," he instructed as the car surged forward and stalled.

Oh no! The signal had gone again. Had he heard her? Had he managed to get her location? What was she going to do now? It was decision time. She didn't dare wait any longer. If she was following the Ripper, as seemed likely, he could be in the back of that van now, cutting up his next victim. She couldn't just sit there and do nothing simply because she had no backup. She was a police officer, after all. This was what she was paid to do.

With trembling hands, she reached into her bag for her ASP gravity friction lock baton. Somehow its weight didn't give her as much comfort as she'd hoped it would, but it would have to do. She got out and closed the door quietly.

Treading as softly as she could, hugging the building line, where the shadows were thickest, she slowly crept towards the van.

Her chest was tight with fear, but she kept telling herself that everything would be okay, repeating the words like a litany.

Doubt quickly began to erode her earlier resolve. Perhaps the van was empty after all. Perhaps the driver had gone to the warehouse for a reason that was totally unconnected to the Whitechapel murders. Perhaps there was a perfectly innocent explanation for all of this. Perhaps she should just wait for more units after all. Perhaps... *What was that?* There was a strange noise coming from the van.

Oh my God, he's in there! Kelly felt her blood run cold. She faltered and almost turned back. Her legs were refusing to obey her mental commands, but she willed them on, a step at a time, each one sapping her reserves a little more than the last. *Please let it be my imagination,* she prayed, *or cats rummaging around for scraps. Cats would do nicely.*

There it was again, coming from inside the van: a low moaning sound. Flowers cocked her head to the side, listening carefully. The noise sounded human in origin. She racked her ASP. The extendable metal baton sounded crisp and businesslike in the silence of the night.

Kelly was only a few yards away now. She could actually hear the van's suspension springs creaking as its occupants moved around inside. Crouching low, she approached the Sherpa from the rear. And then she realised that she had a problem: to reach her objective she would have to break from cover and lose the protection of the shadows. Without any streetlights to illuminate her, it was relatively dark in the open space around the van, but the human eye is drawn to movement and she would be doing a lot of that.

There was no easy way around it.

Hell, there was no way around it.

For a few brief moments she would be exposed and completely visible to anyone who happened to be looking.

Did she go on or turn back?

Was there really a choice?

Taking several deep breaths, she broke into a sprint and dashed out into the open. *Please God, don't let him see me,* she prayed as she ran on tiptoe.

Dropping down beside the rear doors, she pressed her back against the van, listening for the slightest sound.

Her nerves were raw.

The engine was off but the exhaust pipe was still warm. Breathing quickly, she risked a glance around the passenger side, hoping to spot any movement inside the cabin by its reflection in the side mirror.

Nothing.

She edged across to the driver's side and repeated the manoeuvre.

Nothing there either.

Phew!

Okay, it meant that he was in the back and he probably hadn't seen her, but was he alone?

"Help me...please...help...me..."

The voice, weak and disorientated, came from inside. Kelly nearly jumped out of her skin.

The Ripper had a victim in the back of the van with him...and she was still alive.

But for how long?

"Please, if anyone out there can hear me, help me before he comes back... Please..." The voice faded into a final hoarse plea.

Before he comes back...?

The Ripper wasn't in there.

But how long would he be gone for?

There was no doubt he would return.

Kelly jumped up, hyped for action. There was no time to lose. Perhaps, if she moved fast enough, she could get the woman away from here. Then she could wait outside for back up.

She tried to turn the handle, pulling hard. It was locked. "Hang on," she whispered. "I'm a police officer. I'm here to help you."

There was no reply.

Kelly ran around to the front, trying both the driver and passenger doors. They were also locked. She would have to smash the window to get in. Did she dare make that much noise?

If she was going to do it then she had to move quickly. She looked around, scanning the horizon for movement. The warehouse was at least a hundred yards away, right on the edge of the wharf. The killer had to be in there; there was just nowhere else.

Perhaps it was his hideout. That would make perfect sense. This was the ideal location: quiet and secluded, well off the beaten track.

Kelly returned to the driver's window. Leaning as far back as she could, shielding her face with her left hand, she struck out at the window with her ASP.

WHACK. It made a hell of a noise.

To her amazement, nothing happened and the window remained intact. "Shit!" she said breathlessly. She hit it again, harder this time.

WHACK. The glass shattered in an explosion of sound, falling inwards, into the cabin. There was no time to worry about discovery now; she was too committed to even consider retreat, and hopefully, the deepening mist would act as a sound suppressor.

Reaching inside, trying to avoid the jagged shards of glass that stuck up like stalagmites, she undid the lock. "Hold on in the back, it's the police," she called as she slid back the door and climbed in. Despite her great urgency, a small part of her mind was conscious of the need to avoid contamination or obliteration of forensic evidence. The van was a crime scene. It could yield all sorts of important evidence: fingerprints, DNA, and fibres, to name but a few. She had to move carefully, avoid touching anything unless she absolutely had to.

The faint smell of chemicals pervaded the cabin, and she began to feel a little light-headed.

A thick curtain separated the cabin from the rear compartment. "Hello – is anyone there?" she asked, drawing it to the side. It was pitch black inside. She ferreted around for a switch that might control the lights in the back. *Where on earth can it be?* She wondered, fighting the panic that was spiralling inside. She gave up after a short while, unable to find it.

Kelly pulled the curtain as far back as it would go, hooking it over the passenger seat to allow as much ambient light as possible inside. Moving ever so slowly, she climbed into the back, pausing to let her night vision take hold. The inside was repellent to her. She felt confined, totally trapped. She wanted to turn around, run away while she still could.

There, at the back of the van, she could make out a shape on the floor. Was it a person? If so, were they still alive?

She had to fight off her claustrophobia, and think of the victim, not herself. "Hello?" she said nervously, thinking she sounded pathetically weak.

Suddenly, the shape moved, only slightly but enough to convince her that it really was a living person. Kelly leapt back, banging her head against the metal partition. As she rubbed the back of her skull, she could hear the shape breathing, slow and shallow, like someone in a deep sleep.

The chemical smell was significantly stronger back here.

She had to get this poor woman out before the Ripper came back. She wasn't naive enough to think that she could take him on her own. Kelly began to crawl forward, towards the woman.

"What the...?" She realised that the interior was coated with thick sheets of plastic, which rustled and creaked every time she moved. A wave of nausea gripped her stomach as she contemplated its sinister purpose. Had his four previous victims died right here, on the very spot where she was kneeling? Kelly closed her eyes tightly, trying to focus her mind on the task at hand, instead of succumbing to the torrent of terrifying images that threatened to engulf her. This was not the time to ponder such things.

Come on Kelly. You can do this; don't fall apart on me now. She opened her eyes, taking several deep breaths, and then reached out a hand, gently touching the woman's shoulder.

"Can you hear me?" she asked, shaking the woman softly. Sarah Pritchard's moan startled her, and her hand recoiled automatically. She reached forward again, more firmly this time.

"Please, you've got to wake up. We have to get away from here," Kelly said forcefully.

As she knelt down beside the killer's latest captive, she realised that her vision seemed slightly blurry. Her eyes felt gritty, and her limbs suddenly felt heavy, weighted.

What was wrong with her? She shook her head, trying to clear it. Why was she having trouble focusing?

"W – where am I?" The voice, when it came, was weaker than before.

A wave of relief flooded over Kelly. At least if the woman was conscious there was a chance to get her away from the van; hopefully, they would both see this hellish episode through.

"You're in the back of a van in Wapping," Kelly explained. "But we're both in great danger. We've got to move quickly. Can you sit up?"

"Can't move...tied up, I think..." The woman croaked, her every word a supreme effort.

Kelly checked the woman over. Tied up was an understatement. The woman's ankles and knees were securely bound, as were her arms. Kelly turned her over gently. Sure enough, just as she'd feared, the victim's hands were cuffed behind her back. Underneath the cuffs, her wrists had pieces of cloth wrapped around them to prevent marking.

There was no longer any doubt that she was dealing with the Ripper. Everything she'd seen fit his Modus Operandi perfectly. He'd brought this poor woman here for one reason only: to die.

And that was bad news for both of them because it meant he'd be coming back very, very, soon.

Kelly examined the cuffs closely, wondering if her cuff key would fit. They were rigid, police issue cuffs. A shudder ran through her as a disturbing new thought hit home.

My god, he's one of us. The Ripper's a cop.

Kelly began to feel around the floor of the van, frantically searching for something to cut the ropes with.

CHAPTER THIRTY-NINE

The old warehouse was cavernous, and it had taken The Disciple far longer to explore than he'd expected. When he finally emerged from the hole that he'd made in the boarding to get in, he took a few moments to brush himself down; the entire place had been covered in grease, grime, and cobwebs. Then he set off through the mist, which had noticeably worsened since he'd gone in. it seemed like a long walk back to his van, which agitated him because he was desperately impatient to get on with things. He hated having unfinished business.

The old building was spot on. He could hole up in there until the early hours without any problem. Everything he needed to complete the final ritual was contained within his bag, and he would be able to take his time sacrificing his controlling wife, the third bitch responsible for ruining his life.

The mist soon began to thin out, and before long it had been reduced to a few wispy tendrils. As he left the uneven footpath and regained the cobbled surface of the service road, Simon Pritchard spotted his van up ahead. As soon as he saw it alarm bells began to go off inside his head. Something was not as it should be, but what?

And then he saw it. The driver's door had been slid back.

It was open.

NOOOO!

He stopped in his tracks, sniffing the air like a wild animal. There was no way that the Queen of Whores could have broken free without outside help. That meant that someone must have found the van.

But who?

And how many of them were there?

His mind spun as he pondered what to do. He couldn't abandon the van, and he *wouldn't* abandon his final target, not after coming this far.

He had promised Tyler that he would kill again within twenty-four hours, and he wouldn't give that son of a bitch the satisfaction of failing. Slipping back into the safety of the shadows, he began to creep towards the van, ready to turn and run if things looked really bad.

His first thought, on seeing the driver's door open, was that the police had found him, but he'd dismissed it almost at once. There would be patrol cars and flashing lights, and he would have heard lots of excited chatter on the handheld radio he carried.

But what if the police had found the van, rescued Sarah, and retreated to a safe distance, where they could watch without being seen? They could be keeping it under observation in the hope that he would return. He could be walking into a trap.

No, he decided, this wasn't the work of the police. Subtlety wasn't their style, and anyway, they wouldn't have had time to pull off a stunt as elaborate as that.

But if not them, then who was it?

The obvious answer was thieves, drug takers or vagrants, plundering his hard-earned spoils. A ripple of anger surged through his body.

How dare they!

He felt for the hilt of the knife concealed at the rear of his waistband. Someone had just made a fatal mistake, fatal being the operative word. As he reached the side of the van, he heard muffled voices inside. There were two of them, both unmistakably female,

What the...?

His mind raced. There were two women inside his van. One was the Queen of Whores, the other was a stranger – an unknown quantity, but probably a drug addict or a tramp looking for somewhere quiet to lay up for the night.

He tried to imagine the look on her face as she'd broke into his van and came face to face with his handiwork. The anger began to subside, replaced instead by a mixture of curiosity and excitement. Number five had attracted number six. Who would have believed it possible? He was going to have a bonus kill!

What a strange turn of events, he thought, pondering tonight's roller coaster sequence of ups and downs. Still, his unexpected good fortune was not to be sneered at. The completion of the ancient sacrificial ritual, which would give him the power and influence over lesser mortals he so desperately craved, was in sight.

The blood of five maidens must be shed...

He could – no, *he would* – kill another two tonight. They were mere feet away from the cold, unfeeling, steel of his knife. The most delicious part of it all was that they had no idea just how close to death they were. They probably thought they still had a chance to escape. He could hear them moving around inside, making urgent scuttling sounds like rats in a sewer.

He was overcome by a desire to prolong the experience, to feed off of their fear for as long as he could. He would let them build up their hopes inside the van. Then, just as escape seemed a certainty, he would shatter their illusions and put an end to their petty, meaningless lives.

He wondered what birth sign the stranger had been born under. He would refrain from killing her until he had acquired that information.

The Disciple cocked his head to one side, listening carefully. He could hear it quite clearly above the noise the whores were making: his lovely little tune:

What a ride, what a thrill. All I wanna do is kill, kill, kill...

―――

"Come on, don't give up on me. We're nearly there," Kelly said, breathlessly. Unable to find anything sharp on the plastic-coated floor, she had snapped, torn and ruined every nail on her hands trying to undo the thick knots that bound the ankles of the killer's latest victim.

Powerless to help, Sarah Pritchard was forced to lay very still while Kelly worked on the ropes. The pain in her shattered shoulder was astronomical, and it was getting worse by the second. The ropes were so tight that she could hardly feel her limbs. Every time Kelly pulled at the knots, it sent a wave of pain through her.

"What's your name?" Kelly asked, trying to keep the victim's mind from dwelling on their predicament.

Sarah moaned softly, a cry of pain and fear. "Sarah...Sarah Pritchard. My husband, Simon – he's a killer... he's the Ripper."

Kelly paused. Wasn't Sarah Pritchard the woman Steve Bull had recruited to help the team canvass the local working girls?

"You've got to hurry," Sarah cried, trying to make Kelly understand the urgency of the situation. "If you don't untie me before he gets back, he'll kill us both." Sobbing hysterically, Sarah Pritchard tried to get up. She had to get out of the van.

"Shush!" Kelly soothed, gently pushing her back down. "Stop struggling. I'm nearly done." And then, with no prior warning, the knot on the rope around Sarah's ankles came free.

YES! Kelly almost punched the air with relief. She unwound it frantically, ignoring Sarah's protests of pain. There was simply no time for finesse. The woman's knees and arms were still securely bound but they would have to wait. Kelly crawled over her, feeling across the rear doors for a handle. Her hands came into contact with a coarse, thick material, which was draped over the doors from top to bottom.

A curtain!

She pulled it aside roughly, and the inside of the van suddenly became a little lighter as ambient light filtered in through the blacked out rear windows. She looked over her shoulder, familiarising herself with the interior of the van, remembering as much detail as she could. They would want to debrief her when she got out of this.

When?

If I get out of it, more likely!

She shook her head angrily. She couldn't entertain thoughts like that. What would Jack Tyler think of her? Even when faced with danger, the thought of Tyler made her heart flutter.

Kelly spotted the handle halfway up the door. She reached forward, hardly daring to breathe as she took hold of it. Her palm was slippery with sweat as she twisted it, gently at first and then harder, as hard as she possibly could.

It creaked and groaned and gradually began to move. But nowhere near enough. Kelly put her full weight behind it, pushing for all she was worth. And then, all of a sudden, it was open and she nearly fell out, face first, onto the hard-concrete floor.

Kelly jumped down quickly, and uneasily scanned the shadows around her. Nothing moved.

The damp swirling mist was much denser down by the warehouse then it was up here. She half expected the Ripper to burst out of it and run towards her, like something you'd see in a horror flick. The lower floors of the old building were totally obscured by an opaque wall of mist, although the uneven outline of its roof still dominated the horizon like a gothic castle.

The fresh air was starting to clear her head, but the cloying chemical smell of the van lingered on her skin and clothes as unpleasantly as the smoke that always used to cling to her after a long night in the pub.

Kelly quickly opened the other door, cringing at the horrible squeaking its hinges made. She leaned in and helped Sarah up into a sitting position.

"Come on, love, we've got to get you away from here," Kelly whispered. She gently pulled Sarah's Pritchard's legs around until they dangled over the edge of the van, resting her feet on the small back step. Sarah winced and cried with every movement, but she didn't resist.

"My car is at the end of this road. I'll support you all the way, but we've got to go now," Kelly told her urgently. Sarah nodded obediently. Kelly put her arm around the woman's waist and began to pull her out.

Suddenly, Sarah stiffened. Screaming hysterically, she tried to drag herself back into the van, violently shrugging Kelly's arm off.

What the...?

"Look, I know it hurts but –" One look at the woman's face was enough to make her realise that Sarah wasn't screaming because of anything she had done. Kelly went rigid with fear. The hairs on the back of her neck prickled and, suddenly, the presence of death became a tangible thing. It was *him* – the Ripper.

He'd come back.

Tyler's anxiety was making him feel very agitated. He had already driven the length of Wapping High Street without seeing any sign of Kelly, and they were now doing a reciprocal route. "Try her number again, Dill," he ordered impatiently.

"I can't, Jack. There's no signal," the big man replied.

"Damn it. Come on Kelly. Where the hell are you?" Tyler's eyes darted left and right, scanning the streets for her. There was no sign of life anywhere. The place was like a ghost town. All that was missing was the tumbleweed.

"What car did she book out, Dill?" Tyler asked.

"I don't know, Jack," Dillon said. No one in the office ever booked the cars out properly – himself included – so he hadn't bothered to check the register.

"She was listening to the chase on the Main-Set," Jack said. "Apart from the Omega, how many of our cars have one?"

"Bloody hell, you're right, Jack," Dillon said wondering why he hadn't he thought of that. "The only other car with a Main-Set in it is the blue Escort – it's an R registration, I think."

Kelly stood up quickly, every muscle in her body tensed for action. The ASP was tucked into her waistband, still fully extended. Quick as a flash, Kelly pulled it out and spun around, raising it in preparation for a strike.

As fast as she was, the killer was even faster. His fist lashed out, catching her on the side of her chin. His whole weight was behind the blow, and Kelly fell back, banging her head against the van door. The ASP flew from her hand, landing with a metallic clang on the floor nearby.

Everything began to spin as Kelly slumped to the ground. Through tunnelled vision, she watched helplessly as the blurred shape of a man bent over her. She was powerless to resist as he reached down and took her chin in his hand, roughly twisting her head from side to side, as if examining a piece of meat.

"Hello," he said, pleasantly. "And who might you be?" His voice seemed to echo inside her head like a grotesque sound effect. He let go of her head and it sagged forward onto her chest.

The last thing she saw before passing out was the giant thirteen-inch Bowie knife in his left hand. The last thing she heard was Sarah Pritchard's spine-chilling scream.

―――

Jack spun the car around when they reached St. Katherine's Way and began their third trip along the now familiar stretch of road. A cat ran across the road in front of them. It was the first living creature they'd seen in ages. He slowed down on the approach to each side street he came to, in case she was waiting for them off the main road, but there was no sign of her or anyone else in this godforsaken place.

Tyler began to consider the possibility that the van had moved off again. If it had, she would have gone with it. And if that were the case, she could be miles away, unable to update them with her new location because of the poor signal on her cell phone. He was about to suggest this to Dillon when he spotted a dark coloured Escort parked up ahead on the right.

Dillon saw it too and pointed. "Hang on, Jack. I think that's it."

Tyler drew level and Dillon jumped out to check. Cupping his hands against the window, he peered inside. "This is the one, Main-Set and all. She must be around here somewhere," he said, looking up and down the road.

Tyler pulled in behind it. Seconds later, he joined Dillon on the pavement. "I suggest we split up. You go right and I'll go left. We'll cover more ground that way," Tyler said.

"Good idea. But we'd better not stray too far from here. If one of us shouts for help, I want the other one to hear it," Dillon said, wishing they had radios.

"Agreed. I'll check this turning," Tyler indicated the junction almost directly opposite the car, "and that one off to the left. You take the two further up on the right. Just a cursory look – if there's no trace of her we come straight back here and summon help, got it?"

Dillon nodded. "Absolutely."

"Good, let's do it," Tyler said, crossing the road hurriedly.

He jogged into the turning opposite Kelly's car, noting the dead-end sign. After a dozen steps he stopped, struck by how isolated the place was; it was as though, having entered, you were completely cut off from the rest of the world. The bulb in the lone streetlight, which was back at the junction, had long since been vandalised. It flickered at half power, causing his shadow to dance on the floor in front of him.

About fifty yards further in, a bank of fog was slowly drifting towards him. He assumed it was coming up from the river. In the distance, he could see what looked like a series of turrets jutting up into the sky through the fog. They were as uninviting as a Transylvanian castle.

This was a forgotten road, he decided, without character or warmth. There were no houses, no shops and no sign of human occupation, recent or otherwise.

He guessed the cobbled turning was a disused service road leading down to the Thames.

As he stood there, the streetlight flickered a final time and went out.

"That's just great," he snarled, throwing his hands up in the air. Needless to say, he hadn't thought to bring along a torch. Well, there was no point in cursing. He would just have to continue without lighting.

Tyler pressed on, squinting to penetrate the stygian darkness ahead. After a few seconds, he thought he could make out a faint shape in the distance. Could it be the van Kelly had followed?

As he tried to make up his mind, a shadow suddenly detached itself from the rest and glided towards the shape. Either his eyes were playing tricks or someone was prowling around up there. He began to quicken his pace, possessed by a growing sense of urgency.

Before he'd taken half a dozen steps the silence was shattered by an ear-piercing scream.

Jack immediately broke into a fast run. Something was horribly wrong up ahead.

"Kelly!" he shouted at the top of his voice. He strained his ears for a reply, but all he heard was the hollow echo of his footsteps on the cobbled road. The streetlight flickered into life again, illuminating the van and a shadowy figure next to it, albeit weakly.

"You! Stay where you are," Tyler yelled angrily. "It's the police."

He'd covered twenty yards already. The figure – he could tell it was a man now – whipped around to face him, crouching like a savage, predatory animal protecting its prey from a rival.

Even from this distance, Jack could make out the shape of the huge knife in his left hand.

Shit! Tyler wasn't carrying his ASP either. Had he managed to bring anything he needed with him tonight?

Jack watched as the man took a slow step backwards, edging towards the side of the van. Tyler was forty yards from him now, running for all he was worth. To his horror, he suddenly noticed someone lying at the man's feet.

Kelly! Please God, no! Jack's arms pumped like pistons as he redoubled his efforts, sucking in air as he ran. His heart and mind were both racing. He would never forgive himself if anything had happened to Kelly.

He became aware of a third figure; this one slouched on the floor of the van, screaming hysterically. It was a middle-aged woman, and the scream he'd heard a few seconds earlier had obviously originated from her.

The suspect began a subtle retreat, keeping as much distance between himself and Tyler as he could. Was this the Ripper, Jack wondered? Was he finally about to come face to face with the monster he had been hunting for the last two weeks?

Two weeks! It felt more like two years.

Instinctively, Jack knew the fiend was going to run. But where could he go? This was a dead end, wasn't it? As if on cue, the suspect turned and bolted along the path towards the old building.

"Stay where you are," Jack raged, overcome by anger and frustration.

This placed Tyler in a dreadful predicament, one that tore him in two. He desperately wanted to catch the suspect, who was almost certainly the killer, but his overriding concern was for Kelly Flowers' safety. He skidded to a halt as he reached the van, slamming into one of the open doors with a loud thud.

"Please help me," the woman in the back sobbed. He ignored her completely. If she was well enough to make all that noise, she wasn't in any immediate danger. He knelt down beside Kelly, examining her for signs of life.

Please be alive, Kelly. Please!

Her chest rose and fell normally, thank God. It meant she was still breathing. He pulled her jacket open, checking her front and back for puncture wounds. Unbelievably, there were none.

He realised that his unexpected appearance at the scene had saved her. Another few seconds and he would have been too late. Jack tenderly brushed the hair from her face. A nasty swelling had already begun to form along the side of her chin. Her condition was stable, but he couldn't just leave her, even if it meant letting the bastard who'd done this escape.

The killer was almost out of sight and there was nothing Tyler could do about it.

"Jack!"

Tyler spun around to see Dillon sprinting towards him from the main road. A wave of relief flooded over him.

"Jack, are you alright?" Dillon shouted from thirty yards away. He was approaching like an express train.

Kissing Kelly's forehead softly, Jack stood up, his jaw set determinedly. "Dillon, stay with Kelly, she's hurt," he yelled. There was no time to say more. With a final glance down at her bruised face, he set off in pursuit. Maybe, just maybe, there was still a slim chance.

CHAPTER FORTY

Tyler ran as fast as he could, trying to relax his body and control his breathing, the way he did on the treadmill at the gym. His adrenal gland was already secreting the hormone into his system, stimulating his muscles for a sustained burst of action.

The killer, still a long way in front, had almost reached the large building up ahead, which Jack figured was a disused warehouse complex. He seemed to know exactly where he was going, and this made Jack wonder if he had his escape route planned.

Jack thundered along the narrow path, gaining on the fugitive with every step. A few seconds later he emerged onto an uneven concrete strip that ran parallel to the river. He would have to watch his step here or he'd end up taking an unplanned swim.

Through a gap in the fog, he spotted a converted barge berthed against a small pier that jutted out from the Wharf. A solitary light illuminated the living quarters; the distinctive sound of big band jazz came from within, carried by the still night air. The occupants were completely oblivious to the drama being enacted just a few short yards from their waterfront home.

The killer ran along the side of the derelict building. He stopped by an arched entranceway that contained two large wooden doors, each secured by a chain and padlock. Jack watched as the killer pulled a couple of slats loose, exposing a hole big enough for a small man to climb through. He shot Tyler a last, hateful glance as he slipped awkwardly inside and disappeared from view.

Tyler reached the door five seconds later, lungs searing, legs aching. There was a huge sign pinned to the door. It read: WARNING! DANGER OF DEATH! DO NOT ENTER.

He tried to squeeze through the gap but he was too big. Stepping back, he angrily kicked the adjacent slat several times until it came away.

He quickly looked around for a weapon, something he could defend himself with if it became necessary. He hadn't forgotten the menacing knife he'd seen in the killer's hand. There was nothing obvious to use, and he couldn't waste time looking.

Treading carefully, conscious that he could be walking into an ambush, he eased himself through the jagged hole in the door into the cold, dank interior of the warehouse.

It was pitch black inside, and he stepped straight into a deep puddle.

Shit!

Something dripped onto his shoulder from high above and he quickly stepped to the side. The smell of damp, decaying wood permeated the air around him.

He guessed that the building had been empty for many years and was, if the sign was to be believed, fraught with hidden dangers. It was the sort of place that kids would find irresistible, a wonderful place to explore and make secret camps in. Until that is, the roof collapsed on them or the floor gave way, or any one of a hundred other tragedies occurred.

Tyler cautiously moved through a short winding corridor until he reached another door. This one opened out into the main body of the building. He pushed it warily and stepped back, half expecting to be jumped.

Nothing happened.

Taking a deep breath, he moved through the door quickly, hoping to surprise the killer if he was waiting on the other side.

He wasn't.

Tyler let out a small sigh of relief and edged away from the door, where he presented too easy a target. It was lighter in here; isolated shafts of moonlight penetrated the gloom in several places. Shadows flickered constantly in the distance, creating false impressions of movement.

He pressed his back into the wall and held his breath, listening intently for the slightest noise. All he could hear was his heartbeat, which sounded like a drum roll. He wished he had a pair of night vision glasses.

Something scuttled across the floor in the middle distance, heard rather than seen, and all the more sinister for it. It meant rats, the one thing he'd hoped not to encounter.

His eyes slowly began to adjust as he stood there, and he was able to make out that he was in a large storage area that seemed to go on forever. Large concrete support pillars were positioned at regular intervals throughout the main building. Tyler was conscious that the killer could be hiding behind any one of them, just waiting to pounce.

Tyler looked around. The central, domed, ceiling was impressively high. His eyes moved down from that to a network of metal walkways that linked one side of the building to the other. The walkways, about thirty feet above ground level, disappeared into big square holes in the walls.

Jack spotted a set of stairs off to his left, directly beneath the first gantry, but he was sure there would be more. He could also make out the shapes of several fire doors scattered along the wall, doors that could lead anywhere.

Searching this place single-handed was going to be virtually impossible. There had to be other entrances at various points around the perimeter. If the one he'd used was accessible, it was likely the others were too.

He couldn't give up, but where did he start? That was the question. With a team of officers, all linked by radio, he would have posted people at every exit and then searched each floor methodically until he caught the bastard. On his own, he'd just have to wing it. He began to move towards the centre of the warehouse, giving the pillars a wide berth.

"Looking for me were you, Jack?" The hate-filled words shattered the silence like machine gun fire, echoing off every wall. Tyler spun around, trying to figure out where they had come from. At least he knew the killer was still in here somewhere.

Making a final stand, Jack wondered?

Or just plain trapped?

Suddenly, something heavy fell from above, missing him by mere inches. It was a wooden crate of some sort, and it shattered as it hit the floor next to him, sending slivers of wood flying in all directions. Instinctively, Tyler dived to the side, rolling across the floor and coming up in a low crouch.

"You're a lucky man, Tyler. It makes you a worthy adversary," the killer shouted. He was up on the catwalk, thirty feet above, leaning over it, arms folded casually.

"Make the most of your last moments of freedom, you madman. When I catch you, they'll throw away the key," Jack shouted up to him. He was livid with anger but he couldn't afford to lose his cool now. He had to outwit the loathsome creature staring down at him by using his brain. He couldn't allow his emotions to get in the way of that.

The killer waved a dismissive hand theatrically, a gesture Jack found annoyingly flamboyant under the circumstances. "Don't make me laugh, Tyler. You couldn't catch a cold. I've lived right under your nose for the last week and a bit and you haven't even noticed."

"Oh, and what makes you so sure of that? If you're so clever, that woman in your van would be dead by now, and you wouldn't be running scared." Jack had to distract him while he stalled for time. Help had to be on the way by now, surely.

"You dare to mock me? *ME!*" The killer screamed. Tyler realised he'd touched a soft spot. He needed to exploit it for all it was worth. He thought for a moment, choosing his next words carefully. "What's the matter? A bit touchy about your many shortfalls, are you?" Jack sneered. He began to edge to his left, towards the staircase. He hoped that it led up to the walkway above; it was a chance he would have to take. The killer moved with him, too angry to notice that he was being played.

"No one mocks me, Tyler. Do you hear me? No one! Once I've killed five whores, the rituals will be complete. I was going to stop there, but not anymore. Oh no, I'll kill seven, just to rub your nose in it. You'll be the one who has to explain why you couldn't catch the legendary Jack the Ripper. You'll be hated, and shunned as a failure by the pathetic sheep you so foolishly serve." His voice rose to a demented crescendo as he screamed the words down at Jack. His eyes bulged madly in their sockets; spittle flew out from his mouth, plastering his cheeks.

Tyler took advantage of the killer's outburst to take several more steps towards the staircase.

"What ritual?" Jack asked, contemptuously. "What a load of bollocks you talk. You're just a –" he tried to recall what the psychologist had said, and turn it into an insult, "– a pathetic little nobody with an over-inflated opinion of himself. The only way you can get back at a world that treats you for what you are is to kill people weaker than yourself?"

"NO!" the killer screamed in angry denial. The sound was frighteningly inhuman.

"What's the matter, mate, can't you find a girlfriend?" Jack said, viciously. "I bet you can't even get *it* 'up', can you? Can't perform like a real man, huh? Do they all laugh at you, call you names?"

The killer's face darkened with every word that Jack uttered. "NOOOO!" he screamed, pounding the railing with his fists. His face contorted into a snarl of unbridled malevolence, and he looked around for something else to throw at Tyler. He spied another crate a few feet away, and ran to it, his feet clanging on the metal walkway.

"I'll show you, Tyler," he screamed defiantly, sounding like a soul in torture. Lifting the crate above his head, he hurled it down at Tyler, hoping to kill or maim him with it – but Tyler was no longer there.

As soon as the killer turned his back, Jack had made for the staircase, taking the winding stairs three at a time. Up and up he ran, searching for a gap that led out onto the walkway.

"Tyler, you son of a whore, where are you?" The killer's voice filtered down to him. As he turned a bend, Jack spotted the opening, a pool of grey in the blackness of the enclosed staircase.

"Tyler?" The killer's voice again, even more manic than before.

Jack sprang onto the catwalk to find the killer just ahead, leaning over the railing and peering down into the gloom. "I'm right here," Jack said, breathlessly. He began to walk forward slowly, determinedly. "It's over," he said. "There's nowhere left to run."

The killer stood up slowly. He turned to face Tyler, a cruel smile slowly spreading across his face. "What makes you think I want to run?" he asked, and Jack was struck by the unnatural calmness in his voice.

For the first time since the chase had begun, Tyler glimpsed the killer up close. The lighting was poor, but the man's features were immediately recognisable to him. "We've been looking for you all evening, Dr Pritchard," he said, enjoying the look of unease that appeared on the killer's face. "Are you surprised that we'd already worked out you were committing the Whitechapel murders, Pritchard? Did you think you were going to get away with it?"

Pritchard looked flustered. Clearly, he had thought he was going to get away with it, Jack realised.

"My name is Jack. Jack the New Ripper. Whoever I was before that is of no consequence," the killer told him stiffly. The voice was taut, and it sounded very different to the one Jack had heard during their previous encounters, but he knew voice patterns were liable to undergo dramatic change under conditions of extreme stress.

"It's over," Jack said softly. "Give me the knife and let's put an end to this."

The killer's face was unreadable, his eyes two dead pools, cold and unblinking. He studied Jack intently, his gaze hypnotic in its intensity.

Neither man moved; the warehouse was silent apart from the coarse sound of their heavy breathing. Eventually, the killer looked down, unable to meet Tyler's steady gaze any longer.

Pritchard licked his lips nervously. "Of course," he sighed. "You're quite right." His shoulders seemed to sag as he reached behind, slowly pulling the knife from its sheath in the small of his back. "As you say, let's put an end to this, once and for all." Without looking up, he slowly extended his hand, holding the Bowie knife out for Tyler to take. Jack began to reach for it, his hand moving closer and closer to the blade.

At that moment the killer looked up and their eyes met again. What was it that Jack saw flicker in them? Certainly not defeat. He hesitated, millimetres away from the killer's knife hand.

"What's the matter, Tyler? Don't you want to take my knife?" Pritchard asked, a little too meekly.

"Why don't you put it down on the floor, just to be on the safe side?" Tyler said, withdrawing his hand and taking a step backward.

The killer frowned, pondering this. "What's the matter, Jack, don't you trust me?" he asked with a smirk.

"Just humour me," Tyler said, flatly.

"Sure," Pritchard said, and then gave a defeated shrug. He began to bend down, pointing the knife towards the floor. "Whatever you say, Jack." In one swift movement, he lunged forward, thrusting the knife at Tyler's chest with the speed of a striking cobra. As Tyler sidestepped the killer's advance, the tip of the blade effortlessly sliced through his jacket lapel. The killer changed direction in one fluid move, going from a jab to a backhand slice without breaking his step. Jack ducked under the blow and tried to shuffle backwards, but he snagged his foot on the mesh floor of the catwalk and stumbled backwards, landing heavily on his rump.

The killer reversed his grip, holding the flat of the blade against his forearm in the concealed position. "You didn't really think you could win, did you?" he mocked as he came forward, raising the knife for a downward thrust. Now that Tyler knew his identity, Pritchard couldn't allow him to leave the building alive. He didn't buy the bullshit about them already knowing he was the Ripper for one moment; that was just Tyler playing mind games to unsettle him.

"Fuck you," Jack replied. He kicked out at the knife hand as it came down, deflecting the blow from its intended target. He hooked one foot around the killer's left ankle and kicked out at the killer's left knee with the heel of his other foot, knocking him over with a ju-jitsu move he hadn't practised for years.

Jack rolled over on his back in a reverse somersault, coming up to his feet less graciously then he would have liked. The killer was already halfway up, holding the knife out in front of him to deter Tyler from counter-attacking.

"Very good," he wheezed. "But it won't save you for long."

There was little room for manoeuvre on the catwalk, and it vibrated and shuddered with their every move. Jack couldn't help but wonder if it was up to this sort of thing. He had visions of it collapsing under their weight.

The killer was advancing again, slicing left and right in a vicious figure of eight. He certainly knew how to use that damn knife, Jack noted, wishing he had something to fight back with – preferably a Glock 17 pistol. There was nothing like an ounce of lead, strategically placed between the eyes, to slow down a crazed knifeman. He was being forced backwards, towards the stairs, and he had to find a way to turn the tables before it was too late.

The killer lunged forward again, but this time Jack was ready for him. He stepped inside the blow and pivoted. As the knife shot past his face, he grabbed hold of the killer's wrist, trying to shake the knife loose. Unfazed, the killer tried to turn the knife inwards, towards Tyler's stomach. Jack hung on tightly. In this position they cannoned off the railings, bouncing from side to side as though they were in a pinball machine. As each one struggled to gain the upper hand, the two men swayed dangerously over the side, both trying to pin their opponent down.

Pritchard managed to pull his knife arm free of Tyler's grip. Twisting around, so that he was now on top, he stabbed downwards with all his might. Tyler somehow blocked the blow, halting it inches away from his face. For several seconds they remained locked in that position before gravity began to take its toll and the knife began to creep downwards, edging ever closer to Tyler's face. Then, just when all seemed lost, Tyler twisted the killer around, using his own momentum against him. The killer's body slammed into the metal railing, stunning him. Making the most of the sudden advantage, Jack banged the knife hand hard against the solid metal railing, once, twice, three times, until it sprang from the killer's hand, falling thirty feet to the ground below.

It landed with a dull thud.

Tyler drew his right fist back to deliver a haymaker of a punch. Without the knife, Pritchard was no match for him.

"No!" Simon Pritchard screamed, wide-eyed. In a sudden frenzy, he grabbed hold of Tyler's jacket and threw himself backward, taking them both over the edge of the railing and out into space.

CHAPTER FORTY-ONE

Kelly opened her eyes to find a giant figure bending over her. As an out of focus hand reached for her face, panic mushroomed inside her chest; she didn't want to die. "No!" she screamed, raising her arms to fend off the monster. The last thing she remembered, before losing consciousness, was the killer leaning over her with that horrible knife in his hand.

"It's alright, love. It's me, Tony Dillon," a familiar voice soothed.

"Tony Dillon?" she repeated automatically, only half understanding.

"That's right, Kelly, it's just Dillon." He waited until the fear drained from her face and her hands lowered of their own accord before reaching forward again to help her. This time she didn't resist.

Kelly's head was throbbing, her skin was covered in sweat, and any movement made her feel violently sick. She closed her eyes and tried to concentrate on her breathing until the nausea receded. Her mind was slowly coming back online, and it was telling her that she had a mild concussion.

"You're safe now, Kelly. Everything's gonna be okay," she heard Dillon say.

She opened her eyes and nodded sluggishly, and immediately regretted doing so as it made her feel queasy again.

Dillon made her as comfortable as he could before moving on to the distraught woman in the back of the van. "It's alright, love, I'm a police officer. Can you tell me your name?" He was trying to work the knots that were binding her knees free as he spoke.

"Sarah," she told him between sobs. "My husband…"

"Don't worry, my love. We'll let him know you're okay as soon as we can," Dillon promised, only to be taken aback by the look of abject horror that appeared on her face.

"No," she cried, shaking her head violently. "You don't understand. My husband did this to me. He's…he's the Ripper."

"You're Simon Pritchard's wife?" he asked, stunned.

Sarah stared at Dillon in utter disbelief, which quickly morphed into anger. "If you already know he's the Ripper," she demanded, "why the hell isn't he already in custody?"

"Calm down, love," he told her. "We only found out a couple of hours ago, and we've been searching high and low for him ever since."

That seemed to mollify her a little. "I see," she said, relaxing slightly.

"I know you've just been put through hell," Dillon said, trying to comfort her, "and I can't even begin to imagine how you must feel, but I give you my word that you're safe now."

"Where…where is he? Where is Simon?" she asked, scanning the surrounding area nervously, as if afraid her husband might pounce on her at any second.

"That's a good question, love," he replied, looking over his shoulder towards the bank of fog that concealed the old warehouse.

Dillon dug out his phone and tried to summon help, but he couldn't get a signal down here. It occurred to him that if he could get Kelly and Mrs Pritchard back to the road, he would at least be free to come back and assist Jack. He had a horrible feeling that his friend was in need of help.

"Kelly, I've got to get back to the main road so I can get a signal to call for help, but I can't leave you two here alone. If I carry this lady can you walk?"

"I think so, boss," she said, holding her hand out. Dillon took it and gently pulled her to her feet. She wobbled badly, and he held onto her in case she fell back down.

"I'm okay, really I am," Kelly lied. She felt rather giddy and very sick, but she knew Dillon wouldn't leave unless she was capable of going with him. "Where's Jack?" she asked, suddenly aware that he was missing.

"He went after the killer. To tell you the truth, he's been gone a few minutes and I'm getting a little worried about him," Dillon admitted.

Kelly's eyes widened, her injuries instantly forgotten. "Tony, you've got to go after him. Don't worry about us. I'm fine now. I can get her back to my car without your help," she said.

Dillon shook his head. "We go down to the car together, sweetheart. Then I'll come back on my own. Jack wouldn't want it any other way." She opened her mouth to protest but he raised a finger to his lips, silencing her. "Let's not waste time arguing, Kelly," he said firmly. "I'll get the woman."

As he tumbled over the edge, Jack caught a fleeting glimpse of a rope dangling in front of him. It was looped through a corroded metal pulley, which was suspended from a rotting joist just above the gantry. The rope seemed to stretch all the way down to the floor, thirty odd feet below.

Ignoring the killer, who still clung to him as they fell, he reached for it, knowing it was his only chance of survival. The fingers of his right hand brushed against the badly frayed rope, but his left hand missed completely, grasping only empty air. They plummeted downward, spinning violently in mid-air. Jack clawed at the rope again, first with his right hand, then with his left. On his third attempt, miraculously, he caught it.

With gritted teeth, Jack hung on for dear life. The descent was broken, suddenly and painfully, in a bone-jarring jolt that nearly wrenched his arms from their sockets. The rope cut deep into his hands; a pain almost beyond tolerance.

Jack hung there, listening to the old rope creak; he knew he couldn't hold on for much longer, not with the added weight of the killer to contend with.

Suddenly, the rope slipped through his fingers and they dropped another couple of feet before he recovered his grip. Tyler looked down gingerly, calculating his chances of surviving a fall from this height intact. His feet were swinging twenty feet above the floor, and it seemed a very long way down.

To make matters worse, immediately below them were several plastic dustbins, a stack of empty crates and a loose pile of bricks. The bins were filled to the brim with rubbish, long since discarded. What really worried Jack was the small cluster of wooden timbers and the rusted metal pipes that protruded from the clutter below, sticking up like spikes on an iron railing.

Jack couldn't believe his eyes. In a place the size of a football pitch, why did there have to be a huge pile of trash, much of it sharp, all of it dangerous, in that particular spot?

If he landed on it, sod's law dictated he'd either be impaled or break both ankles – knowing his luck, probably both. He could feel his grip loosening, and he doubted he'd be able to hold on for very much longer.

"Grab the rope," he called down, trying to suppress his panic.

"No," Pritchard called back defiantly; his arms remained tightly wrapped around Tyler's chest in a perverse embrace. He began twisting and wriggling, like a worm on a hook, trying to pull his legs up in order to wrap them around Tyler's waist.

"Let go or we'll both fall," Jack shouted.

"Noooo!" Pritchard screamed, squeezing even tighter.

What was the matter with the man? Did he want to die? Jack could hardly breathe. His ribs felt as though they would snap if the pressure wasn't eased. He had to get rid of the extra weight, and fast – or they would both fall to their doom.

Jack brought his knee up hard into Pritchard's testicles, stunning him. The killer convulsed and let out a cry of pain. Jack kneed him again, harder, but the blow only connected with Pritchard's inner thigh. He pulled his knee back for a third blow.

"No, please," Pritchard pleaded in a hoarse voice.

Tyler felt a small twinge of satisfaction.

This is for what you did to my Kelly, you bastard.

As he lashed out, again and again, the rope swayed back and forth, gaining momentum. The supporting joist started shaking violently as its restraining bolts gave way. Brick dust began to rain down on them.

"Let...go...you...swine," Tyler grunted between blows. Pritchard slid further down Jack's body, and then onto his legs, at which point Tyler managed to knee him straight in the face. The blow jarred the killer's head backwards and he slid all the way down to Tyler's feet.

"NOOOOO!" he pleaded, bug-eyed. A trickle of blood had leaked from the corner of his mouth.

"I hope you...break...every bone...in your fucking body," Jack said, finally kicking him away. He watched as the killer fell to the floor and landed in a crumpled heap on top of the dustbins. Pritchard sprawled forward and a small cloud of dust billowed around him like a miniature burst of nuclear fall-out, obscuring his body from view. Jack closed his eyes and drew in several deep breaths before lowering himself painfully down to ground level.

As Tyler's feet touched the floor there was an ominous crack above him and the rope went slack in his hands. He looked up to see the pulley plummeting down towards him, dragging a huge timber joist behind it.

"Shit!" he said, instinctively diving to his left and curling into a foetal position. The metal landed on the exact spot he'd occupied a second before with a loud metallic clang. The joist made a much deeper noise, partially disintegrating as it hit. Dust and fragments of splintered wood rained down upon him.

When it stopped, Jack stood up, coughing. Without thinking, he started brushing at his clothes, which were white with dust. The pain in his hands was immediate and severe. Looking down he saw they had both sustained nasty friction burns. Gingerly flexing his hands, he walked over to the pile of debris the killer had landed on to see...

Nothing!

What the hell...?

The killer had gone. But how could that be? He had landed badly, and from that height...

Wait a minute; if I was twenty feet up and he was hanging from my feet then he was probably only about thirteen feet from the ground...

A fall from thirteen feet onto a bunch of dustbins was still risky, but it was far less likely to cause serious damage than a fall from twenty plus feet, unless you landed directly on your head, which the killer obviously hadn't, or got yourself impaled, as the killer should have done but, again, clearly hadn't. Even so, there was no way he should've been in a fit state to get up and run away. Jack shook his head in frustration. *Now if that had been me instead of him...*

He looked around frantically. The killer had to be nearby. Pace, time and distance dictated he couldn't have gone any further than –

BANG!

A pair of swing doors in the opposite corner of the massive storage area slammed shut, producing an echo that resonated throughout the empty building. Jack immediately broke into a run, jumping over several of the dustbins and their recently spilled contents. He nimbly dodged bricks, loose floorboards and broken crates alike, his burning hands temporarily forgotten.

It took him six seconds to reach the thick, rubber swing doors. Without breaking his stride, he kicked them wide open and carried on through, throwing caution to the wind. Had he been going slower, he might have noticed the grime covered sign on the door that indicated he was heading towards a chemical storage area containing highly flammable materials.

Tyler found himself in a long downward sloping tunnel, which he figured ran all the way down to the river's edge. A long way ahead, a weak beam of light reflected off the walls, bobbing up and down as the killer ran.

The son of a bitch had a torch!

Jack ran after him, taking full advantage of the killer's light until it faded and disappeared around a right-angle bend. Without the benefit of the killer's light to guide him, the passage quickly became as dark as the grave. In the few brief moments that the tunnel had been illuminated, he'd seen that several boxes and an old discarded trolley lay at various intervals in his path like an obstacle course. He cursed out loud and reluctantly slowed to negotiate the first of the hurdles.

He tried to regulate his breathing, but the stale air in the tunnel was thick with newly disturbed dust, making him cough uncontrollably.

Although he couldn't see the killer anymore, he could still hear the steady patter of receding footsteps. The sound infuriated him.

He wondered just how long the tunnel was; it seemed to be going on forever. With one hand held out in front of his face, probing the way ahead, and the other touching the side of the wall for balance, he began to advance. His progress was painfully slow and soon the killer's footsteps faded into silence.

He needed to go faster, but it was dangerous to run. *Fuck it, life's dangerous*, he decided, angrily. Tyler began to jog. His movements were slow and clumsy at first, but at least he was moving faster than before. As he became more confident, he increased the pace. And then it happened.

His left shin collided with something solid and he stumbled forward, his momentum driving him down onto the soggy floor. Something metallic snagged on his foot and whipped around, falling on top of him.

The old trolley!

He clumsily kicked it aside and struggled back to his feet, his leg throbbing, his face and hands covered with dirt and slime. "Why is nothing ever easy?" he complained bitterly. Ignoring the pulsating pain in his hands, he brushed himself down and continued to jog, knowing there was every chance he'd take another tumble and not giving a fuck.

He reached the bend in the tunnel and followed it around to the right. About fifty feet ahead there was a tiny glow of light. As he got nearer, he realised that the light was coming from the other side of another set of double doors, similar to the ones he had entered the tunnel by. Only they appeared to be made of metal, not rubber. Each of the doors had a small glass panel, about a foot square, set into it at head height. It was through these windows that he could see the thin beam of light dancing around on the other side.

It could only be the killer.

Tyler bunched his fists and immediately cringed at the searing pain from his burns. "I'm coming for you, you bastard," he growled.

Pritchard was battered, bruised and bleeding, and it was all Jack Tyler's fault. His face and groin were in excruciating pain; every muscle in his body ached from the fall, and a deep gouge ran the length of his left forearm, where he'd caught it on a sharp piece of wood that jutted out of one of the bins he'd landed on. He'd be lucky not to end up with Septicaemia.

He shone the torch around, looking for something he'd seen on his first trip to the underground storage area, when he'd searched the building earlier.

There was no time to lose. Tyler wasn't far behind, and although he'd heard the good Inspector take a fall in the tunnel behind – the killer hoped he'd broken his neck in the process – he couldn't count on that, or anything else, stopping Tyler for long. The detective was too stupid and too stubborn to know when enough was enough.

An insidious thought had occurred to him after the fall, as he lay stunned on the floor, surrounded by a whirlpool of dust. It was one of those rare moments of undiluted insight that could only be described as inspirational – like the moment he'd decided to let Terri Miller listen to him torturing Sarah.

Tyler had become a thorn in his side, turning up unexpectedly, thwarting his plans, ruining the sacrificial timetable and – most importantly – spoiling his fun. Two whores, both equally undeserving of life, were still breathing thanks to Jack bloody Tyler – and one of them was the third bitch who was responsible for ruining his life. If she survived, she would reveal his identity to the world, and he couldn't allow that. However, before he went back to the van to finish her off, his nemesis had to die – and The Disciple knew just how it was going to happen.

Tyler was going to go out with a very big bang.

He'd run down here, using the cloud of dust to mask his movements. It had given him the few precious seconds he'd needed. The storage room was approximately thirty-foot square with a low ceiling. It was cluttered with old equipment, including two acetylene cylinders sitting on a welder's trolley, an assortment of rusted tools and stacks of general rubbish.

He'd entered through a metal fire-proof door, and when he was finished, he would exit through an identical door at the far end of the storage area, which led down to the loading area on the pier.

He ran the beam of light over the ceiling, which was covered with a series of anodised black pipes, and around the circumference of the room. More pipes: grey this time. A small, old-fashioned, emergency generator, mounted on a heavy-duty trolley, sat in the corner immediately to his right, and he dragged it over to the door, to use as a barricade. Next, he knocked an old filing cabinet over and wedged it behind the generator. Breathing like an old man with chronic asthma, the Pritchard grunted with satisfaction.

That should hold Tyler for a while.

He crossed to a giant metal cylinder that was at least ten-foot long and three foot in diameter. It lay flat on the floor, parallel to the wall, facing the doors he'd come through. Two thin pipes came out of the top end, ran up the wall, and disappeared into the ceiling.

A half-dozen identical cylinders were bracketed to the wall above it, each one slightly offset from the one below. All had the same twin set of pipes leading upwards. He shone the light over the bottom cylinder until he found what he was looking for, a circular turn valve set into the furthest end. If they contained what he thought they did, he would use the cylinders to devastating effect. He would introduce Jack Tyler to Hell – and then send him there.

The Disciple scanned the cylinder for 'Hazardous Chemical' or 'Flammable liquid' warning signs. He wiped a thick layer of condensed grime away from the centre, where he thought it should be, with the sleeve of his jacket. Sure enough, he found a large diamond-shaped sticker coloured in bright red. The words 'DANGER – HIGHLY FLAMMABLE' were written on it in big, bold letters, and accompanied by a picture of a single flame.

If, as the killer suspected, this set up fuelled an outdated cooling system for a cold storage facility somewhere within the building above, then it probably still contained plenty of chlorofluorocarbons, which are a highly flammable propellant. He brushed the cobwebs away from the valve. Although dormant, the whole set up still appeared to be in working order. This was a very dangerous game to play, but Tyler had upped the stakes, forcing his hand.

"You think you've got me, don't you, Tyler? You think you've won. So help me, I'll kill us both before I let that happen," Pritchard promised, as he tried to turn the valve, which was stiff from years of inactivity.

"Turn, damn you," he grunted. His face glowed red from the effort, but the handle had rusted and wouldn't budge an inch. Pritchard looked around, desperate to find something to use as a lever. The torch beam cut through the darkness like a white laser, until it came to rest upon a thin rod of iron protruding from beneath the old generator. About two-foot-long, it was perfect for his needs. He slid it into the valve and started rocking back and forth violently, until, with a loud creak, it began to move. As the valve turned a gentle hissing began to fill the silence, growing steadily louder as the colourless, odourless gas escaped into the air. He knew it wouldn't take long to saturate the atmosphere of a room this size. He immediately started working on the valve in the cylinder above, which, to his surprise, wasn't nearly as hard to move.

Suddenly, the door thundered as something powerful crashed into it from the other side.

Tyler! He quickly shone the torch across his barricade, afraid it might have collapsed. Neither the generator nor the filing cabinet had moved, and he breathed a small sigh of relief.

"Pritchard, open the damn door," Tyler called. The Disciple could hear the anger in his voice.

"Losing your temper, are you, Jack? Not very professional is it?" he taunted. With the second valve now opened he turned his attention to the valve in the third cylinder. He had to use the iron rod on this one, just to get it going.

"Pritchard, I'm warning you," Tyler shouted, banging the door with his fist.

"Ooh, I'm shaking in my shoes," the killer responded sarcastically. The valve in the third cylinder was now spewing its flammable contents out with great gusto, and he quickly started work on the forth. Figuring that four canisters would be more than enough to cause the destruction he wanted, The Disciple moved over to the door, pressing his face against the glass panel.

"In fact, you're scaring me to death." Holding the torch under his chin so that it illuminated his features from below, he distorted his face into a caricature of a death mask.

The door jolted forward, almost banging into his face as Tyler kicked it from the other side. Instinctively, the killer shrank back, an agitated scowl on his face.

"Okay, Jack – my very own Inspector Abberline – if you want me, come in and get me. I'm waiting for you and I'm ready to go out in a blaze of glory. The question is, are you?" The killer stepped backwards, into the centre of the room. He held the torch tight against his chest, shinning it upward. It gave him a ghostly appearance. As he finished speaking, he switched it off, sending the world into darkness.

———

Tyler couldn't see a thing now that the torch had been extinguished, but from what little he'd been able to make out when it was on, he reckoned the killer was trapped in a storeroom of some sort. He doubted there was another way out. Pritchard would have been long gone if that were the case. He pushed on the door, lending all his weight to the effort. To his surprise, it only moved an inch or so. He tried again, quickly establishing a steady rhythm. Push, pause for breath, brace in readiness to push again...Push, pause for breath, brace...

Slowly, ever so slowly, the door began to open inwards. It soon became evident that a large piece of machinery had been wedged behind the double doors, blocking them.

"Fucking asshole," Jack cursed through gritted teeth.

Jack stopped shoving as soon as there was enough room for him to squeeze through. The entry was going to be a very dicey manoeuvre, and he wasn't looking forward to it.

The killer had too great an advantage. For a start, Jack didn't know where in the room the fucker was hiding. Pritchard, on the other hand, knew exactly where he was. Another advantage the killer had was that he knew the layout of the room; he'd had plenty of time to familiarise himself with it. He knew what obstacles were in it and where they were. And, if he needed it, he could always turn his ruddy torch back on. Jack didn't have that luxury.

There were other, more poignant dangers, to consider. Jack knew that Pritchard had dropped his knife up in the warehouse, but did that mean he was now unarmed?

Somehow, that seemed unlikely.

Could he have retrieved it when he fell?

Possibly.

Could he have other weapons concealed on him, brought along as a backup?

Probably.

Had he found something lying around that he could improvise with to create a do-it-yourself club or spear?

Almost certainly.

Jack had learned the hard way not to underestimate this particular killer. He might be mad, but he sure as hell wasn't stupid. Tyler listened carefully, hardly daring to breathe. The only noise coming from inside was a strange hissing sound, like steam escaping from a pipe.

Tyler shouldered the door, knocking it back another couple of inches. Stepping back, he crouched down, waiting to see if there was any response.

There was nothing. No movement, no noise – just the constant unexplained hiss. Tyler sniffed the air, worried that it might be a gas leak, although he couldn't smell anything unusual.

There was no easy way to handle this situation. He couldn't afford to stay where he was in the hope that help would arrive, but the more he thought about going in after Pritchard, the less he wanted to do it.

He began to focus his breathing, filling his bloodstream with as much oxygen as he could. This would have to be fast and furious. Jack couldn't help wishing that Tony Dillon were here to back him up.

He figured that the killer would try and take him as he entered the room, which meant he would be hiding immediately to the right or to the left of the door.

Another possibility was that the killer had somehow managed to climb on top of the machinery without being heard, and was poised to jump down on him as he entered the room. Jack had watched the killer take half a dozen steps straight back, towards the centre of the room, before turning off the torch. It told him that the middle of the room was clear of obstruction.

Dropping to his hands and knees, Tyler edged forward, feeling his way into the gap he'd created. As soon as his head cleared the door, he dived into the room in a rolling break fall, hoping to catch his opponent off guard. Twice he rolled before coming up and spinning to face the door. He froze, crouched in a defensive stance; his hands stretched out in front to fend off the sudden frenzied attack he expected to come at any moment.

After thirty seconds, during which nothing happened, he found himself having doubts. Maybe there was another way out of here after all? Lowering his hands slightly, he began to shuffle sideways, towards the hissing noise. If there were pipes then they would be attached to a wall, and he needed a wall to get his bearings again.

His nerves were raw after waiting for an attack that had never come, and he found himself longing to give up the chase, turn around and get out of this creepy place. But the fact of the matter was that he couldn't turn back. He needed to find the other exit and get back on the killer's trail, and sooner rather than later.

Tyler stopped in his tracks as a small powerful draft hit him. It hadn't been there a second ago. A rusty hinge creaked as a door opened close behind him. The hairs on the nape of his neck began to rise, and a shiver ran down his spine. He wasn't alone after all.

Dillon had managed to carry the injured woman back down to Kelly's car, and she now sat in the front passenger seat. Flowers sat next to her, in the driver's seat, holding the side of her face. She was still badly dazed and had only just managed to negotiate the walk back to the car unaided.

"Are you sure you're okay, Kelly?" Dillon asked, placing a shovel sized hand on her shoulder.

"I'm fine. You should go and help Jack. I'm really worried about him," she said.

"So am I," Dillon admitted. He paused for a moment before making up his mind. "Alright, but lock both doors and start the engine. If anyone shows up, apart from me or Jack, floor it and get the hell out of here. Promise?" he asked, sternly.

"I promise," she said, meaning it.

"Oh, and keep trying to ring out on my mobile." He passed the phone through the open window. "If you can get a signal, dial all the nines and yell loudly for help, lots of it."

"I'll try."

"And close that bloody window," Dillon ordered. With that, he set off for the warehouse at a brisk trot.

CHAPTER FORTY-TWO

Simon Pritchard froze on the spot, silently cursing the squeaking hinge that had stolen the element of surprise. There was no way that Tyler could have missed it and now he would be forewarned of the killer's approach.

He had slipped out of the other set of fireproof doors the moment he'd turned the torch off, hiding in the damp corridor that ran down to the pier. Then, cupping his hand around the torch to prevent its light from spilling back into the room, and alerting Tyler, he had rummaged around on the floor in search of something to set fire to. Almost immediately, he had found a long length of rag, which he'd crumpled into a ball.

He now stood poised in the doorway, ready to run. But he couldn't leave without letting Tyler know who the better man was. It wasn't enough just to kill Tyler; first, he had to tell his arch-nemesis exactly what was going to happen to him.

He switched the torch back on, shining it directly into the detective's eyes. "Did you think I'd gone, Jack?" he asked in a soft sibilant voice.

Tyler shielded his eyes against the sudden, painfully bright light, which was blinding after the total darkness of the underground boiler room. He took an uncertain step towards the voice, ready to pounce on its owner if the chance presented itself.

"Stay where you are, Tyler," the killer warned, and something in his voice made Jack stop.

"Do you hear that noise, Tyler? Do you know what it is?" The killer shone the torch around the room, bringing it to rest on a stacking unit containing several long cylinders, over by the far wall. A ball of ice formed in Tyler's stomach as he recalled his earlier fear of a gas leak.

"Those little beauties contain a highly flammable propellant, Jack. For the last few minutes, the contents of four of them have been filling this room. Can you imagine what would happen if someone were to spark a flint down here? Or, perhaps, set light to a piece of rag like this..." He shone the torch on his other hand, which contained the balled-up rag and something else, something small.

A lighter.

"Pritchard, don't be stupid. I know you hate me, but doing that would kill us both. Is that what you really want?" Tyler asked. His mouth had suddenly gone dry. He quickly calculated the distance between them, and the chances of knocking the lighter from his opponent's hand before it could be used. The odds were poor at best.

The door he had entered through, seconds earlier, was about eight feet behind him. The killer stood in another doorway roughly fifteen feet ahead of him. Trying not to make it obvious, Jack took a small step backwards.

Things suddenly seemed very bad.

"Come on, Simon, put the lighter down. Let's walk out of here together and get you some help," Jack cajoled, hoping to dissuade him from turning the building into a smouldering inferno. Just to be on the safe side, he took another backward step.

"Oh, but I don't want any help. I'm a very bad person, and proud of it." The killer smiled contentedly. Without taking his eyes off of Tyler, he transferred the rag to the hand that held the torch and positioned the lighter directly under it.

"No!" Tyler shouted, raising his hands to stay him.

As the killer thumbed the flint, a blue spark leapt into the air and fizzled out. Tyler cowered down, half expecting them both to be vaporised on the spot. When he realised that it hadn't happened, and that he was still alive, he turned hard on his heels, running full pelt for the door.

"Run, Tyler, run Tyler, run, run, run. Don't let the Ripper have his fun, fun, fun," Pritchard screamed in an insane parody of the old wartime song.

As Jack clambered over the generator, towards the fire door, The Disciple tried the lighter again. This time a bright blue flame burst into life.

Jack glanced fearfully over his shoulder in time to see the rag ignite. He was aware of the killer throwing it towards the cylinder; then he was back in the corridor.

"Run Tyler, run Tyler, run, run, run..."

Jack continued running, legs pumping like pistons, as he tried to distance himself from the danger zone behind. With every step he took the deranged cackle echoed in his ears a little less.

WHUMP!

The storage room exploded behind him. The heavy fire proofed door was blown off its hinges as a powerful concussion wave blew it outwards like a twig, spinning it a full 180-degree arc in mid-air before pummelling it into the thick concrete wall less than a foot from Jack's head. An enormous fireball blasted out of the doorway, chasing Tyler along the corridor, leaving a trail of blazing flame in its wake.

Somehow, Jack managed to stay just ahead of the expanding ball of fire, which moved like a living thing, hungrily consuming everything in its path. He reached the bend in the corridor and threw himself around it, diving onto the floor and covering his head with his hands. After several seconds he gingerly lifted his head and saw that the flames had begun to recede.

Out of breath, Tyler stood up unsteadily. Poking his head around the corner, he peered into a thick cloud of acrid smoke that was drifting along the corridor towards him. There was no sign of the killer. He wondered if Pritchard had got out in time. No one could have lived through the intense heat of that fireball.

WHUMP!

The second explosion was completely unexpected and it nearly knocked him off his feet. It was a completely different type of detonation to the first one, with much more substance to it. A violent tremor vibrated through the ground as the blast wave resonated along the narrow corridor. The ceiling cracked under the weight of the massive explosion and, as debris fell all around him, he instinctively raised his arms to protect his head.

Like a cork being popped from a well-shaken champagne bottle, a large chunk of metal piping from the old generator shot out of the boiler room, careering across the fifty-foot length of corridor at phenomenal speed, making straight for Tyler. Jack pressed himself against the side of the tunnel as the jagged piece of machinery shot by him, embedding itself into the wall where the tunnel forked around to the left.

Jack realised that something very substantial had just exploded. Instinctively, he understood that the first explosion was a result of the CFC's contaminating the room's air supply igniting, sucking all the oxygen from the room and creating a huge fireball. The second blast had occurred when the cylinder, itself, had gone up, causing serious structural damage.

He wondered how long he had until the other cylinders blew up.

Coughing violently, Tyler headed back towards the surface, this time managing to avoid the trolley he'd fallen over on his way in.

As he entered the main warehouse building, he experienced an overwhelming sense of relief. After the claustrophobic darkness of the tunnel below, this place seemed positively light and airy. He retraced his steps back to his initial point of entry, slipping out through the dislodged wooden slats in the old door into the freshness and freedom of the cool night air.

As he moved away from the building line, the third and fourth cylinders ignited.

WHUMP!

A ten-foot high pillar of flame shot out of a manhole cover in the ground between the warehouse and the dock. Half the windows on the ground floor shattered in sequence as the blast wave hit them, one after the other, sending shards of glass flying in every direction.

"What the hell?" Dillon gasped. For a moment all he could do was stand and stare. He had reached the front of the building seconds earlier and, finding it locked and secure, had drifted around to the back looking for an alternative way in. He began sprinting along the wharf towards the small docking area that connected the warehouse to the pier, where a cloud of fresh smoke billowed into the air.

WHUMP!

Another explosion, seemingly right underfoot, sent him to his knees. Large cracks appeared in the pavement all around him. "Jack!" he yelled at the top of his voice.

Smoke escaped from a series of fissures that had appeared in the wharf floor and a section of concrete, off to his left, crumbled and gave way, falling into a newly formed chasm. A small mushroom-shaped cloud of dust spewed up into the night air from the heart of the hole.

There was another tremor, and a large section of the warehouse began to collapse.

He wondered what on earth had just happened. It couldn't possibly be an earthquake; perhaps an underground gas main had exploded? Surely these explosions couldn't be connected to the suspect they were chasing. After all, he was a psychopath, not an international terrorist.

Dillon moved to the edge of the pier, looking down into the murky water below. Nothing unusual there, although he'd half expected to find dead fish floating on the surface.

The tiniest sound of gravel being crunched underfoot warned him that someone was trying to creep up on him, and that could only mean one thing: danger. Dillon spun around, lithe as a cat. The sudden movement saved his life. A wickedly sharp blade slashed through the air where his body had been a split second before.

A dark shadow lunged at him, and he caught a flicker of crazed red eyes, glowing in a face that had turned black from exposure to smoke and dust. The killer had lost his Bowie inside the building, but he still had his trusted Finnish skinning knife, and he slashed at Dillon with this, driving him back as its point missed his stomach by millimetres.

The scream that filled the night air was so bestial that, had Dillon not already seen his assailant, he would have believed that it came from a wild animal.

His heart pounding, Dillon quickly retreated towards the end of the wharf. He looked around desperately for an escape route, but there were none available. He was trapped; there was nowhere left for him to go.

The knifeman had systematically closed him down and was now thrusting and slashing furiously as he moved in for the kill. Dillon tried to sidestep the attack but he tripped on the uneven concrete at the edge of the wharf, falling heavily. As Simon Pritchard loomed over him, he realised he had two choices: Stay here and die or get wet.

The tip of the blade struck concrete, sending sparks into the air, but Dillon was no longer there. Rolling frantically, he went over the crumbling edge of the wharf, plunging into the dark waters below.

It was bitterly cold underwater, but he didn't have time to dwell on that as the deceptively strong current dragged him towards the pier. He surfaced to see the killer peering down.

"Dillon!" Tyler's voice pierced the silence. The killer's head whipped around in the direction it came from. With a final snarl at Dillon, he turned and disappeared.

Dillon swam over to a wooden ladder on the pier and climbed up. As his head cautiously rose above the edge of the wharf, he caught a brief glimpse of the killer running back down the path towards the old van. He pulled himself over the edge and stood up wearily, his sodden clothing streaming water.

"Dillon!" Jack's voice again, nearer this time.

"Over here!" Dillon responded, breathlessly. His expression became grim as he heard the killer's engine cough into life, followed by the screeching of tyres.

"After all that, he got away," he said, shaking his head in disbelief.

Just then, he heard the unmistakable impact of two vehicles colliding and, in the distance, just over the horizon, a plume of smoke rose into the air. Dillon immediately started jogging back towards the road. As soon as it came into sight, he saw the killer's van had T-boned a blue car that was blocking its path. Even from this distance, he recognised the hatchback as the unmarked police vehicle that DC Flowers had been driving.

Heart sinking, he broke into an all-out sprint.

CHAPTER FORTY-THREE

WHUMP!

The sound of the first explosion startled Kelly Flowers so much that she nearly jumped out of her skin. "Oh my God, what was that?" she said, praying that the detonation hadn't come from the warehouse where Jack and Dillon were chasing the killer.

Within moments, a second, third and fourth explosion – each far more powerful than the last – reverberated through the night air, and the sky above the warehouse began to glow orange.

"Oh Jack," she whispered to herself, "please be okay."

The first thing she'd done, after Dillon had set of to find Tyler, was remove Sarah Pritchard's remaining bindings and massaged her aching limbs to get her circulation going again. Kelly had then released her from the rigid handcuffs, having found a key in her bag. It quickly became apparent that Sarah's collarbone was broken and – after putting her in a makeshift sling and making the poor woman as comfortable as she could – Kelly immediately started trying to contact the emergency services. Dillon had given explicit instructions for her to remain inside the vehicle, but when she couldn't get a signal on either of their phones she had resorted to walking up and down the road in an effort to acquire one, not that it had done any good. Kelly had just returned to the car, intending to drive further along the road, in case reception was better there, when the deafening sound from the first two detonations shattered the silence around her. She found herself hoping that her colleagues were safe, but she had a terrible feeling that they weren't.

Two more explosions, which were even more powerful than their predecessors, had followed in quick succession, and as flames lit up the night sky, Kelly Flowers feared the worst. No one could have survived that.

Suddenly, Kelly heard the killer's van spark into life, and when she saw the dazzle of its headlights bumping towards her over the uneven path leading back to the road, she knew that she had to act, and act fast.

"Get out," she told Sarah Pritchard.

"Why? What're you going to do?" Sarah asked, horrified.

"GET OUT!" Kelly shouted. There was no time to explain, and she couldn't risk endangering a civilian.

Sarah Pritchard opened the door but then hesitated, looking at Kelly imploringly.

"Get out," Kelly ordered, and there was steel in her voice.

Sarah nodded and reluctantly forced her aching body out of the car, doing her best to ignore the incredible pain from her shoulder. "Don't do anything stupid," she warned. "He's mad. He won't stop."

Kelly nodded, grimly. "I know that, which is why I don't want you in the car with me. Now move aside."

Sarah hobbled away as the Sherpa rocketed towards them, its engine screaming. It was going very fast, and if Kelly was going to do what she thought she was, someone was probably going to get very badly injured. She could only prey it would be her wicked husband and not the kind woman detective who had just saved her life.

"I must be mad," Kelly said as she engaged first gear, slipped the clutch and began to rev the car into the red. "Steady, steady," she told herself, waiting for the optimum moment. If she moved too quickly, he would simply swerve around her and then he would be free.

The van was really motoring now, and she could see the driver's face clearly enough to see that the bastard was smiling.

He thinks he's going to get away, she realised. *Well, we'll see about that.*

A chilling thought occurred to her; what if he had caused the explosions? What if he had deliberately blown up that building, killing her colleagues – her friends – in the process, just to evade capture? Suddenly, all that mattered was stopping him, even if it meant putting herself in harm's way.

At the last moment, when the van was almost upon her, she lifted the clutch and floored the accelerator, gripping the steering wheel so tightly that her knuckles turned white. The wheels spun and the Escort surged forward into the path of the advancing Sherpa.

The sound of the impact was deafening from inside the Escort. As any science student knows, anything that has mass and velocity also has kinetic energy; the heavier a vehicle is and the faster it is travelling, the more kinetic energy it has. That's all very well and good, but when said vehicle suddenly decelerates – as it does in a crash – the kinetic energy has to go somewhere. In this case, it went straight into the side of the Ford Escort, crumpling it into the shape of a boomerang.

Despite wearing a seatbelt, the violent momentum of the collision whipped Kelly's head sideways, smashing it straight into the driver's door window – and although the front impact airbag went off with a loud bang, deploying at 300 kilometres per hour, it did very little to help.

Everything went silent for a moment as the world around her froze. But that moment passed quickly, and then the world sped up with a vengeance. The frame of the Escort contorted around her as it was shunted sideways with tremendous force and, for a terrible moment, Kelly was convinced that the car would flip over and go into a roll. Her windshield seemed to disintegrate, showering her with glass fragments. The sound of metal twisting and shearing as the mangled frame of her car caved in around her was agonisingly loud – but Kelly was too busy drifting in and out of consciousness to pay much attention to any of this.

When she came around, seconds or hours later – she wasn't sure – she found herself slumped forward in her seat. The car had stopped moving but she could still hear the engine clicking over, and steam was coming out of it. As her senses returned, the first thing Kelly noticed was the smell of radiator coolant; there was something else, too – something much stronger. It took a moment for her befuddled brain to process that the smell was leaking petrol. By some miracle, her car hadn't rolled over. She groggily unfastened her seatbelt and forced open the driver's door, which protested noisily. Somehow, she managed to drag herself out of the car, motivated by a fear that it might catch fire at any moment. She staggered around the front and, as a wave of dizziness swept over her, leaned on the bonnet to catch her breath.

Inside the van, Pritchard's chest slammed into the steering wheel during impact, knocking all the air out of his lungs, and breaking three of his ribs. His head collided with the inside of the windshield with a sickening thud, which seemed louder than the crash itself.

His ears were ringing as the van came to a jarring halt, and the coppery taste of blood filled his mouth. It really hurt to breathe, and he suddenly coughed uncontrollably, covering the dash in frothy crimson. He knew he was badly injured. The blood he'd coughed up was most likely a result of a broken rib puncturing one of his lungs. He ignored the pain; he needed to keep moving or they would catch him and it would all be over. There was so much more than his freedom at stake if he failed to complete the fifth and final ritual.

What the hell had the brainless idiot driving the car that had just pulled across his path been playing at, he wondered? Not realising that the act had been deliberate. He hoped that they were in a far worse condition than him. Had it not been for his pressing need to get away, he would have gone after them with his knife.

Clutching his side, he stumbled out of the van and started to head for the road. And that was when he saw her, standing beside the bonnet of the little blue car he'd crashed into, swaying like a drunk.

"You!" he said, shocked to see the whore who had been with his wife when he returned from reconnoitring the warehouse. "What are you doing here?"

Kelly turned to face him. She had to squint to make him come into focus because her vision had gone all blurry. At the moment, there seemed to be two people standing in front of her, but then they merged into one. *Why are your words so slurred,* she wondered, feeling very confused, *"and how are you making your voice echo like that?"* To her, he sounded like one of the Clangers from the children's TV show.

Simon Pritchard realised that she was badly concussed and that he was unlikely to get any sense out of her. "Oh well," he said reaching for the Finnish skinning knife, "I haven't got time to get to the bottom of this, so you'll just have to die without revealing your secrets." He advanced towards the whore, realising that she had no idea of the danger she was in. "This shouldn't take a second," he said, moving behind her so that he wouldn't be caught in the arterial bleed. Pritchard yanked her hair back roughly and raised the knife to slit her throat. It was a pity he didn't have the time to establish which sign of the Zodiac she had been born under. Ah well, those were the breaks.

As he was about to slice open her throat, he became aware of people running towards him, panting from their exertions. "What now?" he snarled, pulling her close to him, in case he needed to use her as a shield. "Stay where you are," he shouted at the two figures that had just appeared out of the mist. "If you come any closer, I will kill her."

The figures slowed down, but they continued to walk forward, warily. As they stepped into the light, Pritchard immediately recognised the first as his nemesis and the second as his oversized colleague.

As battered as they looked, it was pretty obvious that there was still plenty of fight left in them. "What have I got to do to make you stay dead?" he asked Tyler.

"It's over, Pritchard," Jack growled. "Put down the knife."

Pritchard grinned nastily, exposing blood stained teeth. "Oh, I'm only just warming up," he promised. As he spoke, he began backing away, dragging Flowers with him. He needed to get to the main road and flag down a car.

"Let the girl go, Simon," Jack said. "If you do, we won't pursue you from here. If you kill her there's no way you'll get away. You know that."

"What? You're just going to let me walk away, are you?" The Disciple smirked. "You must think I was born yesterday."

Jack shook his head emphatically. "We'll catch you, whether it's today or tomorrow. All I'm offering you is a chance for it to not be today. What do you say?"

Pritchard considered the offer, and he was sorely tempted. Tyler was right, if he killed the girl there was very little chance that he would get away. But, if he let her live, and if Tyler kept his word, there was still a chance that he would be able to complete the ritual. If he did that, it wouldn't matter that they knew his name – he would be invincible. They would never be able to find him, and after things died down, he would be able to come back for the third bitch responsible for ruining his life. He licked his lips nervously. "How do I know I can trust you?" he asked.

As Jack was about to speak, the sound of approaching sirens reached their ears. From the sound of it, there were a lot of emergency vehicles en route.

Pritchard sneered. "I knew it was a trick," he snarled. "You were just biding your time until reinforcements arrived. You have no intention of letting me go, do you?" He yanked Kelly's hair back, causing her to scream out in pain. The blade of the knife moved towards her throat, and Jack could tell from the look in the madman's eyes that he was going to kill her out of spite.

"No! Please!" he begged, raising his hands in surrender. "They'll do what I tell them to," he said, taking a step forward. Beside him, Dillon crouched, ready to pounce.

Pritchard's face darkened as he came to a conclusion. "I'll take my chances without your help," he hissed. Taking a deep breath, his grip tightened on the engraved handle of his favourite knife and he pressed the blade against Kelly's flesh. "Say goodbye to the whore," he told them.

The sound of the rock smashing into the back of Simon Pritchard's head reminded Jack of the noise a dropped egg makes. Pritchard's eyes went wide with pain and shock, and then they flickered and closed. The knife slipped out of his limp hand, falling on the floor with a clank. Pritchard followed it down, sinking to his knees and then falling face forward into the dirt.

As he released her, Kelly staggered forward, falling onto her knees.

Sarah Pritchard stepped out of the shadows, holding the bloodstained rock in her left hand. "I had to do it," she cried. "He was going to kill her." She stared at the rock as though it would bite her, and then, with a tearful shudder, released it, allowing it to join Pritchard and his knife on the floor.

Ignoring the killer, Tyler ran over to Kelly Flowers, pulling her close to his chest. Then he held her at arm's length and checked her over for injuries. She had cuts and bruises, and a nasty bump on the right side of her forehead, but her pupils were evenly dilated and her throat was in one piece. To his enormous relief, it looked like she was going to be okay.

Tyler looked over to Dillon, who was kneeling beside Simon Pritchard, taking his pulse.

"How is he?" Tyler asked.

Dillon shook his head. "Not good, Jack." Pritchard's skull was caved in. Mass and velocity equals kinetic energy, and in this case, the rapid deceleration of the rock had left the kinetic energy with nowhere else to go, other than into the back of the killer's skull.

The sirens were getting louder. "Either Kelly managed to get through to the Yard or someone's called the explosion in," Tyler speculated.

"Not me," Kelly told him, groggily. "I couldn't get a signal."

"It must be Trumpton," Dillon said. An explosion as powerful as the one at the warehouse would have been seen and heard for miles around. The entire London Fire Brigade was probably on its way.

Tyler put a protective arm around Flowers and helped her to her feet. "We'll get you straight to hospital and have you checked out," he promised.

"Will you come with me?" she asked, longingly.

He shook his head sadly. "I'd like to, but I can't," he told her, squeezing her shoulders affectionately. "I've got to stay and sort this mess out, but I promise I'll be there as soon as I can get away."

After what she had been through, he suspected that Kelly would be kept in for overnight observations at the very least.

Within minutes, the scene was awash with fire engines, ambulances, and uniformed cops. Dillon had been right: the LFB had been inundated with calls about the four explosions, which had been heard from as far as two miles away.

At least half of the 80-metre long building was being hungrily consumed by flames, and a thick black cloud of foul-smelling smoke was now polluting the night sky. Twelve pumps had been dispatched to the scene, but Tyler wasn't sure if that would be enough. The Senior Fire Officer had ordered that a twenty-five-metre exclusion zone be put in place. Fortunately, the warehouse was in a remote location and could be cordoned off without the need for mass evacuations.

Simon Pritchard had been taken to hospital on blues and twos, with a Traffic car providing an escort. His chances of survival were regarded as slim, and even if he pulled through, there was a good chance he would end up as a vegetable. Personally, Tyler hoped that he would do the decent thing and die. The case had been solved, and he saw no reason to waste tax payers' money on a convoluted, and very expensive, trial – or on keeping a monster like Pritchard locked up for the next thirty odd years.

Kelly seemed to be feeling much better, and she was protesting about going to the hospital. "I want to stay here and help out," she insisted.

Tyler resorted to pulling rank. "DC Flowers, you're unfit for duty through injury, and you will go to hospital and have a check-up," he told her in a mock stern voice. And then he smiled warmly. "If the quack clears you, you can come back in tomorrow. If not, relax and enjoy a few days off. You've earned it after tonight."

"I'm sorry about wrecking the car," she told him. "I hope the Traffic skipper who reports the collision will take pity on me."

"The way I see it, Pritchard deliberately rammed you to get at his wife, who you were in the process of driving away from danger. And, as you were on the main road, and he was joining it, you had right of way." It wasn't quite how it had happened, but it was close enough to satisfy a garage sergeant's curiosity.

Kelly smiled. "Oh yeah, I didn't think of it like that."

"Go and get checked out," Tyler told her. "I'll come up after, and we can grab a coffee – if you want to, that is?"

"I want to, very much," she told him, smiling. "Tell me," she asked, studying him inquisitively. "Was I dreaming, or did you kiss me earlier, when I was lying on the floor after the killer ran off?"

Tyler blushed. "Well, I...that is..."

Luckily, he was spared any further embarrassment by the appearance of George Holland. "So, is it true?" The DCS asked, leading him to one side. "Have we finally got him?"

Tyler nodded. "We have," he said. "And we have all the evidence we could ever need to put him away for the rest of his natural, not that he's likely to live very long." Tyler then talked Holland through the rather harrowing events of the last couple of hours.

Dillon found Sarah Pritchard sitting in the back of an ambulance, receiving treatment from a paramedic. "How do you feel?" he asked.

"My shoulder is in agony," she said, grimacing. "I dread to think how much damage that bastard did when he hit me with a hammer."

Dillon winced at the mental image of Pritchard attacking his wife in the back of the van. "That's not what I meant," he said, softly. "How are you feeling after – you know – having to do what you did?"

She gave him a wan smile. "I don't really know. Numb, I suppose."

"It's understandable," he told her. "For what it's worth, I think you're an incredibly brave woman. You saved Kelly's life tonight. Without your intervention, she would be dead."

"Am I going to get into any trouble?" Sarah asked. "You know, for hitting Simon on the head with a rock." She mimed the act, just in case Dillon hadn't understood the question.

"Don't worry, Sarah," he said, taking her hand. "You won't get in any trouble. In fact, you'll get a bloody medal, if I have any say in the matter."

"It all feels so unreal," she said. "My life has been a sham. The man I thought loved me was a monster. How do you move on from that?"

Dillon shrugged. "I don't know," he admitted, "but you're a strong woman and I'm confident that you will find a way."

As he waved the ambulance off, it occurred to Dillon that the majority of the team was still out searching for Pritchard, and probably had no idea what had been happening here. He pulled out his phone to update them, but there was no signal. He supposed he should be grateful it still worked at all after his recent dunking in the Thames. Feet squelching with every step, and shivering from the cold, he set off to find a car with a Main-Set. He would have to radio the SCG Reserve and get them to ring each of the skippers to give them the news.

There was still a ton of work to do before the case was match fit for court – if Pritchard survived long enough to stand trial, but with a bit of luck, the team might actually get a day off this weekend.

EPILOGUE

Saturday 13th November 1999

For most of the team, the weekend was one to remember for solving one of the most challenging homicide investigations the Metropolitan Police Service had been faced with in a very long time.

The van had contained Pritchard's murder kit, including the lambskin parchment and a thick notebook explaining how he planned to kill his victims and consume their organs. It also contained a lot of information about Alice Pilkington, who he referred to as The Infector; Geraldine Rye, who he referred to as The Blackmailer, and Sarah Pritchard, his wife, who he referred to as The Controller. Finally, they understood his motive.

At the hospital, a set of keys had been found in one of Pritchard's coat pockets, and the fob had the address for a lockup at a railway arch in Three Colts Lane written on it. That morning, DS Susan Sergeant had obtained a search warrant for the venue, and had taken a POLSA team over to pull it apart. The initial results were staggering. They found the missing underwear from each of the killer's first four victims hidden in a duffle bag. They found traces of blood in an old chest freezer – no doubt this would match Geraldine Rye's. They discovered make-up props and a variety of disguises, including a long wig, a droopy moustache and a pair of George Harrison style glasses.

The lock up was steeped in mysticism; ranging from an inverted crucifix hanging over the door to a chalk-drawn circle containing a pentagon and a host of symbols that no one understood. There were also some very interesting occult books on ritualistic sacrifices. It would take some time to go through all the evidence the lockup contained, but Susie was confident this little hoard would solve any remaining gaps in the mystery behind the killer's motivation, and provide a clear link between him and each of his victims.

At the mortuary, a dead set of his fingerprints and a sample of his DNA had been taken, and these would be sent to the Yard and the FSS respectively, but it was only a formality now. Lastly, to no one's surprise, Pritchard's name had been on the list that Chris Deakin had prepared of people using the ATM in Whitechapel.

For Sarah Pritchard, it was the day that her husband, the monster – a psychotic serial killer who had dubbed himself 'Jack the New Ripper' – died.

Pritchard had never recovered consciousness. Upon arrival at the Royal London Hospital, he had undergone a CT scan and been rushed straight into theatre. In spite of the best efforts of the neurological surgeon and his highly specialised team, Pritchard expired on the table.

Sarah had been kept in due to her injuries, and when she had awoken after being operated on to repair her shoulder, the first thing she saw was Charise sitting at her bedside, filing her nails and eating the last of the grapes that she had brought up for Sarah.

For Terri Miller, it was a day where record numbers of the London Echo were sold, all thanks to her exclusive story about the New

Ripper. His capture, and subsequent demise created an overwhelming demand for her to do more TV and radio interviews – and not just news bulletins this time; there were even offers to appear on morning talk shows and breakfast TV.

From her perspective, things couldn't have gone any better – she was suddenly a household name and an important reporter for the paper. There had already been a couple of calls from rival rags, to sound her out in case she was interested in taking a position with them. Giles Deakin, being the wily old sod that he was, had offered to make Julie Payne a permanent staffer, but only if she was going to be working with Terri.

It was amazing how much influence she suddenly had, and even the piss takers who ran her down at every opportunity were suddenly treading warily around her now, sensing that the wind had changed.

Even her father, who never praised anyone but himself, had called to say how proud he was of what she had achieved. "You get that determination to succeed from me," he'd had the gall to tell her.

For Rita Phillips, it was the day that she received a telephone call informing her that the man who had murdered her daughter had finally been identified, and that he had died at the hands of a woman he was trying to murder. The evidence against him, she was assured, was overwhelming.

Rita was delighted to hear that justice had been done – not just for Tracey, but for all the victims and their families – although a part of her felt cheated at not getting the chance to see the vile creature responsible for her baby's death stand trial before his peers and receive a life sentence in prison when he was properly convicted by a jury of twelve.

Her sense of relief was, of course, massively tempered by the staggering loss that she felt all day, every day. She would never forget her daughter, and she would never stop loving her. She only wished that she could have told Tracey these things on the fateful night that she had stormed out of the flat, never to return.

Despite the great sense of loss she had felt since Tracey's passing,

Rita felt incredibly blessed to have been granted such a special relationship with her granddaughter, little April. She vowed that the child's life would always be filled with deep, unconditional love, and that she would do everything within her power to ensure that the angelic little girl followed a very different path to poor Tracey. The two of them would get through this together. They would start their journey with a surprise trip to the shops later this morning, where Rita planned to buy her a Belle doll from Disney's Beauty and the Beast.

For Colin and Carmel Franklin, the weekend was one they would remember forever for reasons completely unconnected to the Whitechapel murders investigation.

As of eight-thirty, Saturday morning, after a labour that had lasted sixteen-and-a-half-grueling hours, they became the proud parents of an eight-pound-two-ounce baby boy.

The event was beautiful beyond description. It was a magical moment that no words could ever do justice to, and the euphoria Colin had experienced on holding the fragile infant for the first time, so small and insignificant in his large hands, humbled him to the core.

As Jack had anticipated, Kelly had been kept in overnight for observations, but she was released with a clean bill of health at midday on Saturday. Through no fault of his own, he hadn't made it back to the hospital to see her the previous night, but he had sent his apologies via the night sister on the ward.

When she walked out of the observation ward, having been told that someone from work was coming to take her home, she looked around for her driver, wondering whether it would be Paul Evans, George Copeland or even Steve Bull.

"Taxi for Miss Flowers?" a gruff Cockney voice asked.

Kelly turned around, expecting to see an unshaven slob of a minicab driver waiting for her. She was a little disappointed that none of her colleagues had come, but she knew how busy they must be, and she understood that it must have been impossible for the boss to release anyone – hence the mini-cab.

When she saw Tyler leaning against the wall, her face broke into a big smile. "I wasn't expecting you," she admitted.

"I hope you're not too disappointed," he said, taking her arm in his and guiding her towards the exit.

"On the contrary," she explained. "I'm very pleased that you came."

"Well, I did promise you coffee," he said, "and I always like to keep my word."

Coffee was a good start, she thought. Coffee could easily lead to dinner, and from there? Well, who knew?

FURTHER READING

UNLAWFULLY AT LARGE
The second exciting instalment in the DCI Tyler Thriller series

Claude Winston has been on remand for the past two months awaiting trial for the attempted murder of two police officers. The evidence against him is overwhelming and he knows that he's looking at spending the rest of his life behind bars.

When the unthinkable happens, and an opportunity to escape arises, Winston seizes it with both hands, leaving an ugly trail of death and destruction in his wake.

DCI Jack Tyler and his partner, DI Tony Dillon, are the murder squad officers who sent Winston to prison, and now that he's unlawfully at large it's up to them to recapture him before he can be smuggled abroad to begin a new life in a country without an extradition treaty.

It soon becomes apparent that this is not going to be easy; faced with a wall of silence on the streets, and having very few leads to follow, Tyler and Dillon find themselves being run into the ground as they battle against the clock to locate Winston before he slips out of their grasp for good.

As the chase goes down to the wire, and things become increasingly frantic, Tyler realises that he is going to have to pull something pretty special out of the bag if he is to prevent Winston from getting away.

THE HUNT FOR CHEN
A DCI Tyler Novella only available from Mark's website:
www.markromain.com

Exhausted from having just dealt with a series of gruesome murders in Whitechapel, DCI Jack Tyler and his team of homicide detectives are hoping for a quiet run in to Christmas.

Things are looking promising until the London Fire Brigade are called down to a house fire in East London and discover a charred body that has been wrapped in a carpet and set alight.

Attending the scene, Tyler and his partner, DI Tony Dillon, immediately realise that they are dealing with a brutal murder.

A witness comes forward who saw the victim locked in a heated argument with an Oriental male just before the fire started, but nothing is known about this mysterious man other than he drives a white van and his name might be Chen.

Armed with this frugal information, Tyler launches a murder investigation, and the hunt to find the unknown killer begins.

GLOSSARY OF TERMS

AIDS – Acquired Immune Deficiency Syndrome
AC – Assistant Commissioner
AMIP – Area Major Investigation Pool (Predecessor to the Homicide Command)
ARV – Armed Response Vehicle
BIU – Borough Intelligence Unit
BPA – Blood Pattern Analysis
BTP – British Transport Police
C$_{11}$ – Criminal Intelligence / surveillance
CAD – Computer Aided Dispatch
CCTV – Closed Circuit Television
CID – Criminal Investigation Department
CIPP – Crime Investigation Priority Project
CRIMINT – Criminal Intelligence
CSM – Crime Scene Manager
(The) Craft – the study of magic
CRIS – Crime Reporting Information System
DNA – Deoxyribonucleic Acid
DC – Detective Constable
DS – Detective Sergeant

DI – Detective Inspector
DCI – Detective Chief Inspector
DSU – Detective Superintendent
DCS – Detective Chief Superintendent
DPG – Diplomatic Protection Group
ESDA – Electrostatic Detection Apparatus (sometimes called an EDD or Electrostatic Detection Device)
ETA – Expected Time of Arrival
(The) Factory – Police jargon for their base.
FLO – Family Liaison Officer
Foxtrot Oscar – Police jargon for 'fuck off'
FSS – Forensic Science Service
GP – General Practitioner
GMC – General Medical Council
HA – Arbour Square police station
HAT – Homicide Assessment Team
HEMS – Helicopter Emergency Medical Service
HIV – Human Immunodeficiency Virus
HOLMES – Home Office Large Major Enquiry System
HP – High Priority
HR – Human Resources
HT – Whitechapel borough / Whitechapel police station
IO – Investigating Officer
Kiting checks – trying to purchase goods or obtain cash with stolen / fraudulent checks
LAG – Lay Advisory Group
LFB – London Fire Brigade
MIR – Major Incident Room
MPH – Miles Per Hour
MPS – Metropolitan Police Service
NHS – National Health Service
Nondy – Nondescript vehicle, typically an observation van
NSY – New Scotland Yard
OM – Office manager
Old Bill – the police
P9 – MPS Level 1/P9 Surveillance Trained

GLOSSARY OF TERMS

PC – Police Constable
PLO – Press Liaison Officer
PM – Post Mortem
PNC – Police National Computer
POLACC – Police Accident
PTT – Press to Talk
RCS – Regional Crime Squad
Rozzers – the police
RTA – Road traffic Accident
RT car – Radio Telephone car, nowadays known as a Pursuit Vehicle
SCG - Serious Crime Group
SIO – Senior Investigating Officer
Sheep – followers of Christ; the masses
Skipper - Sergeant
SNT – Safer Neighbourhood Team
SO19 – Met Police Firearms Unit
SOCO – Scene Of Crime Officer
SOIT – Sexual Offences Investigative Technique
SPM – Special Post Mortem
TDC – Trainee Detective Constable
TIE – Trace, Interview, Eliminate
TSG – Territorial Support Group
VODS – Vehicle On-line Descriptive Searching
Walkers – officers on foot patrol
Trumpton – the Fire Brigade

AUTHOR'S NOTE

Let me start by thanking you for taking the time to read my debut novel. I really, really hope that you enjoyed it. If you did, can I ask you to do me a big favour by sparing a few moments to leave an honest review on Amazon. It doesn't need to be much, just a line or two to say if you enjoyed it or would recommend it.

I can't stress how helpful this feedback is for indie authors like me. Apart from influencing a book's rankings, reviews help people who have not yet read my work decide whether it's right for them.

Unlike the stories we see unfold in our favourite TV shows, where everything falls neatly into place and all the loose ends are tied up by the time the end credits roll, things tend to happen very differently in real life.

As a general rule of thumb, I think most police officers would agree that, for every minute of excitement experienced during an adrenalin rush on the street, you end up having to complete five-hours' worth of boring paperwork – and sometimes considerably more.

It takes time to put a solid case together: CCTV can take days to retrieve and weeks to view; forensics can take days, weeks or even months to come back; witnesses can take ages to track down, and they don't always want to play ball. And don't even get me started on the rigmarole of analysing telephone and financial data!

The point is, police work is often slow and methodical, and not remotely glamorous. Detectives – especially DCI's – spend far more time tied to their desks going through files than they do zooming around in fast cars, chasing after suspects and then rolling around on the floor with them. So, while I've tried to be as procedurally accurate, and as realistic as possible, with 'Jack's Back', I do confess to having used a liberal sprinkling of artistic license where necessary in order to ensure that the smooth flow and dramatic tone of the book is maintained.

A few people have asked me if Jack Tyler or any of the other characters are based on me, or on other people I have known or worked with over the years. The answer is a resounding no! Every character featured in this book is completely fictitious and a product of my overactive imagination.

Likewise, the sacrificial rituals The Disciple carries out in this story, along with the book containing his source material, are entirely made up and are not based on real occult practices.

Finally, you might wonder why I've chosen to set my story in 1999 instead of in more recent times. Well, the truth is that that I actually started writing this book way back in 1999, but soon discovered that having to work extended shifts on a regular basis wasn't particularly conducive to writing fiction. I eventually gave up trying and decided to shelve the project until I retired. So, when you actually think about it, this book has taken me the best part of twenty years to complete! Don't worry - I plan to be a lot quicker at writing the next one!

ABOUT THE AUTHOR

Mark Romain is a retired Metropolitan Police officer, having joined the Service in the mid-eighties. His career included two homicide postings, and during that time he was fortunate enough to work on a number of very challenging high-profile cases.

Mark lives in Essex with is his wife, Clare. They have two grown up children and one grandchild. Between them, the family has two English Bull Terriers and a very bossy Dachshund called Weenie!

Mark is a lifelong Arsenal fan and an avid skier. He also enjoys going to the theatre, lifting weights and kick-boxing, a sport he got into during his misbegotten youth!

You can find out more about Mark's books or contact him via his Facebook page or website at:

www.facebook.com/markromainauthor

www.markromain.com

Printed in Poland
by Amazon Fulfillment
Poland Sp. z o.o., Wrocław